PRAISE FOR SHAYLIN GANDHI'S *WHEN WE HAD FOREVER*

"A lyrical debut, full of heartbreak, surprises and loss, tempered with a generous shot of humor. Original and fast-paced, *When We Had Forever* packs the best kind of wallop!"

—Kristan Higgins, *New York Times* bestselling author

"Beautifully written with a twist you won't see coming. I couldn't put it down!"

—Helen Hardt, #1 *New York Times* bestselling author

"Captivating and emotionally charged with a storyline you won't see coming. Shaylin Gandhi writes with the depth and finesse of a seasoned author. All the stars in the sky."

—Mia Sheridan, *New York Times* bestselling author

"There are plenty of unexpected twists . . . culminating in a bombshell . . . readers won't see coming. Anyone on the hunt for angsty romance should snap this up."

—*Publishers Weekly*

"Shaylin Gandhi is a writer to watch (and read!). *When We Had Forever* is lovely, smart, and layered with emotion and heart. I can't recommend it enough."

—Emma Scott, *USA TODAY* bestselling author

"I've got a new favorite writer! Shaylin Gandhi's ability to weave beautiful prose with relatable characters and an unexpected plot twist has resulted in a book that's impossible to put down. I loved every minute of it and can't wait to read what she comes out with next!"

—Lacie Waldon, author of *The Layover*

"Addicting and deeply romantic, *When We Had Forever* is a powerful story of unwavering love."

—Alexandra Kiley, author of *Kilt Trip*

"Gripping, sensual, and twisty, with beautifully evocative prose, this book will keep you turning pages in a fever of discovery. Shaylin Gandhi is one to watch!"

—Maggie North, author of *Rules for Second Chances*

"I was obsessed with *When We Had Forever* from the very first page to the last. The tension. The angst and the plot twist that literally made me gasp out loud and still lives rent-free in my head. Shaylin's writing is pure magic."

—Nisha J. Tuli, bestselling author of *Trial of the Sun Queen*

"Clear your calendar! Once you start reading, you won't be able to stop. Haunting, erotic, and by turns infuriating and satisfying, *When We Had Forever* is a must-read love story that isn't afraid to walk on the dark side and emerge, victorious, in the light."

—Emily Colin, *New York Times* bestselling author of *The Memory Thief*

"Beautifully written and masterfully plotted, Gandhi's *When We Had Forever* is an intriguing romance with an emotional journey Colleen Hoover fans will love!"

—Kate Robb, author of *This Spells Love*

ALSO BY SHAYLIN GANDHI

When We Had Forever

LOVE LETTERS FOR OTHER PEOPLE

SHAYLIN GANDHI

CANARY STREET PRESS

ISBN-13: 978-1-335-01696-6

Love Letters for Other People

For questions and comments about the quality of this book, please contact us at CustomerService@Harlequin.com.

TM is a trademark of Harlequin Enterprises ULC.

Canary Street Press
22 Adelaide St. West, 41st Floor
Toronto, Ontario M5H 4E3, Canada
CanaryStPress.com

HarperCollins Publishers
Macken House, 39/40 Mayor Street Upper,
Dublin 1, D01 C9W8, Ireland
www.HarperCollins.com

Printed in U.S.A.

For the readers who like their heroes dangerous,
broody, and emotionally available.

For the readers who like their heroes dangerous,
broody and emotionally vulnerable

1.

It was one of those nights, the kind on which Nick Thacker needed three things: to work himself to exhaustion, to drown any surviving discontent with tequila, and to then undo all that hard work by rereading a letter he'd done his damnedest to forget.

He'd already checked the first two items off the list. Nick sat on his bedroom floor, his skin slick with the sweat he'd wrung from himself at the gym. The metal bedframe dug into his back. A fifth of tequila dangled from his grip.

He sipped. He hated the way the liquor's fire writhed in his gut—already, he dreaded the price he'd pay tomorrow. But at least bravery came in liquid form, because he sure as hell didn't have the courage to unearth the letter on his own. Never mind that the thing had called to him all day.

Hell, it called to him *always.*

Usually, he ignored its siren song. At work, he'd brave the blast furnace's heat as if wading through oil. He'd watch the glowing iron pour from the hearth until sweat misted his reflective suit and his lungs throbbed in the blistering air. Until the furnace's roar subsumed the hungry ache inside him.

But today, that hadn't been enough. Today, he was going to do something incredibly fucking stupid.

With shaky hands, Nick set aside the tequila and slid a shoebox from beneath his nightstand. He let a few desperate heartbeats pass by, in case his faulty sense of self-preservation decided to intervene. But he'd known since this morning that the day would end this way. On the way to work, he'd caught the tail end of a talk-radio segment while flipping through stations—some guy had called in, confessing that he'd hired a ghostwriter to pen love letters for his girlfriend—and Nick's fingers had frozen on the dial. The letter Aubrey had once written, never far from his thoughts, had leapt to the forefront.

It hadn't left since.

He swallowed and opened the box. He didn't know which hit harder—the hand-written sheets inside, or the tequila rocketing through his bloodstream—but the impact made his chest clench, regardless.

He lifted out the letter. The sheer number of times he'd folded and unfolded these pages had reduced the paper to fragile silk, but seventeen years hadn't dulled the ostentatiousness of the purple title at the top.

An Inexhaustive List of Things I Love About You.

Nick traced Aubrey's handwriting. It'd been forty-six days since her words had last stung his eyes. Forty-six days since he'd vowed to stop doing this to himself. Yet here he sat.

Again.

1. I love your way with words.

No one writes a love letter like you do, Nick, least of all me. But here's my attempt to try, because yours have changed my life. I'll never forget the first one I found in my locker. It was nothing like those awful books we read for English, which are really just some dead guy's long-winded attempts to sound smart. No, your words were alive. They shifted the world beneath my feet. And they were all for me.

Please, don't ever stop writing to me.

Nick dragged a hand down his face. God, had Aubrey ever really loved him like that? With such wholehearted purity?

He tried to feel his way back to that long-dead breath of sunlight, but he couldn't manage. Probably because, even in high school, he'd never truly settled into her adoration. He'd known he could never do anything for a girl like that except hold her back.

People who shone as brightly as Aubrey MacLean didn't belong in places like Henderson, Indiana.

Good thing, then, that Nick had broken her heart. Good thing Aubrey had left town and never returned. Good thing he hadn't seen her in seventeen years and never would again.

Good. Fucking. Thing.

He gulped more liquid flame and thunked the bottle down.

2. I love that you never back down from a fight.

Not that I approve of guys beating each other up. But you don't fight for fun. You just stand your ground when your honor is on the line, and always let the other guy throw the first punch. Then, when you hit back, it's . . . god, what can I say, other than 'beautiful'? I know I'm not supposed to think of it that way. I'm not supposed to lie in bed at night and replay the way you defended yourself against Gallant on your first day. But I'd never seen anyone fight like that before. So calm. So focused, like you were completely sure of yourself.

A dark chuckle scorched Nick's throat. *Some* things hadn't changed. He still fought. Daily. He had to, in order to keep the well of words inside him quiet.

He wondered whether Aubrey would still find it beautiful. If she'd seen him and Jackson pummeling each other at the gym earlier, would she have caught the way Nick funneled his regret into his fists, one punch at a time?

Footsteps sounded. He shoved the letter under the bed, nearly knocking over the tequila in his haste to stand. Thankfully, the mattress shielded everything from view, because Tansy filled the doorway, dripping rainwater. She fluffed her blond waves, scattering droplets across the carpet.

"Hey. What're you doing?" She sounded flat. Bored. Like she didn't have the faintest interest but had gotten so used to asking she couldn't be bothered to do otherwise.

Accurate, really.

"Just taking a breather," Nick said. "I had a hard day at the mill."

Her watery blue gaze swept up and down.

He toed Aubrey's letter under the bed. After six years of separation, Tansy counted as his wife in nothing but name, and he had no reason to hide. But he would've rather stripped naked than let her see, so he schooled his expression to nothingness. "You're home late. Where were you?"

She shrugged.

He knew what that meant—she'd been out indulging in one of the flings she would manage to forget before the day ended. Meanwhile, he'd been holed up in his bedroom like a lovesick teenager, reading a decades-old letter from a girl he'd never deserved.

"Did Paige tell you about her internship?" Tansy said. "There's a fee."

Nick tensed. "A fee?"

"Yep. She needs money."

A headache materialized behind his eyes. "All right. But I'm already pulling overtime at work. Six shifts a week is all they'll let me take."

Tired judgment weighted her gaze. "I'm not asking for me. It's for our *daughter*. You know, the one you impregnated me with and agreed to help raise."

Nick pinched the bridge of his nose, but Tansy was right. She usually was. "Yeah. Okay. How much does she need?"

"Four hundred dollars."

He nearly choked. "Four *hundred*? For an internship? I thought Paige was supposed to be working for them, not the other way around."

She crossed her arms. "This is her ticket to a good college, Nick. It's the most presumptuous internship in Henderson. So yeah, it costs money. Like most things."

"Prestigious," he corrected, without thinking. "The most *prestigious* internship in Henderson."

Tansy huffed. "Whatever."

Silence hung between them. Nick held her gaze, but his awareness pulsed somewhere low, alongside the letter and liquor he'd shoved beneath the bed. He imagined he might shove his failings under there, too, and maybe the dull, anxious thud that invaded his chest whenever he confronted the familiar disdain in Tansy's eyes.

Two more years. Then the bond they'd forged on the night they'd accidentally made a child together would cease to exist. They would no longer be bound to each other, or to this house. Yet the weight of the coming years bore down, an ever-present load on his shoulders.

He cleared his throat. "What happened to the extra three hundred I gave you last week?"

"Gone. It's not like our refrigerator just fills itself."

He sighed. But he already knew he'd find the money somewhere. Of course he would. He would lie down in front of a screaming train if it meant getting his daughter into a good college and helping her build the life she wanted. That was why he stayed, after all. Why he did anything.

For Paige. His precious baby girl. His only real family.

"Okay," he said. "I'll figure it out. Just . . . give me a few days, okay?"

Tansy's expression didn't flicker. "Great."

Without another word, she walked off, leaving him to find a towel and blot the rainwater from the carpet himself.

Later, in the dark, while Tansy snored down the hall, Nick laced his fingers beneath his head and stared at the ceiling. Incessant rain beat on the shadowed windowpanes.

Four hundred dollars. Where would he find that much on short notice? Maybe he could ask Jackson for a loan—with no family to support, the guy had managed to accumulate a decent-sized savings—but he hated relying on his best friend.

No, he'd rather handle it himself.

Nick pushed the covers down, then pulled them back up. Why the fuck couldn't he get comfortable? He contemplated sneaking to the kitchen for the tequila he'd restashed, then decided against it. Tansy's interruption of his pity-fest had been well-timed, and as long as he didn't drink any more, he could avoid a headache tomorrow.

Aubrey's letter, though . . . That still lay under the bed, its purple words shining from the pages like lasers, burning holes through the mattress and gathering into a hot ache in the pit of his stomach.

No one writes a love letter like you do, Nick.

Was that true? Maybe, but only because writing to Aubrey had once come to him as naturally as his own heartbeat. Even now, words smoldered in his belly. Sentences swam in his blood. Paragraphs piled in his rib cage.

Directing them at Tansy had never felt right, so he'd spent seventeen years swallowing them down. Back when he'd first gotten married, he'd tried bringing his new wife flowers, instead. Fake it 'til you make it, or some shit like that.

The first time, Tansy had tolerated the gesture well enough. She hadn't thanked him, but she'd arranged the flowers in the nursery, a welcome gift for the impending baby. When he'd tried again a few months later, though—after her eyes had gone bleary from lack of sleep and the constant soothing of a colicky newborn—she'd curled her lip, scornful.

"Is this really what we should be spending money on? You could've bought another baby bottle, instead. I can't seem to wash them out fast enough."

"I was trying to be romantic," he'd said, stung. "It's my way of saying thank you. For everything you're doing."

Tansy had made a face, then scooped up a wailing Paige from the baby swing and bounced on the balls of her feet in an effort to stop the crying. "If you want to be romantic, why don't you try feeding our kid in the middle of the night? That'd be a lot more useful than bringing me something that's going to be dead in a week."

Her bluntness had shocked him, even though he should have been used to it by then.

But she'd had a point, so Nick had started handling Paige's midnight feeding himself, at least on the days he hadn't worked second or third shift. Even though it had meant concentrating twice as hard at work the next day in order not to topple into the blast furnace's volcanic river and incinerate himself.

He'd never brought Tansy flowers again. Now, all these years later, he understood he should never have tried. The zenith of her interest had already passed, on the night she'd chosen him to distract herself with, for whatever reason. When he'd been so broken he'd unwittingly chained his future to hers.

Still, for all that, Tansy was a good mother—fiercely loving toward Paige, for which she'd earned Nick's undying respect. But her emotional range didn't extend beyond maternal adoration. Sappy love movies bored her. During their marriage, she'd forgotten their wedding anniversary every year. And she'd never once told Nick she loved him.

As far as he knew, it had never occurred to her to try.

Meanwhile, he bled inside. He pretended otherwise, mostly for Paige's sake, and masqueraded through adulthood with his poker face firmly intact. But in reality?

He felt like a boy, sometimes. Like the scrappy kid from the wrong side of the tracks who'd given his heart away at seventeen and never gotten it back. Who still boiled with white-hot self-loathing when he thought about hurting a girl he'd once loved down to the roots of his soul.

Who now spent hours at the gym, silencing the words he still wanted to say to her.

Because if he'd married Aubrey, he would've penned her something every day. Spilled ink like so much lifeblood across the page. He would've written about her garnet hair and green eyes, about that look of hers, the one that made him feel like they were sharing a secret.

His breathing quickened. If only there was some way to alchemize this regret into a way to pay the bills, because lately, the stacked-up words had begun to fester, as if he'd stuffed his jagged crevices full and had no place else to stash the leftovers. He'd tried to feed the words to the blast furnace. Sweat them out, punch them out, anything.

But maybe they had another use.

He sat up in the darkness, this morning's radio segment still heavy in his thoughts. Somewhere, someone was getting paid to ghostwrite love letters. Meanwhile, here he was, overflowing with words he couldn't say.

He threw the covers back, then crept down the hall on quiet feet, past Tansy's door to the cramped office, where he flicked open the sleeping laptop.

He typed a few words into the search engine. *Ghostwriting love letters for pay*. After scrolling through the results, he sat back. No job postings that he could find, but that didn't prevent him from trying on his own, did it?

He navigated to one of those websites where freelancers could offer gigs to the public. After registering for an account, he typed *Nick Thacker's Love-Letter-Writing Service* and pieced together an ad. For four hundred dollars, he would personally craft love letters for someone for up to six months.

He erased the ad, doubtful, then wrote it out again and posted the damn thing. What was the worst that could happen? He shut the computer and sat amid the muted roar of the rain.

Yet the corrosive heat in his gut gnawed deeper, so instead of going back to bed, he ventured to the front door, then outside.

In the driveway, the chilly autumn downpour assaulted him, more like a hail of bullets than actual rain. He tilted his head back and gulped the icy droplets. Maybe, on the off chance that someone responded to his ad, he could finally free himself. Crack open his chest and let the words gush out until the flames died back.

Not that he'd actually be writing to Aubrey. But he could always pretend he was.

Maybe that way, he could finally say goodbye.

Aubrey MacLean hadn't believed she would truly return to Indiana until her feet touched Henderson's broken sidewalk. The Greyhound bus trundled off, leaving her on an unmarked street corner halfway between farmland and civilization.

She breathed deep. To a stranger, the late-September evening might have seemed serene—cricket-song wafted on the air while clouds as fuzzy and soft as ripe peaches drifted overhead. But to Aubrey, menace lurked within the quiet.

This place had nearly broken her. She'd never wanted to return.

But here she was anyway, with a single purpose, and it didn't involve standing around feeling sorry for herself.

She set off with her suitcase, her stiletto heels finding wobbly purchase on the buckled cement. In the distance, the steel mill exhaled gray steam, and she wondered who worked there, these days. Probably most of the people she'd gone to high school with.

At the thought, her heart rattled out a few gunfire beats. While boarding the bus in New York, she'd vowed not to dwell on Nick, but now questions crept in. Was he still living here in Henderson? Raising the child he'd had with Tansy? What did he even look like, after all these years?

She told herself it didn't matter. But the darkened windows of the passing row homes roused memories of familiar black eyes, and the tangled shadows edging the sidewalk looked for all the world like tousled, night-dark curls.

She gritted her teeth and focused on the staccato tap of her heels. *Click, clack, click, clack. One, two, three, four.*

After a minute or two or twenty, the ironclad perfection of numbers repelled the onslaught of memories. Nick Thacker might have had power over her once, but no longer. He probably didn't live here anymore, anyway. Like her, he'd never wanted to stay.

The thought loosened a knot within her.

In town, her passing met with curious stares. The men all wore the dark, utilitarian coveralls of steelworkers, while the women enjoyed sweatshirts and messy buns. Meanwhile, Aubrey sported a shoulder-length red bob, dangly earrings, and a tailored boyfriend blazer.

She tugged at her clothes. She probably shouldn't have donned her corporate armor, but old habits died hard. Without meaning to, she'd dressed for proving herself. For holding her own in a male-dominated industry. Which she just about had, right before she'd gotten booted out the door.

One sky-high heel caught a ridge in the sidewalk, and she stumbled, pain knifing through her ankle. She caught herself, barely, and lowered herself to the curb with a whimper.

A massage of her ankle revealed a joint already ballooning beneath her fingers. "Shit," she muttered.

Cars rumbled past. When she tried to stand, a hot spear of agony rewarded her, so she sank back down, wondering how she would possibly get her luggage across town to her old house now.

She was still pondering when a car pulled off on the street's far side—something meteor-gray and fancy, every bit as out of place here as she was. A tinted window rolled down, revealing an undeniably handsome face.

"Hi, miss. Do you need help?" The man's teeth gleamed in the gathering dusk, somehow familiar. A heartbeat later, recognition hit Aubrey like a tidal wave.

"Gallant?" she breathed. "Gallant Nobel? Is that you?" God, she hadn't thought about him in ages. She'd nearly forgotten he existed.

His brow furrowed. "Uh, hi. Have we met?"

"We grew up together. It's me, Aubrey MacLean."

Gallant's expression slackened. He blinked once, then again. "*Aubrey?* The cheerleader?"

She offered a half-smile. "Yep."

Within moments, he was out of the car, crossing the road with long strides. "My god. What're you doing back? Are you okay? Where's your car?"

She gave a weary laugh. "I live in New York. I don't have a car."

He grasped her outstretched hands and helped her to her feet. "Do you need a ride?"

"Actually, that'd be great." She gestured at the offending frost heave. "I've been back for all of twenty minutes and already managed to sprain my ankle."

He nodded. "These sidewalks'll get you, if you let them."

"Right. I'd forgotten." Apparently, her prolonged absence had taken an eraser to *some* memories. Just not the ones she wanted.

Gallant squeezed her fingers and perused her up and down. "Wow," he said. "You look . . . different."

Aubrey inspected him right back. For the most part, he looked the same, still blessed with the sort of face that graced clothing ads and served as an example of perfect human symmetry. Seventeen years hadn't dulled the rich bronze hue of his hair or the crystalline blue of his eyes. But there *was* something subtly different. An aura of confidence, maybe. An easiness.

Not like the overly cocky boy she remembered.

"It's been a while," she said.

He let go of her hands. "It really has. I can't tell you how great it is to see you."

"You, too." To her surprise, she actually meant it.

Gallant's eyes crinkled as he scooped up her suitcase. "Here, why don't I get this? Can you walk? Or should I bring my car around?"

She tested her hurt ankle, pleased when it took her weight. "I can get there on my own, I think. It just won't be pretty."

He opened his mouth, then closed it again.

Aubrey couldn't stop an eyebrow from arcing. The old Gallant would've seized the opportunity to tell her she looked pretty doing anything. But maybe he'd changed. Either that, or he wasn't in a position to flirt. Yet when she glanced down, both of his ring fingers were bare.

He wheeled her suitcase across the road. Aubrey hobbled after him and situated herself in what proved to be a Tesla. The vehicle's interior reminded her of a spaceship, sleek and dark and polished. As she latched her seat belt, Gallant rolled up his window, shutting out the evening chorus of crickets and frogs. "Where to? Your old place, I'm assuming?"

She nodded. "That, but maybe the grocery store first, if you have time. I could use an ACE wrap and a few things for the house. Nobody's been inside for a while."

Gallant made an affirmative sound and eased the car into motion.

The quiet startled her. She'd been in electric vehicles before, mostly Ubers in New York, but the city's din had prevented her from appreciating the lack of engine noise. Here, the silence was almost eerie.

Gallant's gaze flitted between her and the road. "So, what brings you back to Henderson? Now, I mean?"

She didn't miss the subtle emphasis on *now*. "You mean, why didn't I come back when my dad died?"

"Yeah." His look turned sympathetic. "I'm sorry about that, by the way. He was a good guy. But I was pretty surprised we didn't see you afterward."

Aubrey turned to the window. Outside, single-level homes rolled by, backdropped by a twilit sky. The warm colors belied the chill in the air, which struck her as the perfect metaphor for her feelings toward her dad—warm and cold at once. "I'm sure you weren't the only one. But my dad never wanted a funeral. He just wanted us to spread his ashes somewhere beautiful. So my mom and I went to Switzerland."

Gallant nodded. "That sounds like a nice way to honor him."

"It was."

He didn't seem flustered by the macabre subject and smoothly moved on. "And how's your mom doing out in . . . California, was it? She got remarried, right?"

"Yep. LA suits her. And my stepdad treats her like gold, which makes me feel a lot less guilty about living thousands of miles away."

Gallant turned onto Main Street. A heavy silver watch glinted on his wrist—something expensive, though Aubrey didn't recognize the brand.

"I'm glad she's happy," he said. "When she left Henderson, though . . . I kept thinking you'd show up. Put her house on the market, maybe."

Aubrey wondered if she was imagining the wistfulness in his tone. As if he really had thought about her, more than once. "I didn't need to. Rich is . . . well, he's rich, so my mom hasn't needed the money." She paused, then decided Gallant deserved the truth after offering her a ride. "My mom's been wanting to deed me the house, but to be honest, I've been avoiding coming back."

He glanced over with curious eyes. "How come?"

She hesitated. "You know."

"Nick Thacker," he said. Not a question.

"Yeah." She swallowed the thousand other words scrabbling for purchase on her tongue. She wouldn't ask if Nick still lived here. It didn't matter. Her stint in Indiana would only last for as long as it took to convince her ex-boss to rehire her. She would hole up in her childhood home rent-free, put her nose to the grindstone, and glue the shattered pieces of her professional reputation back together. The moment she got her job back, she'd disappear.

Gallant filled the heavy quiet. "So now you're here to . . . what? Visit? Stay?"

"Visit." She ejected the word with force. "I should be back in New York by the end of the year."

"Oh yeah?" He chuckled. "Funny. That's where I'm headed. Probably in February."

She missed a beat. Henderson was the kind of town that sank its claws into people and didn't let go. "You're moving?"

"Yep."

"To New York City?"

"Yep."

A pang clamped around her chest. He said it so easily, like it was something just anyone could do, any time they liked. "What prompted that?"

He shrugged. "I'm just ready for a bigger pond. You can only go so far in this town, you know?"

She nodded. She *did* know.

"Hey," he said. "Last I heard, you were doing something brainy out there. Something mathy, like you always said. Accounting, maybe?"

Aubrey mustered a limp smile. People who didn't work with numbers rarely grasped the distinctions, so she doubted Gallant had demoted her on purpose. "I'm a mathematician, actually." Or had been. Right now, she wasn't anything, except disgraced.

"Wow." His eyes flared. "That sounds important. Good for you."

"Thanks." She smoothed over the wobble in her voice with a cleared throat. "Seems like you did pretty well, yourself. Fancy car, fancy clothes . . ." She gestured to his charcoal blazer and pressed black slacks. "I'm guessing you didn't end up at the steel mill."

He laughed. "Nope. Real estate."

"That's fantastic."

He slid the Tesla into a parking spot outside the Kroger. Glowing neon letters arced above the store's front doors, backlit by the fading sky. In the distance, the mill crouched like a watchful spider.

"Just tell me what you need, and I'll grab it," he said. "No reason to make that ankle any worse."

Aubrey bit her lip, hesitant to indebt herself further. Gallant didn't seem to expect anything in exchange for the ride, but she didn't think she'd imagined the appreciative glow in his eyes.

The corners of his mouth flicked up. "I can't get over how incredible you look. Really."

Nope, not imagining it at all. "Thanks," she said crisply. "But I'd better go in myself. I have extra shoes in my suitcase, so I'll just change real quick. I won't be long."

His forehead knitted. "You sure?"

"Yep."

He shrugged and pulled out his cell phone, settling in to wait. Aubrey limped to the trunk to swap her stilettos for ballet flats. By the time the store's sliding doors hissed open, the throb in her ankle had her questioning her decision, but she straightened her spine and pushed onward.

Inside, more men in coveralls and women in jeans browsed beneath fluorescent lights. A poster soliciting donations for Henderson's homeless pets met her front and center.

She paused and dug through her purse for a twenty, then pondered the wisdom of parting with it. Breaking her lease in New York had also broken her bank account, but she would earn more money, eventually. Worthy causes couldn't usually wait.

That decided, she stuffed the bill into the bucket and found a cart, letting the pushbar take most of her weight. She rolled over to a display of firewood. If there was one thing she *had* missed about Henderson, it was the rambling old Victorian she'd grown up in. The majestic two-story boasted a wood-burning fireplace, which would come in handy, given that the furnace had been switched off for years and Aubrey had no idea how to rectify that. Tomorrow, she'd hire a handyman, but tonight, her plans involved a steaming mug of tea and a good, old-fashioned roaring blaze.

After loading up on firewood and basic groceries, she found the first-aid aisle. Now that she was moving around, the sprain didn't feel as debilitating as it had initially, but a brace wouldn't go amiss.

Aubrey was gazing down, trying to decide between the ACE wrap in one hand and the lace-up brace in the other, when the hair on her neck lifted. A tingle flooded her skin.

And she knew. She just *knew* Nick Thacker hadn't moved away. Somehow, the cadence of his footsteps still lived within her memory.

He came up behind her and stopped.

Her lungs quavered, but she stayed still, determined not to give him the satisfaction of turning around. He'd have to ask, and even then, she might walk away without even showing her face.

Except when he rasped a single word, it dropped straight into her.

"Aubrey?"

She squeezed her eyes shut. Holy god, it was just her name, but the way he said it unzipped her skin, reached into her chest, and rearranged the beat of her heart. The mutinous thing pattered inside her ribs, its rhythm suddenly alien.

"Jesus," he said. "Is that really you?"

Shit, shit, shit. He sounded exactly the way she remembered, like they'd stood here just yesterday instead of decades ago. His voice was still so husky, still filled with quiet fire, like a match struck against rough stone.

She couldn't help it. She turned around.

The sight of him hit her like a one-two punch. Nick might have sounded the same, but he didn't look it, not at all. He was all grown up. Tall enough that he could look down on her now, which made her wish uselessly for her stilettos. Another five inches would have put her on par with his eyes, at least.

Not that anything could have prepared her to meet them. The color there reminded her of something depthless, so black she had trouble distinguishing where his irises ended and his pupils began. And while his eyes still tipped up at the corners, that once-noble upsweep now lent him an air of lethal intensity. He looked so . . . *male.* So big. So mature.

Gone was the boy who'd snuck into her heart and ripped it apart with his bare hands. In his place stood a man, his face an opus of sharp lines and hard angles.

She dropped her gaze, trying to escape the sudden flurry of her breathing, but the rest of him only compounded her problems. As a teenager, Nick had been skinny—frighteningly so—but now he'd filled out. And then some. A gray tank top showcased the breadth of his shoulders while the sleeves of his unzipped navy coveralls knotted around a trim, muscular waist.

He looked ridiculously fit, like he could punch through a concrete wall, if he wanted.

Knowing him, he probably could.

"It *is* you," he said softly.

A shiver skimmed down her spine. She searched for something to say. Absolutely anything. "You cut your hair," she blurted, then winced.

God, of all the things she could've come up with after seventeen years—chief among them being *how can you stand there looking so casual after you destroyed me?—that* was what emerged. *You cut your hair.* Fan-freaking-tastic.

"Um. Yeah." Nick scrubbed a hand across his scalp. His hair was as black as ever, but he'd shorn the unruly curls in favor of a buzz cut no more than a quarter inch long.

She wished it made him ugly. It didn't. If anything, it only heightened the impact of those angular features, the way they conspired to rob her of breath. Somehow, Nick Thacker was more beautiful—more wildly dangerous—than he'd ever been.

"I get too hot at work, otherwise," he said.

A long silence unspooled. Aubrey focused on the smudge of ash adorning his sculpted cheekbone. She wanted to break the brittle quiet by screaming—at herself for internally falling to pieces, or maybe at that blackened smear. It looked strategic, as if someone had painted it there, deliberate, for the express purpose of driving home how devastating he'd become.

Why couldn't he have just gained weight? Or lost his hair, like a normal person?

Whatever. It didn't matter. She needed to escape the suffocating buzz of the overhead lights. *Now.* "Well, it was nice seeing you. Or something. But Gallant's waiting for me outside."

"Gallant? As in, Gallant Nobel?" His shoulders tensed, the reaction seemingly unconscious, because his eyes never changed.

The impassivity there made her want to throw something. Once, she'd understood every flash within those depths, but now his eyes were a cool dark secret, a word inked in an alphabet she'd once cherished but since forgotten. He could've been pondering his grocery list or cursing her existence, and she wouldn't have known the difference.

"Yeah." She did her utmost to mirror his composure. "I sprained my ankle, and he's helping me out."

"Is he."

God, she needed out. Away. Mustering all the dignity her injury would allow, she tossed both ACE bandage and brace into her cart and limped off.

Just before she rounded the corner, Nick called out, "Aubrey, wait."

She looked back. She shouldn't have, but she seemed just as incapable of ignoring him now as she had been as a teenager.

His raven-dark brows crooked. "Seventeen years, and that's all you're going to say to me?"

Her breath caught at the way *seventeen years* rolled off his tongue as if he'd held the number in his mind already. As if it meant something to him. As if he'd kept track.

But the calculation was straightforward enough: their age now, less their age the last time they'd seen each other. Thirty-five minus eighteen. Her calculator brain could do that in a nanosecond. She knew his could, too.

It meant nothing.

"Yes, Nick. That's all there is *to* say." Lifting her chin, she muscled her cart away and prayed this would be the last time they ever spoke.

But in a town like this, she probably wouldn't get so lucky.

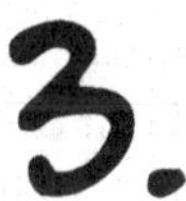

3.

By the time Aubrey slid back into Gallant's Tesla, she was trembling.

He took one look at her and frowned. "Are you okay? What happened?"

She hunkered into the seat, hoping it would do her the favor of swallowing her up. "Nothing, it's fine. I'm fine. I just . . . ran into Nick in there."

Gallant's lips compressed. He started to reach out, then dropped his hand onto the gearshift without making contact. "You look like you saw a ghost."

She scrubbed her palms against her tailored pants, which did nothing to relieve the clamminess there. "Yeah, well. I hadn't seen him since we were kids. I honestly didn't think he lived here anymore."

Gallant nodded.

Her fingers curled, seemingly by themselves. God, how could this possibly feel so *real*, still? So fresh? She and Nick had broken up nearly twenty years ago. Maybe she'd thought about him on occasion—okay, *many* occasions—but she was over it. She'd *been* over it. "Sorry. I think I just need a second."

Gallant's neon-blue gaze held hers, steady and unblinking. In the silence, she forced her hands to relax and her serrated breathing to even.

Whatever he saw in her face must have reassured him, because he eased into a smile. "Take all the time you need. I'm just going to load up your things, okay? Then we'll go."

She blinked, then glanced out the window to her still-packed cart, which stood ten feet away. In her haste, she'd simply left it. She'd been *that* desperate to put a layer of steel between herself and Nick. "Yeah. Okay. Thanks."

Gallant slid out and loaded her things into the trunk. Aubrey narrowed her focus to the clatter of firewood, to Gallant's labored breaths.

Nick probably wouldn't have broken a sweat.

She groaned, her head falling back against the seat. Nope. She wouldn't think about him. It was over and done with and had been for years.

By the time Gallant pulled out of the parking lot, Aubrey had mostly regained her composure. He drove in silence, his expression contemplative, though there wasn't much to concentrate on. The road was arrow-straight. There was no traffic to dodge. She searched for a way to break the silence and came up empty-handed.

"I always wondered what you saw in him," he finally said.

Her breath hitched. Of course she wouldn't escape that easily. "In Nick?"

"Yeah. I mean, to be fair, I didn't know him that well. But you were always so outgoing, and he was so quiet. Or angry. Or . . . something. I never really figured it out."

She studied his profile, searching for some veiled meaning. Had Gallant forgotten the way he'd instigated Nick in high school? The two black eyes he'd earned for his trouble?

It seemed so. His expression was neutral, as if age truly had mellowed him. Meanwhile, the years had honed Nick into something beautiful and cutting, something that sliced beneath her skin and dredged up hurts long since buried.

Gallant glanced over. "I think the whole school wondered, actually. How the two of you ended up together."

She cleared her throat. The encounter in the store had clearly stripped her of her defenses, because she didn't even try to deflect. "That's easy. Because he wrote me love letters. Every day. I'd never read anything like them. Still haven't, actually."

"Really?" Gallant seemed taken aback. "Nick Thacker wooed a cheerleader with . . . poetry?"

In any other circumstances, she would've laughed. Trust cheerleading to be what he remembered about her. "Not poetry. Just these raw, heartfelt letters that convinced me we'd be together forever."

"Huh."

She spun one of her bangle bracelets around her wrist. Honesty welled up, bitter on her tongue. "The truth is, I always thought I'd find another guy who'd write me letters like that, someday. But it never happened. I just ended up dating coworkers. Friends of coworkers. Math people. None of them had the kind of . . . depth Nick did." Mist slicked her eyes, and she angled her face away. Gallant would probably think she was about to cry.

She wasn't. It had just been a long day, and she was tired, and her ankle throbbed, and she'd lost the job she'd loved so dearly and . . . All she wanted was to curl up with some hot tea and an even hotter fire and figure out how to fix it.

Gallant seemed to sense her mental retreat, because he didn't press. Two minutes later, he pulled into her cul-de-sac, then her driveway. Her old house loomed, dark and imposing, but the Victorian didn't look nearly as run-down as she'd expected. Scarlet leaves littered the yard, but there were no cobwebs, no climbing vines, no peeling paint or broken shutters.

Gallant sucked in a long breath. "I owe you an apology."

Aubrey swiveled. "An apology? For?"

He flashed a rueful smile. "For high school. I know I hit on you way too much. And I was a complete jerk about it. But it wasn't because I was trying to carve another notch on my bedpost, I swear. I just had no idea how to tell you how much I liked you."

Her chest hitched. That sounded . . . unlikely. "You carved notches on your bedpost with half the girls in school, Gallant."

"Yeah. I know." Something flickered in his too-blue eyes. "But there was only one girl I actually wanted. Turns out I should've been writing to her instead of screwing around with everything that moved. I just thought . . . I don't know. I thought it made me a stud, or something. I thought it would make her like me."

Aubrey's breath grew harsh in her ears. She had no idea what to make of that. "Gallant, I—"

"It's fine. I'm not asking for anything, except forgiveness. Unless maybe you'd consider letting me take you to dinner sometime."

She gave him a level look.

"Okay, I guess I *am* asking for something." He grinned, again with those bright white teeth. "But I don't have any expectations."

She hesitated, but the earnestness of his smile softened something inside her. He *had* changed, it seemed, and she of all people could appreciate the value of second chances, considering all she wanted was one for herself.

Not to mention she'd probably need weeks to work her way back into her ex-boss's good graces. A distraction might help.

Dating Gallant probably wouldn't lead to anything, but if it did, it wasn't like he would ask her to stay. He was headed to New York, same as her. "I guess we could give it a shot."

"No pressure," he said. "We'd just be two old friends, catching up and seeing what happens."

She weighed that. "Okay."

His smile widened. "Saturday, then? There's this great little seafood place that opened up last year. I could pick you up at seven?"

"Sure."

He punched her number into his phone. By the time he'd helped her bring her groceries to the kitchen, Aubrey's ankle felt ready to give out. She smiled gamely and waved to him from the front stoop.

When the Tesla's taillights faded, she limped back inside and went the frosty living room. Hulking white shapes populated the space—her mother had left sheets draped over everything, apparently.

Aubrey whisked the makeshift slipcover from the couch, grateful for a dust-free surface to lie down on. The thing was a long, low chesterfield, its blue velvet worn to a well-loved shine. It offered all the comfort she remembered, and she huddled into the cushions, hunting for warmth.

God, she was tired. Cold, too, but building a fire would require more energy than she had. Maybe she'd just lie here, gather her strength . . .

Within seconds, fatigue won out, and Aubrey closed her eyes.

When the dreams came, they dragged her down into memory.

4.

Seventeen years ago

AUBREY HATED ENGLISH CLASS.

She always sat at the back, as far from Mrs. Hayes's attentive eyes as possible, and passed the time with a book of logic puzzles she kept tucked on her lap. Why waste time studying a language she'd grasped at the age of three, anyway?

She crossed out a box on her puzzle chart, the classroom melting to a blur of light and chatter. She never tired of the mathematics behind the deduction work, how the puzzle's facts layered in her mind like crystal lattice. Not to mention the incomparable sense of completion at the end, that jewel box *click* when the last tick mark found its place.

Up front, Mrs. Hayes started droning. Probably about *Wuthering Heights*, which Aubrey had skimmed the CliffsNotes for. Since her cheerleading uniform did little to hide her contraband puzzles, she fluffed up the pillowy parka she'd donned to ward off the January chill. Let Mrs. Hayes think she was cold. At this point, Aubrey was only marking time until graduation, anyway. Four months. Exactly five thousand, five hundred and eighty more minutes of English class. Then, at summer's end, she'd be bound for New York. She'd already applied to NYU early decision and gotten her acceptance letter.

Life was waiting. *Math* was waiting.

". . . new student today. Let's make him welcome."

Okay, so maybe they weren't being tortured with books just yet. Aubrey lifted her head just as a stranger slid into the empty desk beside hers.

Her classmates twisted in their seats. The newcomer clearly wanted no part of the attention, because he hunched over his notebook, his pencil poised above a fresh page, as if begging Mrs. Hayes to move on.

Aubrey drummed her fingers against her desk. Huh. Henderson rarely got new students, and never so close to year's end. This one was doing his best to meld with his seat, but his slouch couldn't disguise his ranginess.

A thicket of black curls obscured his face, so her focus strayed to his wrists. The frayed cuffs of his olive green sweatshirt fell short, the garment at least two sizes too small, and his wristbones jutted as if trying to lance through his skin. His hands were similarly devoid of fat, long-fingered and knobby-knuckled.

She frowned. Either he went hungry at home, or he had the metabolism of a nuclear reactor.

Her gaze slid upward again. A flash of glistening black eyes met hers before the boy retreated behind his hair.

"Hi," she whispered. "I'm Aubrey. It's nice to meet you."

He gave no indication of having heard. Up front, Mrs. Hayes launched into a diatribe about Emily Bronte's commentary on passion and obsession, and eventually, Aubrey shrugged and returned to her puzzle book. Clearly, the new kid wasn't the friendly type.

Which suited her fine. By summer's end, Henderson would be in her rearview mirror, and this silent boy and his bony hands with it.

After class, Gallant caught up to Aubrey in the hallway.

He walked backward in front of her, matching her pace. "Hey, MacLean, looking good. That uniform does you all kinds of favors. You should wear it more often."

She rolled her eyes. "I wear it every Wednesday, Gallant. Just like every other cheerleader in school."

"Which officially makes Wednesday my favorite day of the week." He snapped his gum and grinned. "Hey, so you wanna skip next period? We could head out to the quarry, maybe—"

"I've got calculus." She tried to step around him, but he adjusted his trajectory to move with her. "Which I never skip. Not even for someone as charming as you."

If he picked up on her sarcasm, he gave no indication, and she suspected her insult had gone entirely unappreciated. Pity. With his bronze hair and luminous blue eyes, Gallant pretty much did whatever he wanted and had long ago gotten used to hearing *yes*.

But Aubrey had always found something . . . empty about him. As if no amount of lavished attention could ever satisfy. Gallant Nobel was like a hole in the ground—no matter how much water you poured in, you could never fill it up.

"C'mon. Who cares about math when—" Gallant stumbled, then righted himself with a huff. He'd backed into someone who stood unmoving in the middle of the hallway.

It was the new kid, scribbling in a notebook. He turned slowly, as if annoyed by the fact that his failure to move had almost bowled someone over.

A thread of curiosity tugged at Aubrey's insides. Despite the curls falling into his eyes, he couldn't hide from her here, and she seized the opportunity to scan his face. Like his hands, his features were prominent, his cheeks hollowed beneath their bladed arches almost to the point of gauntness. That, along with his squared chin and flinty dark eyes, gave him an austere beauty, a stark sort of allure that reminded her of a doomed hero in a postapocalyptic tragedy.

Gallant brushed off his letterman jacket with contrived concern. "Yo, new guy. Watch where you're going."

The boy said nothing.

"Hey." Gallant waved a hand in front of the kid's face. "You hearing me?"

The boy stared, flat, and a thought occurred. Maybe he hadn't actually meant to ignore her in English. Maybe he hadn't answered her because he *couldn't.* Maybe he was writing things down in the middle of the hallway because that was his only method of communication.

She tugged at Gallant's sleeve. "Hey, don't be rude. I'm not sure he actually speaks."

That got a reaction. The boy's attention slid to her, his expression withering.

"I speak," he said, each word weighted with condescension. Then, to Gallant, "And *you* walked into *me*."

Gallant's expression darkened. He stood eye to eye with the kid, but had a forty-pound advantage, at least. "Hey, man. You were in *my* way. Just say sorry. That's all I ask."

The boy's lips thinned. His entire being seemed to compress inward.

Aubrey's heart ground out a sympathetic beat. Gallant Nobel—captain of the football team, homecoming king, Mister Popularity—could probably break this twiggy newcomer in half with hardly any effort. No wonder the guy looked scared.

"Hey." She pulled at Gallant's arm. She had no desire to watch the new kid get beaten up in the hallway. Or at all. "Do you still wanna skip?" Words motored from her mouth. Anything to wrench his attention away. "I don't know about the quarry, but if you wanted to see a movie . . ."

Thankfully, Gallant let himself be dragged away. When Aubrey glanced back, the new kid stared down at his hands, as if wondering which finger Gallant would have broken first.

"What a freak." Gallant's voice was hard. "What the hell was his problem, anyway?"

Before she could respond, he shook off her grip and stalked away, the offer to skip class forgotten.

Hours later, when the last bell rang, Aubrey headed to cheerleading practice. She was cutting through the frosty brick alley between the cafeteria and the gymnasium when she ran straight into a wall of people. Which only ever meant one thing, here.

A fight.

She groaned and delved into the throng. She was at least mildly interested in finding out which hotheaded jock had caught another guy eyeing his girlfriend, but mostly she just wanted to get to practice on time. Then she glimpsed two heads at the crowd's epicenter—one bronze, the other dark and shaggy-curled—and stopped as abruptly as if she'd face-planted into a wall.

Oh, god. The new kid. Why hadn't he stayed out of Gallant's way? Why hadn't Gallant just *let it go*?

She flung out elbows, forcing her way to the front. The students had formed a ragged ring, and Gallant swaggered within, fists up. The new kid stood uncannily still, assessing his opponent with hard black eyes. He wore a threadbare bomber jacket he'd clearly acquired secondhand. His backpack lay discarded on the asphalt.

"Gallant!" Aubrey shrieked. "Stop! Don't hurt him!"

Gallant didn't hear or, more likely, didn't care. He darted forward, his letterman jacket flapping open on the icy air.

But the new kid turned to look straight at her. The touch of his eyes harpooned her to the spot.

She flung up her hands in a *stop* gesture just as Gallant's fist connected.

The boy's head snapped sideways. His curls straightened and sprang back like stretched rubber bands. He stood there, hunched, his hair shielding his face, while Aubrey wondered wildly whether she could catch him before he toppled.

But he didn't go down. A hush blanketed the crowd.

Gallant retreated, glancing from his clenched fist to his opponent and back again, as if he couldn't figure out what had just happened. After a long moment, the new kid straightened, then hauled his hair back with one hand.

And smiled.

It wasn't much—just a thin, hard flash on a mouth that was split and bleeding—but it did something funny to Aubrey's stomach. A tiny sound snuck from her throat as the boy raised his fists. The gesture looked so . . . fluid. As if he'd done this a thousand times. As if he'd come into the world already knowing how to curl his fingers in that particular way.

Gallant blanched and edged backward. The new kid moved with him, surefooted, then pounced.

Aubrey's breath hung suspended, her need for air receding. She'd seen fights before, lots of them. Inevitably, they involved more grunting and huffing than anything else, and usually ended with a few panicked, graceless swings that rarely found their targets.

This was . . . not that. This was something else entirely. Because this kid was ferocious. And beautiful. And he knew exactly what he was doing.

He spiraled around Gallant, his fists flicking out with bruising precision. He delivered a strike to the jaw. One, two to the torso. He melted from Gallant's answering bludgeon like so much air parted by a blown breath, then slid back in and drove a knee into Gallant's stomach.

The whole time, his face never changed. He looked . . . calm. Certain. The hardness from just moments ago gave way to a resolve so serene that Aubrey swore she'd been made privy to something extraordinary. With a backdrop of brick wall and packed bodies as his canvas, the boy blurred across her vision, a living artwork of sinew and grace.

Her heart quit beating, then restarted again, double time. In another life, he would've been a warrior, she decided. Because what she'd mistaken as fear in the hallway was instead a sort of smoldering poise—fury distilled into a purer, harder form.

And yet she couldn't reconcile this with the boy who'd shunned her in English. Who'd stopped in the hallway to write in his notebook. He was like an equation she couldn't work out—too many variables, not enough data.

She wanted to know his name.

Gallant's swings grew wilder. The boy responded with a few measured strikes, and as quickly as it had begun, it was over. Gallant crashed to his knees on the frigid asphalt, trapped in some kind of chokehold, his face purpling. The new kid set bloodied lips beside his ear.

"Leave me. The fuck. Alone."

Aubrey heard, but couldn't be sure anyone else had. The kid tossed Gallant aside like a sack of rotten potatoes. The crowd rushed in, fawning over their fallen hero.

But she only had eyes for the boy. He snatched up his backpack and slipped through the surging crowd, vanishing around the side of the cafeteria.

She pushed against the tide, curiosity like flames licking at her bones. Where had he learned to fight like that? And why had he refused to talk to her? What had he been writing in that notebook?

If only she could solve for X, she could solve for Y. And Z. And the dozen other variables she suddenly hungered to define.

She cleared the throng, then the cafeteria. The boy was already halfway across the parking lot, headed for the highway at a pace she couldn't match.

But she had a car, so she scrounged in her backpack for her keys. Two minutes later, she pulled alongside him in her hand-me-down Subaru, the passenger window rolled down.

"Hey," she called. "Do you want a ride?"

He flicked her a glance without slackening his pace. He walked in the same direction as traffic, right atop the white line, heedless of danger.

Aubrey checked for oncoming cars, then edged across the double-yellow to give him room. "Come on, get in."

"Go away," he said.

She feathered the gas. "No. Town's two miles away. You'll get yourself killed, doing this."

He snorted. "What do you care? Or did you just come to yell at me for punching your boyfriend?"

"Boyfriend? *Gallant?*" She scoffed. "Definitely not."

"Whatever. Shouldn't you be at cheerleading practice?"

She glanced down. She'd zipped her jacket to the neck, which meant he must've paid her more attention than she'd realized, earlier. The knowledge only fueled her determination. "I'd rather skip it than let you get run over."

He kept walking.

She changed her angle, trying for lightheartedness. Maybe humor could break through that icy wall. "Come on, you're just lucky it's not Friday. If it was, I'd let you turn yourself into roadkill."

He grunted—ninety-eight percent *fuck off,* two percent grudging interest. "Why, what's on Fridays?"

"Math club. Which I never skip."

His stride faltered. "You're a cheerleader who likes math?"

She smiled. Clearly, that had slid past his defenses, however much he wished it hadn't. "No. I'm a cheerleader who *loves* math. Who lives and breathes it. Sees holiness in it."

He stopped. "Okay. That's . . . unexpected."

She braked to a halt. "Yeah, well, so is you beating the shit out of Gallant Nobel. But here we are."

He sighed, then looked up at the sky as if searching for guidance. After what seemed like an eternity, he laid his knobby hands on the doorsill and stooped to look in.

Aubrey met his gaze squarely. Something about his regard made her heartbeat relocate to the roof of her mouth.

"Is that really his name?" His voice was rough. Sultry enough that she could practically feel its texture against her skin. "Gallant Nobel?"

"Yeah."

"Wow." He rasped a graveled laugh, then spat a red gob onto the road. His bottom lip dribbled a fresh rivulet, which he swiped at with the back of a hand. "That's rich."

"Rich? How so?"

"Come on, his parents were laying it on *thick*. Gallant Nobel? They were probably trying to compensate for what a dick he is."

She cocked her head. "What're you talking about?"

"*Gallant?* And *noble*? Two words that mean practically the same thing? Don't tell me you've never noticed."

She blinked. Then laughed, because she *hadn't* noticed, which seemed unbelievable, now that he'd pointed it out. Gallant Nobel.

That really was absurd.

When her amusement had run its course, she said, "What's *your* name?"

He considered her for a long, breathless moment. She'd never seen eyes that dark before, and found them both piercing and impenetrable, like he could take her precise measure without giving away anything in return.

"Nick," he finally said.

Nick. She turned the syllable over in her mind. So abrupt, like a punch. It suited him. "Well, hi, Nick. I'm—"

"Aubrey. Yeah. I know."

A flush crept up her neck. "You heard me, then? In English? Why didn't you say anything?"

"Because. I don't like cheerleaders. And they definitely don't like me."

A normal person would have been stung by his dismissiveness. Maybe driven off and left him standing in the road. But his words sparked all the opposite desires, because they sounded like a challenge.

And she'd never been much good at backing down. Not when there was a puzzle in need of solving.

"Cheerleading isn't something I actually care about," she said. "It was just to round out my college applications. It doesn't define me."

He dipped his chin. "Mmm. I'm getting that."

"Okay, well, good." She tugged at her seat belt. "Does that mean you'll get in the car now?"

The corner of his mouth curled. His lips were uniquely plush amid the ascetic lines of his face—the top one pouted out, fuller than the bottom, and she stared at it while a long silence unraveled.

Abruptly, Nick withdrew from the window. Aubrey started to protest, but he didn't walk off. Instead, he jerked the door open, flopped onto the passenger seat, and slammed the door with an arch of expectant black brows.

"There," he said. "Happy?"

Surprise knotted her tongue. She sat there until the blare of a horn jolted her. When she glanced in her rearview mirror, an impatient driver gesticulated.

Aubrey stomped the gas. What was wrong with her? She'd stopped in the middle of a two-lane highway. How stupid.

"Put your seat belt on," she said.

Nick gave her an appraising look. "A cheerleader who likes math *and* safety? This is getting weirder by the second."

Warmth stung her cheeks. "Well, I went to all this trouble to rescue you. I can't have you dying on me now."

He let out a scuffed laugh. "I don't need rescuing. Not in the hallway, and not when dickhead jocks decide to punch me."

"Clearly," she murmured.

"You didn't think Gallant would actually listen when you told him not to hit me, did you?"

"No. But it was worth a try."

When Nick didn't respond, Aubrey searched for another topic. "So . . . you just moved to Henderson?"

"Yeah," he said.

"From?"

"Baltimore."

"Did you get in a lot of fights there, or something?"

He gave a stiff shrug. "Some."

Okay. He clearly had no interest in that subject either, so she tried another. "How come you moved four months before graduation?"

"Fuck if I know. Ask my dad. I learned not to question that asshole a long time ago, but you're more than welcome to, if you feel like trying to have a conversation with the wall."

She weighed that, slotting it into her mental calculus of him.

Nick apparently had no interest in further conversation. He gazed out the window at the skeletal trees. Beyond them, the steel mill loomed against a crystalline winter sky.

"Where do you live?" she ventured, once they'd reached town.

"Doesn't matter," he said. "I'm not going home."

She paused. "Okay. Where to, then?"

"I don't care. Just . . . not there."

His clipped tone silenced her again. Definitely not a happy home life.

She drove on, stealing sideways glances, lingering on the contour of Nick's cheekbones, which looked even more prominent with his face angled away. Those, along with the upward tilt of his eyes, gave him a regal look, spoiled only mildly by the ruby bead welling on his lip.

She should probably get him cleaned up. If he didn't soak the blood from his sweatshirt soon, it would stain. The *how* didn't pose much challenge—her parents would be at work for a few more hours, so she continued through Henderson and into her neighborhood.

Nick finally roused from his ruminations when she killed the engine in her driveway. "Where are we?"

"My house."

He leaned forward for a look through the windshield. "You brought me to your *house*?"

"Yeah. But don't worry. No one's home."

"What? That's even worse." He twisted to look at her, his mouth a beautiful, bloodied slash. "I mean, I could be anybody. I could be some psycho trying to take advantage of you."

"I'm pretty sure you aren't."

His brows knitted. "No, you're not. You don't know the first thing about me."

Her fingers twined in her lap. He sounded almost affronted that she'd dared to trust him. "Yeah, I do. You let Gallant hit you. On purpose, just so he'd be the one who started it, not you. That tells me more than you realize."

He sat back, blinking. "No. I wasn't being . . . honorable, or anything. I just know what happens when the broke-ass new kid is the one who picks the fight. And it's never good."

She studied him. Spots of color battled for purchase on his cheeks, a betrayal.

"I think there was more to it than that," she said. "I think you're better than he is."

"Not even a little."

She chewed her lip and changed tack again. "Okay, fine, if not better, then more . . . gallant. More *noble*, if you will."

That did the trick. His frigid standoffishness cracked. "You have to admit, that name is fucking ridiculous."

A chuckle bubbled out. "It really is. Now come inside."

She popped her door and climbed out. Nick stayed behind, frowning at her through the windshield, but eventually, he grabbed his backpack and emerged into the bracing air. He followed her to the front door, where she fumbled with her keys. Normally, she had the door open in seconds, but with those watchful dark eyes weighing her efforts, her fingers moved in slow motion.

When she eventually stepped into the entryway, he stayed on the stoop, first gazing up at the house, then at her. He seemed to wrestle with something.

Finally, the slope of his shoulders lowered, and he came inside. But not before he muttered under his breath, words Aubrey just barely caught.

"Why do I have the feeling I'm going to regret this?"

5.

NICK PACED OUTSIDE the Kroger, one hand mashed to his thumping chest. Holy shit, Aubrey MacLean.

Aubrey fucking MacLean.

She'd just . . . appeared, out of nowhere, like some kind of ghost. Or hallucination. Or, more accurately, the physical incarnation of a wound he'd carved into himself seventeen years ago and never let heal.

It was her hair that had given her away. He'd passed the aisle and caught that singular glimmer of garnet, and, for a moment, thought he was dreaming.

But no, Aubrey had been all too real, and she'd nearly knocked him senseless just by existing. And damn, had she looked different. So polished, with her red hair cut on an angle, longer in front and shorter in back—the kind of haircut only women with pin-straight hair could get away with. Not to mention her clothes. Fashionable in a way that left him excruciatingly aware of the thread coming unstitched from the hem of his tank top and the grime still clinging to his skin.

He'd probably repulsed her, and now he groaned just thinking about it. But that hadn't even been the worst part. No, that had been the frosty glint in her eyes, so cold he still felt clammy all over, despite the thunder in his veins.

Aubrey hated him. *Still.* One glance had made that painfully clear, so he'd defaulted to what had always come so naturally. He'd shielded himself. Retreated behind a hard blank wall, even while his heart had clawed itself to ribbons.

Now he turned a circle and stared at his empty hands. He couldn't remember what he'd gone into the store for. He couldn't think at all. He just needed . . . hell, he couldn't even say. Probably the same thing he always did.

He pulled out his cell phone and shot a text to Jackson. **Meet at the gym in 5?** A moment later, he added an uncharacteristic **Please.**

His phone buzzed in seconds. **Does 15 work?**

I'll be waiting, Nick typed.

The MMA gym was eleven blocks away, but he elected to jog. Just minutes ago, he'd been too exhausted to even consider an after-work gym session, but now he blazed with the fiery need to move.

Aubrey MacLean. The woman who haunted his dreams. What the hell was she doing back in Henderson?

Nick was already waiting on the mat when his best friend strode into Wilder's MMA Academy. Thankfully, Jackson had shown up in his gear. All the guy had to do was toss down his duffel and slip on his gloves.

"Hey, asshole," Nick said, mostly because Jackson never swore and always fought harder if Nick said something dickish beforehand. "Took you long enough."

Jackson glanced at the wall clock. "Jeez, man. You kiss the ladies with that mouth? What're you all fired up about, anyway? You texted me twelve minutes ago."

In lieu of answering, Nick put his fists up. The truth was, he *didn't* kiss the ladies with that mouth. Except for that one time, four years ago, when he'd taken Nisha Hansen to dinner with the misguided notion that if Tansy was dating, he should be, too. They hadn't even made it into the restaurant when Nisha had grabbed him by the collar and pulled him down for a kiss, saying she couldn't resist a face like his.

Funny, since she'd resisted just fine in high school. Back then, she hadn't even given him the time of day.

Even so, he'd been hopeful, at least for a moment. But then the great white nothingness had set in, that depressingly familiar desert of feeling, as if someone had bleached him of all emotion. Close on its heels had come the equally familiar jab of guilt, like a knifepoint drilling into his sternum. That one felt suspiciously similar to how Nick imagined cheating did, which was more than a little incredible, considering you couldn't cheat on your high school ex-girlfriend's memory.

But his heart didn't seem to realize that. Why would it? It hadn't with Tansy, either.

So he'd ended the date with Nisha right there in the parking lot and hadn't bothered to try again.

Now he bounced from toe to toe, his gloves on and his mouth guard in, impaticnce like a snapping whip inside him. "I'm not fired up. Come on, let's go."

Jackson stepped onto the mat. The overhead lights warmed his ebony skin and gleamed on his freshly shaved scalp. "*Something's* got you wired. What's up? Tansy hounding you for money again?"

Nick dropped into a fighting stance. Tansy *had* asked about Paige's internship fee again. Seven times, to be exact. And in the almost-week since he'd posted the love-letter ad, not a single person had responded. Which meant if the idea didn't pan out soon, he'd have to come up with something else.

But that was the least of his worries right now. "Paige just needs money for this internship thing. Not a big deal." Nick punctuated his answer with a right hook.

Jackson dodged without any apparent effort. "You don't have it?"

"Not yet." Nick followed up with a low kick.

Jackson danced away. "You wanna borrow it?"

"Nope."

Fuck it. This was taking way too long, and Nick wasn't in the mood. He dove, abandoning any pretense of strategy or form.

Surprise flitted across Jackson's face, but he didn't call Nick on the breach of code. He just met him grapple for grapple, punch for messy punch. The conversation devolved into an exchange of grunts and splattered sweat. Gloves slapped bare flesh.

Nick nearly wept his relief as rational thought receded. His world shrank to a blur of effort. Punch. Kick. Grunt. Pain.

Fire bloomed in his muscles, scorching away the frigidity in Aubrey's eyes.

Jab. Uppercut.

The in-and-out pull of air scraped at his lungs, erasing her scent.

Overhand. Sprawl. Dance out of reach.

Damn, there wasn't anything else he'd rather be doing.

Still, desperation made him sloppy. Within minutes, Jackson had him in a clinch, using it to rain knees against Nick's torso. Each strike left a blossoming flower of hurt behind. Nick jostled for position, but Jackson, taller and stronger, took him down. Nick hit the mat on his back, air driven from his lungs. Before he could counter, Jackson locked him in an arm bar.

The sinew of Nick's shoulder popped and stretched. He gritted his teeth, his mind clouding with a blessed haze of white.

Jackson grunted. "What're you doing, man? Tap out."

Nick didn't, which prompted Jackson to pull harder. Only when Nick's humerus bent in a way it absolutely shouldn't did he finally slap the mat.

Jackson let go and scrambled away. Nick lay there, his arm throbbing, his chest working like a bellows. Overhead, the lights swam in and out of focus. "Thanks," he said. "I needed that."

"Dude." Jackson shook his head. "What is going *on* with you? That was a hot mess."

True. But it had also swept Nick clean inside.

He levered upright and pulled Jackson into a sweaty hug. His best friend clapped him on the back in that perfunctory way that said Jackson had him covered, even if he didn't understand why.

"Don't worry about it," Nick said. "Same time tomorrow?"

"Sure, man." Jackson huffed. "I'll beat the crap out of you whenever you want."

"Yeah, yeah. Why else do you think I keep you around?"

Once outside, Nick walked the eleven blocks back to the Kroger. He still couldn't remember what he'd stopped for, so he climbed into his truck and headed home. He should've been back half an hour ago, anyway. At least for Paige's sake. Tansy never cared.

When he walked in, his co-parent and his daughter sat at the dinner table. Tansy barely glanced up, but Paige squealed like she hadn't seen him in weeks.

"Daddy! You're back! How was your day?"

Nick dropped into his chair. "Hey, Peanut. It was . . . uh, interesting. How was yours?"

She launched into a gleeful accounting of her latest math team competition.

He sat back, basking in her youthful effervescence. For all that he'd fucked up everything else in his life, at least he'd done this one thing right. He had the sweetest sixteen-year-old daughter on the planet.

Other parents griped about the challenges of teenage girls, but privately, Nick pitied them, because Paige was a breeze—smart, driven, curious, responsible, perpetually happier than a pig in mud. Everything he could possibly have wanted for her, she had in abundance. Sharing a house with her felt like living with a spill of sunshine.

Which was astonishing, considering her parentage. She didn't resemble him or Tansy in temperament and hadn't inherited much from Nick physically. Paige's pleasant features came straight from Tansy, right down to the blue eyes, the only real difference being the addition of a strawberry tint to Paige's otherwise buttery hair.

"Isn't that amazing?" Paige cooed. "No one else got that problem right. Only me."

Nick grinned. "It really is, Peanut. You make an old man proud."

"Yeah, well . . . you are pretty old." She scooped lasagna into her mouth, then dodged his attempt to ruffle her red-blond ponytail. "Hey, so can I sleep over at Maria's tonight? She promised to take me to school in the morning."

"Is your homework done?" Tansy cut in.

Paige looked affronted. "Of course."

"Your room's clean?"

Paige rolled her eyes. *"Mom."*

Nick suppressed a chuckle. Tansy would say yes, of course. Even her stoniness crumbled in the face of Paige's unending enthusiasm. And as far as he was concerned, their daughter had earned the right to come and go as she pleased, provided no boys were involved.

That was where he drew the line. No getting pregnant. No getting *trapped*.

Mother and daughter traded a few more comments, a rare smile blooming on Tansy's face. Once acceptable terms had been reached, Paige dropped a kiss on Nick's cheek and sashayed out. Maria lived half a mile away, and Paige liked to walk.

The moment the door closed, Tansy's warmth cooled to neutrality. "So. Any luck with—"

He held up a hand. "I said I'd handle it. When have I ever said I'd do something and not delivered?"

She nodded, conciliatory. "Okay. But she needs the money by next week."

"I know." He'd already decided he'd give the ad two more days. Then he'd resort to . . . well, something. A loan from Jackson, which he could pay back by getting a second job bagging groceries. Whatever it took. "I'll make it happen."

"Fine," she said. "There's lasagna on the stove."

"Yeah. Thanks."

He went to the kitchen, filled a plate, and returned to the table. Tansy ate without looking at him, and he chewed without tasting his food. In Paige's absence, bewilderment crept in, as it usually did.

How had his life turned out this way? How had he ended up sharing a home with a woman who couldn't have been less interested in him if she'd tried? Not that Tansy hated him; she didn't. She just . . . didn't care. Briefly, he wondered what would happen if he wrecked his truck and landed himself in thc ICU.

Tansy would probably only show up if Paige asked her to.

Then again, they'd never promised each other caring, or even friendship. They'd gotten pregnant and resolved to give their child the best life possible, which had meant getting married and buying a house and committing to all the other forms of adulting that came with trying to raise a decent kid in a fucked-up world.

Which Nick had resigned himself to long ago. But seeing Aubrey today had thrown open doors he'd done his damnedest to close. How different would things be if *she* greeted him at the end of the day?

He could say one thing with certainty. He sure as hell wouldn't have let her limp around the grocery store with a cart full of firewood while he waited outside. It came as no surprise that Gallant had, because that selfish asshole never did anything that didn't directly benefit himself. Which meant Aubrey was probably alone in that drafty house of hers right now, trying to build a fire, except that was more difficult than people realized, and it was getting cold outside, and she was probably freezing, and—

"What're you glowering about?"

Nick jerked back to reality. "What?"

Tansy watched him, intent. "What's wrong with you?"

"What? Nothing."

"No. Something happened. You're glaring. More than usual, I mean."

He stared, hoping she'd go back to her food.

When she didn't, he sighed, then . . . told the truth. Probably because he didn't have enough energy left to lie, or maybe because he wanted to inject some actual meaning into his life, for once. "I, uh . . . saw Aubrey MacLean. At the grocery store."

Tansy swallowed and set her fork down. "Oh."

He fidgeted. "Yeah."

She knew what it meant; she'd been there. Hell, she'd been part of it. And while Nick had never told Tansy the full extent of what losing Aubrey had done to him—that, at times, he'd wondered whether a person could die of heartbreak—he knew she knew. Tansy was many things, but she wasn't stupid.

She fisted the napkin on her lap. "Is that going to be a problem?"

A bitter snort snuck out of him. "Would you actually care, if it was?"

Well, shit. He hadn't meant to say that, but the words fell heavily and sat there, like a lobbed bomb he now had no choice but to watch explode.

"Sorry," he finally said. "I didn't mean—"

"No, it's fine. You have every right to ask me that."

He froze, wondering if he'd misheard. They'd never spoken about their relationship candidly. Or at all, really. Tansy was unfailingly practical and never talked about feelings. Even the decision to separate had been businesslike, a transactional exchange of emotionless facts.

At least for her. For him, it had been a knife slipped expertly between his ribs. Not because he'd lost her, but because the end of their marriage had confirmed the death of the thing he'd wanted so badly. The thing he'd broken Aubrey's heart for. The thing he'd broken his *own* heart for.

Family.

He pushed a chunk of lasagna around on his plate. "Sorry. That was a shitty thing to say."

Tansy let out a long exhale. "Not really. Look, I know our life isn't what you pictured. It's not what I pictured, either. You know if it wasn't for Paige, I wouldn't have chosen you. And you definitely wouldn't have chosen me."

He startled, his head jerking back. She'd said it just like that. As if it were self-evident. Which it was.

Still.

"I also know you had a different plan when we met," she continued. "One that involved Aubrey. And I know you've kept her letter, all these years. I know you still read it, too."

His fork clattered to the table, his fingertips numb.

"The thing is, Nick, I don't care if you're still in love with her. All I've ever cared about is Paige."

He groped for a response and came up empty.

"So if Aubrey MacLean is back in Henderson, my only question is, what does that mean for us? For our *daughter*?"

He wondered if he was having a stroke. Was this how people felt right before their brains shriveled up and died? "Nothing. It means nothing."

"Come on." Tansy's nose wrinkled. Nick had the dizzying sense that he'd disappointed her, somehow. "Be realistic. You're not going to let it go, just like that."

The room's air thinned, too insubstantial to support his fumbling lungs. Of course he wouldn't let it go. He'd obsess over it. Lose sleep. But that didn't change the fact that Aubrey hated him, even after all these years.

"If you try to stay away from her, you'll only fixate more." Tansy's mouth tightened. "And I don't think I can handle even *more* brooding around here. I've just about reached my limit as it is."

"What?" he huffed. "I don't *brood*."

Her look turned reproachful. "What do you actually *want* to happen? With her? Be honest."

He went still. Fuck. So many things. *Everything.* To go to Aubrey and beg her forgiveness. To write her love letters until his fingers bled, to confess the endless times he'd dreamed of her over the years and wished he could rewrite history.

Tansy's fingernails drummed against the table. Nick searched her face for some kind of clue as to what she wanted, but it felt like trying to see underwater. Everything looked blurry, and he couldn't manage to catch his breath.

So he simply gave the rawest, truest answer he could. "I want to go see her. Right now. Even if she tells me to fuck off, I just . . . need to make sure she's okay."

Tansy sat back, looking almost satisfied. "Okay. Then go. As long as you come back."

"Come back? Why wouldn't I come back?"

"I don't mean tonight," she said matter-of-factly. "I just mean if you stay, you come home tomorrow. And the day after that. Don't get carried away."

He stared, his mind spinning. The idea that Aubrey would do anything besides slam the door in his face was laughable.

But Tansy apparently disagreed, because her gaze was level. "Paige needs her dad, and this family needs a provider. But you have to get your needs met somehow."

"My *needs*?" He scoffed. "No, it's not like that. At all. Aubrey hates me. She barely spoke to me in the store."

Tansy's gaze thinned. "Why? None of what happened was your fault."

His jaw tightened while silence spread like a stain. How he wished that were true. "She doesn't see it that way."

"She will, if you talk to her. So go. Blow off some steam. I mean, when's the last time you actually enjoyed yourself with someone?"

He swallowed, then slid his gaze away. Fuck this whole conversational blazing of trails if it led them *here*. "Um . . ." He played with his fork as if riveted by it.

Tansy's eyes scanned back and forth, reading his silence. "My god. You can't be serious. You haven't been tending to yourself this whole time, have you?"

He flinched at the bluntly personal question. He absolutely had. He'd been fucking his own hand in the shower for six years, all the while knowing he was the kind of person who could only fall in love once. And who apparently couldn't fall back out. Who would never see anything behind his closed eyelids but garnet hair and green eyes and the world's lightest dusting of freckles strewn across seashell-pale skin.

When he didn't answer, Tansy clucked her tongue. "Wow. No wonder you glare so much."

Nick gripped the dining table's edges, as if he could grab

hold of her accusation and throttle it. "I don't *glare* any more than I *brood*."

"Right. My mistake. Look. Why don't I make this easy?" She gathered the plates and took them to the kitchen. A moment later, she returned and set his truck keys on the table. "Go. Get Aubrey out of your system. Just don't get her pregnant. And don't let Paige find out. And clean yourself up, first. You have dirt on your face."

She walked away. Moments later, the hiss of running water emanated from the kitchen. Dishes clanked. Tansy hummed some pop hit from the radio, a tune Nick recognized but couldn't name.

He sat unmoving. What had just happened? It was so fucking surreal he couldn't even swallow the saliva that pooled in his throat. But the longer he sat there, clutching the table, the louder his blood buzzed in longing.

Right now, Aubrey was hurt, and probably cold and alone in that massive old house. Unless Gallant had stuck around to help, but that wasn't likely. Or, if he *had* stayed, it was only because he'd managed to convince Aubrey to . . .

Heat rocketed through Nick's chest. He didn't allow himself to complete the thought, just snatched up his keys and went to his bedroom, where he threw on clean clothes and wiped down his face. Not that his appearance mattered. Aubrey would turn him away the moment he showed himself. But he needed to lay eyes on her, if only for a second. Make sure she was safe.

No reason to look like a vagrant while doing it.

At the front door, he paused. Tansy still hummed in the kitchen, lightly, as if someone had just brightened her day.

A minute later, he was gunning his truck out of the driveway.

Gallant hated coming home. In the nine months since Lena had moved out, he hadn't grown used to the silence that greeted him when he opened the front door, or the way his keys jangled into the bowl like the saddest welcome imaginable.

Tonight, he tried to avoid the stillness by going straight to the living room, where he flicked on the gas fireplace and poured himself a bourbon. Maybe he should just bite the bullet and get a dog, but that seemed extreme. He was rich. Successful. He shouldn't have to resort to an animal for company.

He flopped onto the couch and punched the remote to bring his 150-inch flat-screen to life. A football game came on, which didn't interest him much, considering he wasn't the one playing. But if he closed his eyes, he could pretend the cheering crowd was here, filling the polished rooms with their excitement, and for a moment, he was in high school again. The life of the party. The football star, the prom king, all the clichéd honorifics other people only made fun of because they hadn't gotten to enjoy those titles themselves.

Man, he missed those days. Tonight, they'd come to the forefront of his mind, thanks to Aubrey MacLean. Back in high school, she'd been pretty, but now? She was a knockout. Polished and put together and clearly on the same page as him about what mattered in life.

Which was to say, leagues ahead of any woman in Henderson.

He swirled his glass. God, he needed to do something with all this keyed-up energy she'd left him with. He pulled out his phone, then thumbed through his contacts, filtered to show only the entries he'd starred.

Marissa? He sipped his bourbon. Nah. Last time, she'd cried afterward. Awkward.

Nicole? Nope. Married to one of the foremen at the mill. He'd indulged a couple times anyway but had no desire to push his luck.

Pauline. He considered, then grimaced and tossed the phone aside. Who was he kidding? He was done playing with these girls. Lately, all the meaningless sex had started to feel like just that. Meaningless. He needed a real woman. A powerhouse. Someone who was going places. Someone headed for New York, like him.

He sipped again and congratulated himself on doing so well with Aubrey today. Back in high school, he hadn't yet learned the subtleties of salesmanship and had pushed his agenda way too hard. That she'd chosen Nick Thacker over him *still* stuck in his craw.

But a career selling houses had taught him restraint. He now knew when to apply pressure and when to play it cool. How to read someone's hesitations and secret desires. How to tell the difference between someone who wanted to be convinced and someone who actually needed convincing, because they weren't at all the same thing.

And Aubrey was the type who needed convincing. She always had been. He just hadn't understood that distinction at eighteen.

Gallant drained his glass. Not that this would be easy, of course. She'd probably be the most difficult sale he'd ever made, but he'd planted the seeds already, and Aubrey had laid out the next step herself.

I always thought I'd find another guy who'd write me letters like that, someday.

He chuckled and carried a fresh drink to his office, where he sat before his double monitors. He didn't presume to think he could write a decent love letter, but apparently Nick Thacker could. Which came as a surprise. The guy worked at the steel mill like every other grunt in town, and had never seemed like the literary type. But maybe Nick had published or posted something online that would give Gallant an idea of what Aubrey was looking for.

He typed the guy's name into Google.

And nearly sprayed bourbon across the screen.

Nick Thacker's Love-Letter-Writing Service

The words burned black and crisp, as if the universe had presented him the key to Aubrey's heart, tied up neatly with a bow.

Gallant clicked the link, his nerves humming. The details proved even better than he'd hoped. A set of personalized letters would cost him four hundred dollars, but what was that, in the scheme of things? He'd gladly fork over thousands for a slam dunk like this.

He registered with a fake screen name—MontanaBirder81, to keep Nick oblivious—then created an alias PayPal account that linked back to his credit card. When he got to the checkout page, he hesitated. The ethics behind what he was about to do were thorny, at best.

But any worthy salesman used every tool at his disposal. And that was all this was: a tool. It would still be *him* taking Aubrey out to dinner, wooing and seducing her. Moving to New York when she did.

Not Nick.

Satisfied he'd done his due diligence, Gallant clicked, then raised his glass when the confirmation filled his screen.

Here I come, Aubrey.

She wouldn't even know what'd hit her.

AUBREY WOKE TO the sound of chattering teeth. Hers, to be precise. They snapped like a frenzied animal's, rattling her skull.

She clamped her molars together and pulled her hands to her chest. How had she managed to pass out when someone had clearly injected ice into her bones? And how was September in Indiana so abysmally *cold*?

Outside, darkness had fallen. She pushed up from the couch, then swallowed a cry when pain shot through her ankle. She'd need the brace she'd bought at the store, but first, warmth. Gallant had stacked some firewood by the hearth, so she hobbled over, trying to remember what, exactly, to do with it. She'd never paid much attention when her parents had built fires. Maybe they'd lit a newspaper first?

She didn't have one, but a hunt across the mantel yielded a long-stemmed lighter. She clicked and held the flame against the smallest log. The wood caught, but the newborn fire died the moment she released the button.

She tried again, but her frozen hands quaked so badly she had to go rummage through the hall closet for a blanket. To her disappointment, the chilled quilt felt more like a mantle of ice than a source of warmth, so she returned to the fireplace and tried the lighter again. Nothing.

A curse slipped out. If given a set of differential equations, she would've known exactly what to do, but fire-making didn't seem to play by similarly predictable rules. At least not the ones she knew, where flame plus wood equaled fire.

She tried again, then chucked everything across the room in a fit of frustration. Just as the shivering set in, a knock sounded at the door.

Aubrey frowned. Gallant? It had to be. No one else knew she was back.

She pulled the quilt close and limped to the front hall. Maybe Gallant had forgotten something. Maybe he knew how to light a fire. She flipped on the porch light and swung the door wide.

And promptly quit breathing.

Nick Thacker stood on her stoop, staring through the screen. "Hi."

Aubrey forced air into her lungs. Or tried. But he'd changed into dark jeans and a cranberry wool sweater that did little to hide the powerful lines of his body. The ash adorning his cheekbone had disappeared, and a newspaper dangled from his hand. Which had to be the most ridiculous coincidence of her life thus far.

"What're you doing here?" she said, then pressed her lips together. She hadn't meant to sound so accusing, but oh well.

His hooded gaze revealed nothing. "I came to make sure you weren't cold. You had all that firewood in your cart, but no way to light it, so . . ." He trailed off, holding up the paper.

Okay, not a coincidence, then. She marveled that she'd managed to conjure a newspaper out of thin air.

Still, she hadn't wanted it to come attached to *him*. "Does your wife know you're here?"

"My wife?" A strange current swirled in his tone. "If you mean Tansy, she's not my wife. We're separated."

Her pulse skipped. "Separated?" The word struck deep, like a bolt of lightning zipping along her bones.

"Yeah." His dark eyes never changed. "I mean, we still live together. Still parent together. We're just not . . . *together* together."

Thickness crowded her throat. Which was ridiculous, because Nick's marital status, or lack thereof, had no bearing on anything. Tansy hadn't even been what tore them apart, not really. It shouldn't feel as if a nuclear bomb had just laid waste to her gut.

So Nick Thacker was single. So what?

He sighed. "Look, I won't stay long. Just let me get you set up. You're obviously freezing. Your lips are blue." He peeked past her into the house. "Figures Gallant didn't stick around to help."

Aubrey swallowed the weapons-grade emotions marshaling behind her breastbone. She should say no. Send him home, then huddle under a blanket until sunrise, shivering and jamming her hands into her armpits for warmth.

But that sounded like a perfectly miserable end to a perfectly horrible day, so she pushed open the screen, stepped aside, and said, "Fine. Come in. I can't seem to get a fire going myself."

Nick's stolid expression slipped, as if she'd surprised him as much as she had herself. But he recovered quickly and brushed past, arrowing down the hall.

Because of course he knew where the fireplace was. Of course he remembered.

At the thought, faint heat bloomed in her cheeks—the sum total of warmth her body could muster. She trailed Nick to the living room, where he knelt by the fireplace, wrestling with some kind of lever inside.

"What're you doing?"

"Opening the flue," he said. "Step number one. You didn't even get that far?"

She smoothed a self-conscious hand over her hair. "I had no idea what the hell I was doing, to be honest. I tried to catch a stick on fire with a lighter."

He paused. "Well, good thing that had no hope of working. You would've smoked up the whole house, if so."

"Oh. Right."

A smile ghosted over his mouth. "Right." He bent to his task.

Aubrey settled onto the sofa to watch. As much as she hated admitting it, she found something about his competence . . . hypnotic. She mapped his every movement, so swift and economical, while he built a nest of shredded newspaper on the grate and split kindling with a pocketknife. Halfway through, he pushed up his sleeves, revealing tendoned forearms. Each smooth undulation pulled her mind toward another time.

This place, but a different year. She'd lain underneath him in this very spot, shivering not with cold, but with nerves. He'd soothed her then with a similar dance of his hands. Reassured her with a finger trailed down her side, with the heated nuzzle of his nose against her neck. Then he'd pulled back, his curls falling over his forehead, his night-sky eyes expansive and unshuttered, the way they always were when they were alone.

A question—what did she want?

Such surety had filled her then, a wave of heat with no end and no beginning. She'd wanted it all, of course. For him to be her first and her only. Because it would always be the two of them, just like this, forever and ever, 'til death do us—

"There you go."

Cold reality washed over her. Aubrey blinked, finding herself once more in the frigid present. Nick crouched by the fireplace, facing her. Behind him, fledgling flames licked at an elaborate arrangement of wood. His expression was mild, maybe even borderline disinterested.

She pulled the blanket tighter. Clearly, his mind hadn't traveled to the same place hers had, but why would it? She wasn't even a blip on his radar now. She would never again watch his expression open up, never see his eyes turn soulful and welcoming, a private invitation just for her.

Aubrey swallowed against a prickly throat. God, what was wrong with her? "Thanks," she forced out. "I'm warmer already."

He nodded and stood, apparently not knowing what to say. She didn't, either.

He turned an awkward circle, then toed a slatted vent in the floor. "Looks like you have central heat. Where's the furnace?"

"I don't know. In the basement, maybe? Why?"

"I'll go get it lit. This fire's only going to last for so long, and I don't want you running out of wood in the middle of the night."

Before she could protest, he vanished through the kitchen—again, so sure of where he was going. This time, Aubrey didn't have the energy to follow. She eased toward the fire and stretched out her hands.

Heat bathed her skin, every bit as soothing as if she'd stepped into a steaming shower after a week of camping. Such blessed, beautiful *warmth*. It permeated her by degrees, thawing the frost in her bloodstream.

Nick was gone a long time. Eventually, Aubrey's core temperature reached a normal level, enough that she vacated the fire in favor of the kitchen, where she found an electric kettle in an ancient cabinet. She boiled enough water to fill two mugs, tossed a teabag into each, and carried her spoils to the living room, killing the overhead lights on the way.

The fire crackled in earnest now. She set the mugs on the hearth and sat staring into the dance of orange and blue. As a kid, she'd spent evenings here, doing her homework by firelight while her dad had solved sudokus. Afterward, they'd launched into their nightly deliberations, discussing life. Dreams. How to chase what you wanted until you caught it.

A grimace surfaced at the bittersweet reminder. It had been so easy, then, to look up to him. To *believe* him. Her classmates had mocked her aspirations to become a mathematician—because what kind of cheerleader went on to crunch numbers?—but her dad had never made her feel small or silly. Never suggested she was too young to know what she wanted. No, he'd given her the tools to succeed, encouraged her to apply to NYU, and pushed her to get out of Henderson.

Pushed her a little *too* hard, as it turned out.

Nick appeared in the doorway, pulling Aubrey from her reverie. Confusion flitted across his face at the lack of lighting, but she shrugged it off.

"The furnace is lit," he said. "And I got the water heater working. It'll take a while for the house to heat up, so you should probably sleep in here tonight, but I programmed the thermostat to seventy. The unit's in the back hall, if you want to change it."

She said nothing. She still hadn't processed his presence here, in her living room. In her life. She especially hadn't processed the fact that his marriage had ended and he hadn't even bothered to look her up. Then again, that one fact told her all she needed to know.

In the face of her silence, Nick strayed closer. After a moment's hesitation, he arranged himself on the floor, facing her, his elbows draped over his knees. "Did you make me tea?"

Aubrey contemplated the second mug. Apparently, she had. "Yeah. I'm pretty happy to not be freezing to death anymore. So . . . thanks."

"You're welcome," he murmured.

Silence pooled between them. God, what went on behind those guarded eyes these days? Did he let down that wall for some other woman, now? He must. No one who stole all the air from the room like he did could possibly evade female company for long.

"What're you doing here, Aubrey?" he finally said.

She looked away. The question sounded innocuous, but he hadn't asked casually. Nick didn't do casual.

She dredged up the same serene expression that had reassured Gallant in the car. "I'm just on sabbatical. New York was getting . . . chaotic, and I needed a break. I won't be here long." Lies, lies, and one hopeful not-lie.

"You're okay, though?"

"Of course. Why wouldn't I be?"

"I don't know." He squinted. "Now that I'm seeing you up close, you just . . . have that look."

She frowned. "What look?"

Nick sipped his tea while holding her gaze. "*That* look. Like something's wrong and you're trying to pretend it isn't."

"I . . . I . . ." Her words turned to ash in her throat.

His eyes changed. She finally caught a glimmer there—a dark softness, the fleeting edge of an invitation.

She burst into tears.

The breakdown hit her hard and fast, utterly beyond her control to stop. *Not now*, she thought desperately, but here she was, sobbing her heart out to the one person she least wanted to see.

"Oh, Aubs." Nick reached out.

She couldn't explain why she did it. She should have pushed him away, but instead, she tipped forward and buried her face in his neck. Her nose squished against the wool of his sweater. His chest felt like warm iron beneath her cheek.

He pulled her close. Aubrey's back heaved, each sob bringing another rush of him into her lungs—fire and soap and something metallically sharp, like a birthday candle that had just been snuffed out. His grip felt so much stronger than she remembered, yet the effect was somehow the same. Years peeled away, and here they were again, safe together in a circle of fireglow, each other's refuge, and god, why had she turned off the lights? Why had she let him set foot in this house? What had she *thought* would happen?

"You can tell me." His warm breath filtered through her hair. "Whatever it is, I've got you."

That only made her cry harder. Aubrey groped in the direction of wherever her sanity had gone and came up with a handful of mettle, which she used to disengage from Nick's embrace and scoot back. He watched her go, looking strangely bereft, but that must have been a trick of the firelight.

She took a few calming breaths and scrubbed at her cheeks. "Sorry. I don't know where that came from. It's nothing."

His mouth thinned. "You'd never cry if it was nothing. So tell me."

She *tried* not to. She hadn't even told her mother yet. But somehow, the confession leapt from her like it was jumping ship to freedom. "If you really want to know, I lost my job, okay? My *dream* job. That's why I'm here. Because I couldn't afford my place in New York anymore. And I had nowhere else to go."

His brows lowered. "Lost your job? *You?* That . . . doesn't sound right."

"Yeah, well. *Lose* isn't really the right word. It was more like someone stole it from me."

"What?" The air around him thickened. Darkened. "How?"

She sniffled and pinned her focus to the facts. Facts were simple. Quantifiable. "It's complicated, but . . . you know I'm a mathematician, right?"

"Yeah. Though to be honest, I don't know what that actually means."

"It means I work with patterns. Figure out how to measure and make sense of them. Kind of like solving a puzzle. And ever since I finished my PhD, I'd been working for a company called Osos. We . . . or *they*, I should say . . . manage paired kidney donation."

Nick shook his head as if she'd spoken Greek. "Kidney . . . what? Like transplants?"

"Yeah." She swiped at her nose with a hand. She probably looked like a mess. A fact that shouldn't bother her as much as it did.

"What does that have to do with math?"

She smiled faintly. It was a common enough question. "A lot. Paired kidney donation is for transplant recipients who have willing donors that can't donate to them directly, for whatever reason. Their blood type doesn't match, or some other incompatibility. So Osos figures out who the donor *will* match with and arranges a swap. As in, A's donor gives their kidney to B, and B's donor gives their kidney to A. Everyone goes home happy."

He did a slow blink. "Wow. I didn't even know that was a thing. Could you do a three-way exchange?"

Her breath caught. She'd explained this process to laymen countless times, but none had ever grasped the implications as quickly as he just had. "Yeah, and that's where the math comes in. You can do a three-way swap, or four. Theoretically, if you could write a powerful enough algorithm, you could build a whole daisy chain of transplants. A's donor gives to B, B's donor gives to C, C's donor gives to D, on and on until it circles back to A. But it takes a lot of data and a lot of math to figure out the best way to do that. To maximize the number of transplants and minimize the chances of organ rejection."

"So *that's* what you've been doing all these years?" He sounded awed. "Saving people's lives? With math?"

"Well," she said. "Yes."

"That's fucking incredible."

"Like I said." She sniffled. "It was my dream job."

His breath caught and held. "That someone stole from you."

"Yeah."

"But *how*?" Acid coated his words.

She searched for something that might occupy her hands and settled on her tea. The mug gifted her palms with warmth. How Nick had goaded her into sharing, she couldn't say, but confessing to someone at last felt like shedding a steel weight. "Well, for the past year, I'd been working on a project on the side. Our biggest limitation with building daisy chains is that the pool of donors is only so large. A lot of the registries are regional, which means someone in New York might match with someone in North Dakota, but we'd never know because the donor pools are fragmented. So I built a program that could compare data across regions, then came up with an algorithm that would wade through all that information and build prospective swaps. *Big* ones. It effectively knit a whole bunch of smaller databases into a national one, and made the match process way more powerful. But I kept it secret, because the company awards a prize every year, the Innovation Cup. Whoever does the most to help the company wins a two-week vacation, plus a trophy, and this was going to be my year to win. The first time *any* woman would've won in ten years. Except when I finished my algorithm, I made the mistake of telling a coworker about it. *Before* I told my boss."

Nick's eyes slitted. "And let me guess. That coworker took the credit?"

"Yeah." Heat prickled at her throat again, but she tamed it. "He took me out for drinks, supposedly to celebrate, then swiped my thumb drive and brought everything to my boss. And when I tried to explain, this guy accused me of trying to steal *his* work. I . . . didn't handle it well. I freaked out. Which looked bad. It made me seem guilty, and it was a death sentence for my career."

Nick's fingers curled into fists. "Who was this guy, exactly? What was his name?"

She raked her gaze over him. Uh-oh. She knew that look. "It doesn't matter. It's my problem. That's the other reason I'm here—to write an appeal that'll convince my boss that nobody but me could've created that algorithm."

He considered. "That sounds time-consuming."

"Things worth doing usually are."

"Or you could just tell me this asshole's name."

She leaned back but couldn't seem to open any distance between them. He dominated her vision, every feature sharpened to fierceness by the firelight.

"Nick," she warned. "This has nothing to do with you."

"Yeah, I get that." His eyes flashed. "I know I'm no one to you, anymore. Just some jerk you used to date who now makes steel and likes to fight."

The words pricked at her, each one a bloodying jab. "What? God, no. You're not a jerk. You're . . ."

She clamped her lips together. She couldn't admit the truth—that ever since leaving Indiana, she'd compared every man to him and found them lacking. That even after all these years, she still considered Nick Thacker the blueprint for the ideal human, minus one very specific flaw she could never forgive: he'd let her go.

When it became clear she had no plans to continue, Nick squared his shoulders. "The point is, I might not save people with math, but I still have some sense of justice. And nobody should be allowed to get away with what this guy has."

"Maybe not, but it's not your job to defend me. Not anymore."

He swallowed, the long column of his throat rippling. "I know. But you could let me, anyway."

She turned her mug around to cover the catch in her breathing. She'd lost control of this conversation in the most spectacular of ways. "Look. Obviously it would be great if someone could just magically solve my problem, but . . ."

Her tongue twined around a cold chuckle. The idea of him fighting for her now, after he hadn't when she'd needed him to, was laughable. "What's this really about? The fire, the furnace . . . you threatening my coworker? This isn't because you still feel guilty, is it?"

He flinched.

"Oh, wow," she said slowly. "It *is*. Seeing me has brought back memories, and you think you can fix the past by fixing this. Well, news flash, you can't. Nothing'll ever change what happened. How it ended."

"Aubs, I—" He cut himself off, strangled. "I know that. I know you'll never forgive me. And you shouldn't, because what I did was stupid. *I* was stupid. But I'm not that dumb fuck kid anymore. Or . . . Jesus Christ, maybe I am. I don't even know." He slammed his eyes shut and pinched the bridge of his nose.

Aubrey plunked down her tea, her throat dry. She hadn't even been back a day, and here she was, having a heart-to-heart with the man who'd broken hers. "Look, thanks for the help, but I shouldn't have told you all that."

His eyes shot open. Those black mirrors reflected the firelight, and suddenly she could see everything—the dark heat brimming behind them, inside him, a whole seething landscape he kept locked away and only let show in the rarest of moments.

Like this one.

Her heart lurched around in her chest as if searching for a place to hide. She inched back. "This was a mistake. I think you should go."

"Yeah, I fucking *know* I should go. I really, really do."

But he made no move to leave. Silence piled in, freighted with memory, saturated with heartbreak, and she fled its weight by getting to her feet. Anything to sunder the open connection his eyes were begging her for.

She couldn't remember why she'd wanted to see that vulnerability in the first place. Last time, answering it had nearly cost her everything.

"You know the way out." She scooped up both mugs and hobbled away as quickly as her bad ankle would allow.

But when she reached the doorway, something stopped her, some awful pocket of yearning his presence had drilled down into and broken open. She paused and spoke over her shoulder. "I just want to know one thing. Do you regret it? Would you change what happened, if you could go back?"

There it was. The question that had haunted her for years, out in the open now.

Behind her, Nick made a throaty, broken sound. Aubrey tensed, already knowing what it meant, already collapsing like a shell of ashes around a burned-away heart of wood.

"I regret hurting you," he said. "But no, I wouldn't change it."

She closed her eyes and dragged in a breath while her bones dissolved like wetted plaster. Honestly, what had she expected?

"But," he continued, "it's not that simp—"

"Good night, Nick."

She brought the mugs to the sink and washed them out with water that emerged from the tap miraculously hot, then took her time setting them in the drying rack.

By the time she ventured back to the fire, the living room was empty, even though she hadn't heard him go.

Nick didn't leave right away.

Maybe he should have, but he needed to know Aubrey was warm. Since he refused to hover in her yard like some kind of creepy stalker, he backed his truck out to the cul-de-sac, then parked along the curb. There. Now he could only see the same thing as every other passerby out walking their dog.

On the other side of the bay windows, Aubrey stood at her fireplace, staring down. Probably thinking about what an asshole he was. Which apparently required a lot of contemplation, because she didn't move for a long time. Neither did he.

He knew when the house started to thaw, because she finally left the room and reappeared looking ten years younger, her fancy clothes swapped out for flannel pajamas, half her hair pulled up and her makeup wiped away.

Fuck, she looked beautiful. Vulnerable, too, and in the most unapologetic of ways, like the girl he remembered.

He wished she'd felt comfortable showing him that side of herself, but of course she hadn't. Especially not after he'd fucked everything up by telling her he didn't regret what he'd done.

He groaned. That was the most brutal question she could have asked. The same one that had rotted inside him for half his life.

But he'd forced an honest answer, because Aubrey deserved that much. So, yes, while he despised having hurt her with an intensity that sickened him, no, he wouldn't undo it. He *couldn't*, because it had ultimately brought Paige into existence. And his daughter was his life, his whole world. His single greatest contribution to planet Earth.

He just wished Aubrey had let him explain. There was still so much she didn't understand, things he'd never gotten the chance to tell her.

Inside, she lay down on the blue-upholstered antique couch. His fists tightened around the steering wheel as he imagined himself still in there, pulling her head onto his lap, stroking her hair until she fell asleep. He fantasized about murmuring to her as she dreamed, telling her that underneath the slick city polish, he still saw the same girl he'd fallen in love with. A woman with passion and heart. Someone destined to achieve greatness, one equation at a time.

A telltale heat invaded the back of his eyes, which he scrubbed away. Fuck, he probably should've just lied to her. Maybe then she would've let him hold her again. Granted him another moment of euphoria like the one in front of the fireplace, when she'd cried and sought comfort in his arms.

That had felt incredible, even more so because he'd expected her to shove him away. When she hadn't, every cell in his body had screamed not to let go, to never let her go. Then the urge to point out where they were had nearly overcome him. For that brief, exultant moment, they'd sat in the exact place in which they'd traded their virginities to each other on what Nick still considered the best night of his life.

His phone chimed in his back pocket. With a grumble, he pulled it out, anticipating a text from Jackson or Tansy, but the notification brought him to a browser page he didn't recognize.

He squinted, then did a double take. MontanaBirder81 had just signed up for his love-letter-writing service. Which meant four hundred dollars, in the bank.

A message icon blinked at the top of the screen. He clicked.

Hi Nick,

How lucky that I came across your ad this evening. I've been looking for a service like yours, but haven't found it anywhere else. I'm hoping you can help me.

Here's the story. There's a woman who just moved back to Billings after spending a couple decades away. We went to high school together, but back then, I never got up the courage to act on my feelings. Now's my second chance, and I don't want to screw it up.

Thing is, she's the love-letter type, but I don't trust myself to do it right. She's high-class and needs a soft touch, nothing too forward.

Think you can help?

John

A harsh laugh erupted from Nick's chest, sending a silvered jet into the chill of the truck. An old flame from high school had shown up and thrown this guy into a tailspin? The fuck? The universe was clearly flipping him the middle finger right now. Even while helping him out.

He tapped Reply.

Hi John,

Thanks for the booking, and for the vote of confidence. I can definitely help. What kind of letter are you looking for first, and what about this woman entices you?

Nick

He clicked Send and glanced up. Inside, Aubrey looked to be sleeping. Her skin glowed like abalone in the firelight. Even from here, he could tell how soft it was, could trace the way her nose turned charmingly upward at the tip.

She would probably never speak to him again.

His phone buzzed.

Nick,

Her name's Jane. She's the total package. Think beauty queen credentials with a fashion sense to match. We're having dinner this weekend, and I want to give her the first letter then. Like I said, she needs a soft touch, so I won't push for much on our date. I'm hoping the letter can do the heavy lifting for me.

John

Nick read the message twice. Jane. And John. What bland, boring names—like aliases on a poorly written crime show. But whatever. He hoped they lived a long and happy life together, even if John sounded a little shallow.

He hit Reply. Okay, he typed, here's what you write. Dear Jane . . .

He wrote the whole letter in one go. The words were for Aubrey, of course. They were his ripped-up guts, splattered onto the screen in the rawest and most visceral way possible.

Because he knew this was the closest he'd ever get. He'd never touch her again, never regain her trust, never sink into her the way he ached to down to the roots of his being. Even if by some miracle she someday forgave him, she'd made it abundantly clear she had no plans to stay in Henderson.

Which meant their situation hadn't changed. Even if it had, what would he say? *Hey, I know you're a superhero genius who can have any guy she wants, but would you consider one whose pastimes include getting punched in the face and trying to fall out of love with you?*

Yeah. Sure.

When he finished the letter, he hit Send and flicked the truck key. The engine sputtered to life, but thankfully, Aubrey didn't stir.

He drove home slowly, not in any hurry to face Tansy. What was it she'd told him? *Don't get carried away?*

Un-fucking-believable that she could say that with a straight face. She might as well have commanded him not to swim, then shoved him into the deepest end of the pool.

But he'd do his damnedest, for both their sakes. After all, he'd indulged himself. Gone and made sure Aubrey was safe.

Now he would leave her in peace.

When he got home, Tansy had already gone to bed. In his room, Nick tried to read an old standby, *The Alchemist*—he would never tire of the dreaminess of Coelho's prose—but tonight, the words drifted past, insubstantial. He finally gave up and turned off the light, then lay in the dark, a tight ache pulsing low in his stomach. He couldn't stop reliving how Aubrey had felt in his arms, so warm and soft and brokenhearted over the injustice some nameless asshole had dealt her. She'd smelled incredible, too, like sun-warmed cashmere, and he'd wanted to tear someone apart for her. Punch whoever he had to punch in order to funnel her life back onto its rightful course.

Sleep eluded him. He tossed and turned, the ache inside him tightening like a turned screw. When he could stand it no longer, he got up, took a shower, did all that came with it, and dropped back into bed again.

Hours later, when he finally slept, Nick dreamed Aubrey didn't hate him.

That somewhere, a world existed in which she never had.

9.

Seventeen years ago

Now that Aubrey had the new kid in her house, she didn't know what to do with him.

She ran through her options, then settled on leading him to the living room, where she tucked herself onto the old blue-velvet chesterfield her mom had once bought at an estate sale.

Nick set his backpack on the claw-footed coffee table and claimed the sofa's opposite end, doing a slow perusal of the room. "So. A cheerleader who likes math and safety. And lives in a mansion."

Aubrey took in the dated furniture, the curling wallpaper, the hulking, ash-stained fireplace. "Mansion? This place is a hundred years old and looks every minute of it."

He snorted. "It's a palace, compared to my place."

She hesitated. His acerbic tone made her suspect he'd drawn a line between them on purpose. He seemed determined to maintain a layer of prickly distance between himself and the world—already, he'd made a public enemy of Gallant, ensuring people would shun him at school.

But beneath the bristly exterior, Aubrey had glimpsed something very different during the course of that fistfight. Something heated and vivid she couldn't get out of her mind.

"If you're trying to convince me you shouldn't be here," she said, "it won't work."

He cleared his throat and looked down, telling her she'd hit the mark.

"Anyway." She gestured to his sweatshirt, where his blood had dried black. "Why don't you take that off? If we scrub it with soda water, it shouldn't stain."

"I'm not wearing anything underneath," he said. "So . . . no."

"Oh." She flushed. "Well, how about some ice for your lip?"

"I don't need any."

"It looks painful."

"I've had worse." He sucked away the blood and braved her gaze again. "This'll heal. Even if your friend with the stupid name *can* throw a punch. And take one, surprisingly. Most people can't."

Aubrey didn't protest the subject change. At least Nick was talking, which was more than she'd gotten in the car. "Gallant's not my friend."

His look turned speculative. "You really don't like him?"

"No. I mean, I don't *dislike* him, he's just not a person I think about. There's nothing to discover about him, you know? Nothing to unravel."

Those dark eyes sharpened, less opaque by the moment, and she forced herself to withstand the assessment. Nick looked like he was trying to tally her up in his head, the same way she was doing with him.

"Is that a hobby of yours?" he said. "Unraveling people?"

She lingered over the potential double meaning. "Sometimes."

"What if they don't want to come unraveled?"

Oh, yes. He'd definitely sharpened the words on both sides on purpose. "I still try. It's always worth going after what you want."

His head tilted. "Is that really what you think?"

"Is that not what *you* think?"

"I think that's something only someone who already has everything would believe."

She hesitated, trying to tease out whether he'd insulted her, but there was no bite to the comment. Just a skeptical sort of consideration, like he couldn't decide whether he respected her philosophy or expected her to fall flat on her face because of it.

Maybe both.

"It's how my dad raised me," she said carefully. "He has these sayings he's drilled into my head since I was little. *If life puts something in your way, go around it. If life knocks you down, get back up. If life sticks you between a rock and a hard place, split the difference and aim straight down the middle.* I used to think they were so cheesy, but the thing is, they work."

He absorbed that. "So . . . you're someone who doesn't take no for an answer?"

"Not when there's something I want."

"Which is how you got me into your car."

"See?" She risked a smile. "Maybe there's something to it."

Nick seemed to weigh her, turning his mental tape measure this way and that. "Explain something to me." He expelled the statement all in one breath, as if he'd tried to hold it back and failed. "About you."

Aubrey's chest fluttered. "Sure."

"What you said earlier, about seeing holiness in math . . . what'd you mean by that?"

Warmth bloomed inside her. This, at least, she could talk about for hours, assuming he had any desire to listen. "Are you sure you want to know? It'll make me sound like such a dork."

"*Are* you a dork?"

"Oh, yeah." She grinned. "Definitely."

He grinned back, then abruptly snuffed it out, as if the smile had been drawn from him against his will. "Then go for it."

"Okay. Well, I've always loved numbers, the way they fit together. I don't know if you're into math, but—"

He jerked his head, a vehement denial.

"Right." She laughed. "Most people aren't. But only because they haven't looked closely enough to find the grace in it. It's there, if you take the time. The way numbers weave together is so . . . pure. I mean, math exists outside of us. Beyond us. It's too flawless for any human to have invented. Like . . . have you ever done proofs? The first time I worked through the laws of derivatives and understood how they work, I swear I saw god. Because only a perfect consciousness could've created something *that* elegant out of thin air. Math is what makes our existence possible, and numbers have always made me feel like the divine, or whatever's out there, is whispering in my ear."

He stared. Hard.

Her cheeks stung. Maybe that had been too much. "Does that make sense?"

"Yeah." His voice grew even smokier. "And . . . this'll sound weird, but I know that feeling exactly. Except for me, it's words. The universe whispers to me in language."

She breathed a laugh. "As in . . . books? Writing?" That would explain the hallway notebook-scribbling.

"Yeah."

"So you and I are opposites."

He held her eyes. "Like I told you."

"Okay. I'm still not kicking you out."

A divot formed between his brows. "I honestly wish you would. It'd make this whole thing a hell of a lot easier."

A pang twanged in her chest. What kind of life must he have led, that he didn't feel comfortable sitting and just . . . talking? Sharing himself? "Would you rather we got in a fight, instead? I could always tell you how wrong you are, if that'd be easier."

One corner of his mouth lifted. "I do like fights."

"Okay, great. Then you want to know what I think? Books are boring."

"Jesus." He gave a strained cough. "You philistine."

Philistine? "I . . . don't know what that means."

"No? Maybe you should read more." He paired the jibe with a smirk.

Aubrey's blood hummed, stirred by the widening curve of that beautiful, pouty mouth. It was like he was coming to life before her eyes. "No way. Books are made of words, which were invented by people. By definition, they're just as flawed as we are. Meanwhile, math is immaculate. Symmetrical. It existed long before humans did, and it'll still be here long after we're gone. Language just dies with us. It'll vanish someday, along with its creators."

His eyes flared. "You know . . . I've honestly never thought about it that way. But damn. You're actually kinda . . . right."

She stuck a finger in the air, victorious. "So you admit I have a point."

"I admit you haven't looked at words closely enough to find the grace in them. But it's there, if you take the time."

Warmth jolted through her. He'd been *listening*. Meanwhile, her classmates' eyes glazed over the moment she waxed poetic about math. Even her best friend Megan had an allergic reaction to numbers.

"Books don't have their elegance built in, though." She pulled her legs up and crossed them. "Their grace isn't inescapable."

"Bullshit." He blew a stray curl from his eyes and leaned in. "You're telling me you've never read something that made you stop and just . . . *marvel*?"

"No."

He gave a sharp shake of his head. "Come on. You've never once wondered how something as enormous as ideas can be captured with something as small as words? You've never felt kinship with someone who died hundreds of years before you were born, because you recognized a piece of yourself in what they'd written?"

"No." Aubrey's breath sped. The more she protested, the more she drew him in, it seemed. "Whenever Mrs. Hayes assigns books for English, I just read the CliffsNotes."

"Oh, god." He buried his face in his hands and peeked through his fingers. "You do not."

"Oh, I do. *If* that. Sometimes, I just watch the movie."

He shuddered. "That's fucking sacrilege. This literally hurts to listen to. Next, you're going to tell me you never write, either."

She couldn't conceal her mounting delight. "God, no. I'd rather watch paint dry."

He groaned. "You mean you've never *once* been so full of something, a feeling, or a need, that you felt like it would burn its way out of you if you didn't get it down on paper?"

"Never. Have you?"

"Are you kidding? All the time."

A stupid grin claimed her face as the pattern of him took shape in her mind. His penchant for words made so much sense, because hadn't she already glimpsed poetry in the way he moved?

"What a fantastic fight." Her breath came short and sharp. "Maybe my favorite I've ever had."

Now that his eyes had latched onto hers, they refused to stray elsewhere. "I'll admit, it didn't suck." He sounded half-winded, too.

He stared into her. She swore if she'd lit a match, the span between them would have caught fire.

"Who *are* you?" he finally said. "I never talk to anyone about this shit. Ever."

"Just a cheerleader." She smiled. Clearly, people didn't usually come at his defenses with guns blazing. "Who likes math and safety and lives in a mansion."

"I'm getting the sense there's more to it than that," he said.

"Maybe. Stick around, and you could find out."

Nick held her eyes for longer than most people would have, but his gaze finally flickered away. He unfolded from the couch and slid his hands into his scuffed pockets. "Um. Anyway. Where's the kitchen? I think I'll take you up on that soda water."

For a raw moment, she mourned the obvious retreat. But he'd essentially just agreed to undress in front of her, which probably counted for something. "Yeah. Sure. This way."

In the kitchen, Nick shrugged off his bomber jacket and draped it over a chair. Aubrey delved into the fridge, shoving aside various Tupperware containers and seizing a can of fizzy water from the back.

When she emerged, Nick had already stripped off his sweatshirt.

She froze. He could have covered himself, but instead, he stood straight-backed, his hands at his sides.

God, his bones. They stood out in stark relief, his sternum like a ship's keel, each rib etched in shadow by the overhead light. She wondered how he'd bested Gallant so effortlessly, yet the longer she looked, the more she read a hidden vitality in those acres of sinew and bone. He was all bladed edges and pitiless lines, as if some inner fire had reduced him to a finely honed weapon.

Her grip on the can tightened. "I . . . owe you an apology."

"For?" he murmured.

"Thinking you didn't speak." Her voice echoed, husky in the stillness of the kitchen. "It was just that when you didn't answer me in class, or the hallway, I thought maybe you couldn't."

His lips quirked. "Because someone like me would never ignore the gorgeous cheerleader for any other reason?"

"I . . ." Blood rocketed into her cheeks. Which surprised her. Gallant complimented her looks all the time, and it never flushed warmth through her like this. ". . . didn't mean it like that."

"Sure you did. Girls who look like you aren't used to being ignored."

The corners of her mouth ticked down. "That's presumptuous."

He huffed a chuckle. "Is it?"

"Yeah. I might not get ignored very often, but that doesn't mean I'm not constantly misjudged."

His lips thinned, but she sensed an invitation to continue.

She gestured at her uniform, on display now that she'd hung her parka in the front hall. "People see this and assume I only care about hooking up with guys or screaming my head off every time Henderson wins a football game. Every time I talk about math, they think I'm being delusional. Or trying to sound smarter than I am. But you of all people should see past that."

"Me? Why me?"

She shifted the freezing can to the other hand. "Because. There's more to you than you let on. A lot more."

Nick sucked in a breath. "Okay. I'll admit, you *are* surprising the shit out of me right now."

They stood like that for long moments. His eyes looked so different than they had at school. She still couldn't read them, exactly, but the hard wall had given way to something else, like he had a whole continent inside him, just waiting to be discovered.

"You said you write a lot," she ventured. "What do you write? Stories?"

"Letters, mostly." He swallowed. "To my mom."

"Do you give them to her?"

"She's dead. So, no."

"Oh." Aubrey deflated. "Damn. I'm sorry."

He shrugged a bony shoulder. "It happens. I don't even remember her, to be honest. Just snippets. I have these memories of . . . soft hands. Short fingers. This smell, like some kind of flower. And she used to tell me stories. She'd get up close to my ear and tell me the same few fairy tales, over and over. I remember that much, that they were always the same. I just wish I could remember what they were about."

Her gut tightened. "Couldn't you ask your dad?"

Nick shook his head. "He's a dick. She might've been an angel, but the other half of me is pure, grade A asshole.. For better or for worse."

"That doesn't make *you* an asshole, though."

He grated out a laugh.

Silence welled. She couldn't stop her attention from straying again. His leanness broke her heart, each sparse line a testament to scarcity.

Somehow, the fact that he'd let her see felt monumental. Not like he stood half naked in her kitchen, but as if he'd peeled back his skin to allow her a glimpse of the glistening bones beneath, the rhythmic squeeze of his heart.

"Are you hungry?" she heard herself say.

He chuckled without humor. "What, right now? Or always?"

"Both."

"Yeah," he said simply.

"Well, I've got plenty to eat." She held out a hand for his sweatshirt. "I'll clean that. You can help yourself."

He nodded and moved to the fridge, the voltage in the air cooling to something resembling normality. Aubrey scrubbed at Nick's sweatshirt in the sink. While she worked, he tore through three meals' worth of leftovers. He didn't bother to reheat anything, though a microwave sat in plain view.

The water ran pink, chilling her fingers. When she finished, she handed back the soaked shirt. "I'll go grab something dry from my dad's closet. You can bring it back to me at school."

"Okay." Nick carried his dishes to the sink. "Thanks."

She mounted the stairs to her parents' bedroom, where a quick search of her dad's closet produced a checkered flannel.

Downstairs, she found the kitchen empty. Nick's dishes had been dried and put away, so she continued into the living room. She found him by the coffee table, stuffing his wet sweatshirt into his backpack. The knobs of his vertebrae marched down his back.

She drew close, her pulse a wild tangle. He'd pulled out a few books and set his notebook on top with the cover folded back. Tight words crowded the page, not spaced out or bulleted, the way class notes would be.

Nick caught her looking and flipped the notebook shut.

"Can I read one?" She offered the flannel, which he pulled on. "Of your letters?"

He layered his bomber jacket over the borrowed shirt. "Not those. They're for my mom. But I could write one for you, if you want."

"Really?"

"Sure." He smiled faintly. It warmed his whole face, and she had the strangest desire to smooth a thumb across his split lip, or maybe brush a curl from his eyes. She rubbed her fingers together until the itch faded.

"I think I owe you an apology, too," he said.

"For what?"

"Being a dick. And misjudging you." He shouldered his backpack and tucked the books under his arm. "The first is just habit. But I don't have any excuse for the second. Because you're right. I should've known better. Anyway. Thanks. For everything."

"No problem. Do you want a ride home?"

"Nah. I'll walk. It'll take longer."

He made for the door. Aubrey trailed after him.

Out on the stoop, her uniform did nothing to block the January wind, but she hardly felt the cold. Nick made his way down the creaking wooden steps, then turned. "You're sure you want me to write to you? Absolutely positive?"

She measured the question. The way he searched her face made it seem like he was asking something else. Like she was standing on some precipice with him behind her, his breath in her ear, asking if she wanted him to push.

"The thing is," he continued, looking up at her, "words are more personal than numbers. A four is a four is a four, whether it's here or in Iran or on the moon. But words . . . Ten different people can use the same word to mean ten different things, and the choice says as much about the message as it does about the person sending it. Words are like windows. They let you see straight into whoever's writing them. So when you ask for a letter, you're asking to look. At me."

Her breath thinned. "I know."

Those black eyes bored into her, as if willing her to understand. "The thing is, you might regret seeing."

She pondered that. "I might."

Strangely, that seemed to satisfy him. He nodded once and turned away. The wind ruffled his curls like it was trying to pull them off his head.

Even after he shrank to a speck, Aubrey still stood there. She only went inside once she started to shiver.

The next day, Gallant showed up with two black eyes.

Aubrey had expected him to hide the proof of his defeat, but he came right up and leaned against her bank of lockers as if it were just another day.

"Hey, MacLean."

"Hey." Pity softened her voice. "How're you feeling?"

Gallant resorted to his usual cocksure grin. "Better than I look. I mean, the new kid's clearly some kind of karate freak, but at least everyone knows he cheated during our fight."

"Cheated?" She busied herself with her combination lock, already regretting offering sympathy. "How would he have cheated?"

"Oh, come on, didn't you see the way he . . ."

Whatever he said next turned to mush, because a sheet of notebook paper lay inside her locker. Someone had folded it into thirds and pushed it through the slats.

She snatched at it, yanking it open so quickly it almost tore.

Dear Aubrey,

I couldn't sleep last night. I wish I could say it was because I regretted, because as a rule, I don't open up to people. Especially not about the things I told you yesterday. Those were confessions I haven't made to anyone in years. If ever.

But it wasn't regret that kept me awake.

The thing is, before I came to Henderson, I assumed this town would be just like the last one. I expected fights, a constant battle to be left alone. I even expected to have to prove myself on my first day, because of course everyone would need to know where on the food chain I fell.

What I didn't expect was you. A girl with a mind like a diamond and no hesitation about sharing it. But you came from nowhere yesterday and just . . . shone for me. Like it was easy. Like you trusted me to see.

I won't lie, I'd already dismissed you in English. I saw a cheerleading uniform and a waterfall of red hair and figured I'd taken your measure.

But that hour with you at your house turned my assumptions upside down. Then, last night, your words swirled together in my head again, a fever dream I wanted to crawl back into and live inside of.

I couldn't sleep because I couldn't stop wondering if you would've let me kiss you.

It's something I've never done before. Kiss someone, I mean. Not that I haven't wanted to. I have. But there are myriad things I've wished for and never gotten. Sometimes, it feels like that's the natural state of my existence. Just . . . wanting. The sheer power of craving hollows me out sometimes, carves an empty ache into my bones.

Which isn't normal, I know. I'm not normal. Especially because sometimes, I can't even name whatever it is I'm wishing for so fiercely. But last night, I knew.

I wanted to kiss you. A fucking cheerleader, of all things. But not just that. A girl with perfect pink lips who looks at numbers and somehow sees god.

Would you kiss the same way you talk, I wonder? With all that passion?

I should clarify I'm not actually asking for that. I don't have your faith that, given enough trying, I can have whatever I want. I also know that after getting a letter like this, you'll probably never speak to me again. I wouldn't, if I were you. But you asked me to write, so here it is, assuming I muster the courage to actually deliver this.

I think maybe what I'm really trying to say is thank you. The truth is I have surprisingly few afternoons like yesterday's in my collection, and that hour together meant something to me, regardless of whether it's ever repeated.

So, thanks.

Nick.

PS—I told you you'd regret seeing.

Aubrey battled for breath. Gallant droned on, but her blood roared so loudly it drowned him out.

She mashed the letter against her chest and stepped back from her locker. From far away, down the hall, dark eyes collided with hers. Nick's expression was pained, his jaw flexed, like a man whose fate had just been sealed at the gallows. A sea of people heaved between them.

She started toward him. She had no idea what she would say, only that he'd been right, holy shit he'd been right, there *was* a god in words, because the ones he'd written had rocketed straight into her, like stars imploding as they fell to earth.

Gallant called after her, but Aubrey barely heard.

But by the time she reached the spot where Nick had stood, he'd gone.

10.

In her first week back in Henderson, Aubrey dove headfirst into writing. Every morning, she opened her laptop along with her eyes, then immersed herself in creating a detailed analysis of her program and its daisy chain algorithm, complete with her reasoning for every line of code. Her progress was slow, hampered by the need to re-create it all from memory, but hopefully that would only strengthen her case, in the end.

Still, she would need weeks to finish. But she would expend any amount of effort. *If life puts something in your way, go around it. If life knocks you down, get right back up.*

In the afternoons, once she'd wrung out her brain to the consistency of a damp handkerchief, she spent her time deep-cleaning the house and mimicking Nick's fire-building process until she could conjure a blaze with ease. Each evening, she live-streamed a Pilates class from her old studio in New York and followed along as best she could without a reformer, then drank tea and did logic puzzles by the fire.

The whole time, that evening with Nick buzzed in her awareness. She tried to ignore it, but as the days wore on, the hum grew louder, spiraling into an idea so concrete she could no longer set it aside.

She didn't want to have dinner with Gallant.

Because those moments with Nick at the fireside—however fleeting, however inconsequential for him—had solidified something she'd long suspected.

Uncomplicated men didn't interest her.

She'd mostly known it after things had fallen apart with her last boyfriend. As an actuary, Luke had led a life as predictable as the numbers he juggled. He'd read the same newspaper each morning. Smiled the same smile each time she'd walked in the door. Vacationed on the same week each year, never once gotten angry, and done not one single thing to surprise her.

He'd definitely never gazed at her with eyes so bottomless she wanted to tip into their abyss.

Which, at the time, had been fine. Maybe even safe, now that she thought about it. Until the night Luke had cooked his regularly scheduled Friday steak dinner and added an engagement ring to the dessert.

Aubrey had ended it then and there. Not because she didn't want to get married. She did. She wanted the whole shebang—the kids and the picket fence *and* the meaningful career. But the moment she'd spotted that ring atop her tiramisu, she'd known she hadn't wanted it with Luke.

Now she had no desire to repeat that experience. And Gallant, despite having changed, was every bit as uncomplicated. He didn't have layers to uncover. He was simple. Straightforward. The kind of guy who would make a perfectly decent husband . . . for someone else.

By the time Saturday arrived, Aubrey had decided. She'd go on the date—at this point, it'd be rude not to—but then she'd gently snip Gallant's ambitions off at the roots.

With that resolved, her stomach only heaved mildly as she stood before the bathroom mirror and swept mascara onto her lashes. She donned a ruched cocktail dress she'd once found in a bargain bin in Hell's Kitchen, then shrugged on a knee-length wool coat and settled on the chesterfield to wait. Headlights swept through the cul-de-sac at exactly 7:00 p.m., followed by a knock at the door.

Aubrey's heart jittered as she swung it open.

Gallant grinned from the stoop. "Hi. Wow. You look great." Like her, he'd buttoned up against the chilly evening, but his navy peacoat and pressed slacks conveyed the time he'd taken, regardless.

"Thanks," she said. "You don't look half bad, yourself."

His smile brightened a watt. "How's your ankle?"

She raised her eyebrows. He'd remembered. "Better, thanks. Almost like new."

He offered an elbow and accompanied her down the walk. In the car, her seat warmer had already been turned on, and the leather welcomed her with all the sumptuousness of a Jacuzzi.

Huh. How thoughtful.

As Gallant backed out of the driveway, Aubrey swiveled and took a long, hard look at him.

Even in the dark, his eyes seemed to glow with their own inner light. "What?" he said. "Why're you looking at me like that?"

"I'm just . . ." She searched for tactful phrasing. ". . . surprised. Or impressed. I had no idea you were so considerate."

He laughed. "You haven't seen me in almost twenty years. How would you?"

Well. Fair question. Maybe he'd changed more than she'd realized.

At the restaurant, Gallant guided her in with a hand laid against the small of her back. Aubrey paused to absorb the sleek, undersea-themed decor. Blue recessed lighting shimmered on silvered walls while clusters of globe chandeliers dangled from the ceiling.

"Wow," she breathed. "In Henderson? This is . . . unexpected."

Gallant chuckled. "I'm full of surprises. Just wait. I'm saving the best for last."

She shot him a look of alarm. "Wait, what happened to no expectations?"

"Oh." He threw up spread hands and laughed. "No, not *that.* I just meant I wrote you a letter. For after."

A letter. The words dropped straight into the stillest, most secluded pool of her heart. She did her best to follow the hostess, but shock waves made her waver on her feet.

At the table, Gallant pulled out her chair, and Aubrey forced her confetti emotions to settle. He might have written her a letter, but his words wouldn't be anything like Nick's. *No one's* words would ever be like Nick's.

She shed her coat and draped it across the back of her chair.

"Wow," Gallant choked out. "That is . . . one hell of a dress."

Aubrey slid into her seat and glanced around. None of the other diners had gone to the lengths she had, but this outfit had been her only choice for an evening out. It did look somewhat painted on, and she grimaced. "Is it too much?"

He shook off his daze and sat. "Your entire existence is too much for a place like this."

She frowned. That, at least, sounded like the Gallant she remembered.

He seemed to realize as much, because he smoothed over the comment by calling to the waiter for some sparkling water. When the man had gone, Gallant smiled. "Don't worry. It won't hurt Henderson to get a little taste of New York."

She nodded and spread her napkin over her lap.

"Anyway," he said. "How've you been? Are you staying busy in that big old house?"

She deflected with a smile. Despite having bared her soul to Nick, her mission to recover her job felt fiercely personal, not like fodder for casual conversation. "Yeah, I've been working on a . . . ah, project. But to be honest, I should probably get out of the house more. I'm getting pretty tired of staring at my screen all day."

The waiter delivered a carafe. Gallant poured and pushed a glass across the table. "Sounds like you need a hobby. How'd you spend your time in New York?"

A rueful sigh escaped. For the past year, she'd devoted herself to her side project. Its mathematics had filled her lungs. Powered every beat of her blood. God, how she missed that, the depth of it. The way she could lose herself transcribing numerical elegance into code. "Working, mostly. And Pilates. Then more work."

He nodded along. "You know, I admire that. Seems like hardly anyone's actually trying to get ahead, these days."

Her tongue twined around a denial. "It wasn't because I was angling for a promotion, or anything. It was more like I needed something to be consumed by. If that makes sense." That, and she'd wanted to win the Innovation Cup. The badge of honor would've lent credence to her life's work.

"Sure," Gallant said. "You like to stay busy."

She pressed her lips together. "Yeah. Something like that."

He scanned the menu. "I respect that. And hey, Henderson might not have much going for it, but that doesn't mean there's nothing to do here. Maybe you could volunteer."

"Volunteer?" A spark fired in her belly. Now, *there* was an idea. "For what?"

"Harvest Days, maybe? The parade's not 'til November, but it seems like half the town comes out to help build the floats."

That inner spark flared to a full-blown glow. Getting out of the house and away from that memory-laden fireplace would help clear her head. "That sounds great, actually. Who would I talk to about that?"

"Megan Shimamoto, probably. She chairs the volunteer committee."

"Megan Shimamoto?" Aubrey searched her memory and came up empty.

"Sorry," he said. "Tomlinson was her maiden name. Weren't you two besties, back in the day?"

Aubrey straightened. Megan Tomlinson *had* been her bestie, and the closest thing she'd had to a sister—not only a fellow cheerleader, but captain of the squad. It came as no surprise that pert, outgoing Megan now chaired a volunteer committee.

"Wow," Aubrey breathed. "I'd love to see her again. Do you have her number, by chance?"

"No." Gallant's tone took on an edge. Before she could divine its source, he moved on. "You could probably find her online, though. Anyway, do you know what you want?"

Aubrey shifted her attention to the menu. Once they'd ordered, the conversation turned to the past seventeen years.

Gallant spent the bulk of the evening talking up his accomplishments. He'd gone to college in Indianapolis, then returned to Henderson for his real estate license. Now he owned various properties around town, most of which he leased to businesses. He'd also renovated a run-down apartment complex into upscale condos for the mill foremen and their families.

As he talked, Aubrey's earlier interest faded. She savored her sea scallops, but her responses turned mechanical.

As she'd suspected, Gallant was uncomplicated. He aspired to wealth and not much more, and while she didn't begrudge him that, his life could be described with simple arithmetic.

Meanwhile, someone like Nick required advanced regression analysis and still left her feeling like she'd overlooked a hundred data points or two. She could probably spend a lifetime trying to solve the equations that made that man tick and never puzzle through them all.

Catching herself, she set her glass down with enough force to chip it. God, she *had* to stop thinking this way.

"Sorry," she said, aiming the word like a dart into Gallant's latest stream of braggadocio. "Look, it's been great to catch up, but I should probably go. Early morning, and all."

His smile dimmed. "Oh. Okay. You don't want dessert?"

"No. This has been nice, but the truth is, Gallant, I—"

"Hey." Concern crossed his brow. "No buts, okay? At least not until I give you your letter."

She swallowed her impatience and nodded. She almost couldn't bear to read whatever he'd written, because she couldn't stand to compare. Which she would, of course. She already had. "Okay."

He flashed a strained smile, paid the check without fanfare, and trailed her to the door.

At the entrance, she stepped aside for an incoming couple, her heels clicking on the ocean-patterned tile. The man and woman had nearly brushed past when Aubrey registered a familiar black pixie cut and sparkling blue eyes.

"Megan?"

The woman stopped, her expression pleasant, if blank. Then astonishment took hold. "Oh my god. *Aubrey?* Is that you?"

"It is!" Aubrey leaned in for a quick hug, then stepped back and held her friend at arm's length. Megan hadn't changed much—still cute, still tiny, with dimples so perfect they looked painted on.

"It's been forever!" Megan squealed. A man with jet hair and impressive cheekbones accompanied her, his hand cupped loosely around her elbow. "What're you doing here? I thought you'd gone off to New York and forgotten all about us."

Aubrey laughed. "How could I forget the girl who taught me a back handspring?"

Megan trilled a giggle. "Jeez, you look incredible." Her gaze traveled up and down, and she fiddled with the cowl neck of her glittery gold sweater. "I mean, *really* incredible. I think I might be underdressed."

"Oh, please. I got lucky and found this dress in the discount bin. And you look absolutely amazing. I mean, how're you glowing like that?"

"Oh. Well." Color blossomed in Megan's cheeks. "Sixteen weeks of pregnancy is doing me *some* favors."

"Pregnancy?" Aubrey's heart swelled. "Really?"

Her enthusiasm earned a smile from the man who must've been Megan's husband. As eager as Aubrey had been to leave, now she wanted to stand here all evening, learning every detail of her friend's life, her marriage, her baby—

Megan's grin faltered as her gaze slid past Aubrey's shoulder. "Oh. Gallant. Hi."

"Megan." His voice was cool. "Great to run into you."

A tense pause ensued, and Aubrey glanced from one to the other. Whatever lay between them, it didn't seem to match the civil words.

Megan's brows crooked. "You two aren't . . . together, are you?"

Aubrey paused, hesitant to put a damper on the reunion by explaining. Better to change the subject and get specifics later. "Gallant and I were just catching up. Funny we ran into you, actually. He suggested I talk to you about volunteering for Harvest Days."

Megan's smile recovered. "Oh, really? I'd love to have you. Why don't you call me this week? Everyone's meeting up next Saturday to get started."

The awkward tension faded. A few minutes later, Aubrey slid into Gallant's Tesla, Megan's number tucked safely in her clutch. Seeing her oldest friend had made the whole evening worth it. Now she simply had to let Gallant down easy. She'd accept his letter, then tell him the truth: that she simply didn't feel the *spark*.

When he pulled into her driveway, he circled to her side and escorted her up the walk. On the stoop, he took her by the elbows, searching her face with those luminous blue eyes.

Aubrey's gut tangled when he leaned in, but his lips merely brushed her cheek.

"The last thing I want to do is pressure you," he said, pulling back, "because I know we said we'd see what happens. But I've been thinking about you. A lot. And I hope you won't write me off until you read my letter. Sometimes it's easier for me to get things onto paper than to say them out loud."

Something inside her coiled tight. Gallant dug in his peacoat and produced a crisp, expensive-looking envelope. When she took it, the warmth of his body clung to the paper.

"Thanks." Her voice came out rough. "I'll read it tonight."

"That's all I ask." He smiled. "And I'll wait to hear from you."

She nodded and returned his murmured good-night. When the Tesla's taillights faded, she unlocked the front door, then set the letter on the coffee table in the living room. The thing seemed to occupy the entire space, familiar yet not.

She scolded herself for her reaction. This wasn't from Nick. For one thing, he'd never used a fancy envelope like that. Paper had simply been a vehicle, a tool he'd used to bare his marvelously complex soul. Which he'd done almost compulsively, as if she were the only one he trusted with it.

Unnamed emotions tangled in her chest, and she banished them by going to her bedroom, where she exchanged her cocktail dress for pajamas. In the kitchen, she brewed tea, then circled back to the living room, where she built a fire and sized up Gallant's letter the same way she might eye an opponent from across the ring.

She should just read the damn thing. Get it over with so she could let Gallant know that while she appreciated the effort, they weren't a match.

"This is stupid," she announced to the empty room, then tore open the envelope before she could reconsider. She read the words by firelight. Then again.

To her astonishment, her heart didn't sink.

Instead, it took flight in a way she'd thought it never would again.

Seventeen years ago

The new kid hadn't spoken to Aubrey in three weeks.

On his second day in English, he'd claimed a desk at the front of the room without so much as looking her way. She'd tolerated that for four whole days, then moved up, at which point Nick had promptly relocated to the back and continued to ignore her. When she'd switched again, so had he. And every time class ended, he somehow slipped from the room before she'd even made it out of her seat.

In the hallways, she'd spotted him a dozen times, but whenever she beelined toward him, nothing awaited but empty space. If she went left, he went right. If she went right, he disappeared entirely.

Nick was, very clearly, avoiding her.

Which, under normal circumstances, Aubrey would've thought meant he regretted their bizarrely intimate afternoon together. But every morning, when she opened her locker, another letter waited inside.

Nick's confessions varied in length and content, but they all contained the same painful honesty as the first. One said simply, *I couldn't stop thinking about you last night. I fell asleep with your name on my lips.* In another, he delved into his hatred for his father.

When I was seven, he wrote, *my dad cheated on my mom. Or maybe I should say that's when my mom found out. I'm sure it wasn't the first time he'd done it.*

I don't remember how everything happened, at least not in detail. I was too young. But I've read the police report enough times, and it says my mom had some painkillers left over from a surgery she'd once had on her ankle. She took too many that day and didn't wake up.

It wasn't intentional. At least, that's what everyone says. She just went looking for a reprieve from her heartbreak, and accidentally went too far.

I barely remember her anymore. But she permeates some level of my memory, enough for me to know that, of my parents, she was the good one. The reliable one, who kept the rent paid and food in the fridge. The one who tucked me in and told me stories and made sure my shoes didn't have holes in the bottom.

When she died, my life changed overnight. My dad started drinking and hasn't held a steady job since. He always has some excuse, some delusional plan that involves moving us to a new place where he'll miraculously start showing up for work on a regular basis.

That's when he's speaking to me, at least. Which is rarely. Mostly, he forgets I exist. On the few occasions he remembers, he expects me to take him seriously. As if he didn't kill our relationship the day he killed my mom.

I wish I didn't feel her loss so deeply, still. But it's like a hole in me, a permanent knot in my soul, a rupture where the family I should've had was torn out by the roots.

That's why I write to her so much. And, as fucked-up as it might sound, she's the parent I'm closest to. My dad is just some asshole I live with. Some guy I'll never forgive. I'll never stop hating him, either. And no matter what happens, I'll never betray anyone the way he did.

Now you know why I spend as little time in that house as possible.

That one brought tears to Aubrey's eyes. Nick's agony dripped from the page, staining her soul, and she ached to sit with him on the chesterfield again, to trade her secrets for his. Such a simple desire, but one she couldn't fulfill, because she couldn't get anywhere near him.

Meanwhile, the letters kept coming. Just as he'd warned, each one was a window, illuminating some new facet of the darkly glittering jewel that was Nick Thacker. Sometimes he showed her beauty. Sometimes yearning, or shame. He handed himself over fragment by fragment, each letter a piece in a puzzle so vast and intricate Aubrey could barely comprehend its scope.

She thought about him all the time.

Every morning, when she spun the dial on her locker, anticipatory lightning crackled across her skin, and her next full breath never arrived until after she'd finished reading. Then, when she glimpsed tangled dark curls in the distance, frantic wings beat inside her chest.

Yet as January dwindled, Nick continued to elude her. February dawned gray and bleary. In the hallways, Gallant continued to be Gallant, proclaiming to anyone who would listen that the new kid had cheated during their fight.

Aubrey paid no attention. Each word from Gallant's mouth dissipated before reaching her, no more impactful than smoke on a breeze. Meanwhile, the words in her locker made her bones quake. She reread Nick's letters so many times they inked themselves on the backs of her eyelids.

Last night, I dreamed of you, he wrote. *When I woke, I couldn't breathe. I'm not sure I even wanted to.*

It wasn't normal, she knew. He'd even said as much in his first letter. But the more he wrote, the less she wanted it to be. What was normal, anyway? Gallant? Megan? Probably. They were predictable. Solvable with a single swipe of the pen. Which had its place, certainly. Aubrey considered Megan an invaluable friend.

But this—this was something else entirely. Nick had spent one afternoon with her and fallen head over heels into *something*—obsession, maybe, or fascination—and she wanted nothing more than to draw closer, to burn herself on the flame of his fixation, because his words never stopped pulling her deeper. And god, how she wanted to hear that raspy voice again, let it roll through her, down to her toes.

She longed to unravel him. The same way he was unraveling her.

So . . . Nick could keep avoiding her, if he wanted. Maybe he'd even succeed, for a little while longer. But this game of his had failed to factor in one thing.

The lengths to which she was willing to go when she wanted something.

Today, Aubrey sat at the back of the classroom, awaiting the start of English. Nick appeared his usual millisecond before the bell and slid into a front-row seat.

She had no idea how he did that—acted as though she didn't exist. Especially when her entire being realigned in his presence like iron filings around a magnet.

Mrs. Hayes started talking, but Aubrey's stare didn't budge. A month ago, she'd looked at Nick and seen frailty. Now she understood there was nothing wasted when it came to him, nothing extra. He was all longing and fire and fight, a lit furnace that incinerated anything unnecessary.

She just hadn't understood what she was looking at, at first. She hadn't realized how breathtaking he was.

Aubrey let five whole minutes pass, then raised her hand. "Mrs. Hayes, can I move? This desk keeps wobbling. It's making it hard to concentrate."

Mrs. Hayes expelled the world's longest sigh, probably because Aubrey never concentrated. But the puzzle book had stayed at home for the past few weeks, which hopefully counted for something.

"Be quick," Mrs. Hayes snapped. "And no interruptions from anyone else hoping to play musical chairs, please."

Triumph coursed through Aubrey's bloodstream as she toted her things to the desk beside Nick's. She sat, then stared at him so hard he would have no choice but to feel her laser concentration boring into his skin.

Mrs. Hayes turned her back, squeaking some kind of chart onto the markerboard. Nick studiously refused to acknowledge her.

"Hi," Aubrey whispered.

He mashed his lips together and hunched over his notepad. The handwriting there kickstarted her heartbeat. She could have traced it in her sleep.

Still, not a glance.

"I need to talk to you," she breathed. "Tonight. I'm cheering the boys' basketball game, but I can find you afterward, if you'll come. Please?"

Nick closed those beautiful, elongated eyes of his, as if in pain. When he reopened them, he looked straight at her, and she had the most ridiculous urge to fist-pump the air.

Incredible. A boy had *looked* at her, and she may as well have gold-medaled in the Olympics.

"Fine," he said.

Victory dawned inside her. She gathered her breath to answer, but Mrs. Hayes's strident tone sliced through the quiet. "Is there a problem, Miss MacLean? Because if this desk wobbles, too, I'm sure the desks in the principal's office are more sturdily built."

Aubrey ducked. "No, Mrs. Hayes. Sorry. No problem at all."

In a show of contrition, she actually took notes for the rest of the period. But she fisted a hand against her mouth the whole time, trying to hide her grin.

The gym stank. Mostly like sweat, but also like the limp, boiled hot dogs the chess club was hawking in order to raise money for the state championship at year's end.

Aubrey had bought one of the rubbery things in the first quarter, if only to support a game so blatantly based on mathematics, then promptly dumped it in the trash. Now, with the second quarter running down, she huddled on the bottom row of bleachers with her squad.

As Megan chattered about the halftime routine, Aubrey resisted the urge to look around again. She hadn't spotted Nick, but he could have been anywhere amid the sea of colorful jackets filling the gym. Or not there at all.

The timer buzzed. As the basketball team jogged off the

court, Aubrey sprang up. The band blared as her squad took to the floor.

Raucous cheers sounded. She burned with the need to scan the stands, but as one of the bases for Megan's liberty, she couldn't look away, not even for a moment. The stunt required her total attention.

Aubrey lifted, tossed, caught. The heated atmosphere scorched her lungs, her muscles catching fire. Megan came down safely, then tumbled away.

Finally, *finally*, they made it to the dance portion of the routine, and Aubrey whipped her gaze across the bleachers, seeking—

There.

Nick sat in the top row, his elbows draped over his knees, staring at her with such intensity she swore she felt a *thunk* when their eyes connected.

The crowd dissolved to a wash of color. Time slowed to a trickle.

Then it didn't just feel as if she performed for him, she *did* perform for him. The dance couldn't come close to reciprocating all he'd shared with her, but with every pull of muscle and lift of her body, she scripted a response to his letters. She told him every last secret she'd ever kept. She sank her whole self into the routine in a way she never had before.

Those infinite eyes never looked away. Aubrey swore she glimpsed words within, calligraphy scrawled atop itself until the ink bled black as midnight.

The band blasted to a crescendo. Her squadmates cheered and cavorted, but Aubrey stood motionless, locked in communion with this incredible boy who dreamed of her at night.

Abruptly, Nick stood. He wove down the bleachers and loped out through the gym's side door, letting it slam behind him.

She nearly shrieked her frustration. "Wait, what?"

She spent a precious moment deliberating, then broke formation. Megan called after her, but Aubrey flung open the side door and shot through without looking back.

Outside, the cold bit into her bare skin. Orange sodium lights flooded the alley, gilding her exhales and illuminating emptiness in both directions. A scream rushed up her throat, but she throttled it.

Nick couldn't have gone far. She just had to find him.

Which she would. There was no way in hell he was getting away from her again.

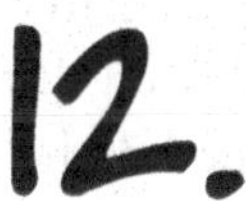

12.

Seventeen years ago

NICK HURRIED THROUGH the freezing night, wondering what in the ever-loving fuck he'd been thinking.

The amount of real estate Aubrey MacLean had staked out in his head already tortured him, but this would burn him alive. Had he *really* needed to know what the precious underside of her thigh looked like, or that she could lift her leg up beside her head with no apparent effort? Had he absolutely *had* to memorize the dewdrop glisten of sweat on her neck, the way it made damp red tendrils out of her hair?

Ugh. Now he would never get her out of his thoughts.

He sucked in a breath so cold it stung his lungs, then upped his pace. Aubrey probably wouldn't have left the game at halftime, but on the off chance she'd followed, he needed to put as many frozen shadows between himself and the gym as possible.

How stupid that when she'd asked today in English, he'd thought he could face her. One glimpse of that *dance*, and he'd known he couldn't stand to let her end this . . . whatever it was. Which was borderline hilarious, since he would gladly get into another fistfight with Gallant. A hundred fistfights. A fucking thousand.

But let Aubrey tell him to stop writing to her, even once?

He'd rather die.

Still, it would happen, no matter what he did. He'd known it from the moment he'd shoved that first letter into her locker and stared, wondering whether he had the means to punch through the flimsy metal and reclaim the paper before Aubrey could see it. See *him*.

Except the look on her face while reading it had done something to him. Her eyes had deepened, her bottom lip folded between her teeth, and some kind of detonation had taken place beneath his ribs. Now he couldn't stop writing to her, and it made him feel crazy. Like someone addicted to a drug they'd only done once.

"Nick!"

A sick jolt shot through him. Shit, *had* Aubrey followed him? She must be desperate to put a stop to the messed-up therapy sessions he was unilaterally conducting with her locker.

"*Nick*," she said, right behind him, now.

He stopped, shooting panicked glances left, then right, but the night offered no escape. Nothing but frosty brick walls and darkness.

With no other options, he turned.

His insides twisted. She stood there in her cheerleading uniform, her hair like a flaming torch beneath the lights. Fuck, but she was beautiful. Cruelly so.

"Why do you keep running from me?" she said.

A dead laugh needled at his throat. *Why?* Gee, where to begin? Because he didn't want to have to leave her be? Because he needed to go on believing she actually valued his confessions? Because he didn't want confirmation that she'd never again look at him the way she had at her house, like she hoped to take him apart and cradle the pieces safely in her hands?

"I'm sorry about the letters," he rushed out. "I got carried away, but I'll stop."

He made to flee, but she flung out a *wait-a-minute* hand. "Stop?" She sounded hoarse, her voice rubbed raw by the cold. "God, no, I don't want you to *stop*."

Nick hovered there, uncertain. He suddenly seemed to be anyplace and no place, floating in some nameless auburn darkness, his only anchor the girl who gleamed before him like a freshly bloomed rose. "You . . . don't?"

She drifted closer. "No. Of course not."

He couldn't move, couldn't make himself back away.

She drew dizzyingly close. "Did you mean everything you wrote?"

He meant to say, *no, not even a little*. An easy out. But his stupid mouth betrayed him. "Of course. I meant every word."

Her eyes shone. "Then you were right. About language. It's magic. I had no idea."

He shifted his weight. He had no clue how to stop the barrage of inhalations piledriving into him. He was freezing. Or melting, he couldn't fucking tell.

"And . . ." Her fingers twined at her waist. "I think about you, too, you know."

He could hear himself breathing. Why the hell was it so loud? He sounded like a bull about to charge. "You think about getting me to leave you alone, you mean."

"No." She hugged herself across the middle. "I think about *you*. About the things you've written. Especially the part about you wondering what it would be like to kiss me."

He stared. That made no sense at all.

Her teeth dug into her bottom lip. "Say something. Please."

He surveyed her, searching for the lie. But she looked sincere. More importantly, she looked cold. Goose bumps bristled as she rubbed her palms along her bare arms.

"You're freezing," he said. A true master of words, indeed.

"Yeah, a little. Can I use your coat?"

In nanoseconds, he'd unzipped the bomber jacket he'd "inherited" from a kid who'd picked a fight with him at lunch two years ago. It was too small in the arms now, but would swallow her trim frame with room to spare.

"I meant with you still in it," Aubrey said.

He paused with the collar down around his elbows. "What?"

"Like this." She sidled closer, hesitant. When he didn't move, she pulled his jacket back into place and slipped her arms underneath, around his waist.

At the contact, his heart ballooned to block his throat. His mind fuzzed out. Yet somehow, his body responded, his arms folding open to cocoon her into the jacket. Into himself.

Aubrey burrowed against his shoulder and sighed, her breath a molten caress that seeped through his shirt. "That's better."

Seconds whirled past, each one tightening confusion's hold on him. What? Just . . . what? One minute he'd been running from her, and now he was holding her, and the interval separating the two was a dissonant blur, like a needle-skip over a scratched record.

And Aubrey was trembling. Why was she trembling? She hadn't been, a moment ago.

She lifted her head. She was tall for a girl, just an inch or two shy of his five foot ten, and her breath feathered against his mouth. Her pupils expanded, their swell visible even in the orangey sheen of the lights.

His lungs kept exploding, over and over. This wasn't happening. Aubrey MacLean couldn't possibly be pressed to his body, her heartbeat battering at his sternum like a thrashing bird. Her face couldn't be inches from his, or her cheeks so flushed, or her green eyes heated and expectant, as if she really had thought about him kissing her.

But oh god, what if he *did* it? What if he just did the same thing he'd done at her locker that day, and silently screamed all the doubts into shutting the fuck *up* for once, because couldn't he just pay for his idiocy later?

His body ran away with that line of thinking, because somehow he was easing her backward, maneuvering her until her ponytail hit the nearest wall. His hand landed beside her head, the brick an icy sizzle against his palm.

Aubrey reached up. He braced for her to shove him away, but her fingertips landed on his cheek, gentle. Heat blazed wherever she touched. An involuntary sound worked free of him, a wispy kind of moan.

She didn't seem to want to talk. Thank fuck, because he wouldn't have had any idea what to say. It was enough of a challenge trying to figure out how to keep himself upright, especially when she insisted on staring at his mouth like that.

"Well?" she finally whispered.

"Well, what?"

"Do you still want to find out?"

Jesus, he was shaking. She was, too. His attention strayed to the side of her neck, where her pulse beat recklessly fast, a hummingbird flutter in the darkness.

None of this made any sense. But god, yes, of course he wanted to find out. He wanted it more than anything, ever. Some circuit clicked off in his brain, a whole bank of neurons going dark. Probably the ones responsible for self-discipline, or self-doubt, because when she tipped her chin up, he didn't think. He just dipped his head and slanted his mouth across hers.

Her lips molded to his, and it was everything he'd wanted and more, a shot of liquid heaven, a lightning infusion to the nervous system. Desperately, he wondered if he was doing it right, but the noises she whimpered into his mouth, her whispered *oh, thank god*, the way her fingers scrabbled at his chest—it intoxicated him. Emboldened him. Instead of pulling away, Aubrey pulled him *closer*, and he couldn't help but part her lips with his tongue. She tasted like honey and vanilla, like lip gloss, maybe, or some kind of fancy-ass toothpaste. Whatever the source, it made him feel drunker and dizzier than if he'd stumbled off a carnival ride after a thousand spins.

He tried going further, twining his tongue with hers.

She made a new noise, this one even more encouraging, and it exploded warmth into the pit of his stomach. Without consciously deciding to, he palmed the back of her head, his hips tilting against hers. She must have felt him pressed up against her belly, but she didn't recoil, just kept clutching at him as if she wanted to meld her body with his.

He realized, then, that this whole thing was a dream. It had to be. But he didn't want it to end. He just kept kissing her, kept abandoning himself to her softness and her hot wet tongue, and decided this wasn't at all something a person needed to learn, just something they needed to surrender to, because some feral, ancient part of him knew exactly what to do. How to possess her mouth with his, and oh fuck, he wanted more, so much more, and if he woke up now it would crush him, just please don't wake up, please don't wake up, please don't—

"Oh. Ahem. Whoops. Didn't see you guys there."

Nick lurched back, opening a foot of space. Off to the side stood a girl. He had a vague impression of pale hair, flat blue eyes, and combat boots, but aside from that, he couldn't process. Nothing existed between his ears but a splatter of heat and color.

"Sorry," the newcomer said. "Didn't mean to interrupt."

"We weren't kissing," Nick said inanely.

"Oh." The girl cocked her head. "Really? 'Cause it kinda looked like you had your tongues shoved down each other's throats."

Her frankness unnerved him, and he scrabbled for a rebuttal, some way to give Aubrey plausible deniability. She wouldn't want to be seen with him, not when he'd made sure the whole school would—

"We were definitely kissing," Aubrey said.

Nick looked to her wildly.

"Okay, cool, well . . ." The girl scuffed a sole against the asphalt. "Carry on, I guess." She walked off.

He groped for something to fill the silence. "Who the hell was that?"

"Tansy Burroughs."

He shook his head. Why had he even asked? He didn't recognize the girl's name any more than her face. "Okay. I don't . . . She's not going to tell anyone, is she?"

Aubrey's brow knitted. "Um, probably. Is that going to bother you?"

"No, I just . . . Won't it bother *you*?"

She studied him. "No."

"Oh." He wondered where all his words had gone, how he could possibly boil over with them in private, yet not have the faintest clue of how to talk to her in person.

She cocked her head. "Why would you even think that?"

"Because." Wasn't it obvious? "You're a cheerleader. Who likes math and safety and lives in a mansion. And I'm . . ."

When he didn't continue, her expression softened into quiet understanding. "You're . . . what?"

"No one. Just a guy who likes words."

Silence pulsed between them. At last, she blew out a breath. "Can I tell you a secret? Since you've told me so many of yours?"

He couldn't help it. He drifted closer.

"I'm just a girl." She held his eyes. "Who likes numbers. *And* you."

His mental gears ground. "Me?"

"Yeah. Now will you come share your jacket again? I'm cold."

He stood there for half a second, his brain a melted lump of candle wax. But he couldn't have denied her anything, so he wrapped her up again, then buried his face against her neck when she nestled into him. The clean tang of her sweat rushed in, a rising brightness inside his head.

She liked him. Aubrey MacLean *liked* him. Even though he'd shoved enough letters into her locker to decimate a small forest. Or . . . he dared imagine . . . maybe *because* of that.

She pressed herself even closer.

"My god," he groaned in her ear. "A cheerleader who likes math and safety and lives in a mansion and can touch her ankle to her ear and smells like fucking *paradise.* I don't even know what I'm doing here."

He was drunk on her, clearly. Or maybe still dreaming, because when she made a hungry sound, he cupped her jaw and nipped at her bottom lip. He didn't know if he'd thought of that himself or seen it in a movie somewhere, but the way she shivered in response made him marvel.

"I have a favor to ask," she said, breathy. "I have to go back inside soon, but—"

"You want my jacket?" he murmured against her lips.

"No. I want you to sit next to me. In English. Tomorrow."

He pulled back. Her eyes were wide and intensely green, a breadth of springtime on this frigid night.

"And talk to me in the hall," she continued.

"You mean . . . in front of people?"

"Yeah."

"That's two favors," he said, for lack of anything else.

A shy smile slid across her mouth. "Yeah. Actually, can we make it three?"

He dared to settle his fingers against the pulse in her neck. It felt like touching something holy, and he already knew he would do whatever she asked. He'd go find a fucking dragon to slay, if she wanted. "What?"

"Don't stop writing to me."

A searing hope lit his chest.

She reached up to brush his hair from his eyes. "And maybe kiss me again, if you don't mind. That was . . . incredible, and I'd really like to do it some more."

"That's four favors." He limited himself to three words, because if he didn't, too many would emerge. A cyclone would pour out. He'd never stop.

"So is that a yes, then? Or . . . four yeses?"

"Yes," he said. "Yes, yes, yes. Anything."

She leaned up and kissed him, or maybe he kissed her. He didn't know, only that she tasted even better, felt even headier against him, the second time. She finally broke away and left him leaning against the frosty wall, panting.

"I have to go, but . . . see you tomorrow, Nick?"

"Yeah." He didn't recognize his own voice. "See you tomorrow, Aubs."

He couldn't have said where the nickname came from, but her eyes crinkled in pleasure, so he committed it to memory as she melted into the darkness.

He stood there for a few thousand years, trying to get his brain to work again, but it refused, so he eventually gave up and went home.

Only when he was halfway asleep did he finally realize the dream still hadn't ended.

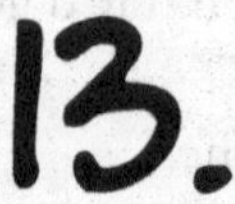

13.

Dear Aubrey,

Have you ever looked back and asked yourself how you got here?

I have, so many times over the years. Sometimes I turn to trace the path behind me and can't say how it led me to this place.

The funny thing is, I laid every stepping stone myself. I'm responsible for every crooked turn, every dead end I stumbled into, every blind alley I had to squeeze out of. And so I have no one but myself to blame for the fact that I didn't end up where I wanted to go.

I sometimes wonder what the turning point was. With which choice did the road diverge? How many steps would I have to retrace in order to make it all turn out differently, to see what life would have offered you and me?

Too many, I'm sure. And of course, I can never retrace anything. But that's the strange and beautiful thing about life: every once in a while, it offers us another chance. Even when we lose ourselves in the twisting detours and unmarked side streets, we sometimes still manage, miraculously, to stumble out in exactly the place we belong.

That's what reconnecting with you has felt like.

I'm sorry I didn't get it right when we were younger. I hope you'll forgive me for that, and I hope you realize I paved my path without knowing what I was doing. I put the stones down in all the wrong order, staked the signposts in mixed-up directions, then had the audacity to wonder how I'd managed to wander so far afield.

But the other day, seeing you again after so many years, I wondered if maybe I'd somehow reached my destination, after all.

All this to say . . . I hope you'll give me a second chance. Or maybe a first one, a new one. Turns out, I'm a much better wayfinder than I used to be.

Gallant

During her second week back in Henderson, Aubrey buzzed with barely contained energy. She logged countless hours on what she'd affectionately come to think of as her manifesto, and did Pilates daily, but each night, she forewent her logic puzzles in favor of reading Gallant's letter. Again. And again.

And again.

Days had passed since their date. As promised, he hadn't contacted her, which relieved her. She needed the breadth of the week to absorb what he'd written. To accept that he was, in fact, far more skilled at putting things onto paper than at saying them out loud. Because, while his efforts to impress her at dinner had done little to pique her interest, the letter revealed a whole new side, one she found both vulnerable and arrestingly human.

Now she felt herself hovering, just like with Nick all those years ago. She stood on the cusp of something immense, something she both craved and feared. She only needed . . .

Well, who knew. A push, maybe.

On Thursday night, after even an extended Pilates session failed to quiet her mind, Aubrey ventured out her front door. Her ankle had healed, so she turned up her collar and let the chilled wind push her down whatever street it chose.

She wandered Henderson, Gallant's letter like a burning weight in her pocket, and absorbed the scenery with eyes that felt both new and old. So much had changed. So much hadn't. The corner of Ivy and Harkness sported an unfamiliar café with Edison bulbs and exposed-brick walls, but old man Sajak's yard still had four rusted-out cars piled like checkers, probably the same ones that had teetered there when she'd been born. Five blocks later, she saw that the Siegels' ramshackle bungalow had finally been torn down, yet the steel mill kept watch over the empty lot, as it always had and likely always would.

Aubrey memorized the changes, superimposing a new mental map over the old. Sometimes, things stayed the same. Other times—she fingered the letter—they metamorphosed.

Two blocks later, she rounded a corner and came face-to-face with a plate-glass window. The building looked newly constructed, the window offering a view of a gym-like space, complete with red floor mats and a cage-like structure at the back.

She stopped. Strange. The place didn't have much equipment, just a few punching bags, plus lots of open space, and—

Oh.

Blood rocketed into her cheeks. Nick was in there.

She hadn't seen him since that night at her house, and now she took an involuntary step back. A glance at the gym's door revealed *Wilder's MMA Academy* in arched red letters.

Which made a strange sort of sense. She'd seen MMA fights on bar TVs over the years, and now had no difficulty imagining Nick involved in a sport that included blood and punching and sheer, unbridled intensity.

Thankfully, his attention was elsewhere, so she stood on the wind-scoured sidewalk and watched. Inside, Nick shared a mat with a broad-shouldered Black man, discussing something that clearly displeased him. Dark brows slashed over eyes like smoldering coals. The overhead lights accentuated the planes of his face, his tank top clinging to every line and ripple. He knocked gloved knuckles together, then said something that prompted his friend to clasp a compassionate hand on his shoulder.

Aubrey's heart caved in. Nick Thacker had been beautiful in high school, but now he'd grown into something else entirely, some otherworldly being that shot fist-sized holes in her ability to draw breath. He hardly even looked real. More like some scowling warrior angel, or an errant god with a world to overthrow. And yet nothing about his glower intimidated her. It was so real. So *him*, enough that her belly turned a slow pirouette.

Skeletal leaves skittered past. God, had she ever been free of him? She'd thought so, but standing here now, she understood that part of her had never left this place. Her work in New York had meant the world, but it had also served as an escape. A way to ignore the fault lines along which she'd fractured long ago. So had her boyfriends.

Distractions, every one.

Because all this time, a secret sliver of her had been waiting. A last, starved hope had stowed away, whispering that someday, Nick would come for her. That she could pass her time with mathematical men all she liked, but in the end, she would always belong to a dark-eyed tempest with words swirling in his bloodstream.

One glance through that window, though, and the depth of her foolishness became clear. Nick had *told* her he didn't have regrets. Straight to her face. He'd taken those words of his, honed them to a killing point, and skewered her with them.

Meanwhile, Gallant was the one who'd reflected about the road not taken.

The wind gusted, blowing wet against Aubrey's cheeks. She glanced around for rain, then realized she was crying.

She let it happen, because something was ending, right here in this moment. Some small, bitter death was taking place as the imaginary future she'd nurtured for seventeen years curled away into the shadows.

Nick glanced up, startling when their eyes connected. Aubrey offered a wilted smile. Hopefully he couldn't see her tears from this distance.

He started for the door, but she hastened away. She turned a few aimless corners and, once certain he hadn't followed, pressed her back against a building and pulled Gallant's letter from her pocket. The wind tried to snatch the paper away, but she held on and fished out her cell, finally making use of the phone number he'd left at the bottom.

Gallant answered on the third ring. "Aubrey?"

"Hey." The word sat softly on her tongue, rich with her tears.

"Uh, hey." Cautious hope infused his voice. "How are you?"

"Good. I read your letter."

"Oh." A few beats of silence unfurled. "And?"

"And . . . what're you doing? Right now?"

His breath caught. "Drinking wine. And wishing I had someone to drink it with."

She screwed her eyes shut and took a fortifying breath. "Well, maybe you do. Could you come pick me up?"

"Of course. Where are you?"

She rattled off the intersection, then hung up and tipped her head back against the wall of the hair salon she'd taken shelter beside. Nick might be her past, but the time had come to move forward. To stop holding back. To stop *waiting*.

Time to turn her gaze to the road ahead. And maybe, just maybe, it led to the man who'd written her this letter.

14.

ON SATURDAY, AUBREY woke renewed. For the first time in weeks, she had a purpose. One that involved more than just doing job-related damage control.

She dressed in a fitted brown tunic sweater, jeans, and slouchy ankle boots. Today marked her first day volunteering for Henderson's Harvest Days. And, she supposed, her third day dating Gallant Nobel.

Which sounded odd even to herself, so she focused on getting to her morning coffee meet-up on time.

The café was only a handful of blocks away, so she struck out on foot, tilting her face to soak up the cheery sunlight. High above, the sky glowed turquoise. Even the steel mill looked less dour today, sending spurts of silver steam into the blue.

By the time the café on Ivy and Harkness came into view—*Windy's Place*, read the script on the window—Aubrey felt light inside. She reached the door just as Megan pulled up in a maroon Jeep.

"Hey, you!" Megan hopped out and wrapped her in a hug. "Thanks for coming."

"Thanks for inviting me."

Inside, they took their place in line, and Aubrey snuck a

sidelong glance. Megan was barely showing, and even then, probably only because of her diminutive stature. But there were other tells, like the airbrushed quality of her skin.

"You look phenomenal," Aubrey said.

"Aww, thanks." Megan blushed and smoothed her short dark locks. "No pregnant woman dislikes hearing *that*."

They ordered coffees and claimed a table near the window, where Megan clasped Aubrey's hands over the polished butcher-block. "I'm so glad we're finally catching up. I still can't believe you're here."

"Me, neither. I think . . . I probably should've come back a long time ago. At the very least, I should've kept in touch. Seeing you again has already made this entire trip worth it."

A sheen sprang to Megan's eyes.

"Hey, now. That wasn't supposed to make you cry."

Megan gave a wet laugh and wafted air toward her face. "Sorry. I get emotional at the drop of a hat these days. Hormones. And believe me, I understand why you cut ties. I never held it against you. Though I did wonder how you were doing, out in New York. Whether you . . . recovered or not."

Well, that was as diplomatic a way of asking about Nick as any, Aubrey supposed. She reclaimed her hands and fiddled with the swizzle stick in her cinnamon latte. "It took a while. Losing Nick was the worst thing that ever happened to me. Especially because of *how* it happened. But then I went and did all the things I'd dreamed about. Got my doctorate, got a job doing something meaningful. Now I actually make a living doing math all day."

"So it all worked out." Megan heaved a contented sigh. "And you're going back to New York soon?"

"Yeah." Aubrey summoned a smile. She *would*, come hell or high water. Already, she'd made decent headway on her manifesto. "I'm only here for a couple months. But enough about me. What about you? You're married. You're pregnant! Tell me everything."

Megan's inner light threatened to boil over as she gushed about meeting her husband, Kenzo, at a concert in Indianapolis a decade prior. They'd been married seven years and were expecting their baby girl in the spring.

"I work at the steel mill, these days." Megan patted her barely there belly. "Not on the line, obviously, but in HR. I like it just fine, but honestly, I *live* for Harvest Days. There's nothing like seeing the festival come together and knowing I made it happen."

Aubrey chuckled. This was the Megan she remembered, who relished nothing more than putting her mark on things.

Megan leaned in. "And honestly, as volunteer coordinator, I do more than just organize the parade. I get to play fairy godmother, too."

Aubrey gave a puzzled smile. "What do you mean?"

"I mean I'm the one who assigns volunteers to each project, which is a lot more influential than it sounds. Last year, I paired up Trina Nguyen and Melanie Farrow."

"What?" Aubrey rocked back in her seat. "No way. Haven't they hated each other since kindergarten?"

"They have." Megan's eyes gleamed. "Or should I say *had.* Now they're inseparable. They're even going into business together. Some kind of mineral cosmetics company."

Aubrey blinked through her shock.

Megan pressed eager palms together. "And do you remember Pippa Huntington and Josh Bristol?"

"The shyest kids in school?"

"Yup. They're married now, *finally*, after being secretly in love with each other for, I don't know . . . twenty years? They were both too scared to make the first move. Until I put them on float-painting duty together." She exhaled against manicured fingernails and polished them on her sweater. "Thank you very much, Megan Shimamoto."

A laugh worked loose from Aubrey's throat. "Wow. But how do you decide? Who to pair up?"

"It's a small town, you know? And I'm in HR. I hear things. Get to know people. See things in them they sometimes miss themselves."

Aubrey shook her head in wonderment. She shouldn't ask but couldn't seem to help herself. "Does Nick work at the mill, still?"

"Mm-hmm." Megan's mouth curled on one side. "He's usually down in the blast furnaces, so I don't see him much. But I come in contact with everyone, from time to time."

Aubrey fiddled with her cup. God, she should really change the subject. But this was simple curiosity, now. A mere gathering of data. "And what do you see in him? Is he . . . happy?"

The gleam in Megan's eyes sharpened. "About as happy as you remember. Which is to say that *very* little about that man has changed since high school, except for the whole tall-dark-and-handsome thing he's got going on now. But I'm about ninety-nine percent sure he wants exactly the same thing he always did."

Aubrey puzzled that over. It wasn't really an answer.

"Why?" Megan's look turned sly. "You aren't still carrying a torch, are you?"

Aubrey spluttered into her drink. "No. What? No. I just . . . wish him well."

One of Megan's lacquered fingernails tapped out a rhythm against her mug. "That's it?"

Aubrey fought the heat spreading up her neck. It wasn't, not really, but she had no desire to add her hang-ups to Megan's mental catalog of Henderson drama. "That's it. At this point, he's no different to me than anyone else in this town."

"Oh. Well, good to know." Megan sipped her latte and licked away the foamy mustache. "But enough about him. Tell me about you. Having dinner at Sea and Be Seen with Gallant? That seems . . . serious."

Aubrey occupied herself with her drink. A few days ago, she would've downplayed the date. But that had been before she'd spent Thursday evening drinking wine with Gallant and staring into eyes almost too blue to be real. It was funny—in person, he seemed different from the man who reminisced so poetically on paper. But now that she knew that side of him existed, it made the real live person so much more compelling.

Still, what they were doing barely qualified as dating. They hadn't even kissed yet. Aubrey had just fallen asleep on his sofa and woken the next morning with a quilt tucked around her and a home-cooked breakfast on the table. Then, when Gallant had dropped her off, he'd slipped another letter into her hand.

This time, she'd wasted no time ripping into the thick, creamy envelope. And the words inside . . .

Warmth rushed into her cheeks. She sipped, giving herself time to think. "We're just . . . getting to know each other. Seeing what happens."

Megan's lips thinned. "I have to say, that surprises me."

"I know. And trust me, Gallant Nobel is the last guy I ever expected to date. But I think maybe we misjudged him. That there's more to him than any of us realized."

Megan nodded along, clearly not sold.

"Why?" Aubrey ventured. She hadn't forgotten the frosty exchange at the restaurant. "Do you . . . see things in him, too?"

"Nothing I'd share in polite company."

She blinked. "That sounds ominous."

Megan buried her face in a long swallow of milky latte. "Sorry. I try not to gossip. He's just . . . Well, he sold us our house last year, and we found out afterward there was a bat infestation in the attic. Which ended up being an incredibly expensive, incredibly stressful mess. But it's entirely possible Gallant didn't actually know about it. That it was an honest mistake."

Aubrey nodded, relieved. Was that all? "I'm sure he had no idea."

"Probably not." Megan stood briskly and straightened her sweater. "Anyway, we should get going. The volunteers are meeting at eleven, and I don't want to be late."

Aubrey toted her empty mug to the bin and followed Megan out. She had no idea where they were headed, only that a local farmer had volunteered his barn for the festival preparations.

In the car, Megan navigated out of town, onto a county road that apparently stretched forever.

"Wow," Aubrey said. "There's no way I can walk this next week."

"No need. There're plenty of volunteers who can give you a ride."

"How about Gallant? Is he coming?"

"No." Megan's lips flattened. "He never volunteers."

Aubrey studied her, but Megan was either very engrossed in driving in a perfectly straight line or didn't want to pursue the subject further.

She shrugged and turned to the window. Really, she didn't care what anyone thought. Even *she* had missed Gallant's complexity, and probably would have continued to, if not for that letter.

Twenty minutes later, they crunched to a stop in front of an ancient, majestic barn. Pastureland billowed away on either side, an idyllic frame of russet and gold.

Aubrey hopped out. A few dozen people milled around, and she approached with Megan, though her ankle boots made for difficult going. The heels stabbed into the soft ground, so she made a mental note to buy sneakers in town.

Suddenly, a thought occurred. "What will I be doing, by the way? I mean, not that you'd do that match-makey thing with *me*, but—"

"Oh, no." Megan's eyes widened. "Absolutely not. I'll put you exactly where I need you, regardless of who it's with. I know that's what you'd want."

"Right. Yes. Good." Aubrey ducked her head. How ridiculous that she'd even brought it up.

"But since you ask . . ." Megan rubbed a hand across her chin and contemplated the sky. "You'll probably be most useful building float skeletons with Paige. That's pretty mathematical, and she's into that sort of thing, and . . ."

Aubrey dutifully absorbed the rest, relieved to hear an unfamiliar name. Not that she'd doubted Megan's intentions, but still. She had no desire to be paired up with someone she had history with.

But not to worry. Whoever this Paige woman was, if she liked math, she and Aubrey would get along just fine.

As it turned out, Paige wasn't a woman, but a teenage girl.

Which Aubrey didn't mind, though the prospect of finding conversational common ground with someone half her age daunted her. What were high schoolers into these days, anyway? Parties? Boy bands? At that age, she'd been consumed by mathematics and her boyfriend. NYU and Nick. Nothing else had existed.

Fortunately, that turned out not to matter, because Paige did most of the talking. Bright-eyed and squeaky-voiced, and with the perkiest strawberry-blond ponytail Aubrey had ever seen, the girl was like a rainbow transmuted into a person. When Megan introduced them, billing Aubrey as "a native Hendersonite back for a visit," Paige pumped Aubrey's hand, then dove straight into a discussion about wire framing.

Aubrey half listened, half glanced around the airy barn at the many volunteers. When Nick proved absent, a knot between her shoulder blades loosened.

". . . we'll have to divide up the chicken wire," Paige was saying. "But first, we'll need to figure out the dimensions of the welded skeletons. Those're made of steel rods, which'll have to be cut to size."

"Okay," Aubrey said.

"You and I are in charge of two floats. A turkey, and one shaped like Indiana. Last year, the planning guys just made drawings and went for it, but a lot of steel got wasted and the floats didn't end up being all that big." She gestured to a pile of rebar poles. "I thought it'd make more sense to approach it like an optimization problem, so—"

"Wait." Aubrey's ears perked. "Did you just say 'optimization problem'?"

"Oh, gosh, I know." Paige rolled exceptionally blue eyes, their color nearly on par with the autumn sky. "It's math, everyone gets all frowny-faced when I start talking about it, but hey, I love it anyway, and I'm not afraid to tell everyone that I think"—she made an impromptu megaphone with her hands and pointed it at the broader crowd—"NUMBERS. ARE. AWESOME."

A few people looked up, then returned to their tasks. Aubrey raised her brows.

Paige dropped her hands, sheepish. "Sorry, I get carried away, sometimes. Everyone says. But math is actually way more useful than people realize, and right now it's gonna help us build some really big floats without wasting any rebar. You know, save the planet, and all that. Doesn't hurt to impress everybody while we're at it."

Aubrey wrestled with a smile. My god, Megan had chosen wisely. This girl was a delight. "I don't disagree with a single thing you just said, actually. So how would you put together this optimization problem?"

"Well, for the turkey, we basically need a big sphere, which we can build from four circles, right? And for Indiana, a rectangle twice as tall as it is wide."

Aubrey nodded along. "So we're maximizing the enclosed areas of the circles and rectangle?"

"Yeah, exactly." Paige's perky brows winged upward. "Wait, are you a math person?"

Aubrey grinned. "You could say that."

"Oh, no wonder Megan put us together." Paige made a *squee* sound, then pulled a tiny spiral-bound notebook and pencil from her back pocket. "Okay, so it's easy enough. We just write an equation that combines the areas of all the shapes, right? We'll call the radius of the circle X, and the width of the rectangle Y."

"Sounds good."

Paige jotted in the notebook. "This is the equation we'll maximize, but we can write another relating X to Y, since we know the perimeters of the circles and rectangle will add up to a hundred and twenty feet of rebar. Solve that function for Y, plug it back into the first—"

"—then take the derivative and solve for zero," Aubrey finished.

Paige's pencil stilled. "Yes. Wait, yes! You're like, a *real* math person, aren't you?"

"If having a PhD in mathematics counts."

"No way!" Paige *squeed* again. "A woman after my own heart. But wait, didn't you say your name is Aubrey? Not . . . Aubrey MacLean? The woman with all those trophies in the math club cabinet?"

Aubrey pressed a hand to her chest. "Oh, wow. They still have those up?"

"Of course!" Paige hopped up and down. "Oh my gosh. Okay, so don't get mad, but I've been trying to break your trophy record for *forever*. This might even be the year. I've got sixteen trophies, you've got twenty-two. Twenty-two! I mean, you're a legend."

Aubrey's startled laugh filled the barn. "I don't know about that." None of her classmates had even acknowledged her trophies, back when she'd earned them.

"Oh, but you are. All the math clubbers know your name. Mostly because you and I are locked in a heated battle." Paige giggled. "Ooh, you know what you should do? Come speak to my club. They'd die of surprise. My archnemesis, coming to tell us what it's like to be a math goddess in the real world. Wait, what *is* it like to be a math goddess in the real world? Do you—"

As Paige rattled off questions, tension tightened Aubrey's lungs. Speaking to the math club sounded wonderful on the surface, but it would mean showing her face at the same high school Nick's son or daughter attended. Paige probably even knew the kid.

Maybe he was in math club.

A vivid, daydream flash lit her mind. She saw herself walking into the musty old math room, only to confront a lanky sixteen-year-old with a dark glower and tangled curls.

What would she even say to the living, breathing proof of the heartbreak she'd barely survived?

Except . . . no. She was moving on, now. And kind of, maybe, sort of dating Gallant. Which might make meeting Nick's kid into a test, of sorts.

Proof of concept.

Aubrey drew a long breath. The faint itch of hay tickled her nose. "You know what? I'd love to talk to the math club. When would be best?"

Paige paused just long enough to squeak a victory. "Really? Oh, Mrs. Runge is gonna be so excited. Why don't I ask her about scheduling, and I'll get back to you. Here, do you have your phone? I'll put in my number and text myself. I promise I won't spam you with math questions. Okay, I *might* spam you with math questions, but you can tell me to back off at any time and I'll totally respect that."

Aubrey chortled and obediently handed over her cell, then tucked it back into her pocket when Paige finished. That done, they migrated to a rickety folding table by the window, where they tilted their heads together and planned the rebar cuts.

Paige scribbled numbers without hesitation. The girl was lightning quick and, even more impressive, confident about it. Not to mention personable and engaged, as if someone had permanently turned her dial up to eleven.

Within the hour, Aubrey's cheeks ached from smiling. Why hadn't she realized teenagers could be so . . . fun?

"So, is this what you want to do with your life?" Aubrey asked, when they'd settled on the final configuration for the rebar skeletons. "Math?"

"No. I mean, I love it and all, but for me, it's just a piece of the bigger puzzle."

"The bigger puzzle being . . . ?"

Paige glanced down, her broad grin tempering to something more restrained. "Um. Astrophysics."

Aubrey sat back. "You want to be an astrophysicist? *Really?*"

Paige stole a glance from under her lashes, and Aubrey kicked herself for her reaction.

She, of all people, should've known better. "Sorry, I just—"

"I know, I know," Paige said. "I'm only sixteen, I have about a million years to change my mind. Everyone says. But I swear astrophysics is it. Ever since my dad got me my first telescope when I was ten, I've been hooked. The idea of all those stars out there . . . forming, falling apart, imploding, *ex*ploding . . . I mean, they're beaming light at us all the time, which takes thousands of years to get here, like some kind of time capsule constantly arriving from the past. I honestly can't think of anything I'd rather do all day than study *that*."

Aubrey's heart swelled. "I'm sorry. I didn't mean to question your conviction. At all. Because you can absolutely know what you want to do at sixteen. I did."

Paige straightened. "Yeah?"

"Yeah. And astrophysics sounds incredible. I mean, you can do whatever you set your mind to. As in, you, specifically. You seem like a . . . force of nature. So don't bother with what people say. Just go out and show them they're wrong. There's a special kind of satisfaction in that, trust me."

"Wow. Thanks. You kind of sound like my dad, actually. He's always like"—Paige squared her shoulders and adopted a mock baritone—"'Ignore the haters, Peanut.' Which is such an old-man way to say it, but I appreciate the message."

Aubrey chuckled. "He sounds like a good guy."

"He is. I mean, I'm a daddy's girl, definitely. But only because he's a really amazing human."

A twinge of envy stabbed at Aubrey's throat. Love saturated this girl's voice, free of qualifications, a bittersweet echo of the way she'd felt toward her father at that age.

Back before everything had gotten broken. Before he'd smashed it to smithereens. And afterward, it had stayed broken. A decade later, he'd lost his battle with hepatic cancer, and that'd been it. A sad story with no ending.

Aubrey cleared her throat. "I'd like to meet this dad of yours. He sounds wonderful."

"Oh, you will," Paige chirped, the damper on her demeanor already dissolving. She glanced at her watch. "In about five minutes, actually. He's volunteering with us, too. He stopped by the fighting gym this morning, but he said he'd be here by noon."

A tendril of disquiet unfurled in Aubrey's stomach. "The fighting gym?"

"Yeah. He's super into this MMA stuff. It's so weird, but I'm all for whatever makes him happy, you know? And—Oh, look! Speaking of!"

Paige jumped up and dashed away. All the blood in Aubrey's body plummeted toward her feet. It was just a coincidence, had to be . . .

But no. When she swiveled in her chair, there stood Nick, in jeans and work boots, hugging a daughter whose personality could not have been more diametrically opposed to his than if she'd been designed that way.

Their gazes snared over Paige's shoulder.

"Well, shit," Aubrey muttered, her heart doing a slow capsize. "Definitely did not see that one coming."

16.

NICK'S MIND WHIRLED. There sat Aubrey, porcelain-pale, her throat working against a painful-looking swallow.

Paige pulled out of their hug. "Come on, come meet our float-building partner."

He forced his muscles to unlock and let himself be towed by the hand, because what choice did he have? *No thanks, Peanut, let's skip the part where you introduce me to the woman I've loved since before you were born.*

"Soooo this is Aubrey," Paige chirped. "But not just any Aubrey. Aubrey *MacLean*. The record-holder for trophies in math club. Although I *am* about to dethrone her, which maybe makes us bitter enemies, except I like her a lot, and . . ."

He resisted the urge to drag a hand down his face. Hearing Paige shape the same name that forever echoed inside his head had him questioning whether he'd wandered into some kind of upside-down reality. As did the fact that his daughter apparently knew Aubrey's name already.

". . . but, wait, didn't you two go to school together? The years on those trophies . . ." Paige smacked her forehead with an open palm. "Right. I'm being dumb. You've probably already met."

"Yeah," Nick choked out. "We've met."

"Wow, what're the chances Megan would pair us up with your old classmate?"

He almost groaned. What *were* the chances? Well, one hundred percent, probably. Fucking Megan Shimamoto, meddling again. The woman barely knew how to do anything else.

"And I can't believe you've never told me you went to school with a real live mathematician," Paige continued. "How could you just not mention that? *Ever?*"

Aaaand there was a question he had no desire to answer. Even so, he couldn't wrench his eyes from Aubrey's. Amid the cool blue shadows of the barn, her hair shimmered like it had been spun from jewels. He just stood there, in some kind of thrall, his heart a painful thump inside his chest.

Thankfully, Aubrey saved him from a response by sliding from her seat. "Excuse me. I think I need to . . . clarify something. I'll be right back." She bustled away. A moment later, she appeared outside the window, huddled in a conference with Megan.

Nick tried to shake off his stupor. Get it together. He'd only come to help Paige out, and if Aubrey didn't want him near her, he'd respect that. He'd *been* respecting it.

"I wonder what that was about," Paige said.

When he forced a shrug, she hauled him over to a stack of rebar, where she fired off a string of numbers that went over his head. Something about polygons and the sum of interior angles. He eventually gleaned that he had to cut the rods into pieces and weld them back together into a circle. No, four circles.

Which would probably take all damn day.

He sighed, but went to work with minimal grumbling. The sooner he finished, the sooner he could leave. His morning workout with Jackson had granted him some measure of calm, and he clung to it now, though it felt like trying to hang on to a bar of soap while standing under a roaring waterfall.

A pair of bolt-cutters lay beside the rebar, so he planted one handle against the floor, set a rod between the blades, and clamped the other handle down by leveraging all his strength. The cut pieces pinged onto the weathered floorboards. Paige nodded her encouragement and bounded away to "do more calculating."

Five minutes later, Aubrey reentered the barn, her cheeks pink with cold. Or maybe with being strenuously opposed to his existence. She strolled over and braced her hands on her hips, her brows raised, as if this had all been his idea.

"Well?" He tried to sound casual. "What'd Megan say?"

Aubrey glanced sidelong at Paige, who sat hunched over her notebook, her tongue peeking from the side of her mouth. She wouldn't be rejoining them anytime soon.

"She said she needs me here." Aubrey kept her tone hushed. "Doing math. And she *did* promise to put me where I fit best, regardless of who with. I guess I just misinterpreted what that meant."

He snorted. "You didn't misinterpret shit."

Aubrey's mouth pinched. "You're saying she paired me up with your daughter on purpose? Paired me up with *you*?"

He shrugged. No point trying to convince her of Megan's machinations if she didn't already know. "Just pick some other job, if this bothers you."

Aubrey hesitated. "I'm not going to . . . run away from you, if that's what you mean. I don't need to."

His heart thrummed a discordant note. No, of course she didn't. That night at her house—when he'd stupidly told her he didn't regret—had been the end of it for her. Case closed.

"Besides," she said. "That'd send everyone the wrong message."

Right. The "wrong message" being that she was still hung up on him. As if anyone would have suspected that to begin with. He bent to the rebar again, working in silence.

Aubrey stood and watched, as if to prove a point.

Which shouldn't have changed anything. But his skin grew hot and prickling under her stare. He manhandled the cutters until sweat trickled down his spine, then peeled off his jacket and tossed it aside. Not because he liked the feel of her gaze on him as he worked in nothing more than a sweat-dampened T-shirt, but—

Oh, fuck it, that was exactly why. Some primal part of him relished the chance to demonstrate the strength he'd never had when they were kids. Because while Aubrey might not care anymore, *he* did. He'd care until he was dead—and probably long after.

And the longer she stood there, the more he dared to imagine that maybe, just maybe, some overlooked ember of their past still flickered. Bit by bit, the stiffness melted from her posture. Her fingers snuck to her waist, then twined together. Her gaze cut from his body to his face and back again while her pulse swelled visibly in the hollow of her throat.

Heat rose inside him. He *knew* those tells, had once been fluent in that language of lowered lashes and half-drawn breaths. Even now, he remembered enough to know that while Aubrey might not care, some part of her, however small, still found him attractive. At least on a physical level.

Cold comfort, but he hoarded the knowledge, regardless.

The afternoon passed slowly, with him working up a sweat and trying not to stare at Aubrey, which, for the most part, failed miserably. Paige did most of the directing, while Aubrey marked off rebar cuts with a chalk-paint marker and arranged the finished pieces in preparation.

Then came the assembly. Nick went to the truck for his MIG welder and lugged it into the barn, then set up in a corner where he wouldn't burn anyone's vision.

Paige and Aubrey stayed outside. In between hissing showers of sparks, he caught their muted chatter, and reality seemed to drift. How mind-boggling that they could coexist like this. That his life's diverging roads could overlap in any way, much less chat casually in the October sunshine.

What in the actual fuck.

If nothing else, though, he appreciated knowing Aubrey had the grace not to hold Paige's origins against her. Even from here, he could make out her tone, warm and encouraging.

Probably talking about math, then. Definitely not about him.

When he finished, he packed up the welder, then paused in the barn doorway. Aubrey and Paige leaned against his truck, smiling. Aubrey kept lifting the heels of her boots out of the ground, then putting them down again, at which point they sank right back in. Paige's giggle drifted on the breeze.

Seeing them like that, laughing together, ripped open a rift inside him, an ache so profound it felt eternal, equal parts pleasure and pain.

Fucking hell, if only he could have had both of them. Done right by one without forsaking the other. If only he could have built himself a family that knitted together the disparate pieces of his torn-up heart.

But he couldn't, and he had no one to blame but himself, so he shouldered the welder's weight and stepped into the sunshine. Aubrey's smile died at his approach.

He tried not to let that bother him, but a weight dragged at his stomach, anyway.

"All done?" Paige said.

"All done." He manhandled the welder back into the truck bed.

"Great," she said. "I'm gonna go check everything over, figure out what we need for next week. I'll see you and Mom at dinner, okay? Oh, and you'll have to take Aubrey home. She doesn't have a car. I'd drive her, but I'm heading to Maria's for a bit."

He opened his mouth, but Paige had already bounced off toward the barn. She called over her shoulder. "Nice to meet you, Aubrey! I'll text you about math club!"

Nick pinched the bridge of his nose. "Math club? Do I even want to know what that's about?"

"Probably not," Aubrey said.

When he dropped his hand, he found her peering up, and this new vantage point struck him. In high school, she'd stood nearly at eye level, but that had been before he'd shot up four inches between eighteen and nineteen, once he'd started at the steel mill and begun filling his refrigerator with as much food as he could afford. His body had soaked it up, maybe making up for all that lost time when his dad had considered a refrigerated bottle of ketchup an acceptable discharge of his parental responsibilities.

Yet in those intervening years, Aubrey hadn't grown an inch. Somehow, that felt right to him, knowing he could tuck her protectively beneath his chin if he needed to.

"Don't worry." She frowned, and he realized he'd been staring for entirely too long. "You're not actually taking me home."

"I'm not?"

"No. I'll ride with Megan."

He surrendered to a bitter chuckle. So damn innocent. "Aubs. Megan *left*."

She reared back and glanced around. Cobalt shadows filled the barnyard. Only a few volunteers lingered, none of whom Aubrey would know. Conspicuously, Megan was nowhere to be found.

"Really?" Aubrey said, her voice shrinking.

"Really."

"You're sure?"

"Very."

She gnawed at her bottom lip. "I could . . . walk, then."

It sounded more like a question. "The hell you could. It's fourteen miles. Not to mention you sprained your ankle two weeks ago. I'm driving you, and that's the end of it."

Her mouth turned down at the corners. "Okay. Fine."

"Okay. Great."

Neither of them moved.

"Ugh," she said, throwing her hands up. "This is so stupid."

"What, me taking you home?"

She rolled her eyes. "No, this *awkwardness*. I mean, why're things so weird? So what if we dated in high school? So what if we were in love when we were kids? So what if we slept together *one time*? That was a million years ago. It doesn't matter anymore."

He stared, a spike of outrage hammering into him from nowhere. If she thought she could . . . "Oh, no. No way. You don't get to do that."

Her gaze thinned at his tone. "Do what?"

"Are you kidding me?" He lowered his voice, pushing words from a graveled throat. "You don't get to talk about it that way. You don't get to *diminish* it. Look, I get that what we were doesn't matter to you anymore. But it did to me. Then and now. So think of it however you want, but don't you dare include me in your dismissal. Don't even *try* to take away what you meant to me."

She blinked so many times he lost count.

He ejected a short, burnt-up breath. He hadn't meant to say all that, but something about her demanded compulsive honesty. It always had, ever since they'd first sat down on her couch and a gut-deep part of him had recognized himself mirrored in her. She'd waxed poetic about math, and a wealth of feeling had shone from her—the very same light that cast its blaze across the inner walls of his heart. He'd already gotten into the habit of shuttering his, but right then, it had spilled forth, because for the first time in years, he hadn't been alone.

After an eon of silence, Aubrey said, "Sorry. I didn't mean to . . . diminish anything. I just meant we should be able to talk to each other. Be civil, regardless of the past."

"I'm being perfectly civil," he snapped.

She huffed and dropped her eyes.

His irritation ebbed. "Look, if this is your weird-ass, roundabout way of asking me to be your friend, then fine. If that's what you want, I can do that." Sort of. Mostly, it would be like lighting himself on fire and trying to smile through it, but for her? Sure.

She toed the ground with a boot. "Maybe that *is* what I'm trying to say."

"Okay. Then we're friends. All right?"

She hesitated, then nodded.

"So will you get in the car now?"

Another nod. In the truck, she huddled against the passenger-side door. He started the engine and urged the vehicle down the lane. Aubrey faced the window, and just like in the barn, he couldn't help but steal glances. Words flooded into him as he drove, ones he wanted to brake for and scribble down. He wanted to capture the way her hair fell around her face, the way her bottom lip sloped inward when she breathed.

She looked so different than she had the other night, when he'd glanced through the window at Wilder's and gotten slapped in the face with the unexpected. Then, the timing couldn't have been more uncanny, because he'd finally admitted to Jackson what had been weighing on him. Then, as if his words had summoned the real live person, Aubrey had appeared.

She'd looked desperate, then. A little wild. But he didn't want to ask about it now, didn't want to risk this progress between them, however tenuous.

Halfway to her house, she broke the quiet. "Your daughter's wonderful, by the way. I mean, it was weird, meeting her. I won't pretend it wasn't. But she's impossible not to like."

His mouth hitched upward. "I'm glad you think so. She can be a little much for some. Kind of like . . . getting shot in the face with a glitter cannon. But I love that about her."

Aubrey half-smiled. "She's so *different* than you."

He rasped a laugh, devoid of mirth. "Yeah. Also what I love about her."

She cut him a glance, but he looked away.

"So . . ." She twiddled her thumbs in her lap. "You'll be back next Saturday? You and me and Paige'll be working together? Every week?"

"Looks that way. Unless you ask Megan to switch."

She mulled that over. "I'd rather not. I *did* tell her I was completely . . ."

"What?"

She bit her lip. "Nothing. It doesn't matter. She's done a pretty impressive job of backing me into a corner, either way."

He cracked a smile. Maybe not so innocent, then. "Don't worry, you're not the first. And you definitely won't be the last."

"Yeah. She even went to the trouble of giving herself a defense *before* I suspected anything. Which is pretty diabolical."

He grinned, relishing her word choice. *Diabolical* was a favorite of his. "She's basically just a tiny, pregnant Machiavelli."

Aubrey snorted. Her green eyes warmed, and the moment of shared understanding flared into connection. Just for a second, but it was one Nick took hold of and stuffed into a mental pocket, for the express purpose of torturing himself with it later.

He eventually pulled into Aubrey's cul-de-sac.

"Thanks for the ride." She was in the process of unlatching her belt when he reached out to stop her. She snatched her hand away, so he raised his in a show of contrition.

"Sorry. Look. There's just something I want to say. Something that's been weighing on me since the other day."

She stilled.

He hesitated, but he had to get this out. It had been crawling around inside him for more than a decade now, trying to find the light of day, and this was his chance. Probably his first *and* last, because once Aubrey returned to New York, he wouldn't see her again.

He cleared his throat. "The other night, when I said I didn't regret how things ended, I only meant because of Paige. Because she's . . . everything to me. My pride and joy. The family I never had. Regretting her would be like regretting my life's meaning, and I can't do that. But that doesn't mean I don't regret hurting you. Because I do. I've regretted it every day for seventeen years."

Aubrey's lips parted. She stared, her chest hitching. Something complex moved across her face, so deep and wide he had no hope of untangling it.

Not that he needed to. This was for her, not him.

"And I want you to understand," he continued, "that if there'd been any way to raise Paige right and keep from losing you, I would've done it. I would've done any fucking thing. If I could've sawed myself in two and given each of you half, I would have. In a heartbeat. But I couldn't, and I'm sorry for that. I'm so sorry for the way I hurt you, Aubs. Really. For losing you. I can't even tell you. I've wanted to say that for years."

A faint whimper snagged in her throat.

He curled his hands around the steering wheel and squeezed, mostly to keep himself from reaching out again. A thousand other confessions piled onto his tongue, about loneliness and longing and guilt. But he knew how it would come across, like he was asking for something, and he wasn't. He just needed to give this to her, needed to hand her his truth so she could do with it what she would.

"I . . . don't know what to say." Her voice warbled. A sheen misted her eyes. "Except thank you, I think. And . . . maybe I understand, now. After meeting her."

Honeyed relief cascaded through him. It was more than he could have hoped for, and he clenched the wheel so tightly his fingers ached. If he didn't, he would do something idiotic, like slide across the bench seat and hug her.

"I guess you should also know that . . ." She fumbled and stopped, deliberating. "You *did* mean something to me. You meant everything, actually. Then and—"

A razorblade breath sliced into his lungs. He waited, but she didn't continue, and the unsaid word dangled in the air, a promise so sweet he couldn't bear to have it broken.

Now. Then *and now.*

He willed her to say it. If she did, he would tell her he still loved her. Fuck everything else, all the doubts, the *should've-known-betters*, because there went her pulse again, a frantic shimmer in the divot between her collarbones. He swore he wasn't imagining it. *Or* the heat in those verdant eyes.

He just needed that word. One *now*, and he would confess everything, even if it changed nothing.

Yet Aubrey stayed quiet. She blinked back whatever emotion had overtaken her and looked away, a fist pressed to her mouth. When she met his gaze again, she'd raked hers to smoothness.

"Sorry. I didn't mean to get heavy on you." Her voice was measured. "And you won't have to take me home again. I'll ask Gallant next time."

The name hit him like a slap. "Gallant?"

"Yeah."

"Why? What does he have to do with anything?"

Her eyes changed. This time, he *could* read them, because a crack zig-zagged down the center of his chest. "Wait. You're . . . seeing him? You two are dating?"

"Yeah," Aubrey said. "We are, actually."

A desolate stillness descended, so complete he couldn't even find his own heartbeat within. Gallant Nobel.

It felt six kinds of wrong, and yet he should have seen it coming, because Gallant was the choice who'd made sense for her from the beginning. The picture-perfect poster boy for all-American maleness. The rich, successful counterpart to Aubrey's genius and drive.

Also kind of an asshole, but probably only in Nick's imagination, because Aubrey would never get involved with someone who didn't treat her like a queen.

He forced a swallow. Someone had clearly deposited a half ton of crushed glass in his throat at some point in the last five seconds. "That's great. That's . . . right. Great. I hope he makes you happy."

Aubrey's lip folded under her teeth. What did *that* reaction mean? He couldn't tell. Not that it mattered. All his deductive reasoning had drained away, along with his stupid, delusional hope and every last red blood cell in his body.

"Thanks again, for the ride," she said softly. "I'll see you next week?"

"Yeah. See you next week."

She thumbed off her seat belt, hopped out, and disappeared into the house.

He sat there for a long time, trying to find his composure. But it had abandoned him, so he eventually slid the gearshift into Drive and crept across town at half the speed limit. He didn't want to go home. He had no desire to face Tansy and Paige like this, hurt and bleeding and freshly shredded.

But he should probably get the fuck over that, and quick, because this seemed to be rapidly becoming his new normal.

Seventeen years ago

FOR THE FIRST time in his life, Nick had everything he wanted.

Three months in, it still didn't feel real, even though Aubrey kissed him everywhere—in the hallway, the school parking lot, the brick alley where he'd fought Gallant.

She also kissed him on the big blue sofa in her living room, where they canoodled every afternoon. At least until one of her parents pulled into the cul-de-sac, at which point Nick disappeared through the back door. Then he'd wander Henderson with his hands in his pockets and, when the upstairs at Aubrey's house went dark, steal around back to her ground-floor window. She'd raise the sash, pop out the screen, and welcome him in so they could kiss some more, this time in her bed, where Nick would ravel his hands in her silken hair and press himself as close as he dared.

He hardly went home anymore. Mostly just to shower and change. His dad had asked why exactly once. Noah Thacker had lowered his beer, narrowed his eyes, and muted the TV long enough to string a whole sentence together.

"Where the hell're you off to this time?"

Nick had instinctively planted his feet, defensive. "My girlfriend's house."

But Noah hadn't cared, of course, and had immediately gone back to his show. "Girlfriend? Huh. Just don't knock her up."

Seething, Nick had loped out into the night. He couldn't have said what angered him so much, except maybe the suggestion that Aubrey was nothing but a *thing* to impregnate, when in actuality, she was the sun around which his world orbited.

Ire aside, though, his dad had no cause to worry. Nick had turned eighteen in April, a mere three weeks before Aubrey had, but even though they'd both officially entered adulthood, she wanted to wait.

So Nick would wait. Happily. Not that he didn't want to have sex with her. He did. All the time. Every time he got near her, and nine-tenths of the time he didn't, some driving force pulsated within him, a scorching command for more, more, more. *Claim her, possess her, make her yours.* But he wouldn't have dreamed of pushing. He'd barely even processed the fact that something about him had apparently earned him the right to hold her hand, to slip a new letter into her locker each morning. To explore her mouth with his at night until they both reached a state of blissful exhaustion and fell asleep with their limbs woven tight.

Asking for more would have been like winning the lottery and daring to complain that it wasn't enough.

It *was* enough. More than that, Nick was in love.

Which he knew would prove agonizing when Aubrey left for NYU. But try as he might, he'd gone careening off that cliff, all the while knowing that nothing waited at the bottom but a bone-shattering impact. Yet he only seemed to have two settings—*full throttle* and *fuck no*, and he couldn't seem to remember the latter's existence when all he felt was the former.

So he would take what he could get, and suffer for it later. That part, at least, would feel familiar.

That simple fact circled in Nick's mind as he stretched on his side in Aubrey's bed and tongued her earlobe. She writhed, her breath a hot tide against his bare shoulder. She'd flung his shirt away somewhere, into her darkened bedroom, while he'd worked her down to a bra and pajama shorts. Their combined weight made the bed dip, and he felt submerged in her, shipwrecked on the headiness of her sunshine scent, on the warmth of the leg she'd draped over his hip.

"Nick," she whimpered as he suckled at her throat. Her fingers bit into his shoulders.

His mouth trailed downward, his tongue skimming the blade of her collarbone. Fuck, she tasted sweet and salty at once, like a delicacy he'd always coveted but had never tried until right now.

She said his name again, this time with enough force that he paused. He'd made it to the valley between her breasts, and he pulled back with a muttered curse.

"Sorry," he said. "Sorry, shit. I got carried away. I didn't mean to—"

"No, don't apologize." In the darkness, she curled close. Her whisper ghosted against his lips. "I want more, trust me. I want *you*. So, so badly. I just . . ."

He waited, but she didn't finish. "What?"

"I don't know. I'm scared."

"Of what? It . . . hurting?"

She laughed, a thick sound that coiled him tight inside. "No. Of disappointing you, I think. Of . . . not being any good. Not satisfying you."

He exhaled through his nose, short and sharp. "That would be impossible. And I'm the one who's supposed to be doing the satisfying, anyway. You're just supposed to lie there and enjoy it. Hopefully."

This time, he felt her laughter more than heard it. "I'm pretty sure there's more to it than that."

"If there is," he said, "I don't care. If you ever decide you want to do that with me, it'll be all about you. What you want. You'll have to show me what you like, but whatever it is, I'll do it."

Her breath caught. "God, see? This is what I love about you."

He stilled. That incomparable word soaked in to the silence, saturating the inches between them.

Nick told himself to relax, that it was just a phrase. Aubrey hadn't said she loved *him*. Just something about him.

"Sorry." She wriggled away.

He let her go, at a loss to do anything else.

"I even promised myself I wouldn't do that," she said. In the faint starlit glow from the window, he could just make her out, lying on her back, a hand pressed to her chest as she stared at the ceiling.

"Do what?"

The shadows hid her expression. "Say it before you did."

His pulse stalled. "Say *what*?"

"Oh, come on, Nick. That I love you. Everyone knows the girl isn't supposed to say it first."

He dragged in a breath laced with fire. A few dozen rockets launched off inside his skull and detonated somewhere in the vicinity of his breastbone. "Do you? Love me?"

She turned his way, her face pale in the darkness, a beckoning light. "Of course I do. But it's fine. You don't have to say it ba—"

"I love you." The declaration barged out, so ferocious he felt like he'd thrown it at her. "I love you so fucking much."

A stream of air staggered into her lungs and stayed there.

"I love you so much," he continued, words gushing free now, "that I just want to be near you, all the time. Because even when we're not talking, you hear me more clearly than anyone else has. You might actually be the only person who's ever listened. And not only that, you shine. Your passion, your drive . . . you're the brightest star in the whole damn sky. The one I steer by, now."

She was quiet. He bit his lip, hesitant, but when he reached for her, he found her cheeks wet.

He scooted close and tucked her against the length of his body. "Was that the wrong thing to say?"

"No." She sniffled. "That's the thing. You never say anything wrong. You only ever say everything right."

"Do I? I worry it's too much, sometimes. That *I'm* too much."

"You're not. I don't ever want you to stop being so . . ."

"Dramatic?" he guessed.

"*Real.* Don't ever stop being so real. So intense."

He slid a hand down her body, skimming past the plane of her stomach to settle on her hip. "I couldn't if I tried. You do something to me."

She tugged him down, and he kissed her with all the tenderness her confession had unlocked. No one had ever said they'd loved him, at least not that he could remember. Probably his mom had, at some point. But that was lost to the haze of time. Now, hearing it from Aubrey's lips—the same lips he nibbled and worshiped and kissed away tears from—redefined all his inner boundaries, as if she'd torn down some wall within him and allowed him to glimpse a faraway horizon he hadn't realized existed.

"I fucking love you," he said into her mouth.

"I fucking love *you*."

He stayed there, breathing her breath, letting his heartbeat align with hers.

"There's something I've been wanting to ask," she said. "Seems like this might be the time."

"Okay."

A long moment passed. She swallowed. "Would you . . . come with me, maybe? In August? When I go to New York?"

His fingers dug into her hip. "Come with you? Like . . . move there?"

"Yeah."

His thoughts tumbled over one another. "I . . . don't know that I could. I have nothing. No money to get to New York. No way to live there, even if I did."

"But you could get a job, couldn't you? After graduation? You could go talk to the union. I bet they'd get you a place at the mill."

He pondered that. They would graduate in just two weeks, and in his descent into this delirious rapture, he hadn't planned for whatever came next. He hadn't wanted to. Yet he hadn't dared dream that the end of high school might mark the beginning of something else.

"You'd have the entire summer to save up," she said. "I could get a job, too. We could pool our money, get an apartment together in the fall."

"You mean live together? Would you really want that?"

"Are you kidding? More than anything."

He choked back a wild rush of emotion. "But . . . what would your parents say about you skipping the dorms? Wouldn't they mind you living with your boyfriend?"

She tensed. He still hadn't met her parents, despite sleeping in their house nightly and raiding their kitchen every day after school. He'd signed away his soul to their daughter, yet never seen their faces.

But he knew what they would think when they saw his, so he'd deflected Aubrey's many requests for a proper dinner. Maybe once he'd filled out more, since having access to her kitchen had already added six pounds to his frame. Or maybe once he'd gotten that job at the mill and earned enough to be taken seriously. To be treated like an adult.

"Let me worry about that," she said. "Though meeting them would help."

"I will," he murmured. "Soon. And I'll go down to the local tomorrow."

She twined her arms around his neck and kissed him again, sweetly, in that dreamy way that meant sleep was calling to her. "Thank you. The truth is, I never want to be away from you. And I know it can work. We'll *make* it work."

He grazed his fingertips up and down her back as she descended into slumber. He really would talk to the union tomorrow. Hell, he'd take a job cleaning toilets, if they offered one.

But try as he might, Aubrey's casual optimism felt faintly dangerous when placed in his hands. She made it sound as if a future together was something they only had to reach for, something they had every right to expect.

Meanwhile, he'd considered this whole thing more of a fever dream. One divine happenstance after another, a series of statistical anomalies that kept piling up and would have to come toppling down at some point.

But fuck it. If she wanted him to try, he would.

Really, he'd give her anything she asked for.

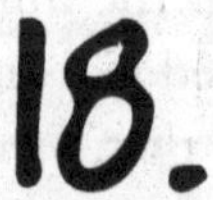

18.

GALLANT STARED AT his computer monitors and sighed. Why had he ever thought this was a good idea?

He knocked back half his bourbon and reread Nick Thacker's latest letter, hoping the alcohol might unveil some brilliant strategy within. But no. The words were pure sap.

Then again, the first two letters had undoubtedly gotten him somewhere, and Aubrey *did* operate in a way Gallant wasn't used to. Wasn't that why she equaled the other half of his ideal power couple, anyway? She was *different.* She had class. Style. Not to mention a tight body he wanted to explore by the handful.

He just wasn't about to write freaking poetry about it. But apparently, that was what she liked, so Gallant sighed again and dutifully whisked a sheet of paper from his drawer.

A good salesman adopted his strategy to suit.

He set to copying Nick's words, making sure to substitute "Dear Aubrey" for "Dear Jane." A few days ago, Nick had emailed asking about "John's" most recent date, so Gallant had written back about drinking wine with "Jane" on the couch. Now that impromptu evening had made it onto the page—only injected with a whole hell of a lot more meaning than Gallant had thought to give it.

That confused him, too. Nick Thacker had always seemed like such a brick wall of a person—stone-faced, cold, not much going on behind the eyes. Turned out, the guy had more feelings than a teenage girl crying into a pint of ice cream. And clearly, at some point in his life, he'd fallen in love up to his eyeballs, because there was no way he'd pulled all this from thin air.

Gallant almost felt sorry for the guy, then paused on a particularly saccharine sentence. Or not.

Whatever. He'd close this deal with Aubrey, then back off with the letters, train her not to expect this mushy fluff all the time.

Soon, she'd realize he had so much more going for him than sugary words. Once they spent more time together, she'd fall for his long list of positive attributes, and the letters would cease to matter.

With any luck, it would all start tonight.

Aubrey had insisted on walking to Gallant's. He'd sounded dubious on the phone, fretting over her safety in a way that charmed her, but she'd insisted, saying it was only half a mile and that the fresh air would do her good.

In actuality, she'd needed a buffer between her house and his. At home, when she cozied by the fire and meandered through rooms that gleamed with the patina of memories, she couldn't help thinking of Nick. What he'd said in his truck kept doubling back on her, often without warning.

If I could've sawed myself in two and given each of you half, I would have.

Aubrey's stomach wobbled as she pulled her collar up against the cold. Clearly, a single sentence from that man could still bring her to her knees, no matter what she'd told herself.

She just wished she hadn't responded by telling him about Gallant, but in that moment, it had simply bristled out of her, a bizarre form of self-defense. Nick's earnestness had invoked a bone-deep, *what-if* yearning, and she'd stabbed at it with the first weapon available. Mostly because the alternative would have involved flinging herself into his arms.

Aubrey shuddered. God, she'd come perilously close to doing exactly that. For a moment, when he'd spoken to her that way—so sincere, so familiar—her resolve had turned to vapor. But she *had* to keep her distance. Nick would never leave his daughter, and rightfully so. Meanwhile, she had a job to regain. Kidney donations to arrange, lives to save. Once Osos reinstated her, she wouldn't see this town again. Even if she'd wanted to stay in Henderson, the company had a strict on-site-only policy, no remote work allowed. Not to mention she was dating someone else.

No, she and Nick had already followed their road to its terminus. Nothing lay at the end but the smoking ruins of heartbreak.

Thankfully, the fresh, cold air cleared Aubrey's head. By the time she reached Gallant's doorstep, her heart thumped out an eager rhythm—partly because of the aroma wafting on the chilly air, and partly because she suspected a third letter waited inside.

She needed to read it. If for no other reason, because each new page recalibrated another fragment of her, reaffixing her inner workings to a new compass point.

When she knocked, Gallant swung open the door, two glasses of white wine already in hand.

Aubrey anchored herself to the moment. To him. "Hi."

"Hey, beautiful." He welcomed her into the polished-concrete entryway and kissed her cheek before handing off a glass. "You look stunning."

She flushed and hung up her coat. She'd taken extra care in selecting clingy black pants and a peplum blouse with a plunging neckline. Funny how, back when Gallant had complimented her on nothing but her looks, she'd found the comments so disingenuous.

Now she relished the spark in his cobalt eyes. Now she knew how much *more* lay behind it.

"Flattery will get you everywhere," she said.

"Good to know." He winked. "Now come see what I've been working on all evening."

He led her to the dining room, where he'd set the table with spotless linen and softly glowing taper candles. The rich scent of roasting poultry warmed the air. And there, propped against her porcelain plate, was a white envelope.

Aubrey's heart catapulted into her throat. She set her wine aside as Gallant pulled out her chair for her. "Can I read this?" she asked, all in one breath.

He hesitated. "Now?"

"Yes."

"Um. Sure. Just . . . while I get the food, maybe? It might be kinda strange if I was standing right here."

She gave a smile that hopefully broadcast her encouragement. Gallant hadn't shared his softer side in person, yet. "Of course. Whatever you need."

"Great. I'll be right back." He squeezed her shoulder and headed for the kitchen.

The moment dishes clanked in the other room, she tore into the envelope, her pulse roaring like a redlined engine.

Dear Aubrey,

Once every few years, life conspires to create a moment. You know, the unforgettable kind, one that sinks into you and makes a home for itself. The kind you slip into your pocket, to be taken out and examined later, like a bright, found penny, or a uniquely flawless stone.

Life gifted me with one of those moments just the other day.

You looked so breathtaking, sitting across from me, your hair falling so perfectly, as if it knew how best to frame your face. For a heartbeat, I lost myself in the shape of your mouth, in the way your bottom lip chased each inhale. And yet you tempted me with so much more than beauty, just then. You looked like tranquility to me. Like peace.

The truth is, I sometimes feel like a storm found its way into me years ago and never found its way out again. I hide it well, I think, but it's noisy in here. Lightning flashes. Thunder booms. Half the time, I'm stumbling, and the other half, I can't tell up from down. Then, just when I glimpse a path through the darkness, the wind snatches me back and crushes the breath from my chest.

But the other night, all of that faded. There was you. Your face, your hair, the slope of your mouth, your laugh, the way your eyes crinkled when I said something that amused you. Then came that singular instant in which your gaze locked onto mine and neither of us needed anything else, only to be there with each other, content, connected, cocooned from the world. Immersed, however briefly, in what sharing space together added up to.

And, for an incomparable moment, I could breathe again.

Gallant

Aubrey set down the paper, her lungs spasming. Her composure had melted somewhere in the second paragraph.

She could scarcely believe he felt this way about her so soon, but it was everything she needed and feared she'd never find again. She wanted passion. Ardor. Someone who could love her with abandon, the way she loved mathematics. Someone she could love back the same way.

And a letter like this . . . it couldn't be faked.

She tucked the envelope under her plate. Her hands felt empty without it. She had just touched shaking fingers to her wineglass when Gallant appeared carrying a roasted chicken.

Aubrey's breath caught. She hadn't looked at him yet, not truly. Now she did.

He wore an earth-colored cashmere sweater and jeans, no shoes. His chestnut hair was uncharacteristically mussed, but it suited the occasion, proof that his guard was coming down. That, coupled with the Technicolor eyes and the letter that had just shaken her world on its foundation, made her throat go dry.

"How did I never know you could write like this?" she said.

Gallant blinked, then set down the food and reached to reposition his perfectly positioned silverware. "I don't know. Probably because I don't let a lot of people in."

She swallowed. It was just like he'd said in the letter. "So all that posturing in high school . . . The fights you got in? The girls you chased? All those times you said, 'Hey, MacLean, looking good'? That was . . . what, a cover-up?"

His lips ticked downward. "A cover-up?"

"Yeah. All that . . . bravado."

He squared his shoulders, considering. "I was trying to get your attention, I think. *Everyone's* attention. Because I didn't know any better. I was just a kid. But . . . I don't have to do that now. At least, I don't want to. Especially not with you."

Heat cascaded through her. God, he looked beautiful, lit by candleglow. How had she missed it before?

He crooked a half-smile. "Any other questions?"

"No." Her voice quavered. "Except . . . Will you sit down with me?"

His smile spread. "Let me get the Brussels sprouts. Then I'm all yours."

They ate dinner leisurely, Gallant refilling her wineglass at every opportunity, Aubrey making rapturous sounds with each bite. Given the intensity of the letter, she was happy to keep the conversation light, and didn't have to feign her enthusiasm for the meal. The chicken melted in her mouth, a chorus of flavors singing on her tongue. Apparently, this man could also *cook*—another thing she hadn't known.

"How'd you learn all this, anyway?" She savored a juicy bite. "I can barely make a peanut-butter-and-jelly sandwich."

He propped his chin on his fist. "My last girlfriend was a chef. Living with her taught me a thing or two."

Aubrey set her wine down. "Oh. Sorry." She hadn't meant to bring up past heartbreaks. If they were, in fact, heartbreaks. Which she suddenly itched to know.

"Don't be," he said. "Lena moved out a while ago. Nine months, now."

"Oh. Was it . . . serious?"

"Probably not as much as she wanted it to be. She was always trying to get me to be more . . ." He took a deep breath. "Emotional."

"You weren't?"

He spun his wineglass in place. "I guess not in the way she wanted. It didn't come to me naturally, with her."

She weighed that. The alcohol had made her head sloshy and turned her vision fuzzy around the edges. Or maybe she was seeing more clearly than ever. "But with the right person . . . you *are* emotional?"

"I don't know." He smiled, the curve of his mouth freighted with significance. "What do you think?"

There was you. Your face, your hair, the slope of your mouth, your laugh, the way your eyes crinkled when I said something that amused you.

Aubrey's heart crowded her throat. "I think . . . yes. Definitely yes."

He chuckled. The silence that followed stretched into something she could fall into.

"You know what?" she said. "This has been delicious, but I think I'm done eating."

His smile wavered. "Oh. You're going? So soon?"

"I didn't say anything about going. Just that I'm done eating."

Gallant held her eyes. She held his. When the silence swelled to a breaking point, he slid from his seat and came around the table, his hand held out.

Aubrey took it. The napkin slipped from her lap with a sigh. She didn't stop to see where it fell.

For a wild instant, she wondered if he would try for the bedroom. But he led her to the living room, instead, where he ignited the gas fireplace and sat on his black leather couch, legs spread wide. He tugged her close, stationing her between his knees.

She stared down into eyes the color of Caribbean waters. "I'm sorry," she murmured.

Gallant cocked his head. "For?"

She let out a laugh, thick enough to sound drunk. Which she probably was, now that she thought about it. "For getting you so, so wrong. For dismissing you in high school. I'm sure I was part of the storm, but I didn't mean to be."

A beat passed. "The storm."

"You know. From your letter. You said you have all this intensity inside you, bombarding you all the time. I never knew."

He processed that, the interplay of emotion in his eyes so complex she couldn't follow it. Finally, he gripped her hands and tugged her down.

Aubrey settled astride his lap. He slid his hands up her thighs to her hips, his expression that of a man who knew he was about to be thoroughly kissed.

"It's okay," he said. "Now you know."

She hovered there, on some perilous brink, snared in eyes she'd met so many, many times before. But this was no longer Gallant Nobel, captain of the football team. No, this was a man who'd scribed beautiful words for her. A man she'd somehow overlooked, even though he'd been right in front of her.

She tipped forward, abuzz with heat and wine and feeling. Gallant angled his face up, his mouth finding hers, and Aubrey closed her eyes. He tasted like thyme and chardonnay. She clutched at his shirt, pressing herself closer, allowing him to part her lips with his tongue. One moment melted in the next.

He kissed her, slowly and thoroughly, his hands roaming from her hips to her back. After a few minutes, he gathered her and swiveled, pressing her into the couch and settling on top. His kisses deepened, his tongue plundering her mouth as his hands kneaded at her.

Aubrey's world spun. She met his mounting urgency, careening too quickly for anything else.

And, for an incomparable moment, I could breathe again.

God, maybe *he* could breathe, but she couldn't. She could only cling to him as her wine-soaked world whirled out of control.

Gallant released her mouth. He tongued a trail down her neck, making her shiver, then spoke heated words against her skin. "Do you want to go the bedroom? I have condoms."

She stilled, the spreading flame inside her slowing. "You . . . what?"

"I want you." He nuzzled his way up again, his breath scorching her ear. "You're so gorgeous I can hardly stand it."

She blinked and edged back, fighting the wine's influence long enough to bring his face into focus. One of his hands had found its way up her shirt, and she tugged it away.

Condoms. Condoms? She couldn't think. They'd had their first kiss all of . . . what, five minutes ago, and he was already jumping to sex?

"What?" he said. "What's wrong?"

"I just . . ." Aubrey tried to keep her words from bleeding into one another. She really should've had one less glass of wine. Or three. "I wasn't trying to sleep with you. Not tonight, at least. We're just at the beginning."

Gallant stared. For a long time, he didn't move, just exhaled slowly through his nose.

"What?" she said. "You're not mad, are you?"

"No." He pulled back. "No, of course not. Sorry. I just got excited. I liked that we were getting somewhere."

That sobered her. She levered into a sit and straightened her clothes. "What do you mean, 'getting somewhere'? I'm not some touchdown you're trying to score."

He took her measure. "No, you're absolutely right. You're not. That was the wrong thing to say. That wasn't what I meant at all."

Her shoulders eased a fraction. That sounded genuine enough.

"I'm sorry." He scrubbed at his hair. "I just . . . got carried away. Because it's so crazy to have you here. To kiss you. Finally."

Okay, maybe not the most eloquent apology in the world, but he'd probably spent hours honing those letters to perfection before writing them down.

"It's okay," she said. "And I'm sorry if I gave you the wrong idea. It's just that I'm a five-date kind of girl. At least."

Gallant's brow creased. He had the grace not to ask what number they were on, though she could practically see him tallying up the mental math.

Might as well cut him a break, since he'd apologized. "This is date three. I think we're allowed to count the first one, even if it wasn't planned. You *did* rescue me off the sidewalk, after all."

A smile flickered across his lips. "I do remember something like that, yes." He leaned in and tucked her hair behind her ear. The gesture was pure tenderness, and she smiled back.

"Why don't I take you home?" he said.

Buttery warmth softened her insides. "Yeah. I'd appreciate that."

"Just let me get my coat, okay?"

He disappeared into what Aubrey assumed was the bedroom. In his absence, she contemplated the glass-enclosed flames and, when that failed to hold her attention, began to wander. Gallant hadn't given her a tour of his home, but she doubted he'd mind if she poked around.

She soon found herself in a hallway with a floor-length mirror at the end. She tracked her reflection's approach, taking in the cherry flush in her cheeks, the sway of her steps. She was clearly on the wrong side of sober, and would feel like hell tomorrow.

Oh, well. No help for it now.

At the end of the hall lay the tidiest office she'd ever seen. On a desk by the far wall, double computer screens glowed. She squinted at the display. It looked like . . . a letter?

Sparks fired in her chest. Was this where Gallant drafted his ideas before committing them to longhand? Could this be the beginnings of letter number four?

She glanced over her shoulder, and, finding the hallway empty, started toward the computer. Just one tiny peek. If it had nothing to do with her, she'd leave it—

"Hey."

She turned. Gallant filled the doorway, bundled into his peacoat and a camel-hued scarf. "What're you doing in here?" Something quavered in his voice.

"Nothing. Just exploring." She retraced her steps and met him at the doorway.

His attention flickered over her shoulder, then back to her. A muscle flexed in his jaw.

"Sorry," she said, laying a hand on the doorframe for balance. She really was drunk. "I probably should've asked, first."

He searched her face, then blew out a breath. "It's okay. I'll show you around next time, all right?"

She cast a glance back at the monitors, but had no hope of deciphering the words from here. "Okay." She let him lead her away.

In the car, Gallant's smile resurfaced. "I hope I didn't make you feel pressured," he said. "Because I can wait. Five dates, six, however many you want. How about seven? Eight?"

She couldn't help but smile, relieved that he'd taken her refusal in stride. Some guys wouldn't have. Most, actually.

In her driveway, Gallant kissed the back of her hand. "Next time, we'll get dressed up and drive to Chicago, okay? There's this great little oyster bar I want to show you."

"Chicago?" She quirked an eyebrow. "That's a two-hour drive. Each way."

"What, you can't handle me for that long?"

A wry smile twisted her lips. She could. So far, their dates had always wrapped up before she'd had a chance to truly dig in, and she relished the idea of changing that.

But she didn't need to dress up and spend two dollars per bite in a fancy oyster restaurant to do it. The idea of spending six hours in his living room tempted her just as much.

"Come on," Gallant crooned, clearly mistaking her silence for hesitation. "If you say yes, I'll write you another letter."

"Really?" Softness bloomed within her like a flower. "In that case, when can we go? Tomorrow? No, scratch that. How about tonight?"

He laughed. "I've got some contracts to draw up tomorrow. And some listings to get done in the next few days. But let's plan for next Wednesday?"

She bit her lip. An entire week. But if he could be patient, so could she. "Next Wednesday. Sounds great." She leaned in for a kiss, then climbed out.

As the Tesla's taillights painted ruby lines across the darkness, she thought of what she'd said. Five dates, but really, she'd meant five *letters.* The first three had drawn her further and further into his orbit.

A couple more like tonight's, and she wouldn't be able to help but fall for him.

19.

Seventeen years ago

AUBREY'S FINAL SUMMER in Henderson was, by an order of magnitude, also her happiest. The June days melted together, a sticky whirl of fireflies, laughter, and stolen kisses sweetened with watermelon juice.

True to his word, Nick got a job at the mill, slinging the scrap iron that fed the blast furnaces day and night. Aubrey racked up hours at the bowling alley, blocking off gutters for kids' birthday parties and handing out rental shoes.

Neither had any love for their work, but their savings accounts grew by the week, and they had each other, and that was all she cared about.

One humid night in July, she and Nick drove out to the old quarry in her battered Subaru. He spread a blanket on the pebbled ground and pulled her down. She loved the way he molded himself against her now, unhesitating, guided by half a year of learning how they fit together best.

She settled her head on his chest—her favorite pillow. Overhead, the sky hung warm and close, the stars a heated prickle.

Tufts of tall grass nodded in the breeze while another couple murmured nearby.

It was always like that out here—private, but not. The scattered knolls shielded half a dozen trysts, mostly high schoolers who'd escaped their parents' watchful eyes. Protocol demanded that everyone keep to themselves, so Aubrey watched the stars, how their light pulsed in time with Nick's heartbeat.

His arm tightened around her. "Aubs?"

"Yeah?"

"I've been thinking."

The brittleness of his tone made her hoist up onto an elbow. She sought his eyes in the dimness. "About?"

"New York. I won't have enough. Not by August, at least. I've been looking at apartment listings, and even if we lease a studio, it'll cost us at least eighteen hundred a month. First and last month's rent, *plus* a deposit, will be five grand, at least."

Her breath caught. "Okay. What're you saying?"

His fingers caressed her arm, long strokes probably meant to reassure her. "That this whole thing might work better if you do a semester in the dorms, first. Your student loans'll actually cover that. I could come out once I've saved some more. After your winter break, maybe. In January."

She tensed. Not because he was wrong, but because he was right. She'd done the math herself and reached the same conclusion, but hadn't wanted to believe it. Or maybe she'd stacked all her faith in the power of her own wanting. If she willed for something hard enough, she could make it happen. *When life puts something in your way, go around it. When life knocks you down, get right back up.*

"No," she said. "I'm not living in the dorms."

"But we don't have *enough*, Aubs. I mean, maybe we could scrape together enough to move in, but afterward? You'll be in school, and it'll take time for me to find another job, and—"

"So I'll wait," she blurted. Her hand fisted his thin cotton shirtfront. "I'll defer my enrollment for a year."

"No," he said, with force.

"Yes."

"No. Fuck no. You want to get out of here as badly as I do. I'm not gonna let you screw that up on my account. Just go to New York. Live your dream. I'll come as soon as I can." He paused. "Unless . . . you decide you don't want me, by then."

"What?" Her mind tripped over the thought. "How can you even say that? That would never happen."

Nick stared up. The fierce black stars of his eyes outshone the sky above.

Aubrey gulped down the stone forming in her throat. She couldn't lose this. She *wouldn't.* The way he held her, the way he looked at her—every moment only deepened her conviction that whatever her path in life, she wanted him walking it with her.

Then a thought wormed its way in. One that soured her stomach and shrank it to a marble. "Wait. This isn't your way of breaking up with me, is it?"

"Breaking up with you?" His grip on her arm tightened. "*Me?* Breaking up with *you*?"

"Yeah." Her voice wobbled. "Like, you send me off to New York and promise to come, but then January turns into August, and August turns into January again, and eventually I give up waiting and realize you've moved on?"

He let out a hiss—harsh, almost angry. He levered upward and spun her beneath him. Her knees fell wide, her skirt pooling around her hips.

Nick settled himself between her thighs without seeming to notice the compromising position. He speared her with a look so intent she swore he could read her innermost secrets. "If you had any idea what you mean to me, you'd never say that."

Her hands clamped around his sides. “I wouldn’t?”

“No.” He sucked in a breath, his rib cage swelling beneath her fingers. “Aubrey MacLean. You’re the best thing that’s ever happened to me. The only person who’s ever really seen me. That’s not something I can *move on* from, and I couldn’t stop loving you if I tried. I’ll be yours for as long as you’ll have me. I’ll write you love letters until I’m too old to see the words anymore, if that’s what you want. Even if you don’t, I’ll still love you until I’m dust in the ground, and probably after that, too, because I’ve never met anyone as fearless or determined or true to themselves as you are, and it makes me a better person just to be near you. Just to breathe your air.”

Her pulse roared, escaping her control. She would never have his way with words, but that didn’t mean she didn’t mirror every inch of his intensity. “I love you, too. So, so much.”

He shook his head as if brushing off the sentiment. “Do you understand what I’m telling you? Why I don’t want you to stay here for my sake?”

“Yes.” She brought her hands up to frame his face. “But you’re forgetting something important.”

His jaw flexed beneath her fingers. “What?”

“That it’s just as much my decision as yours. I know how giving you are, how self-sacrificing. It’s what I love about you. But you don’t get to decide what I do next. *I* do. And I’m not leaving Henderson without you. Which doesn’t mean I won’t go to NYU, or get my degree. I will. But I want it all at once. New York *and* you. Math *and* my other half.”

His eyes glinted, reflecting the starlight. “What if that’s not what life has planned for us?”

“It is. I know it is. And if not, we’ll *make* it the plan.”

He lowered his head, tucking his face against her neck, and hugged her with his whole body. “Jesus. Sometimes I don’t know if you're overconfident, or just the most formidable person I know."

"Overconfidence only counts as overconfidence if you surrender before you succeed."

He laughed soundlessly against her skin. "So that's it? You're staying another year, and I can fuck right off if I try to convince you otherwise?"

"I wouldn't've put it that way." She smiled into his mop of curls. "But yeah, that sounds about right."

He hugged her tighter. The sky gleamed, bathing them in pearly light.

All of a sudden, Nick seemed to realize how tangled they'd gotten. He sucked in a breath and tugged at her skirt, trying to cover her exposed thighs.

She pushed his hand away. "Leave it."

He stilled. His breath hitched, his weight pinioning her to the earth. So little separated their bodies. Just her silk panties, then his jeans and boxers. Beneath his clothes lay nothing but smooth, hot skin. At least, Aubrey imagined it as smooth, hot skin. She hadn't touched him there yet, had never dared.

Now, though, the fervency of his words boiled inside her, cementing a decision she had, until this moment, kept to herself. "There's one more thing, though. Something I want way before New York."

He shifted. "What?"

"I want to . . . be with you. I want you to be my first."

He made a strangled sound. "What, right now?"

"No. But soon."

A fine tremble took hold in his limbs. A quarter century slipped by while she awaited his answer. Finally, he said, "You're sure?"

"Completely."

He buried his face in the side of her neck again. "If you're counting on me being chivalrous enough to turn you down, you're going to be disappointed."

She laughed. "Chivalry is overrated."

"No, it's not." His breath tickled her skin, igniting heat in places she'd dreamed of asking him to touch.

"It is if it'd make you say no," she said. "Because I want you. And I want our first time to be special."

"You mean not when other people are fucking thirty feet away?"

She paused. Sure enough, the neighbors' conversation had given way to rhythmic rustling and bitten-back moans. "Yeah. Somewhere where it's just us. Not with my parents upstairs, either. Which means we might have to wait for the right opportunity. If you're okay with that."

"I'd wait a century, if you needed me to." Naked reverence filled his voice as he brought his face to hers. "And doing this with you . . . it'd be my honor."

"And mine."

They stayed like that for long minutes, foreheads touching, bodies locked together. The stars wheeled overhead as the weight of their pact infiltrated her marrow. Mars hung over the towering wall of the quarry, peering down like a knowing red eye.

When the immensity of the moment finally ebbed, Aubrey untangled herself. Their neighbors kept getting louder, so they bundled into the car with the wadded-up blanket, this time with Nick driving. He swung the car around and flipped on the headlights.

Aubrey lunged for the knob. "No, everyone keeps their lights off here. That's the rule."

Too late. The beam swept over their neighbors, illuminating bronze hair and taut male buttocks. The boy threw a hand up while his companion recoiled, a flash of alabaster and blond.

Aubrey twisted the knob, dousing the quarry with darkness again.

"Oops," Nick said, clearly not sorry at all. But he waited until the tires bit into the graveled service road before flipping on the lights again.

A quarter mile later, Aubrey let go of a snicker. "Was that Gallant Nobel?"

"Looked like it."

"Who was he with? I could've sworn he was dating Gina Abramo when school got out. But her hair's black."

Nick shrugged. "Who cares?"

Aubrey turned to the window, exhaling a silver canvas onto the glass and inking a heart with her forefinger. "I'm just curious."

"You know what I'm curious about?"

She added an "A+N" inside the heart. "What?"

"What your parents are going to think of you deferring for a year. Especially when they find out it's because of me."

The warmth gallivanting around inside her faltered. Her father wouldn't like it. He'd hate it, in fact. He'd pushed her harder than anyone, and he knew what New York meant to her. But hopefully, once she explained . . . "They'll come around. But it's definitely time for you to meet them."

Nick looked over. "Soon," he said solemnly. "Soon."

20.

Nick woke with a pounding headache and a cheery-as-fuck sunbeam assaulting his eyes.

He groaned and sat up, sending a pillow tumbling to the floor. What time was it? Hell, what *day* was it?

He clutched his head and forced himself to think. Right. Saturday. Float-building day. Which meant he would see Aubrey in a few hours. And he couldn't be any less prepared. Or any more hungover.

Last night, with Paige sleeping over at Maria's again, he'd gone out barhopping with Jackson. Which hardly made sense, considering his best friend didn't drink and Nick didn't care for it, either. But Jackson had taken one look at him after sparring, said, "Man, this woman has you strung out," and declared Nick in need of a "recovery" night.

Some fucking recovery.

Now he shut his eyes against the brightness and tried to squeeze the ache from his head with brute force. But the fists pressed to his temples couldn't expunge the throb. Or the images emblazoned on his mind. For days, he'd thought of nothing but Aubrey and Gallant. Talking. Laughing. Kissing. Probably even having—

A wave of nausea threatened. Nick flung the blanket aside, then stumbled to the bathroom and downed four tablets of ibuprofen dry. Jesus, he hadn't been this hungover in years.

In desperation, he sucked water straight from the faucet. Tansy was already up, as evidenced by the scent of bacon weighting the air. His stomach simultaneously revolted and whimpered in anticipation.

In the kitchen, Tansy sat at the breakfast table already. "Morning, Sleeping Beauty."

He grunted and went to the stove. Cream-cheese-scrambled eggs and bacon awaited. Essentially a heart attack on a plate, but it would do miracles for his stomach.

He dropped into the chair opposite her. "Thanks for cooking."

She chewed, her expression mild. "Thanks for paying Paige's internship fee."

"Yeah. No problem."

"Did you have fun last night?"

He scowled. He knew what she thought—that he'd been out with Aubrey. That *he* was the one talking to and laughing with and kissing her. That he'd gotten to taste that hollow between her collarbones again, maybe pressed her against a wall while he lapped at it with his tongue, made her make that little sound where—

Ugh. He crammed some eggs into his mouth to stop his brain from churning out lurid fantasies. That was Gallant's territory, now.

"I'm guessing that's a yes," Tansy said.

"I was with Jackson." Nick moved on to the bacon. "Not . . . her."

She eyed him. "I told you, I don't care. Fuck whoever you want to fuck. I hope she blew your mind. Among other things."

His headache roared back full force. Had she really just said that?

Well, yeah. It was Tansy. "It's not like that. Really. I haven't seen her in days."

Her eyes slitted. "Come on, at least be straight with me. I deserve that much."

He tightened his jaw and plunked down his fork. "I *am* being straight. It's like I said, I wasn't with her. I haven't touched her since she's been back. At all."

"What, I'm supposed to believe you've just suddenly lost interest? After all that pining?"

"I don't *pine.*" His scowl deepened. He totally fucking pined. "And no, of course I haven't lost interest. *She's* the one who—" He cut himself off with a clack of his teeth. "You know what? We're not discussing this. This is too weird, even for you."

Tansy rolled her eyes and rose to bring her plate to the sink, but a quavering voice from the other room brought her up short.

"Daddy? Mom?"

The bottom of Nick's stomach dropped out. Shit. What was Paige doing home? Had she *heard* them? It sounded like it. A hesitant note soured her usual sunshine.

He jumped up and squeezed past Tansy, forgetting her existence before she'd even left his eyeline. "Peanut? I thought you were at Maria's. Didn't you say you weren't coming back until ten?"

In the living room, Paige stood by the couch, her eyes wide, her overnight bag on the floor beside her. "It *is* ten."

He winced. A glance at the clock on the mantel proved her right.

"What were you and Mom talking about?" Uncertainty dampened her tone. "Just now?"

He stuffed his hands into the pockets of his flannel pajama pants. He wouldn't disrespect her by lying, but he wasn't about to provide the details. "Um . . . personal stuff."

Paige's blue eyes were uncharacteristically clouded. "It sounded weird."

Well, it had felt weird, too. But he'd rather stab himself in the face than admit that Tansy had just accused him of having a sex marathon with their float-building partner, so he said, "Mom was just confused about something. And I was explaining."

"Oh." Surprisingly, Paige sounded at least mildly reassured. "Okay. Well . . . I thought maybe we could go grab breakfast before heading out to the farm."

His heart squeezed. "What, just you and me?"

"Yeah."

Despite everything, he melted around the edges. "I'd love that. Just let me go get dressed, all right?"

"Okay."

Nick retreated to his bedroom, where he swapped his pants and undershirt for the first items of clothing he laid hands on. Tansy followed him in, her eyes sparking.

"I had *one* condition," she hissed. "One. And that was that this Aubrey thing doesn't affect her. Which means you need to fix it. Now."

"I know," he hissed back. Never mind that she'd been the one so dedicated to prying. "I *know*."

Two minutes later, he was back in the living room, keys in hand. Paige hadn't moved.

He hustled her to the truck, oddly desperate to get her out of the house. Once they'd climbed in, he jammed the key into the ignition, but didn't start the engine.

"Look." He cleared his throat. "Your mother and I might disagree sometimes, but I don't want you to worry. It's never going to affect you. I won't let it, and I'm not going anywhere. Not ever. You understand that, right?"

A wan smile tugged at Paige's mouth. "I know. It's not even

that, really. It's just . . ." Her eyes slid to her lap. She picked at a fingernail.

"What?"

"Are you . . . happy?" She raised her eyes. "I wonder, sometimes."

He hesitated. Well, shit. Happiness. What did that feel like? Did he even know? His mind searched for experiences that matched the word and dredged up moments from years ago.

Happiness . . .

His first kiss. *That* had been happiness—pressing Aubrey against a frozen brick wall while he ignited inside. He remembered, too, what it had felt like later, hearing her breathing change as they lay in the darkness and sought sleep in each other's arms. Not to mention their night together in front of her fireplace. Jesus Christ, that night by the fireplace.

The moments didn't end there, though. There were more. Ones that had come after.

He thought of how his soul had grown to eclipse the entire known universe when he'd held his baby daughter for the first time. He'd kissed the bottoms of Paige's tiny feet and marveled at their softness, at skin that had never seen a shoe or taken a step. *That* had been happiness. So was the way she'd questioned everything as a child, how she'd made him stop to think about things he'd hardly even noticed before, like why water swirled around a drain and owls only hooted at night.

Then she'd grown into a young woman who made the score to *The Sound of Music* swell in the background whenever she was around.

"I'm plenty happy," he said carefully. "I know it might not seem like it, and I can be a grouchy old man sometimes. But that's just me. It doesn't mean there aren't things I live for. Like being your dad. Being your family. That's the happiest thing in my whole damn life. It always has been."

Paige's eyes softened. She reached for his hand, coaxing open the clenched fist he'd unwittingly pressed into the bench seat. "You know you're the best dad I could ask for, right?"

The band that had clamped around his chest days ago loosened a fraction. "Thanks, Peanut. And you're a hundred times more incredible than I ever expected. I couldn't be prouder to call you my daughter. You know *that*, I hope."

"Obviously." She smiled, lopsided. "I just . . . wish you had everything you wanted. That you were happy every minute of every day. Because of everyone I know, you're the one who deserves that most."

Mist sprang up behind his eyes. Shit, could she be any sweeter?

But he couldn't cry. Not when she was the one who needed reassuring. "Thanks. But it's not your job to worry about me. It's *my* job to worry about *you*. So you just leave my moody bullshit to me, okay? I'll be fine, as long as you are."

She smiled. Not with her usual brightness, but close. "Okay. If you say so."

He tugged his hand away, then started the truck and swiped at his eyes when she wasn't looking. Paige leaned back, her attention on the window. He drove in silence, knowing it wouldn't take long before she banished the lingering shadows with her shine.

Sure enough, she started talking inside of a minute, filling the cab with her chatter.

Nick drove toward that new café on Ivy and Harkness—Lindy's Place? Windy's Place?—while Paige updated him on school, math club, and college admissions. Apparently, she and Maria had decided to apply to the same schools and hoped to room together, wherever they ended up.

He made affirmative noises at every opportunity. Paige eventually moved on to an article she'd read, about astronomers who'd discovered a planet that resembled a giant marshmallow. "Can you imagine? A marshmallow! A *marshmallow*! Maybe I'll get to do that someday. Find a whole planet that could float in a bathtub. Maybe I'll name it after you."

He chuckled. "Me? Why? Because I'm just *so* damn fluffy?"

"No." She giggled. "Because you lighten up my world. Get it?"

"Oh, wow." He shook his head. "We're making density jokes, now?"

"We sure are."

He blew out a breath. "Okay. Whatever floats your boat, kiddo."

She tinkled a bell-like laugh. "I see what you did there. And guess what? It only makes me love you s'more. Get it? Because marshmallows. Ha!"

He groaned. But only because he knew that she knew he loved her cheeseball puns.

"Oh, I almost forgot," she said. "We have to stop at the feed store after breakfast, before we head out to the farm."

He skewed an eyebrow upward. "The feed store? How come?"

"To pick up corn for the turkey."

"The . . . turkey?"

She rolled her eyes in the most endearing way possible. "Come on, the *parade float* turkey. Once we get the frame finished, he's getting decorated with dried ears of corn. Ellis's Feed is donating it, but they said we have to pick it up today. We'll need to keep it in the barn until we're ready to use it."

Nick glanced through the windshield. The weather had turned, and the sky loomed flat and close, the color of iron. He had a feeling it would only worsen. "Okay. But if we put all that corn in the truck bed and it gets rained on, it'll get ruined."

Paige nodded. "I checked the forecast. It's supposed to stay dry until noon, which should give us plenty of time. And—oh! Aubrey will be there. She'll help us unload. And also, I'm kind of buff, in case you hadn't noticed." She popped an underwhelming biceps—not that he would ever say so.

"See?" she chirped. "Nothing to worry about."

Maybe not, but he inched the gas pedal toward the floor, all the same. "Okay. We should make breakfast quick, though."

At the café, Paige flowed from one subject after another. She talked about her internship, which started in January, then some genetics assignment she had in biology. Nick sipped his coffee, his smile growing fonder. The ibuprofen had kicked in, and between that, his greasy breakfast at home, the caffeine, and the unexpected morning with his daughter, he almost felt . . . content. At the very least, the hangover had faded.

His phone pinged just as Paige hit her stride. He pulled it out, intending to make the notification go away, but the screen pulled up a message from MontanaBirder81.

His teeth clenched. He resented the intrusion into his morning, but moreover, he resented the way this whole letter-writing business was turning out. When he'd cooked up this idea, he'd wanted to help nurture a relationship that would've blossomed anyway. And, sure—he could admit it—exorcise his demons in the process.

But John Whatever-His-Last-Name-Was in Billings increasingly wanted to be spoon-fed. The guy didn't have any ideas of his own, and had little to say about Jane apart from the fact that she dressed well and was apparently a total smoke show. Which made Nick wonder if his heart was even in the right place. Maybe? Maybe not? Either way, the whole situation had grown uncomfortable, as if Nick were conducting the relationship himself instead of merely refining John's feelings into words.

"Dad? Can you do it?"

He glanced up. Shit, he'd totally checked out. Talk about a dick move. He pocketed his phone, vowing not to touch it for the rest of the day. "Sorry, Peanut, what were you saying?"

"Your tongue. Can you roll it up? Like this?" Paige curled her tongue into a tube.

He laughed. "What kind of weird-ass question is that?"

"It's for my biology assignment. Mr. Gallegos gave us this whole list of Mendelian traits. Tongue-rolling is autosomal dominant, so since I can do it, that means you or Mom can, too. We're supposed to find out our parents' phenotypes, then compare to ours to figure out our genotypes."

"That sounds . . . scientific."

She giggled. "Yeah, that's the point. Try it."

He stuck out his tongue. Trying to replicate what she'd done felt like chewing on a pretzel.

"Oh, come on." She did another adorable eye roll. "You can do better than that."

He tried again, but his tongue wouldn't cooperate. "Nope. Sorry. You must've gotten that one from Mom." He polished off his coffee and scoped out the café window. The sky looked even more threatening than it had earlier. "Hey, kiddo, I hate to cut this short, but we should probably get going. I don't think the rain's going to hold off until twelve."

A faint divot formed between Paige's brows. She'd only finished half her eggs, but rose and gathered her jacket.

"You don't want to finish?" he said.

"No. This is more than one person can handle."

He helped her into her coat and scooted her out the door. Outside, the temperature had dropped, and Nick's fingers tingled as they sped toward Ellis's Feed. On arrival, Chip Ellis ushered them into the back room, where eighty-eight mesh bags of dried corn awaited. Thankfully, Chip's two sons were on shift, so between the four men and Paige, everything got loaded within minutes.

Unloading would take significantly longer, and Nick tried to shave as many minutes off the drive to Hinkley Farm as possible. The whole time, Paige stared out the window, contemplating the weather. Clearly, the possibility of losing the corn worried her.

"Hey. You okay?"

She mustered a watery smile. "Yeah. Sorry. My stomach just feels weird. That food isn't sitting right."

He studied her. "Are you going to puke?"

"Maybe. I honestly can't tell."

"Do you want me to take you home?"

"No," she said. "If we turn around now, the corn'll get ruined."

"So? Who cares?"

She gave him a level look. "Daddy."

"What?"

"Don't be ridiculous."

"Come on. I care a lot more about you than I do about corn."

That seemed to bring some color back into her cheeks. She smiled. "Just drive faster. I'll get a ride back from Megan, if that's okay. You and Aubrey can unload together."

He quelled a sigh. Him and Aubrey. Of course. "Sure, Peanut. You're the boss."

When they pulled up, Aubrey stood in the barn doorway already, eyeing the sky.

The sight of her hit Nick like a wrecking ball to the chest. She looked different today. No earrings, no makeup. She wore a cozy-looking red flannel over jeans, and had traded her impractical heeled boots for a pair of white sneakers she'd clearly just bought, since they didn't have a single scuff. The front half of her hair was pulled into a bun, the fringed ends radiating outward like a flaming halo.

Her survey of the sky complete, she lowered her eyes and met his through the windshield.

His gut bottomed out. Fuck. She'd never looked as compelling as in that moment. Never looked so *real*. Like a woman he wanted to burn down worlds for. Maybe he even wanted to burn down himself.

The slam of Paige's door brought him back to reality. He shook off his daze and emerged just in time for a fat, icy raindrop to splat against his forehead.

"Hey," Aubrey said as they approached. "It's great to see you, Paige. Did you talk to your teacher yet? About math club? I've been thinking about what to discuss, and—"

"Sorry, I'm not staying today, actually." Paige smiled apologetically. "But I'm excited about math club, and I promise I'll text you soon. Have you seen Megan?"

"Oh." Aubrey frowned. "Um, I think she's around back."

"Great." Paige wandered off. "I'll see you later, Dad."

Aubrey's green eyes turned questioning as Nick jogged to the doorway and scanned the barn's interior. The corn could go over in the corner, next to the rebar.

"Is she okay?"

Warmth flooded his throat. Aubrey had only met his daughter once, but had clearly paid enough attention to realize something was amiss. *And* she cared enough to ask.

"She's not feeling well," he said. "But Megan's going to have to take her home, because right now, we've got eighty-eight twenty-five-pound bags of corn to unload, and about ten minutes before it starts pouring."

Aubrey blanched. "Twenty-two hundred pounds of corn? In ten minutes? Is that all?"

He paused, startled. "Did you just . . . multiply eighty-eight by twenty-five in your head?"

"I'm a mathematician. So . . . yeah. That one's easy, anyway."

"Easy? How's that easy?"

The corner of her mouth kicked up. "Because. Multiplying by twenty-five is the same as dividing by four and adding two zeros. Anyone can do that."

Another raindrop slapped his temple, but he ignored it. He'd never have thought to do it that way. Yet he saw why Aubrey's method worked, and even he could appreciate its elegance.

"You're incredible," he blurted.

She flushed and looked away.

"Sorry." He scrubbed at the back of his neck. "I'm just . . . yeah. Gonna go get that corn."

"Okay." She sounded relieved. "I'll help."

They worked quickly, but the sky opened within minutes. Most of the volunteers ran for cover, and those who didn't scrambled to get their own projects to safety.

Frigid rain slapped at Nick's scalp, quickly turning to stinging sleet. He upped his pace while Aubrey climbed into the truck bed. She tossed bags down into his arms, piling them five or six at a time before he shuttled them into the barn. His lungs burned and his muscles quaked, but he relished the feeling. It was almost like a fight. A pain he could disappear into.

When they finished, slushy rain saturated their clothes. They took cover in the barn. Sleet lashed against the roof, so loud Nick could barely hear himself think.

"Should we open the bags that got wet?" Aubrey shouted over the din. "Spread the corn to dry, so it doesn't mold?"

He nodded. By the time they'd scrounged blankets from the loft and arranged the damp corn, the roar of the storm had lessened. Nick tucked away the pocketknife he'd used to slice the mesh and turned toward Aubrey.

And went silent inside.

Shit. She hadn't complained once, but her lips had turned a painful shade of blue. Her teeth chattered. Wet red tendrils stuck to her forehead.

"You're freezing." Quickly, he wrenched off his sodden jacket and draped it around her shoulders. "Why didn't you tell me? And where's your coat?"

She shivered in his grip. Jesus, those eyes. They burned a hole right through him.

"I forgot it in Gallant's car," she said. "I didn't realize until after he left, and I don't have any service out here, so I couldn't ask him to come back."

Nick's heart burst into a million microscopic pieces. He struggled to swallow them all down. Fucking Gallant fucking Nobel. That asshole must have seen her jacket on the seat and made a conscious decision not to turn around.

The realization made him want to punch something. Preferably Gallant himself. Preferably hard enough to break the guy's nose. "When's he coming back for you?"

"Four o'clock."

"That's hours from now." He clenched his jaw. "There's no way I'm leaving you here until then. Come on, I'll take you home."

Aubrey wavered. Her hesitation knifed into him—clearly, she had no desire to be taken care of, at least not by him.

"Come on," he said gruffly. "We're friends now, remember?"

"Yeah." But her tone told him she hadn't forgotten the way he'd confessed his deepest regrets the other day.

He tried again. "Look, you're soaked. You'll freeze out here with nothing but my wet-ass jacket and a four-hour wait. Which makes no sense when you have a perfectly good fireplace at home."

She lifted her chin as if to argue, then surprised him by nodding. "Well . . . okay."

The fist around his lungs loosened. "Okay."

They darted back out into the storm. He helped her into the truck's passenger side, not caring that his wet eyelashes froze in moments or that gooseflesh pebbled his arms beneath his sodden Henley shirt.

As long as he got her warm.

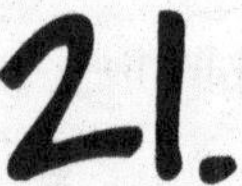

21.

Aubrey had never been so cold.

She huddled against the passenger-side door, quaking within the wet shell of Nick's jacket. He cranked the heater before they'd even cleared the barnyard, but the truck had more than a few miles on it, and air that should have gusted reached her as more of a wheeze.

Her teeth chattered. Nick glared past the thumping wipers and the sleet exploding against the windshield as he edged the speedometer toward eighty. "I've been meaning to fix this heater. Sorry. But hang on. I'll have you home in no time."

Aubrey nodded. He, too, was soaked—his shirt clung to his sculpted frame while rainwater slicked every inch of exposed skin. The bones bracketing his throat reflected the stormy light, giving his wet skin a pearly sheen.

He wasn't shivering, though. She couldn't fathom how. Then again, he radiated intensity the same way a flame threw heat. Maybe that kind of sustained inner force crossed over into the physical. As if she might reach out and warm her hands with the sheer energy he exuded.

"Nick."

His jaw hardened. He wouldn't look at her. "What."

God, she knew exactly where his mind had gone. She'd seen that look dozens of times. "This isn't your fault."

"The fuck it isn't." His staring contest with the road intensified. "I left you standing in the truck while I stacked bags in the barn. You were in the rain twice as long as I was, and then I wasted all that time spreading the corn without even checking to see if you were okay, first."

"That was my idea."

"And my oversight. I should've given you my jacket as soon as it started raining. Better yet, I should've just done the whole job myself and let you stay inside."

She sighed, even while some hidden part of her fluttered. His concern touched the very center of her, like a caress.

God, Megan had been right. Very little about Nick Thacker had changed. He still *cared*, so much that it bordered on selflessness. So much that it bordered on self-neglect, because he'd always put others before himself. Aubrey had no doubt he'd offer his last morsel to someone he cared about, even if it meant condemning himself to starvation. As it was, he'd already given her the clothes off his back.

That part of him had always awed her. It also made her grieve, because she knew where it came from. His father hadn't cared for him, so now Nick cared for others. His noble heart demanded nothing less. Yet no one had ever taught him to treat himself the same way.

Somehow, she'd forgotten that. And, as a result, had been so hard on him since coming back—spurning his overtures, minimizing all he'd done for her. Mostly to protect herself, but that wasn't a decent excuse.

He deserved better.

She swallowed against a raw throat. "You must be freezing, too. Do you want your jacket back? Or for me to . . . scoot over there?"

He shot her a wide-eyed glance. "As in, share body heat?"

She crossed her legs. Uncrossed them. "Well. Yeah. Friends can do that."

His Adam's apple scraped up and down. "It *would* warm you up."

"You, too."

He dragged his gaze back to the road, but the raw energy pouring off him intensified. Aubrey glanced at the visor mirror, halfway expecting to find her hair standing on end.

"Okay," he said. "Come here."

The truck was old. Not ancient, but not the shiny new kind with fancy electronics, either, and it had a broad bench seat, smooth all the way across. Aubrey unclicked her seat belt and slid to the middle. Once she fastened the lap belt, she hesitated. Nick's scent enveloped her, a clean blend of rainwater and lit matches. His pulse ticked beneath his jaw, swelling and retreating, swelling and retreating.

The interval shortened the longer she stared.

"Put your arms around me." His words came out precise. Stilted.

After a frozen moment, Aubrey complied. She hugged the firm breadth of his torso. He snaked one arm under the sodden jacket and clamped her against his side.

He really was freezing. Tiny ice crystals prickled in his shirt, and she angled her face so her exhalations would warm his chest. They drove in silence, Nick stiff in her arms.

She closed her eyes, lulled by the hypnotic thump of the wipers. Memories ebbed and flowed, echoes of a time when this had felt as natural and needed as breathing. Not fraught with doubts or broken promises, but simple. Right.

Gradually, her skin warmed where it pressed against his. His heat leached into her, soothing old scars, and she squeezed tighter, trying to communicate something that felt, in that moment, easier to convey with touch than with words.

Thank you for taking care of me. Thank you for letting me take care of you.

Maybe some fragment of her message reached him, because his posture softened. He didn't melt, exactly. More like he capitulated, inch by inch.

All too soon, they reached her house. Nick shifted into Park, took her by the shoulders, and tilted her away, just far enough to look down into her face. She gazed up, caught in the tidal pools of his eyes. In the hazy silver light, they looked like windows to another universe, opening onto someplace private and lushly shadowed and, best of all, warm.

He didn't ask whether she wanted him to come inside. He just did, pulling her from the truck, blocking the sleet's assault while she unlocked the front door, guiding her to the living room, where he knelt to spark a fire.

He breathed the flames to life. "You should put on dry clothes."

Aubrey pulled his soggy jacket closer, then reconsidered and draped it over the nearest chair. The cold no longer had her in its grip. Far from it. "What about you?"

"I'm fine."

She shook her head and went to her room. He could refuse to look after himself, but now that he'd tended to her, he couldn't stop her from returning the favor. She tossed her wet clothes into the bathtub and pulled on a cozy waffle-knit pajama set, then snuck upstairs to her parents' old room.

There, the stillness had a weight to it, which she resolutely ignored. Her mother had gotten rid of most of her father's things when he'd died, but nevertheless, she managed to unearth a pair of worn sweatpants and a soft, sky-blue button-down.

She returned to find a drenched Nick seated before a roaring blaze. Warm light swelled from the hearth, repelling the muted gray glow from the windows.

"Here." She held out the clothes.

His head swiveled. He eyed the offering like she'd tried to hand off a venomous snake. "Whose are those?"

"My dad's."

He turned back to the fire. "No, thanks."

She stood there, awkward. "What, you hate him that much?"

"I don't *hate* him." He hugged his knees. "I never hated him."

"So you're refusing these because . . . ?"

"I'm pissed."

Her breath hitched. "It's been seventeen years. And he's dead."

"Yeah, well. No one's ever accused me of not holding a grudge. Which I'm sorry about. I'm sure you don't want to hear it. But what he did wasn't right."

She shifted her weight. "It wouldn't have changed anything, you know."

His shoulders hunched, the great muscles in his back knitting. "It would've changed everything, Aubs."

She sucked down a pained inhale. He was right. She'd only claimed otherwise because she *wanted* it to be true. "Okay. Maybe. But . . . you have Paige to show for it. And we've agreed that was for the best."

A long silence spun by. "Yeah."

"So what does it matter?"

When he didn't answer, she set the unused clothes aside and joined him on the floor. The fire lavished her with enough heat to combat the chill of still-wet hair against her neck. "Okay. Moving on, I guess."

"Let's."

She looked down at her hands. Her fingers gleamed red and raw. "Can I ask . . . would it be okay if I checked on Paige? I was thinking of texting her to see how she's feeling, but I don't want to be weird. So I figured I'd better ask you, first."

"Christ." He closed his eyes and massaged between them. "How do you always do that?"

She eyed him. "Do what?"

He tapped the center of his chest. "Say things I can feel, right here."

She stared at the spot he'd touched long after his hand had fallen away. She had no idea how to answer.

"Look." He sighed. "Thanks for worrying about her, but she was only upset because she walked in on me and Tansy arguing this morning. Which understandably freaked her out a little."

"Oh." Aubrey mulled that over.

"Or maybe she really does have food poisoning. But either way, she'll be okay."

She looked down to find her fingers threaded, and forced them apart. "What were you and Tansy arguing about?"

He huffed out a stillborn laugh. "You don't want to know. Trust me."

She searched for a response. She couldn't imagine sharing a home with someone she'd once been partnered with, long after the relationship had ended. Even the three days it had taken for Luke to move out had felt like weeks.

"You know what?" Nick said abruptly. "Screw it. I can't keep things from you to save my life. We were arguing about you."

A low sound of surprise welled in her throat. "What? *Me?* Why?"

"Do you remember the night I came over here? When you first got back?"

"Yeah. Of course."

He stretched one leg toward the fire and hooked his elbow around the remaining knee. "I just came to get your fire lit, that's all. But Tansy wanted me to 'get you out of my system.' Her words, not mine."

Aubrey stared. Then stared some more. "She what?"

"Yeah." He flashed a smile, but something about it glinted, cold. "I'm sure it's the same thing she thinks I'm doing right now. It's what she thought I was doing last night. And my efforts to correct her weren't going so well this morning, at which point Paige walked in."

A low buzz invaded Aubrey's ears. "I . . . don't understand."

"What's not to understand?"

Her mind whirled. He couldn't possibly mean what she thought he did. "You're telling me Tansy sent you over here to . . ." Her throat worked. She couldn't even say it.

"Seduce you?" He laughed, bitter. "Yeah. When she found out you were back, she got it into her head that I'd be less of a pain in the ass if I came over here and 'had some fun for once.' Also her words. Definitely not mine."

She opened her mouth, fumbled for her voice, and tried again. "What do you mean, 'for once'?"

He kept his face aimed at the fire, but a blush burned high on his cheeks. "Yeah. So. I don't know why I can't keep my mouth shut around you."

"What do you mean, '*for once*,' Nick?"

He wouldn't look at her.

Suspicion laced around her rib cage and pulled tight. "You must have someone," she ventured. "Right?"

He cleared his throat, then dragged a hand down his face. "I mean, not really. No. Not in a long time."

A weight hardened in her gut. "So, wait. Exactly how long has it been since you've . . ."

"What?" He finally looked at her, cutting a glance that sliced her to the bone. "Had sex? Made love?"

She flushed. "Yes."

"Well, which one? They're different. If you're asking how long it's been since I've had sex, the answer is six incredibly long and lonely years. And the last time I made love . . . well, that was right here. With you. And it was just the once."

She stilled, her breath a nonsensical whirl. A dagger, poison-tipped with longing, slid into her heart. She . . . couldn't be hearing this right. "I don't get it," she stammered.

"I think I put it pretty plainly."

"How could you go that long without being touched? *How?*"

The black of his eyes seemed, impossibly, to deepen, the air around him crackling with a heat more aggressive than the fire's. "What do you want me to say, Aubs? Do you actually want the truth? Do you want me to say I don't want anyone's hands on me but yours? Do you want me to tell you my heart still stops beating when you're around? You want to know that even though I thought you were beautiful when we were kids, now you're so fucking breathtaking that just looking at you hurts? Especially when I get to see you like this?"

Oh, god, where had all her oxygen gone? "Like . . . this?"

"Yeah," he continued, as if he hadn't just reduced her to a chaotic whirl of disordered heartbeats. "Not that there's anything wrong with the power suit thing. But when you're like this, in pajamas and no makeup, I see you for what you are."

She searched his face while the world fell down around her. "And what am I?"

"A beautiful, incredible genius." His voice thickened, like honey swirling through gravel. "Someone who's going to save the world. Someone who's ten times the human I'll ever be."

Her lips parted. She couldn't breathe. "Nick. That's not true."

"It is."

"It's not." For all that his words had poured into her like rains sweeping across a desert, she needed him to see. She needed to give back, to make him understand how singular he was. "You're miles beyond what most people could ever hope to become. You're honorable. Pure-hearted. Generous to a fault. Not to mention one of the smartest people I know. The total package."

"No." He scoffed and scraped a fingernail across some invisible stain on his jeans. "I'm just some guy who makes steel and reads a lot. I don't save people's lives, with or without math."

"You do, though." Fire ran rampant in her bloodstream. "You saved Paige's life. You know that, right? That first day out at the farm, before I realized she was yours, I couldn't get over how much she adored her dad, how much she worshipped him. And when I found out it was you . . . It took my breath away."

"What? Why?"

Her palms throbbed, and she fought the urge to reach out. Oh, if she touched him, she wouldn't be able to stop, not after what he'd just said. "Because. Your dad gave you nothing, but you were stronger than that. Than him. You grew up and gave everything you had to the luckiest little girl in the world, even though no one had ever shown you how, and Paige grew into an incredible person because of it. And that's real. That's absolutely pure. So much more than me matching up kidney donors."

Nick's breath rushed out of him. He blinked, his eyes as bright as polished onyx. "Is that really how you see me? As . . . a father? A good one?"

"Yes," she breathed. "Absolutely yes. And looking at *you* hurts, too. It always has."

He scrubbed his hands through his barely there hair and sniffed, long and hard. "Fuck," he muttered. "Fuck, fuck, fuck."

Aubrey didn't realize she'd leaned in until he scrambled away and went to the window. He leaned a palm against the wall and stared out through the sleet-slicked pane.

"What?" Her question came out half broken. "What is it?"

He breathed hard, the carven lines of his back heaving. "It's you. This. It's so fucking hard, Aubs. Being around you. Hearing you say this shit to me."

An ache rose in her throat. After a moment of indecision, she rose and went to him, reaching out. "Nick, I—"

He spun and seized her in one sudden motion, pressing her against the wall, hemming her in with his sheer size and *himness.* His hands skimmed down her sides until his thumbs seated themselves against her hipbones.

Her lungs emptied. Nick stared down, caging her in, so close she could taste the heat of his exhales. When her chest finally inflated again, it filled with plume after plume of his searing scent.

"What're you doing?" she whispered.

"Something incredibly fucking stupid. Something you should definitely tell me not to do."

When she didn't protest, his grip tightened. His chest rose and fell, his breath frantic in the silence.

Electric heat churned in her belly. Slowly, ever so slowly, she inched her trembling fingers upward until the tips grazed his abdomen.

He hissed in a breath. "What're *you* doing?"

"Touching you," she whispered. "Someone should."

"No," he said, but he sounded like a man starved. "I've gone without for a long time."

The sentiment hollowed her out. But he leaned closer—unconsciously, almost, as if his body were pleading with her without his permission. Muscle quivered beneath her fingertips, a confession he refused to let cross his lips.

She answered it. She grew bolder, her hands roaming over his wet shirt to explore the planes of his chest. She traced the ridges of his neck and tunneled her fingers through the shorn dark silk of his hair. When he released a shuddering exhale, she reached beneath his shirt to map his body. She charted the divots along his ribs, the hard lines of muscle that dived toward his jeans. Then she worked her way back in the other direction, dragging her fingernails up his sides. Down again. Up. Around. Everywhere she could reach.

Nick angled his face past hers and panted in her ear, hot and ragged. Something finally broke in him. He fisted her hair and yanked her head to the side, then set his teeth against her throat.

Heat raced down her spine, splattering into a molten puddle at the bottom. His breath lashed fire across her skin.

"Someone should touch you," she repeated, on a gasp. She murmured it over and over, chanted it to him, and the incantation drowned out everything else, even the pop of sap-soaked firewood and the whisper of sleet on glass.

Because honestly, *someone* needed to appreciate the long, smooth columns of muscle flanking his spine, the way the groove of his abs hugged a dragged finger. Someone should worship the solid expanse of his chest and the faint dusting of hair that charted a course down from his belly button.

Nick rasped a sound of pure hunger against her throat, then pressed his lips to the tender flesh there. She gave herself up to an endless shiver. She should stop this, but instinct thieved away rational thought. All she wanted to do was climb him, bite him, lick, suck, grab . . .

His mouth withdrew abruptly, leaving her gasping and empty. She glanced down to find her fingers snared in his waistband. She'd undone the button of his jeans and taken hold of his zipper.

He muttered a curse, then gripped her shoulders and lowered his forehead to hers. "Aubs, you can't. If I stay here . . . If you . . . If we . . ."

A whimper slid from her lips. "What, you don't want me?"

He made a broken sound. "Of course I do. Fuck, are you kidding? You're what I want most. I'd ruin myself ten times over just to have you again. Even once. I'd break myself to pieces and thank you for it."

Her voice nearly deserted her. "But?"

"You're with someone," he said, hollow. "And after what my dad did . . . I can't. You know that. I can't even be the other half of someone else's equation."

Each word chipped a jagged piece from her soul. She had no idea how they'd gotten like this, pressed up against a wall together. She only knew she wanted more.

Was that so wrong?

Maybe. She honestly didn't know where the line was, with Gallant. A part of her had tied itself to his letters, but Nick's nearness awakened something, a force as everlasting as the one that bound her to the earth.

She would never, she realized, not feel this way.

Yet opening this door again would mean closing another she'd only just discovered. One that might lead to her best shot at happiness, because she couldn't stay in Henderson. She couldn't give up her dream job, or walk away from her database project, not even for Nick. If she did, she would wither. Slowly but surely, the light that had burned so brightly in New York would fade to ashes.

"You're right," she whispered. She hated it, but he was right.

"I know."

Still, he didn't retreat. His hands found her hips again, pulling her flush against him. Want crackled under her skin like a living thing.

"I need you to do something for me," he finally said.

His pleading tone nearly broke her heart. "Anything."

"Tell me that guy's name. In New York. The one who stole your job."

She tried to reassemble her composure. How could he be thinking of *that* right now? "What? Why're you asking?"

"You know why."

She hesitated, but only for a moment. "It's . . . David. David Ballard."

Nick repeated the name. "Thank you," he said, then released her and stepped back.

An abyss opened within her as she sagged against the wall. Only the unguarded longing in his eyes kept her legs beneath her.

She memorized the hawklike planes of his face, the way his brows tapered to points, as if they'd been shaped, only she knew they hadn't, because they'd always looked that way. "Nick, I don't—"

"I never fell out of love with you," he said roughly. "I never will. But I can never leave Paige. And you can't stay here. I wouldn't ask that of you even if I deserved to. What's more, you have someone else, now. And the last thing I want to do is screw that up."

Just like that, he was gone, and the agony of his absence stole all the air from her lungs. The front door opened and closed. Outside, an engine roared and faded.

Only when the truck's rumble melted into the susurrus of falling sleet did she let herself slide down the wall.

Then she gathered her knees to her chest and sobbed.

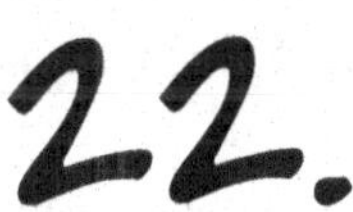

22.

Seventeen years ago

When Aubrey's father finally met her boyfriend, it was by accident.

It was a Tuesday afternoon when she finished her shift at the bowling alley. Twenty minutes later, she met Nick at the Mexican place on Main Street for their weekly date.

They always ate at the tiny two-person table near the window. Outside, steelworkers and their wives strolled by, some holding hands, some swinging children between them, some existing in the comfortable, easy silence of people who'd loved each other for decades and had already said most of what they needed to say.

Watching them always left warm footprints across Aubrey's heart. How would she and Nick look, in twenty years? Would they stop and kiss on street corners? Walk with their pinkies brushing? Would they glance up every so often, trade one of those knowing smiles that carried the depth of years?

The possibilities were endless, and she loved guessing. She especially loved that they would have twenty years to find out.

Today, they ordered their usual—guacamole, tacos, and virgin margaritas. Nick stacked an absurd amount of green dip onto each chip while Aubrey repeatedly darted in with one of her own to halve his load.

He pouted. "Hey. How am I supposed to get all big and burly if you keep stealing my food?"

"Big and burly?" She swallowed her chip, then propped her chin on a fist. "Sorry, but I don't think that's in your future. I can't even picture it."

In truth, he *was* gaining weight, now that he could buy himself food, but the past month had softened the hollows of his cheeks only slightly.

Nick scooped up half the remaining guacamole and crammed it into his mouth. "Just wait. Someday I'll pick you up and throw you over my shoulder."

She giggled. "How caveman of you."

"Yeah, well, isn't that what girls are into? Don't the guys in those romance novels pick women up all the time?"

"Who knows? I don't do books, remember?"

"Mmm. Right." Another chip vanished. "Maybe I'll just pin you down, instead. Make you listen while I read *War and Peace*."

She snickered. "*That's* your plan? To be a muscly caveman who holds his girlfriend hostage and force-feeds her Russian literature?"

"Yeah, why not?"

His smile mirrored hers, and the perfection of the moment engulfed her. She settled back, watching while he ate enough to fill a black hole. In truth, she'd only thieved his guacamole because she knew they'd order another round. And another. On Tuesdays, they always ran up the bill, then waddled out the door groaning. Because Wednesday through Monday, every spare penny went toward saving for New York.

Today belonged to them, though, so they ate and laughed and leaned over the tabletop to steal kisses when nobody was looking. They stole kisses when people *were* looking, too.

Then, after paying the tab, they emerged into the sultry afternoon, their palms locked together.

Hand-holders, probably, she thought. *Even in twenty years.*

In the grassy square, they took shelter from the July sun within the shadows of the bandstand. Aubrey backed Nick against a stone column and kissed him, relishing the flavors of lime and salt.

He groaned as she twined her fingers in his spiral curls. She didn't care that he'd come straight from work, that sweat had dried in streaks on his sunbaked skin or that coal dust smudged his clothes. Nothing existed except the way he pulled her against him, the fingers he splayed against the small of her back. She angled her head to give him deeper access. She could do this for hours. Weeks.

A lifetime.

A nearby snigger shattered the moment. "Man, are those two still at it? You'd think they would've given up by now."

Nick stiffened. Aubrey whipped her head around.

A row of six onlookers leaned against the far balustrade. Among them was Gina Abramo, whose lush black hair hung loose, brushing her equally lush rear end. Gallant stood beside her, a casual arm slung around her waist. "Hey, MacLean."

Aubrey's eyes narrowed, but he sounded friendly, unlike whoever had first spoken.

Gallant's best friend, Brent Reinholdt, smiled nastily. One front tooth gleamed whiter than its neighbors, reminding Aubrey of the first basketball game she'd ever cheered. Brent had fought with an opposing player and lost the original against the guy's kneecap.

"Did you have something to say?" she snapped.

He flicked his cigarette onto the concrete and ground it out with a sneaker. "Just surprised to see you two still hooking up."

"We're not *hooking up*," she said, scathing. "Nick's my boyfriend."

"Uh-huh." Brent sucked on his false tooth. "Well, just be careful you don't climb on top, later. I'm not sure that *boyfriend* of yours can survive those thighs you've got going on."

Everyone in Brent's entourage twittered. Except Gina, who looked scandalized, and Gallant, who frowned.

Nick stepped forward, his eyes cold. "Hey, dickface. You can talk shit to me, but not to my girlfriend. And you definitely can't make asshole comments about her body."

"Oh yeah? Or what? Ooh, wait, I know." Brent waved his hands in mock terror. "You're going to bust out your karate shit and make me say sorry? Oh, no, anything but that."

Sour rage flooded Aubrey's tongue. She started to move, but Nick looped long fingers around her wrist and tugged her back.

"That's exactly what's going to happen." He spoke flatly, devoid of emotion. "Because I'm not leaving until you apologize. So you can either do it with that nice, pretty face you have now, or with a busted lip."

Brent spat on the concrete. "Come on. Cut the crap. Everyone knows you cheated when you fought Gallant."

"Do they."

"Yeah." Brent glanced to his friend. "Right?"

Gallant blinked, then slid his gaze sideways, as if seeking an escape. "Right."

Heat swarmed Aubrey's stomach. She wanted to ask how someone could cheat at something that had no rules, but it would have wasted a breath.

"Your choice," Nick said.

Brent cracked his knuckles. "You know what? Let's do it. If anyone's apologizing here, it's going to be you, to Gallant. I don't like it when people mess with my friends, and it's about time someone set the record straight."

Nick broke into a wolfish smile. "Finally. Something we agree on."

Aubrey should have stepped in. Or, more accurately, she should have *wanted* to step in. But some feral corner of her vibrated with pride, because she hated bullies. She especially detested anyone who tried to elevate themselves by dominating others.

Nick stalked to the center of the bandstand and motioned for Brent to approach. His face was a cold, hard mask, but she glimpsed the secret underneath. The hint of anticipation glittering in the depths.

Still, she braced. She knew who would throw the first punch—who would *always* throw the first punch—and phantom pain bloomed when Brent slammed his fist into Nick's eye.

But she curled her nails into her palms and stayed out of it. Sure enough, Nick recovered in moments, throwing himself into the fight with dark, bullish grace.

The scuffle lasted half as long as Gallant's. Inside of a minute, Nick had Brent's cheek mashed against a column, his arm wrenched behind his back at an angle that reminded Aubrey of twisting off turkey legs at Thanksgiving.

"Any time now." Nick yanked.

Brent yelped and cast wild eyes at his friends. None of them moved. Blood dribbled from Brent's nose, making blotches on his yellow polo. "Uh . . . yeah. Sorry, MacLean."

Nick did something to Brent's arm that elicited another whimper. "We're not in the army, asshole. Her name's Aubrey."

"Right. Aubrey. Sorry, Aubrey."

"For?" Nick prompted.

"I, uh, I didn't mean anything bad about your thighs. I mean, only that they're really powerful. They have to be, right? Everyone's seen that thing you do at halftime, where—"

"Jesus." Nick made a disgusted sound and thrust Brent away. He toppled into his friends, who caught him more out of sheer surprise than anything else.

Nick turned to Aubrey and threaded his fingers through hers. Brent's opening punch had split the skin beneath one perfect brow, and the wound leaked blood into his eye and down his shirtfront.

But she didn't recoil. He looked beautiful like this. She squeezed his hand and turned her back on Gina and the others, leaving them to sort out their opinions about what had just happened on their own.

Around the corner, Nick stopped long enough to rip a square of fabric from his shirt. "How bad is it? Do I need stitches?"

She peered at the cut. She didn't have any experience evaluating things like this, but the gash wasn't gaping. "I don't think so. Maybe just a butterfly bandage. Does it hurt?"

He shrugged. "Not enough to spend time talking about it."

"That was . . . sweet. What you just did."

He snorted. "Sweet? Bringing you flowers would've been sweet."

"No way. I'd take punching over flowers any day. Or a love letter. Or maybe you holding me down and reading Dostoevsky. That'd work, too."

Those tilted eyes crinkled at the corners. "You're the most perfect girl in the world, you know that? Except for one thing."

She arched a brow. "What's that?"

"Tolstoy wrote *War and Peace*. Not Dostoevsky. I mean, come on."

She laughed and planted a kiss on his cheek, not minding the hint of salted iron that came with it. "Let's stop at the pharmacy, then clean you up at my house, okay?"

He hesitated. "Your parents won't be home?"

"Not yet. It's only four."

He nodded. In the car, he pressed his makeshift bandage to his face while she drove the mile-and-a-half to the brick-fronted drug store where she'd bought nickel bubble gum and cream soda as a kid.

She parked along the curb and hopped out. "You stay here."

To her surprise, he didn't protest, just leaned back against the headrest and clamped down on the wadded square of T-shirt. "Okay. Thanks."

She fought a smile as the door jingled on her way in. Nick took care of her. Always. But this marked the first time he'd allowed her to return the favor.

She liked the feeling. A lot.

Inside, she found some butterfly bandages, along with a bottle of hydrogen peroxide and nonstick gauze. The whole place smelled of lemons, which made her feel slightly better about the dust blanketing everything she touched.

Up front, Aubrey dumped her haul onto the wheezy conveyor belt. Behind the counter sat Tansy Burroughs, the same girl who'd borne witness to Nick's first kiss. And Aubrey's second, considering she'd wasted her first on Julian Byrnes in a game of spin the bottle junior year.

Nick had been her first *real* kiss, though. The first one that mattered.

Tansy began a listless search for price tags. The two months since graduation hadn't changed her much—she wore her standard loose T-shirt, dark jeans, and combat boots, and apparently felt no need to engage her customers in conversation. Then Aubrey caught sight of the puffy shadows lurking beneath her eyes.

"Hey. Are you okay?"

Tansy glanced up. "Sure. Why wouldn't I be?"

"I don't know. You just look . . . sad."

Tansy shrugged. "Yeah, well. I got in a shitty fight with my shitty mom. I'm sure it won't be the last time."

"Oh. That sucks. Do you want to talk about it?"

"Nope." Tansy returned to her task, then cut a glance through the grubby front window. Nick sat in the car, silhouetted by afternoon light. "What's all this for, anyway? Did your boyfriend beat the shit out of someone again?"

Aubrey blinked at Tansy's frankness. "Um. Maybe."

"Huh. Did the guy deserve it?"

"Definitely."

"Oh. Good for him, then."

Aubrey didn't answer. She had the distinct impression that this line of questioning had only served as a way to change the subject.

Tansy turned the hydrogen peroxide over four times, then found the sticker on the cap. "What's he like, anyway? The new kid?"

Aubrey's stomach soured. "He's lived here for six months. I don't think he still counts as the *new kid*."

"This is Henderson. In five years, we'll still be calling him that."

Aubrey blew out a frustrated breath. Something about the offhand remark fired a spark in her. "Actually, he's the most incredible person I've ever met. Like . . . a knight in shining armor, or something. He's honorable. And selfless. The kind of person who does the right thing no matter what, even if it hurts him. Which is pretty rare, these days. I didn't think they made guys like that, anymore."

Tansy's hands stilled on the bandages. She glanced up, a flicker of interest lighting her pale eyes. "That is rare."

Aubrey shifted her weight, wishing she could retract the dramatic speech. "Sorry."

"For what?"

"I just get . . . defensive. People misjudge him sometimes."

Tansy held her eyes. Flakes of mascara clung to her cheeks while crimson vessels tangled in the whites of her eyes. She'd definitely been crying.

"Are you *sure* you're okay?"

"Yep." Tansy tapped a fingernail against the total on the register and handed over the bag. "Here you go."

Aubrey counted out cash, wondering if she should push, then shrugged and took her things. Just before shoving through the door, she turned. "Hey, I hope you feel better. And that things with your mom improve."

"Thanks." Tansy twisted to face the window again. "Hey. You said he's like a knight? Always doing the right thing?"

Aubrey paused. The moment tilted, off-kilter, as if the dust motes swimming past had suddenly reversed direction, or gravity had tugged on her from above and taken her stomach with it. "Yeah, he does."

"Huh. That's awesome. Have a nice day."

"You, too." She fled.

In the car, Nick gave her a questioning look. "What's wrong? You look . . . strange."

Aubrey gulped down the bile crawling up her throat. What *was* wrong? She'd gone hot and cold all over. "Yeah, I don't know. Tansy Burroughs was in there, but she was acting weird. For some reason, it gave me the creeps."

He looked blank. "Who the hell is Tansy Burroughs?"

Aubrey laughed, and the heaviness of the moment cracked and fell away. He truly had no idea. She started the car.

"Never mind. Forget I said anything. She's no one."

At home, Aubrey ushered Nick into the kitchen, where he stripped off his torn, bloodied shirt and stuffed it into the trash.

He leaned over the sink and let her fuss over him until the water ran pink. As she dabbed the garnet crust from his eyebrow, he took the opportunity to snake an arm around her and pull her against him.

Aubrey giggled. Ever since they'd agreed to sleep together, Nick had grown bolder. Bit by bit, he was beginning to trust her. To trust *them*. She loved the gentle new possessiveness of his touch, the way his hands said, *mine*. Especially because her body always agreed, answering with a ripple of heat.

She aligned the butterfly bandage over his gash. He snuck his other arm around her waist, lacing his fingers behind her back.

She bit her lip and tried to concentrate, but all the blood in her veins tumbled off course. The part of him pressed against her belly felt much firmer than it had a moment ago.

She stuck down one side of the bandage. "And just what're you thinking about right now?"

He made a low, rumbling sound in his throat. "Take a guess."

"Hmm. *War and Peace*? Dostoevsky?"

He chuckled. "It's Tolstoy, you heathen."

"Oh, right. Well, either way, I had no idea dead Russian writers got you so excited."

He snickered. "I won't be excited for much longer if you keep talking like that."

"Would you rather I talk about something else?"

"Yeah." He tugged her closer. "Talk about us. Tell me when I'm going to get to make you mine."

Heat pooled in her belly. "Soon. The first time we get a night alone."

"Does it have to be a night?" He angled his face to nuzzle her, ruining her aim. The butterfly ended up stuck to itself and she yanked it off, starting over.

"Stop that," she said. "I can't concentrate. And yes, it has to be a night. No one loses their virginity in the daytime. It's supposed to be sexy and romantic. Preferably in front of the fireplace while it's pouring rain outside."

He chuckled, darkly sensual. "You know it's July, right?"

"Yeah, so? I want rain. And fire. Now hold still."

He did as she bade. "Rain and fire. Well, whatever my lady demands, my lady—"

The sound of a cleared throat stabbed between them. Aubrey reeled backward and immediately wished she hadn't. Nick stood beside the still-running sink, shirtless, his left half covered in blood, the butterfly dangling off his eyebrow like a limp flag of surrender. A very obvious erection tented the front of his khaki work pants.

Her heart shrank to a hard, pale speck. Her father filled the kitchen doorway, color splashed across his cheeks, a match for his flaming hair.

"What the hell is this?"

"Umm. Dad. Hi." Her voice skewed upward. "Aren't you supposed to be working?"

"I was. Working. And then I finished working, like always, and then I came home, like always, and why is this person standing in our kitchen, bleeding everywhere and putting his hands all over you?"

Aubrey risked a sideways glance, but Nick's horrorstruck expression told her he wouldn't be much help. She snapped off the water and edged in front, hoping to give him time to regroup, at least. "This is my boyfriend. Nick."

"Nick." Her father's tone was stony. "And he's bleeding because?"

"Because . . ." She trailed off. Shit.

Behind her, Nick sucked in a breath. "I . . . Um . . . Got in a fight. Sir."

Aubrey squeezed her eyes shut. This had to be a nightmare. Any moment, she would wake up. Except when she looked again, nothing had changed.

"It's, um, nice to meet you," Nick stammered. "Sir."

Her father said nothing. He stepped into the room, took Aubrey by the arm, and marched her out to the living room. "You did *not* tell me he's the kind of boy who gets in fights."

She shook off his hand. "Because he's not. I mean, not without good reason. He only did today because Brent Reinholdt said something awful to me and Nick made him apologize."

His jaw worked as he processed that. "He . . . defended you?"

"Yes." She wanted to grab his lapels and shake. "Which you should appreciate, not judge him for."

He thought that over, his flush fading. "Okay. But he's . . . not what I pictured. Why's he so skinny?"

She pressed her lips together. "Because his dad is a jerk who doesn't keep any food in the house."

"You mean he's not being raised right?"

"Dad, it's not his fault. At all."

"Maybe not, but that doesn't mean it's not important."

That stole the protest right out of her mouth. She had no way to refute that, and yet it watered down the beautiful complexity of Nick Thacker to a single bullet point. One that mattered, yes, but certainly not the only one. If anything, Nick's unfortunate home situation only proved his resilience.

"Look." Her father rubbed at his brows with a thumb and forefinger. "Just get him cleaned up, get him some clothes, and send him home. You and I need to have a talk."

She tensed. "About?"

"The future."

She hauled in a breath, then released it unused and went to do as he asked. She found Nick by the kitchen sink, still shell-shocked.

"This is bad," he said. "This is really, really bad, isn't it?"

"It could definitely be better." She fitted the butterfly into place. "But my dad's reasonable. I can make him understand."

Nick nodded, but looked no less stricken.

By the time Aubrey had gotten him into a clean shirt, he'd recovered somewhat, enough to approach her father on his way out through the living room.

Nick straightened to his full height and made unflinching eye contact. "I'm sorry. I wish we'd met under different circumstances. But I want you to know I genuinely love your daughter. With all my heart."

Aubrey's chest swelled. This surpassed his earlier defense of her and left it gasping in the dust.

Her dad raised bushy red eyebrows. "I'm glad to hear that."

"Have a good evening." Nick made for the door. "Sir."

Once he'd gone, her father set her down on the blue chesterfield. He settled beside her with a sigh that added ten years to him, even though he'd just turned forty-five. "So. That's the famous Nick. At last."

Aubrey clasped her hands in her lap. "That's him."

Another sigh. "You're serious about him?"

"Yes."

"How serious?"

"Very." Her fingers tangled together. "He's the most honorable person I've ever met."

"Honorable? He didn't look honorable, with his hands all over you like that."

Her heart wriggled up the back of her throat. How she wished she could go back in time and beg Nick to come to dinner on a night when he could've showed up with a bouquet for her mother and a handshake for her father. A wasted wish. "I know, but—"

"*And* he started a fight over you."

"He didn't," she rushed out, absurdly grateful for Nick's first-punch policy. "Brent started it. Nick just hit back."

Her father grunted. "He's not being *raised* right, Aubrey. That probably means more to me than it does to you, but people learn from their parents. They turn into them, someday."

She hissed in protest. "That's prejudiced."

"It's realistic."

She dug her heels in at that point. So did her father, and Aubrey ended up parroting the same speech she'd delivered to Tansy. She wished, then, that she had Nick's aptitude for words, because hers failed in every way to convey the breadth of what he meant to her. She couldn't explain how his arms offered a haven, or that his letters scorched into her, each word a fizzing star slingshotted across her sky. She had no poetry to describe her certainty that Nick was worth it. Worth anything.

Still, her father listened, and when she finished, he cradled her hands in his. "That's all well and good," he said. "But it's probably for the best that this thing is ending in a few weeks."

She stiffened. "Ending?"

"When you go to NYU."

Ice trickled down her spine. "Well, that's the thing, Dad. I've decided . . . I've, ah . . ."

His hands tightened around hers.

Somehow, the pressure steadied her. "I'm deferring. For a year. I'm not going to New York without him."

There. She'd said it. At the worst possible moment, but anything less would have been a betrayal.

Her father dropped her hands as if stung. "What? No. Absolutely not."

"Yes. I'm staying in Henderson for another year to save up, and then we're leaving together. We're going to move in—"

"No," he thundered. A vein in his temple throbbed. "*Absolutely not.* You haven't told NYU this yet, have you?"

"No, but it's not up for discussion."

"Everything is up for discussion." He rose and paced. A red mottle rose in his cheeks, brighter than the one he'd worn in the kitchen. "And you've worked too hard to defer. You have a plan. I'm not letting you throw it away for some *boyfriend*."

"He's not just a boyfriend!"

The conversation quickly spun out of control, degenerating to a cacophony of raised voices and impassioned pleas.

"Pack a bag," her father said, when Aubrey started crying. "We're going away for a few days. Somewhere where you can think about this. I mean *really* think, away from that boy. You need to approach this with a clear head."

"I don't want to go away. And I don't need to think about it."

"I'm not asking."

"I don't care. You can't force me."

His eyes flashed. "Think about this, Aubrey. It's inertia. Simple physics. If you stay in Henderson, it'll only get harder and harder to leave. And I know that's not what you want for yourself. It's not what I want for you, either."

She sniffled. She had no doubt his heart was in the right place, but he didn't understand.

She struggled to her feet, her hands flexing into fists. His eyes had hardened to chunks of jade, and as she wiped away her tears, she imagined hers had done the same.

"Look, Dad, I love you, but this isn't your call. I'm eighteen now. An adult. And I know what I want. So if you put something in my way, I'll just go around you. If you knock me down, I'll get right back up. If you—"

"Do *not* finish that sentence," he half-shouted. "Not to me."

She took a step. "Yes, to you. You taught me to never give up, and guess what? You don't get to pick and choose when that applies. So yeah, if you stick me between a rock and a hard place, I'll split the difference and aim straight down the middle.

And that's what this is. The middle. The path that gets me where I want to go."

He gaped, but a subtle gleam undercut his fury. Aubrey dared to hope she'd impressed him, if only a bit.

"We're going," he said. The knot of his tie hung askew. "And that's final."

"You know what?" she snapped. "Fine. *If* you agree that when we get back, that's the end of it. If I still want to stay, I'm staying, and we're not discussing this again."

His jaw worked. "Fine. But only *if* you make an honest and open-minded effort to reevaluate your decision."

As angry and affronted as she was, a rush of love shot through her. "Okay. Yes. Thank you."

"Now go pack. We're leaving tomorrow. For a week."

He stormed off to make some phone calls, no doubt rearranging his work schedule. Aubrey retreated to her bedroom to do as she was told.

She filled her suitcase, not caring what went in, then stood in the middle of her bedroom, casting about for more.

Her eyes fell on the desk in the corner. She hesitated only a moment before sitting and ripping a page from a spiral-bound notebook. Any letter she produced would fall miles short of Nick's, but this would serve as a declaration, at least. An assurance, something he could hold on to while she was away.

She uncapped a purple pen and began to write.

An Inexhaustive List of Things I Love About You . . .

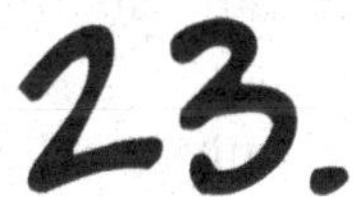

DEEP IN THE steel mill's underbelly, Nick stood staring into the vat of molten pig iron. With the visor of his heat-reflective shield up, the air boiled against his cheeks, a physical force, like a hell-spawned demon roaring in his face.

Which wasn't far off.

It was funny. He'd stood here so many times, contemplating the open maw of the blast furnace and presuming to understand longing. He'd waded to the fringes of the fire, trying to cauterize his internal wounds, all the while believing he'd never see Aubrey again.

That alone had been crippling. But having her back, having to *deny* her, plunged him into a fresh new hell he never could have imagined.

Days had passed, but the echo of her touch still reduced him to a mess of need-soaked nerve endings. Jesus, the way her hands had gifted every inch of him with heat. *Someone should touch you.* By the time she'd gotten to his zipper, his blood had bellowed with the sheer fucking agony of having to refuse her.

It *still* did.

"Hey, man." Jackson appeared, his heat shield firmly in place. The reflected glare of thousand-degree metal obscured his expression. "You taking a sample, or trying to decide whether to throw yourself in?"

Nick grunted. Good question. He had no idea.

But it cost him nothing to reassure his friend, so he went through the motions, his mind approximately eight thousand light-years away.

God, Aubrey hadn't only smelled like paradise, she'd tasted like it, too, in that all-too-brief moment when he'd had his mouth on her neck. His senses had ignited with salt and sunshine and something else he'd wanted to plunge into and suffocate in. Later, he'd put off brushing his teeth until the last possible moment, loath to lose whatever traces of her lingered.

That had been after he'd taken a shower, of course. A very, very long shower. One in which the water had sluiced over him in icy sheets once he'd finished himself off for the second time.

Now he tipped his ladle, trying to focus on the dribble of red-hot iron. Still, Aubrey persisted, draped across his thoughts like a fire-haired goddess.

He shuddered. He couldn't believe he'd turned her down. How. *How?* Had he lost his mind?

"Hey. Earth to Nick."

He turned. Jackson again. What were they supposed to be doing? He'd already forgotten.

Jackson gestured. "Put your heat shield down, my man. You're cooking yourself. Your eyebrows are all curly."

Nick stared stupidly, then snapped the visor down. "Uh. Yeah. Thanks."

"Where are you today?"

He pretended not to hear over the roar of the furnace. He returned to his sample, blinking the sting of sweat from his eyes.

Jesus, he needed to get his shit together. Make a plan.

Right. A plan.

Because when it came down to it, he had two options. He could let Aubrey stay in Henderson while finishing this statement of hers, but it would only be a matter of time before his control snapped and he went over there begging for a redo. She'd probably tell him to get lost, but if not, he'd end up buried too deeply in her to ever recover. Worse, he'd prove, once and for all, that he was no better than his piece-of-shit father. Not to mention he'd jeopardize her thing with Gallant, which he would never forgive himself for.

Or . . . He could do his best to get Aubrey back to New York. Back to the life she wanted and deserved. Back to the job that fulfilled her.

Nick stopped mid-task. Really, what was there to consider? If he had a shot at making her happy, he had to take it.

His attention shifted to David Ballard, whose name rolled around in his head like a rotten grape. Last night, Nick had researched the guy on the internet, in between fielding increasingly demanding messages from MontanaBirder81.

Which posed a whole separate problem. Apparently, John had finally convinced Jane to kiss him, and had sent no less than three requests for a letter that would ensure she climbed into bed with him, next.

Nick couldn't even think about that right now. He'd written back last night, citing a bout with the flu and promising a letter by next week. Then he'd promptly spent the next hour on Google, tracking down David Ballard's address in Brooklyn.

The idea that had followed was stupid. Totally unhinged. But somehow, Aubrey MacLean shattered all his internal logic, and had for seventeen years. He would do anything for her, no matter how dumb, no matter how desperate.

That included hopping in his truck and driving to New York, at which point nothing would stand between his fist and this Ballard guy's face. Then, once he forced the asshole to confess, Aubrey's company would reinstate her. She could return to New York if she wanted. Ride off into the sunset with Gallant, if she liked.

She'd have choices. She'd have everything she'd ever wanted.

Meanwhile, he could return to his quiet life. Work, gym, Paige. *Not* living out his worst fucking nightmare by turning into his home-wrecker dad.

With that decided, he set his jaw. The remainder of the shift passed in a tumult of heat and sweat. When he finally clocked out, he hung his protective equipment in his locker and waited for Jackson outside the mill's gates.

His best friend emerged into the frost-touched parking lot and puffed out a single word. "Gym?"

Nick stuck his hands in his coverall pockets. "Yeah."

He absolutely needed it, though he didn't know where he would find the energy required. Fatigue weighed down his limbs while every step hammered a new ache into his soles. But the alternative involved driving across town, banging down the door of that old Victorian, and begging on his knees.

"Hey," Nick said. "Do you think you could do me a favor? A big one?"

Jackson paused. "You never ask for favors."

"Yeah, well. I don't like bothering people with stuff I should be dealing with myself. But I have to go to New York this weekend, and I was wondering if you could come."

Jackson cocked his head. "Really? What's in New York?"

"A guy. Who needs a little . . . redirecting."

Jackson thought about that. "The kind of redirecting that involves fists?"

Nick scuffed a boot on the iced gravel. "Maybe. Maybe not. We'll see how it goes. But I don't expect you to help with the redirecting part. I just want you to make sure I go through with it. Keep me from doing something stupid, like turning my truck around and going to Aubrey's house."

"Huh. Yeah, all right."

That was it. No *let me think about it,* or *are you sure this isn't the kind of thing that'll get us arrested?* Just ready acceptance, and Nick had to restrain himself from hugging his best friend until somebody's ribs fractured.

"But," Jackson said, "if I go, I have a favor to ask, too."

Nick frowned. "Yeah?"

"Yeah. I've never been to New York, and there's something I've always wanted to do there." Jackson rolled his hulking shoulders and cracked his neck. "We have to go see a show. On Broadway."

"A show? Like . . . with singing and shit?"

"Yeah. With singing. And *stuff.* And by stuff, I mean I want it to have dancing, too."

Nick stared. "I tell you I might have to rearrange some guy's face, and you want to go see fucking *Cats* afterward?"

"Hey, man. Don't judge. I'm not. And I'll splurge for the tickets. That way, you don't have anything to explain to Tansy, afterward."

Nick threw his hands up. Whatever. He'd go see Disney on Ice, if that's what Jackson wanted. "You know what? Sure."

Jackson stepped close and clapped him on the back. "Hey, thanks. It's not every day I get to cross something off my bucket list. You book tickets, I'll pay you back. When're we leaving?"

"Saturday. I gave my shift to Carl. I'll pick you up at six a.m. We won't be back 'til Sunday night, so pack a bag."

"Okay. Sounds good. Meet you at Wilder's in five?"

"Yeah."

In his truck, Nick kept his hands at a perfect ten-and-two. Maybe if he forced his body into line, his mind would follow.

But without the distraction of work, his thoughts slipped the reins, his head filling with one wild fantasy after another. He imagined turning the truck around. Showing up on Aubrey's doorstep, hoisting her over his shoulder, carrying her to the nearest bed, and showing her exactly how much the intervening years had lessened his love. Which was not at all. Even though it'd been ages for him, their second time together would prove even more transcendent than the first. He knew he could please her now in ways he hadn't before.

His fists tightened around the steering wheel. The daydream beckoned to him with the power of a thousand blazing suns, but he would resist. He had to. After all, he'd done this before. Stared down the barrel of a future without her, knowing he had to pull the trigger himself.

He just wished it didn't hurt even worse the second time around.

Aubrey had nothing to occupy herself with, and she hated it.

Yesterday, Gallant had texted to reschedule their Chicago date, saying work had gotten crazy and would keep him tied up all week.

Are you sure? she'd texted back. **I could drive, and you could use that time to work. I've been looking forward to this.**

I'm so sorry, had come the reply. **I haven't had time to write you another letter yet, and I know that was the deal.**

Her chest had clenched, but she'd forced a breezy reply. **It's okay. Though you *could* just tell me those words instead of writing them.** She'd hesitated, then added a grinning emoji to soften the suggestion.

A long pause. Then, **This one will be worth the wait. Trust me.**

At that, she'd sighed and tucked the phone away, then turned her attention to her manifesto, but the words had swum before her eyes. Now, less than twenty-four hours later, she flung herself down on the chesterfield with Gallant's letters. She needed a distraction. A *letter.* If not a new one, then an old one. Anything that might slam the door on the memories running laps in her mind, in which familiar fingers tangled in her hair, baring her neck to gleaming white teeth. In which lush dark lashes swept low against sculpted cheeks, and Nick made that hungry sound while her hands mapped one hard, heated muscle after another.

A ripple tore through her, and she reeled it in by focusing on the page. Her eyes scanned the same paragraph seven times, yet failed to relay a single word to her brain.

Okay, this wasn't working. She lowered the paper, but her gaze strayed to the wall beside the window. A mere glance at that innocuous stretch of plaster rammed a brand-new lightning bolt down her throat.

She jumped up, scattering the letters across the cushions. In the kitchen, she brewed tea and confined herself to the breakfast table. Human contact. That should do it. She pulled out her phone. She hadn't seen Megan since their coffee date two weeks ago, except in passing, and had been meaning to get in touch. Now was as good a time as any. Especially because she could not, under any circumstances, work with Nick out at the farm again. Her budding relationship with Gallant wouldn't survive. Not to mention her sanity.

Hey, she tapped out. How have you been? Still glowing, I hope. I just wanted to say I'd love to get coffee again soon, and I think I need to switch volunteer groups. Working with Nick is . . . well, not working.

She hit Send. Bubbles popped up, followed by Megan's reply.

Why, what happened? Are you okay?

Aubrey dragged a hand down her face. What had happened? Why, nothing. She'd only done her level best to seduce the ex-boyfriend she refused to sacrifice her career for, because apparently she was still violently attracted to him, even though she was dating someone else.

Nothing to see here at all.

Her thumbs hovered over the keyboard, stiff with indecision, when the phone pinged again. The banner at the top gave her pause.

Paige Thacker.

She frowned. Why was Nick's daughter texting her? She exited Megan's message and clicked on Paige's.

Hey, Aubrey, sorry for the last-minute notice, but could you possibly come speak to my math club tomorrow? It'd be at the end of the day, so around three.

Aubrey stared at the words. Something about the tone struck her as off. No emojis or exclamation points. Then again, maybe Paige texted differently than she talked. The girl hadn't sent any messages before, so Aubrey had no way to gauge.

She rubbed at her eyes. She was being paranoid, probably. And she owed Paige some kind of explanation as to why they wouldn't be building floats together anymore. Might as well roll that into the math club presentation. Besides, this would prevent her from staring at that stupid, blank, smug-as-hell *wall* again. Which she desperately needed right now.

She crafted three separate messages before settling on something suitably neutral.

All right. I'll be there. Looking forward to it.

On Friday afternoon, Aubrey chose a black plaid tweed skirt suit and the same skyscraper heels that had resulted in her sprained ankle, only this time, she had the foresight to stash the shoes in her purse and only swap them out once she'd made the two-and-a-half-mile walk to the high school in her ballet flats.

Mrs. Runge, a white-haired, bespectacled toothpick of a woman, welcomed her into the math room with a warm smile and a handshake more vigorous than anyone had a right to expect from a septuagenarian.

"Thanks so much for coming. It's wonderful to have you. Women in mathematics don't exactly get a lot of airtime, so when Paige suggested this, I jumped at the chance to have you speak."

Aubrey channeled her gratitude into a smile. "Thanks. This means a lot to me, because this is where my love for math was born. It's an honor to share that with the next generation."

Mrs. Runge beamed.

As Aubrey took a place at the head of the class, a sea of bright faces followed her. Paige sat up front, but Aubrey directed her attention to the room at large, launching into an impassioned description of her work. She talked about math's utility, not only as a tool to challenge oneself, but as a means to better the world. The possibilities were endless, limited only by the imaginations of those applying numbers to real-world concepts.

Twenty pairs of eyes followed her, each one vivid with the clarity of youth, and a twinge gripped her heart. This room held so much hope. So many dreams. She prayed none of these kids would tie their lives in knots the way she had.

When she finished, a boy with buck teeth raised his hand. "Can I ask how you made the decision not to teach? Isn't that what most math PhDs end up doing?"

"It is," Aubrey said. "And I'd encourage anyone who feels drawn to teaching to pursue it, because teachers are the lifeblood that sustains the future of mathematics. But I needed something hands-on. Non-academia is definitely a less-traveled path, and a tough one to navigate, because it's hard to find the employers that need you. Those jobs don't typically get posted online, and it takes a lot of networking to find them. But for me, it was worth the effort. Knowing I was making a difference fulfilled me in ways nothing else could have. Working at Osos was the most meaningful thing I've ever done."

Her voice warbled at the end, and she clamped her lips shut, clearing the air for another question. The last thing she needed was to lose her cool in front of twenty strangers. Well, nineteen strangers and the daughter of the first, and possibly only, man she'd ever loved.

A girl with tightly woven braids raised her hand. "What's it like, being a woman in math? Have you had more challenges to contend with than a man would have?"

"Yes," Aubrey said frankly. "And it isn't fair, getting held to a higher standard than your male counterparts. Having to prove your chops over and over while your colleagues get accepted at face value. But you deal with it. You keep doing the work, and at the end of the day, no one can argue with results. At least, that's how I always looked at it."

The girl nodded, seemingly satisfied.

When the kids' curiosity had run its course, they applauded. As the students filed out, Paige gathered her things. "Can I meet you in the parking lot?"

"Of course," Aubrey said.

Paige slipped out the door, but Aubrey hung back, letting Mrs. Runge pump her hand with even more bone-crushing force the second time. "That was wonderful," the woman said.

Aubrey blushed. "Thanks. It was my pleasure."

They chatted, and when Mrs. Runge finally released her, Aubrey made her way outside, where she breathed into her chilled hands and surveyed the parking lot. The place had changed so much in seventeen years. In her day, the lot had been dirt.

"Hey. Thanks for meeting me."

Aubrey turned, then stilled, her stomach sinking. Bluish shadows collected beneath Paige's eyes, stark in the jaunty sunshine. A white knit hat with a perky pompom capped off her strawberry-blond pigtail braids, but even the cheeriness of the hat and hairstyle couldn't obscure the tension clouding Paige's expression.

"Hey. Are you okay? You're not still sick, are you?"

Paige let out a mournful chuckle. "Is it that obvious?"

"Well. Yeah. It's kind of like someone turned your eleven down to a five."

"Sorry. I'm just . . . yeah, not feeling great. My stomach's been weird all week."

Aubrey's lips pressed together. Just like with the text, Paige's tone was off, her voice brittle. Aubrey probed her mind for reasons a sixteen-year-old girl might suffer from nausea for nearly a week, then came to rest on one that made her heart shrink.

She scanned Paige again, but the girl wasn't glowing the way Megan was. Far from it.

She was probably way off base, then. At least, she *hoped* she was way off base.

"Do you . . . need to talk?" she ventured.

Paige chewed at the inside of her cheek. "Actually, yeah. I have a question for you. It's going to sound totally insane, but I have my reasons, I promise."

Icy dread slid down Aubrey's spine. She suddenly wanted very much not to hear whatever came next. What if this was about Nick? Their shared past? "This isn't . . . something you should be asking your dad instead, is it?"

Paige glanced down, guilt stamped across her features. "No.

I mean, I know you and he were . . . well, you guys knew each other pretty well in high school, it turns out."

All the blood drained from Aubrey's face.

"But," Paige hastened to add, "I get that that's not a conversation you and I should be having. What I want to ask has to do with something else. It's just not going to make any sense to you."

Aubrey braced. Maybe if she played dead, the earth would take pity and open a crevasse directly beneath her. "I—"

"Please, just tell me if you can do this." Paige stuck her tongue out and rolled it into a tube.

Aubrey stared. Stared some more. "What?"

"I know." Paige fidgeted. "I told you it wouldn't make sense. I just . . . Please. Can you do it?"

Aubrey shook her head, which did nothing to clear her confusion. "I, uh, don't think so?"

"You don't think, or you know? Will you try?" Paige rolled her tongue again, then waved a *you-go-next* hand, her eyebrows tented upward, her eyes as wide as a hunted deer's.

Aubrey stuck her tongue out. She curled. Twisted. Try as she might, she couldn't replicate what she'd been shown. "No. I can't."

Paige plastered her hands over her face. "Oh my god," she muttered, over and over.

Aubrey cast around for help, but the parking lot yawned wide and empty, most of the students having left for the day. After a moment, she said, "I have no idea what's going on, but do you need me to call someone? One of your parents, maybe?"

Paige dropped her hands. Her eyes brimmed with . . . *relief*? "No, no. Nothing like that. God, sorry. I know I must seem like such a mess right now."

"Hey, we've all been there. I just don't know how to help you."

"You already did, actually. I just . . . need a minute."

They stood in silence, until Paige's ragged breathing smoothed out. She swiped at her too-bright eyes. "I'm okay, I swear. Anyway, thanks for coming to math club."

"You're . . . welcome?"

Paige bobbed her head. Miraculously, she seemed to have shed a hundred-pound weight in the past minute, even if a fifty-pounder still remained. "And thanks for trying the tongue thing. I know this is all coming out of left field, but I'll explain at some point."

"You don't have to. Whatever's going on, it's none of my business."

"Yeah," Paige said softly. "I thought for a minute it might be, but you're right. That doesn't mean I won't still tell you, though. I'm kind of an open-book sorta person, if you hadn't noticed. Anyway. I'll see you tomorrow? At the floats?"

Aubrey gulped down the sourness bubbling in her throat. "Yeah, about that . . . You should know I talked to Megan about switching jobs. But not because of you. I've enjoyed every minute of working together."

"Oh." Paige nodded. "Right. You wanna avoid my dad."

Aubrey hesitated. But lying felt disingenuous, and Paige had gotten a step ahead of her, somehow. "I think that'd be best for everyone."

"Look, I get it. But you don't have to worry. He's not coming tomorrow. He went out to the farm last night to finish up the welding, and he's bundling on the chicken wire tonight. All we have to do tomorrow is attach the corn. And I'd really like to finish up with you. If you're okay with that."

Something violent took place inside Aubrey's chest. Nick was avoiding her, too, then, and now her heart was . . . what? Soaring? Crashing?

She couldn't tell. Not that it mattered. It wasn't like she hadn't made the same decision, first. "Wouldn't working together make you uncomfortable, though? It must be weird knowing your dad and I were . . . close, once."

Paige tugged at her braids, a shy smile curving her mouth. Bizarrely, this subject seemed to unsettle her less than the tongue-trick thing. "It's really not. It's kind of a relief, actually. Knowing he's capable. Because I just want him to be happy. Really. I figure it's best if you know that now. Up front."

Aubrey paused, utterly unsure of what to do with that statement. "Uh, I want him to be happy, too."

"Oh, good," Paige said, earnest. Some of her usual brightness had crept back in. "At least *someone's* on the same page with me."

When Aubrey didn't respond, Paige said, "Get it? Same page? Same Paige? With me?"

Aubrey shook her head, her mind full of blank white fuzz.

"Okay, well, puns aren't for everyone, I guess. That's fine. Just don't expect me to stop trying. Anyway, I'll see you tomorrow?"

"Okay," Aubrey said, mystified. "Sure."

"Great." Paige walked off.

Aubrey stood in the parking lot for a long time, replaying the conversation in search of some explanation. But her head drifted somewhere high above—distant, helium-filled, incapable of rational thought.

What in the holy hell had just happened?

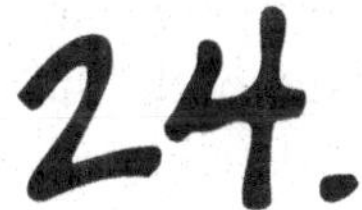

THE GUY WHO'D stolen Aubrey's algorithm didn't look like a douchebag. Exactly the opposite, as it turned out.

Nick squinted through the windshield. Half a block away, David Ballard ambled along the sidewalk, wearing the same coat he'd had on in his grainy Facebook photo. Except the picture hadn't captured the beatific innocence emanating from David's wide-set brown eyes, or the way his rounded cheeks brought to mind one of those baby angels from an Italian painting.

Nick promptly absolved Aubrey of all blame in trusting the guy. He looked about one good deed away from growing a halo and a pair of wings.

"That him?" Jackson rumbled.

"Yep." Nick rubbed his hands together in front of the truck's anemic heater. He'd circled the block nine times before finding a parking spot, and leaned in as David paused at the gated entry to his apartment building.

"Really?" Jackson said. "Because that dude looks like he runs a kitten rescue. Or saves babies from burning buildings."

"Yeah, well, he's actually a dickhead thief who ruins people's lives."

Jackson made a thoughtful sound. "Kind of seems like a crime to hit him, anyway. But hey, man. You do you."

Nick snorted. He waited for a rush of guilt, but . . . nope. Nothing. "You know the rule. He'll have to hit me first. Which I sincerely hope he does. Anyway. Go time."

Before Jackson could respond, Nick slipped from the truck alone and arrowed along the sidewalk. Up ahead, David unlocked his security door and pulled it open.

The block pulsed with vibrancy. Brightly painted fire hydrants competed for attention with whizzing yellow taxi cabs, while the warm waft of roasting shawarma meat softened the November chill. But Nick barely registered the surroundings. His fingertips caught the edge of David's security door just before it snicked shut. He ducked inside.

Ahead of him, David sauntered through a tiled entryway, then down a hall and up a musty flight of stairs. Nick trailed him, but the guy didn't glance back. Apparently, he had the situational awareness of a turtle.

Halfway down a bland hallway, David stopped at an unassuming door. His key grated in the lock, prompting Nick to up his pace. Once again, he caught the door just before it shut. He pushed it open and stood on the threshold.

David paused and turned. He scanned Nick up and down, blinking with those too-big eyes. "Uh, hi. Do I know you?"

A whisper of sympathy ghosted across Nick's mind. He hadn't taken off his beanie or oversized jacket since Indiana, considering the heater in the truck barely worked, and he knew how he must look. Any sane person would assume this was a break-in. Worst-case scenario, David had a gun and would go for it.

Nick primed every muscle. If this guy was armed, he'd have to lunge before—

"I think you have the wrong apartment." David gave a puzzled frown. "Or are you lost? Do you need help?"

Nick paused. Weren't New Yorkers supposed to be rude? Or cautious, at least? Had this guy missed the memo? "I'm not lost. You're David Ballard, right?"

David's frown deepened. "Yeah. What's this about?"

"A . . . friend of mine. Aubrey MacLean."

The guy froze. A complicated procession of emotions marched across his face before his features crumpled. "Oh, thank god."

"Thank . . . Wait, what?"

"I've been hoping she'd get in touch." David pulled the door open wider. "I haven't known how to reach her. Anyway, you should probably come in."

Nick glanced around the hallway. Had he fallen asleep in the truck? Was he dreaming? Could be, except nothing struck him as out of place—tatty brown carpet stretched in both directions, lit by a harsh fluorescent glare.

He cleared his throat. "Uh, sure."

David nodded and led Nick inside, to a compact kitchen with cheery yellow linoleum, where he rifled through an aged refrigerator. "Do you want a beer? Maybe some orange juice?"

Nick took his bearings, searching for hidden cameras peeking from the light fixtures. Maybe this was like one of those reality TV shows where some unsuspecting bystander got pranked.

But also, he was pretty damn thirsty, now that he thought about it. "Yeah, man. Orange juice sounds good. Thanks."

David poured two glasses and pulled out chairs from a nearby bistro table. Nick sat and sipped. The juice was the pulpy kind that left spongy bits in his mouth. His favorite.

But also, what the fuck?

"So Aubrey sent you?" David began. Up close, his saintly aura took on a hint of the bovine.

"Um." Nick sipped again, mostly to distract from the fact that he had no intention of answering that question. "I'm just going to cut to the chase, okay? Because I didn't come to ask you to admit to stealing her project."

"Oh. You . . . didn't?" David's shoulders drooped. He looked, of all things, crestfallen.

"No. I came to *tell* you that's what's you're going to do. I mean, thanks for the orange juice. I love this stuff, with all the little pieces in it. But I'm not leaving until you email your boss and tell her—or him, I guess—what really happened. I'm going to stand behind you and watch. And you'll make sure Aubrey gets credit for what she built. Because you sure as hell don't deserve to benefit from all her hard work."

David's lower lip wobbled.

Nick stared, equal parts horrified and fascinated. "We clear?"

David fiddled with his juice, then lost the battle with his trembling chin and burst into tears. He was an ugly crier, the kind that got blotchy in seconds. Nick set down his glass, nonplussed.

"Sorry." David covered his face with his hands. "It's just been so hard. Oh my god, I can't tell you how hard it's been. I didn't really think it through, you know? And now I've been living in a nightmare."

Nick glanced around for a napkin. The guy was dribbling mucus. "Is that so."

"Yeah." David peeked up through his fingers. "People keep asking me about the program, how does it work, how did I come up with this line of code, when will it be ready to go live, it's endless. And I don't know! I can see how Aubrey built it, mostly, but I don't get how she put all the pieces together."

"Uh-huh."

"That's just never been my strong point, you know? I'm never the guy with the *ideas*. That was her. And I just got tired of it. Being in her shadow. You can understand that, right?"

Nick slitted his eyes. "So you screwed her over because you didn't like that she's smarter than you?"

"Yeah. Er . . . No." David sniffed. "I don't know. I just saw an opportunity and went for it. But it turns out when you do something smart, people expect you to *keep* doing smart things. And I didn't know how much pressure that would be. I haven't been able to sleep. Or eat. I've lost ten pounds in the past month."

Nick jiggled his heels against the stool. He wasn't about to shame a man for crying—sometimes, tears cleansed the soul—but if this asshole wanted sympathy, he could look elsewhere. "I really don't care. I'm just here to make sure Aubrey's reputation is cleared."

David barreled on as if he hadn't heard a word. "It's been awful for me. Terrible. One challenge after another. First, my boss wanted me to do a presentation to the whole department about how I brought the idea to life. Then he upped my workload, said I was capable of more. And now the company's trying to give me the Innovation Cup. The Cup! I'm supposed to give a *speech*."

Nick quirked a brow. "A speech?"

"Yeah, Osos does this big company gala every year, for Christmas, you know? They give an award to whichever employee goes 'above and beyond.' I always thought I should win, but not if I have to make a speech about something I didn't actually do. It's giving me nightmares. I keep having this dream where my name gets called, but when I go onstage, everyone's laughing. Then I look down and realize I'm naked. And I just . . . I need Aubrey to come back. I need for this all to stop."

Nick looked at him, deadpan. "Wow. Sounds tough."

"Really?" David swiped at puffy red eyes. "You get it?"

"No, asshole. I don't."

That quieted David, finally. He wiped his nose. "But . . . you can understand why I did it, can't you? Or do you just think I'm a horrible person?"

Nick drained the last of his juice. "To be honest, yeah. That last one. But where's your computer? You have an email to write."

Nick hovered by David's shoulder as he typed. Now that the adrenaline rush of his arrival had worn off, the clack of keys grated on him, each staccato tick another nail in the coffin that held his hopes of ever touching Aubrey again.

He jammed his hands into his pockets. Think about something else. Anything else.

David paused, then pecked out a couple more words. Nick leaned in, scanning the text.

I understand my actions have effected Aubrey MacLean in an extremely unfortunate manner . . .

He jabbed a finger at the screen. "No, it's *affected*. With an *a*."

David squinted. "What? Where?"

"Here." Nick pointed again.

"Oh. Are you sure? Does it actually matter?"

Nick grumbled. "Of course it matters. *Affected* and *effected* are two completely different words. Just because they sound the same doesn't mean they have identical meanings. And if you want people to take you seriously, you should pay attention to stuff like this. Say what you mean. Mean what you say. Spell it right while you're at it."

David hunkered in his chair. "Fine," he muttered, but dutifully backed up the cursor and corrected the mistake.

Nick read over the final version and fixed four more typos, but at least he agreed with David's wording. It was almost like the guy had been cooking up this letter for a while.

Still, when it came time to send, they both stared at the mouse, awaiting the other's move.

Nick swallowed. Once this email reached its destination, Aubrey would have the option to disappear from his life. Forever.

But . . . she'd also be happy.

He reached for the mouse.

"Are you sure?" David whimpered.

Nick clicked Send. Simple. As easy as cutting his own rope so he wouldn't drag his climbing partner off the cliff with him. Done.

And to be extra sure, he printed out a copy and folded it into his pocket. Just in case.

David started crying again. A grim satisfaction settled in Nick's bones, imbuing his steps with steely weight as he made for the door.

"Hey." David sniffled behind him.

Nick turned. "Yeah?"

"Are you leaving already? Do you want some more juice, maybe?"

He narrowed his eyes. *Were* there cameras in the walls, recording this absurdity for posterity? "No, thanks."

"Who are you, anyway? Are you like, her boyfriend?"

His stomach shrank to a pinpoint. "No. Definitely not."

"Okay. But . . . you'll tell her I did the right thing, won't you?"

Jesus, did this bag of dicks want credit? "I think she'll hear about it eventually, whether I tell her or not."

"Oh. Yeah, you're probably right." David clutched his knees. "But Osos . . . they're going to fire me, aren't they?"

"I really hope so." Nick sailed through the door and let it slam shut behind him, then hurried down the hall, trying to escape David's question. It insisted on bouncing around in his skull, anyway, a mockery. *Are you her boyfriend?*

Not anymore, but he would forever cherish the seven

months in which he'd worn that title. In which Aubrey had bettered his existence.

But now their hourglass had run out. The timer had ticked over to zero.

He'd just made sure of it himself.

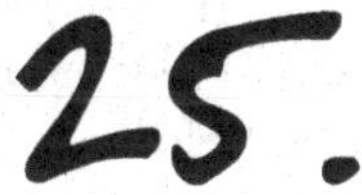

25.

Seventeen years ago

AUBREY HAD NEVER lied to her father before.

She'd misdirected, yes. Arranged the facts to suit her needs. She'd also omitted truths, like the fact that her boyfriend had been sharing her bed for half a year. But she'd never deliberately lied to her father until the morning of their impromptu vacation.

She sat at the breakfast table, gazing dully at a picture of the cabin he'd booked for the upcoming week of "rethinking her future." The rental was an hour and a half away, on the shores of Lake Holiday, and, according to the information booklet, had no phone service. Aubrey would be off the grid for a week, with no way to reach Nick.

Which had undoubtedly been her father's intention.

She quashed a sigh and set the pamphlet aside. Her mother was out in the driveway, packing the car, so she needed to do this now. Easier to lie to one of them than both.

"So . . . here's the thing." She pushed her waffles around on her plate. "I can't take today off work. I talked to Renee this morning, and she said I'll have to come in."

Her dad barked a laugh. "Nice try. But you're coming. No ifs, ands, or buts."

"I know, Dad." She made a face. "I'm not saying I can't go, just that I can't go *right now.* Renee found coverage for my other shifts, but today's my responsibility."

Responsibility. That seemed like a good word to toss in.

He stabbed at his waffle. "No."

Aubrey ground her molars together. "But they'll fire me if I don't show up."

"Then they'll fire you. You don't need that job anymore, anyway. You're leaving for New York in three weeks."

A silent scream sounded in her head. *No, I'm not.*

No use rehashing that now, though. She tried out a smile that could probably cut someone, if she wasn't careful. "Come on. It's my first job. It's important to me to be honorably discharged."

He grunted. "It's not the military."

"No, but it's still my name on the line. My integrity." Integrity. Responsibility. God, she was really digging deep.

He lowered his silverware and surveyed her.

She squeezed her fork until her fingers ached, shunting all her frustration into the metal. "Look. You and Mom can go up today and get everything ready. I have to work until eight tonight, but I'll drive out to the cabin first thing in the morning."

His eyes narrowed. "Are you trying to buy an extra night to go see that boy?"

Heat licked at the base of her throat. *That boy.* As if he didn't know Nick's name. "No. I'll call him and tell him I'm leaving, but I won't see him if you don't want me to."

"I don't. Not until you've had time to think."

"Okay." Aubrey forced her grip to loosen and reached out with an upturned hand. "Then I'll come straight home after work. I'll be in bed by nine tonight, and I'll head to the cabin the second I wake up. You have my word. I just don't want to get fired. I'd rather wrap things up on my terms. All right?"

The seconds stretched. Calculation flashed in his eyes.

Aubrey held her breath. She'd banked eighteen years of trustworthiness, apparently in preparation for this single moment. She prayed it would be enough to tip the tally in her favor.

Her father finally sighed and took her hand, his grip dwarfing hers. "All right. But you'd better be there before ten tomorrow. And you'd better look rested."

Her heart kicked. She smothered the jolt with a tight smile. "Okay. Thanks."

He squeezed. "Someday, you'll look back on all this and thank me."

She didn't dare push her luck by responding, and instead polished off her waffles and went to change into her work clothes. She waved goodbye to her parents, got in her car, and headed for the bowling alley, glancing at the sky the whole time. In a surprising display of cooperation, the weather had delivered an incoming front of leaden clouds.

Aubrey did her best to will rain into existence. *Heavy* rain. The kind she could hide away from and build a fire against, even in July.

At the bowling alley, she parked and went inside. Renee, the manager, raised an eyebrow at Aubrey's khakis and Henderson Lanes polo.

"What're you doing here? I already gave your shift to Angelique. I thought you were going out of town."

"Yeah, I am." Aubrey flashed a lopsided smile. "But if my dad calls here looking for me today, I'm working too hard to come to the phone. All right?"

Renee snorted and snapped her bubble gum. She might be the manager, but she was only twenty and could thus be counted on. "So it's like that?"

"Yeah. It's definitely like that. And . . . one more thing. Can I use the phone?"

"Go for it." Renee pointed to the office behind the counter.

"Thanks." Aubrey shut herself inside the cramped room and dialed the number for the steel mill. She'd memorized it the day Nick had started work, but hadn't had cause to use it yet.

A foreman answered, then issued a gruff harrumph when she asked for Nick. "Is this important?"

"Very."

"Fine," he said. "But it'll be a minute. And don't make a habit of calling here when he's working."

"Right. I understand. Thank you."

Another grunt. Staticky silence swished on the line for what Aubrey gauged as half a lifetime. Then came rustling, and a breathless "Hello?"

"Hey." She smiled into the receiver. God, just the timbre of his voice could soothe her like nothing else. "It's me."

"Hey." His tone softened. "Are you okay? What happened yesterday?"

"Nothing good. My dad's not happy with me. Mostly because he doesn't think I should be deferring."

"You told him?" Nick groaned. "On top of everything else?"

"I kind of had to. And now he's taking me on vacation for a week to 'consider my future.' He thinks he's going to change my mind."

Nick sucked in a breath.

"Don't worry," she rushed out. "He won't. All this week will do is convince him how serious I am. The point is, he and my mom are leaving this morning, but I bought myself another day. I was hoping you could come over later. We'd have the house to ourselves."

Silence.

Bubbles fizzed in her stomach. "I thought . . . maybe it could be tonight."

More silence, unrolling before her like an endless white carpet. She squeezed the receiver so hard her palm ached. "Nick? Are you there?"

"Yeah." His voice dropped an octave. "I'm here. But . . . are you sure?"

"Yes. Absolutely."

"Okay. Then . . . me, too. I'll be there as soon as I can."

Oh, thank god. She dropped into a hard, hurried whisper. "I love you."

"I love you, too. So fucking much."

She clicked off without saying more, wanting those words resounding in her ears instead of a goodbye. Before leaving the office, she smoothed down her polo, but Renee still gave her a quizzical look when she emerged.

"What is *up* with you, girl?"

Aubrey raised her eyebrows. "What do you mean?"

"You look . . . I don't know. Weird. Like you have a fever."

"Huh." Aubrey ran a hand across her forehead. "Yeah, I do feel a little off. Maybe it's best that I won't be around you guys for a while."

"Ugh. Do *not* get me sick." Renee backed away and cast a pointed look toward the door. "Go on, get outta here. And feel better."

"Don't worry, I'm about to." Aubrey laughed at herself the moment she got outside.

As she climbed into the car, her smile stretched even wider. In the few minutes she'd been inside, the sky had gone from brooding to downright angry.

Maybe she shouldn't have derived so much encouragement from that. She had one hell of a fight with her dad looming on the horizon, and life would undoubtedly throw more curveballs before she and Nick made it to New York.

But right now, none of that mattered. She cared about nothing beyond tonight.

Tonight belonged to them, and they would make it perfect.

By the time Aubrey got home, the house was empty.

A weight slid from her shoulders as she went inside, stripped off her work clothes, and proceeded to take the longest shower of her life. She scrubbed until everything turned pink and tingly, then shaved—twice—and worked as much moisturizer into her skin as it would absorb. She wanted to be soft tonight. Soft and clean and warm and willing.

A flutter shot through her stomach. She waited for it to pass, then upended her underwear drawer onto her bed and picked through the contents, settling on a matched set in white lace. She topped off the choice with jean shorts and a cleavage-baring white tank top.

Might as well give Nick a preview. Lure him in so she could do debauched, heavenly things to him the moment he got close.

In the kitchen, she slapped together a lunch. Afterward, a search of the hall closet yielded a few faux fur throws, which she spread in front of the fireplace. Then she waited. And waited. She contemplated going to the pharmacy for protection, but after thinking over her cycle, she calculated the chances as essentially zero. Besides, she didn't want anything between them tonight. Just him and her and the first of many beautiful experiences together.

At four, the heavens opened. Rain battered the house, its drumbeat roar barreling down every hallway. Aubrey perched on the chesterfield in the living room, too wound-up to relax, too weak-kneed to pace. Nick was probably leaving the mill right now, but he'd still have to walk the two and a half miles to her house.

Really, she should go pick him up, but venturing outside now would mean squandering the hair and makeup she'd labored over for the better part of an hour. Not only that, she didn't trust herself to drive, not with the way each heartbeat exploded atop the next like a chain of fireworks popping off.

Very soon, she'd belong to Nick in every sense of the word. In a way no one could ever take from her, no matter how many vacations they dragged her on.

A knock sounded. Aubrey jerked a glance at the mantel clock. Four fifteen. No way he'd gotten here that fast.

Frowning, she went the door. To her shock, Nick stood on the stoop, his thin chest heaving, one hand propped against the doorframe. Rainwater coursed from his curls. The look he gave her scorched a hole right through the screen.

Aubrey pressed a hand to her breastbone, trying to ease the flurry underneath. "Oh my god. How'd you get here so fast? Did you get off early?"

"No. Same time as usual. I ran."

She gaped. "You got here in fifteen minutes? On *foot*?"

A wry smile claimed his mouth—the one he reserved only for her. "Turns out I'm really fucking fast when I want to be."

The thrum of her pulse swelled to join the storm.

Nick pushed his hair out of his eyes. "And look. You asked for rain. You got your wish."

"Not quite yet," she breathed.

That earned her a grin. He opened the screen and stepped inside, all smoldering eyes and wet dark curls and glistening skin.

Her heart cracked down the middle and sighed a single word. *Mine.*

Nick reached for her, molding his hands to the curves of her waist and backing her up until her heels hit the wall. Chilled rainwater dripped from him, soaking into her top, cooling her heat-drenched skin.

"So." His face hovered close. "We're doing this in your living room?"

"That was the idea." She pushed the words through a rapidly narrowing airway.

"Mmm. So, we've got rain. Did you build a fire, too?"

"No. I don't know how. Do you?"

He smirked. "Like any good Boy Scout."

"You're not a Boy Scout."

"Nah. I get the sense that's not what you're looking for right now, anyway."

Her pulse shortened. "Well, I delivered on the weather. The fire's your job."

"Among other things," he rasped, and kissed her.

Aubrey lost time after that. Her world shrank to him, to the way he brought every aching, needy part of her to life. She existed in the liminal space between the places he touched and the places he had yet to discover. Nothing else mattered.

They progressed down the hall one foot at a time. Her hands roved over him, her fingertips coming awake against the abrasive wetness of his shirt. She threaded her fingers through his hair and kissed him until she forgot what it felt like not to.

In the living room, Nick pinned her to one piece of furniture after another as they consumed each other's mouths. Somehow, his shirt ended up on the floor, then his pants. Had she done that? She hoped so. She held him at arm's length and drank in the acres of unblemished skin, the delicate press of bone against flesh, the twin lines that narrowed into the waistband of his boxers.

Dear god, he stole her breath. Her sanity. Especially when he had that *look*, open and naked and ravenous.

They finally made it to the fireplace. Nick broke away long enough to get a blaze going, though Aubrey couldn't say how he did it. Time spun by in a delirious whirl. She bore the weight of herself like never before. There was so very *much* of her inside her own skin, so much everything, so much love and longing she could hardly contain it all.

When the flames gained a foothold, Nick laid her on the furs with heartbreaking tenderness. He kissed his way down her body, alternating featherlight touches with hungry ones. He paused at her belly button, his thumbs hooked beneath the hem of her tank top, a question in his eyes.

She gazed down her cheeks and nodded. "Take it off. Take it all off."

His lashes swept low as he bent to his task. He arced his tongue along every curve and peeled her clothes off. He chased each unveiling with trailed kisses and the skitter of heated breath.

Aubrey trembled. He stripped her bare and acquainted himself with every inch of her. It felt incredible, and also exquisitely, painfully vulnerable, in a way that made her understand she would never be the kind of person to do this with someone she'd just met.

Tremors gripped her in earnest as Nick climbed back up and met her nose to nose. He worked his boxers down and off and settled between her thighs. One hand cupped her jaw, reassuring her with the steady press of his fingers.

"You're shaking," he said.

Aubrey hauled in a breath. She'd meant to reciprocate—to touch him everywhere, to explore *him* with her mouth, to lay him on his back and do everything she could to please him. Not the other way around.

Yet the significance of what was happening pinioned her to the blankets, made her legs ease wider and curl around his hips. Her nerves rattled more than she'd realized they could, but something deeper moved beneath, some elemental need to give herself up. To yield. To submit to him in every way possible.

"I'm nervous," she said. "But I want you."

"Me, too."

"Which one?"

"Both," he said.

She took his measure. He didn't *look* nervous, with his open gaze, the firelight twinning in his eyes. She had no idea how much time had passed, but either it had grown dark outside or the storm had taken the light, because shadows swirled around them. That, and the heat of the fire, added to the burn where his skin met hers. She swore someone had doused her in gasoline and tossed a lit match.

He trailed a finger down her side, then placed a gentle kiss against her throat. "Just tell me what you want."

You. The word joined itself to each beat of her heart.

He shifted his hips. He was so close. He was *right* there. Just another inch, and—

"You're even more beautiful than I imagined," he said. "And if this is as far as we go, it's still more than enough for me."

His night-sky gaze held her in thrall. Aubrey focused on that wide-open expanse, the one she called home.

The world tipped. She fell, upward and inward, into warm, welcoming depths. She wanted to stay there forever. "Do it."

He searched her eyes. "You're sure?"

"Yes," she whimpered. "Please."

"All right." He reached down.

She braced.

"I love you," he said, and pushed.

Reality condensed to crystalline perfection. He sank into her along with his words, and in exactly the same way—slow and deep and binding.

It didn't hurt. That surprised her. Every TV show she'd ever seen had promised pain, but when Nick joined himself to her, her body sang out a high, clear note. She melted, melding with fire and rain and darkness.

Some of that transformation must have shown in her expression, because Nick went still. His fingertips found her face again. "Are you okay?"

"Yes." She inched her legs wider.

"Does it hurt?"

"No. It feels like . . . God, I don't know what it feels like, but you should definitely keep going."

He did, hesitant at first, then surer, with his lashes touching his cheeks and the guttural syllables of her name in his mouth. Time washed over her in waves. She had never felt so full, so *absolute.* And yet her soul seemed to be billowing out from her body, a luscious unstitching of herself she had no desire to fight.

Television did get one part right, though. She didn't orgasm. But Nick did, and she found she liked it better that way, because something deeper than pleasure claimed her in the moment when his breath shortened and the tendons in his neck raveled tight. A mangled curse slid off his tongue as he buried his face in her shoulder.

Her fingers pressed indents into his back as he went rigid against her. A dizzy whirl of pride claimed her. God, look at what they'd done together. Look at what their bodies had created.

She bottled up the moment, storing it on a high shelf in her mind.

Nick gave one last shudder and went slack, surprisingly heavy once he became dead weight. "Holy shit," he murmured. "Holy shit, that was . . . I don't even know."

She ran her nails lightly along his back, up and down.

He lifted his head. Shots of color dusted his cheeks. "Sorry. I couldn't hold back. I'm an asshole."

She sighed, small and contented. "No. That was . . . perfect. That was exactly what I wanted."

"You didn't come."

"But *you* did. And I wanted that more. I wanted to be the reason for you feeling that way."

When she tugged at him, he pressed a kiss to her lips, hard and sincere. "Do you want me to keep going? With my fingers? My tongue? Whatever you want, just tell me."

She hugged him, enamored with the feeling of having him tucked inside her, still. What magic. Like a pact. "No. This was what I wanted. Exactly this."

He sighed. "You're too fucking perfect, you know that?"

"*We're* perfect. Together."

They lay like that a long time. Once they'd cleaned up and tugged their underwear back on, Nick stretched on his side and nestled her backside against his front, propping himself on an elbow to suckle at her neck.

Aubrey pillowed her head on one arm and stared into the dwindling flames. A moan slipped free every time he hit a sensitive spot.

"This whole setup was evil-genius-level clever," he murmured.

"Evil genius? How?"

"You just went and got me hopelessly addicted to you, right before leaving for a week. I won't be able to think of anything else the whole time you're gone."

She smirked and rolled onto her back. "You were hopelessly addicted to me already."

He scoffed. "That's . . . Well, that's true, actually."

She lay there and drank him in. "Thank you. For this. It was . . . everything."

He dropped his eyes. "I really am sorry. Next time will be better for you."

"Hey. Don't say that. I love you. Turns out I also love having sex with you. I couldn't have asked for a more incredible first time than that."

Maybe some measure of her sincerity filtered past his embarrassment, because when she touched his cheek, he tilted his face into her hand and kissed her palm. "I didn't know this amount of happiness existed. I really didn't. But next time'll still be better. I'll make sure of it."

"In that case, I might actually pass out."

He laughed. "God, I'm going to miss you. It'll be like someone's carved a hole into me while you're gone."

"Me, too."

His smile wavered, tilting toward sad. "But I wanted to say . . . I think your dad has a point, Aubs. You *should* take this week to think. Make sure you really want to defer. It's a big decision. I wouldn't blame you if you changed your mind."

She tensed. She hated it when he talked like this. "Don't do that."

"Do what?"

"Doubt yourself. Doubt us."

"I'm just being realistic."

"Well, me too. And my reality is that I want everything. Call me selfish, but I'm not settling for anything less."

He swallowed, long and slow. The reflection of the dying fire wavered in his eyes. "Okay. Then I'll be here, waiting."

"You won't change your mind, either?"

"I won't change my mind ever," he said, his voice thick.

"Good." She kissed him. "That reminds me, actually. I have a letter for you."

Aubrey kept two-thirds of her promise to her father. Part one: she fell asleep by nine, albeit with Nick wrapped around her like a blanket. He didn't say much after she gave him the letter, just read the words several times with the intensity of a hawk bearing down on a mouse. Then he looked up at her, wonderstruck, and pulled her into a whole-body hug that lasted into sleep. Part two: she pulled into the cabin's driveway well before ten the next morning, fully rested and more bright-eyed than ever.

Aubrey waltzed right into the cabin without knocking. She felt . . . new. Freshly forged.

Her dad sat in an easy chair, reading the newspaper. His bushy eyebrows hiked to his hairline. "Morning. You're here early."

Aubrey shrugged off his obvious surprise. Nothing could touch her today. Except perhaps the aches in places she'd never had them before, and the fact that this marked one day down, six to go.

To her relief, the week passed easily enough. She moseyed around the shores of the lake, working on her tan and breathlessly reliving every moment of her night with Nick.

God, if it got any better than that, she really would pass out, next time.

In the evenings, she played cards with her parents and stayed up late with her father, who surprised her on the last night by offering her a beer. Her first. Maybe he had ulterior motives, but she chose to see it as a gesture of camaraderie. Like he'd acknowledged her as a full-fledged adult. An equal.

Still, as they lounged in the living room's worn leather armchairs, their voices lowered so as not to wake her mother, the conversation finally—inevitably—turned to New York.

Aubrey sipped, trying not to wrinkle her nose at the beer's sourness, and endured her father's questions. She wrapped her responses in velvet, but nothing could soften the steel at the center.

Yes, Dad, I'm sure. No, Dad, I'm not leaving Henderson yet. Yes, I love Nick. Yes, I'm still going to NYU. Just not this year.

Her father finally gave up and went to bed, shaking his head. Aubrey stayed up to polish off the beer, wishing she had access to a phone. She wanted to tell Nick about the way the alcohol made her thoughts shimmer at the edges. Had he ever been tipsy before? What was he even doing right now? Not suffering through too much contact with his father, she hoped. Most likely, he was lying in bed, dreaming about her.

In the morning, Aubrey woke in a cold sweat. Her head pounded. Her stomach heaved like a rollicking sea. And someone had apparently taken a hammer to her bones overnight.

She staggered into the kitchen to find her parents leaning over the breakfast table, conferring in low tones. They jerked apart at her entrance.

Aubrey didn't stop to wonder why. She just lurched across the room, leaned over the sink, and puked her guts out.

Chairs clattered. Within moments, her mother had her hair pulled back and a soothing hand traveling up and down her back. "Are you okay?"

Aubrey finished up and spat bile into the sink, clinging to the lip in an effort to keep her legs from giving out. "I don't know. I think I'm hungover. I mean, is this what a hangover's like? Can you even *be* hungover from one beer?"

"I don't think so." Her mother's hand found her forehead. "Oh, honey, you're burning up. No, this is something else. You look like you have the flu."

Aubrey swayed. Her whole body had gone into revolt. "In July?"

"It happens." Her mother spoke with the stoic certainty of a nurse with twenty years' experience behind her. "Come on, let's get you back to bed."

Aubrey did, in fact, have the flu. A fact she only admitted to herself once she'd spent the entire day bed-ridden and aching, lashed by fever and wondering what she possibly could have done to invite such punishment.

Her mother stayed at the cabin with her. After calling to extend the rental, her father headed back to Henderson, having already used his vacation days. Aubrey grasped at his hand before he left, begging from amid the sweat-dampened sheets. "Nick will come looking for me. You'll tell him I'm here, right? That I'm coming back soon?"

"Oh, sweetheart." He swept a damp tendril away from her forehead. There was something in the way he looked at her. Something vast and pointed and frightening.

Probably just the fever spiking again. An hour ago, Aubrey had watched a swarm of black butterflies amass on the ceiling.

"I'll take care of it," he said.

"You promise?"

"I promise."

Her relief lasted only moments before misery wiped her mind clean of anything but the sickness.

Aubrey barely slept. For eight days, she thrashed from one contorted position to another, racked by heat and a cough so deep it tore at her lungs.

The world continued, somehow. Her mother brought soup and crackers that went ignored, and folded-up ice-water washcloths that didn't. When the fever finally relinquished its grip, Aubrey slept for sixteen hours straight, then woke on a bright, sun-soaked Thursday morning with a miraculously clear head. Grit clogged her eyes and her chest ached, but the storm inside her had subsided.

She wriggled out of the sweat-soured sheets and stumbled to the kitchen. A pan of scrambled eggs sat on the stove. Beside the coiled burner, a platter offered triangles of toast slathered in butter. She piled a plate high and scarfed enough food to make her wasted stomach press against the elastic waistband of her pajama shorts. When she looked up, her mother leaned against the doorway, fondness in her eyes.

"You survived."

"Barely," Aubrey croaked.

"Are you ready to go home?"

"God, yes." She hadn't seen Nick in over two weeks. It felt like a lifetime. "Let's get the hell out of here."

Her mother drove. On the way, Aubrey dozed, and the extra sleep restored her even further. When Henderson came into view, she peered past her smiling reflection to the hulking steel mill that would watch over her for another year.

She'd run the gauntlet. Descended to hell, fought through, and clawed her way back. Now her father had no choice but to take her decision at face value. Because she would not, under any circumstances, allow life to come between her and Nick Thacker.

Of course, Aubrey had no way to know, then, that it already had.

26.

ON SATURDAY NIGHT, Nick took Jackson to see *Moulin Rouge.*

He didn't expect much. He'd simply Googled *Broadway singing and dancing,* then bought tickets to the first show available, even though the price had made him choke. Thank god Jackson was paying, because when they walked into the theater, he'd resigned himself to spending the next three hours taking the most expensive nap of his life. But when the lights went down and the glitz and glamor flowered onstage, his spine straightened.

Then everyone started singing.

Within minutes, Nick realized he'd chosen a love story. And not just any love story. One that sucker-punched him right in the gut.

Up onstage, Satine and Christian fell hopelessly in love. The two couldn't live without each other, yet circumstances kept tearing them apart, and it was like watching his own life play out in song.

Well, not quite—Aubrey could definitely live without him. But holy shit, did he know how Christian felt, especially at the end, when Satine succumbed to her illness and left him heartbroken and alone, forever longing for something he could never have again.

When the lights went up, Nick cleared his throat a half dozen times. He fiddled with the zipper on his jacket. Scrubbed at his hair. Sniffed hard enough to suck his eyeballs dry. Only then did he risk a look at Jackson.

And promptly breathed a mile-long sigh of relief.

Tears streaked Jackson's dark cheeks. He'd locked his fingers around his armrests and stared at the now-quiet stage. All around, women in evening dresses and men in suit coats filtered out of the theater.

Nick gave his friend a shoulder bump. "Hey. You okay?"

"Yeah, man. That was just . . . Wow. That was something."

"Yeah." Nick wished he didn't sound so hoarse. "It really was."

"What I wouldn't give to find *my* Satine." Jackson peeled his hands from the seat and pulled a handkerchief from his pocket. He blew, loud and unrepentant.

"Hey, what do you mean? Aren't you dating that woman from the bakery? The one who gives you those orange-cranberry muffins every morning? Giselle?"

"Nah," Jackson said thickly. "She ghosted me. After five *really* good dates. I even went into the bakery last week, asked why she'd stopped answering the phone. She said she'd gotten back with her ex-boyfriend. She made it awkward, too. Like she thought it was weird I was even in there. I guess I have to find a new breakfast place now."

"Shit, that sucks." Nick slumped in his seat. "Those muffins were fucking amazing."

Jackson gave a wet laugh. "That's all you've got?"

"Well. What do you want me to say? The muffins sound like a bigger loss than the girl."

"Yeah, maybe." Jackson sighed. He continued to study the drawn curtains, like maybe Satine would come bursting back through and throw herself into his arms. "I just wish I knew what it felt like to be that sure of someone, you know? Even if my girl left me at the end, it'd have to be better than all these . . . dead ends. I mean, what's that thing people say? It's better to have loved and lost than to never have loved at all? Who was that, Shakespeare?"

"Alfred Lord Tennyson." Nick took a long breath. "But he didn't know what he was talking about, trust me. It's hard enough to find someone who gets you. But to find her and *then* lose her? It's some next-level, you-aren't-coming-back-from-this kinda shit. I wouldn't wish it on anyone. It'd be better not to know. Not to understand what's missing."

Jackson swiveled. The overhead light careened off the tear-tracks on his cheeks. "That was you and Aubrey, then? Like those two up there?"

"Uh . . . yeah." Nick wished he hadn't invited the question. But whatever. No point in lying. "Pretty much exactly that. At least for me."

Jackson shook his head. He opened his mouth, then closed it, but apparently couldn't hold back. "You ever wonder if you should move out? Move *here*?"

Nick tugged at the hem of his jacket. "Trick question. I've got Paige."

"She'd understand."

"No, man. She's sixteen. It's not an option. I promised her I wasn't going anywhere, and I'm not a liar. I'm not my dad."

Jackson heaved another sigh. "Yeah, okay. I guess I don't know how that works, really."

Nick squashed down the urge to sit here matching his buddy tear for tear. "Look, all I'm saying is you're in a better situation than you realize. Because people *also* say ignorance is bliss. And there's a reason for that."

Jackson made a pass over his face with the hankie, then wadded it up and pocketed it. "Yeah," he grunted. "Maybe."

Neither of them made any move to get up. Muted chatter drifted through the open doors, but the theater yawned around them, cavernous. Nick's mind offered up an image of one of those Russian nesting dolls. An empty shell inside an empty shell.

Jackson broke the quiet with a loud sniff. "Hey, I think our hotel has a gym. What do you say we go beat the crap out of each other?"

Nick stood up, rolling his shoulders so hard his neck cracked. "Yep. Good idea. Let's definitely go do that."

On Sunday morning, Jackson insisted on driving, since he hadn't on the way up. Nick didn't argue. He just settled on the passenger side, wishing for a warmer jacket. Maybe he'd finally fix the heater once he got home.

Not that he wanted to spend all night working on the truck. But he had a burning desire to avoid Tansy, who probably thought he'd spent the past two days having another imaginary sex marathon and would have no qualms about asking.

For whatever reason, Nick didn't want to tell her what he'd really done. Aubrey would never know, either, but in his mind, it linked him to her in some intimate way, and he wanted to keep that for himself. He wanted just one damn piece of her that would belong to him alone.

He hunkered in his seat. Stupid, pointless thoughts. It was done, now. Time to go home and get on with life. It might take a week or two before David's confession worked its way through the proper channels and resulted in an offer of reinstatement, but Aubrey would probably hear from Osos before Thanksgiving.

Miles passed. Jackson started humming some riff from last night, and Nick envied the guy for somehow being a morning person, despite never drinking a drop of coffee. Not to mention the fact that no matter how low Jackson's mood dipped, which didn't happen often, he always bounced back. He was like the pop-up mole from that arcade game with the squeaky plastic hammers.

"I guess someone's feeling better this morning," he grumbled.

"Yeah." Jackson grinned. "It's a brand-new day. I feel great. You?"

"The usual."

"Which means . . . what? Heart's all smashed to bits? You got a rabbit hole in your mind deep enough to spit you out in China?"

Nick rasped a flat laugh. "How'd you know?"

"Come on. How many years have we known each other? It's always the same with you. But I still have hope for you, man. There's always hope."

Nick watched the window. New Jersey rolled by, flat and drab and colorless, which somehow gave him the impression of looking in a mirror.

Hope. Ha. He'd packed up all his hope, bought it a one-way ticket to Antarctica, and shipped it off himself with one click of David's email. He'd do it again, too. "Easy for you to say. You still have a shot of finding your Satine."

"I don't mean there's hope with Aubrey. I just mean that someday, you're going to stop holding back and actually go out and do something for yourself."

"What're you talking about? I do stuff for myself all the time."

Jackson ejected a breath that edged on laughter. "Oh yeah? Like what?"

"Like . . . I don't know. Going to the gym. Like . . ." *Writing letters*, Nick almost said, then swerved before he could partake in that particular car crash of repressed feeling. ". . . doing this volunteer thing with Paige. Providing for my family. All kinds of stuff."

"I hate to break it to you, man, but those aren't things you do for yourself. And I know you think you've been fighting all your life, but the truth is, you've been *surviving*. Reacting. Making do with what you got, which wasn't much more than a crap dad and an even crappier hand to play."

Nick grunted. "What're you, my therapist?"

"I'm your friend. All I'm saying is, you've never really fought for anything, not really. For your own sake, I mean."

"Bullshit."

Jackson slid him a *come-on* glance. "Name one thing. *One thing* you've actually gone to war for, just because you wanted it."

Nick pulled his brows low. "I don't know. What've *you* gone to war for?"

"Nice." Jackson nodded. "Deflection. But you know what? I'll bite, if only to prove a point. So here it is: I'm going to war for my Satine. The minute we get home, I'm signing up for Tinder, and Bumble, and whatever that other one is where they put you through an algorithm and match you up using math. I'm going to find my queen or die trying."

Nick's heart squeezed at the word *algorithm*. Then again at the word *math*. Jesus, could he be any more pathetic? "I don't think your Satine's on Tinder."

Jackson shook his head. "Your attitude sucks."

"Tell me about it."

"Come on. Look at all this." Jackson swept a hand to indicate the rising sun, which spilled light across the frosty landscape. "It's a new day. Another chance to go out and seize life by the horns."

"You sound like a fortune cookie." Really, Jackson sounded like a young Aubrey, but Nick couldn't bear to say so.

"Insulting me doesn't get you out of answering the question."

His shoulders tightened. "What question?"

"What have you ever fought for, my man?"

Well, fuck. Put so baldly, the question stared Nick in the face. But there had to be an answer. Otherwise, how had he ended up this way?

No, he'd fought, he decided. Sometimes with his fists, sometimes with everything else. He'd had no choice, because life had started him with little, then given him the world and taken it all away again, and he'd battled and bled and come back empty-handed, left with scars and gaping holes where his vital organs had once been. The only reason Jackson believed he hadn't done enough was because every time he'd fought, he'd lost. But he couldn't have acted any differently. Not without sacrificing his daughter or his integrity.

"I'm waiting," Jackson said.

Nick jabbed at his forehead with his fingers. "I don't know. Ask me again when it's not seven in the morning, okay? It's too early for this. And your cheeriness is fucking with my head."

"Good." Jackson readjusted his grip on the wheel. "I'm glad something is."

Nick grumbled out a response even he didn't know the meaning of.

More miles passed. They stopped in Pennsylvania to gas up the truck and get Nick coffee. Once the caffeine hit his bloodstream, he pulled out his phone. He needed to take his mind off that damn Broadway show, and with nine hours to go, he had plenty of time to cook up a letter for MontanaBirder81.

After all, he owed the guy, fair and square.

He leaned his forehead against the icy window and closed his eyes in a search for inspiration. *Go to war*, Jackson had said. Like it was that easy. But for a moment, Nick pretended he was in a position to do exactly that. He drifted back to last Saturday, when Aubrey had touched him again, after all these years, in ways only she ever had. With possessiveness. And in that single, perfect slice outside of time, he'd been hers again.

He opened his eyes. He knew what his letter would say. He just had to get one thing clear.

He typed out a message to John. *Do you love Jane? And if so, do you want her to know?*

The reply came within minutes. *Sure, I do.*

That galvanized him. Words burbled up. He splashed them across the screen, swiping and deleting and rephrasing until his finest work to date took shape. It was a do-or-die, all-cards-on-the-table kind of declaration.

He hit Send, then settled back in his seat. If Jane had liked his earlier letters, which it seemed she had, then somewhere in Montana, very soon, John would be making love to his new woman.

Meanwhile, Nick would be jerking off in the shower. Again.

Hurray.

He started to tuck his phone away, then paused when it rang in his hand. He frowned down at the caller ID. It was Sunday. Why was he getting a call from Paige's biology teacher?

Years ago, he'd saved Juan Gallegos's number after doing some welding work constructing a firepit for the guy's admittedly impressive garden. The pay had netted Nick enough to take Paige and Tansy to the grandiose water park in Indianapolis for a weekend.

But he hadn't spoken to Juan since.

"Hello?" Nick glanced at the dash clock, his frown deepening. It was only eight o'clock in Indiana.

"Hi, is Nick Thacker there?"

"Yeah, this is him. What's up?"

A beat of silence sizzled on the line. "Hi, Mr. Thacker. This is Juan Gallegos, Paige's biology—"

"I know who you are, Juan. Why're you talking to me like we haven't met?"

"Sorry." Juan sounded breathy. Nervous. Nick imagined him

at his breakfast table in full science-teacher regalia, wearing one of those absurd ties he favored, like the bright yellow monstrosity that had *Science Is Fun!* written all over it.

"Uh, normally I wouldn't call a parent in a situation like this, but since it's Paige, and since she's normally such a stellar student, *and* you and I are acquainted, I thought I'd address it personally, without involving the faculty."

Nick's spine snapped straight. "What're you talking about? What 'situation'?"

"Paige hasn't turned in her genetics assignment." Juan's tone made it clear he expected Nick to understand the significance of this. "I gave her a two-day extension, but when she missed that deadline, too, I confronted her. At which point she told me to, and I quote, 'get out of my face.'"

Nick laughed. "No, she didn't."

The line fizzed and popped. As the silence dragged, the smile slid off Nick's face. "Wait, what? Really? Why would she say that? She's never talked back to a teacher in her life. She's never even talked back to *me*."

Jackson jerked a glance at him, one eyebrow raised. Nick gave him a helpless look.

"I don't know," Juan said slowly. "I was hoping you could shed some light, here. Her track record is pristine, so I'm willing to cut her some slack, but I don't appreciate being insulted by my students. And I'll have to fail her for the assignment if she doesn't turn it in. Like I said, I normally wouldn't circumvent the proper channels, but I'm hoping this is all a misunderstanding."

"It must be." Nick breathed heavily into the phone. "And yeah, I'll talk to her. Absolutely. I'm sorry she said that. But there must be an explanation."

"I hope so. She has until the end of the week for the assignment, but after that, I'll have to give her a zero. It's worth a quarter of her grade, so it'll be hard for her to skate through with anything higher than a C-minus."

"Sure, I understand." Nick went through the requisite ritual before hanging up.

A C-minus. Paige had never brought home anything lower than a B-plus, and even then, only two of those.

When he slid his phone back into his jeans, Jackson looked over. "Everything okay? What was that about?"

Nick rubbed absently at his sternum. He hadn't seen much of his daughter since their ill-fated day at Hinkley Farm, when she'd had Megan take her home. Since then, she'd spent the night at Maria's more than once.

Shit. Now that he thought about it, they hadn't had a substantive conversation all week.

"I don't know," he said slowly. "I think I fucked up. I upset Paige the other day, and it sounds like she lashed out at school."

Jackson frowned. "Paige, lashing out? No way. She's the sweetest kid I know."

"Yeah. Usually. But something's gotten to her. And I'm pretty sure it's my fault."

"You're always pretty sure it's your fault."

Nick gave a brittle laugh. "That's 'cause it usually is." He stewed in his thoughts for the next few miles, then abruptly snapped his fingers in Jackson's face.

Jackson jerked the wheel, then corrected. "Jeez, man. You almost sent us into a ditch."

Nick ignored him. "That's it."

"That's what?"

"The thing I'm going to fight for."

Jackson cast him a skeptical glance.

"Whatever's bothering Paige, I'm going to fix it. I'll go to war for *her*. Un-screw up whatever I screwed up. There's your answer. That counts, right?"

Jackson sighed. "I swear. It's like you haven't listened to a word I've said."

Nick shook his head. He had. He *always* listened when Jackson talked, because Jackson never said anything that wasn't worth taking the time to say. The guy stood head and shoulders above most people in that regard. Well, at six foot five, he stood head and shoulders above most people in general, but especially when it came to meaningful insight.

But Nick didn't feel like arguing, so he turned his face to the window and plotted his next moves while Henderson rolled ever closer.

As soon as he got home, he'd find Paige. He'd coax the truth out of her, then do whatever necessary to get her feeling safe again.

Really, he just had to figure out where he'd gone wrong.

27.

On Monday, five days after originally planned, Gallant finally had a letter.

He parked in Aubrey's cul-de-sac, then glanced at the envelope on the passenger seat. Delivering it would change things. Alter his trajectory with Aubrey in a way he wasn't entirely sure he was ready for. And yet, when he'd copied down the lines last night, he'd glimpsed, for the first time, something more than just gooey declarations. He'd sensed something deeper within the words, some tangible force he'd ultimately decided, almost against his will, was bravery.

Nick Thacker had balls. Not just the run-of-the mill kind, but a kamikaze sort of courage that made Gallant wonder whether the guy was one egg short of a dozen, or the type who would keep everyone around him alive in the zombie apocalypse.

Whatever the case, Gallant plucked up the letter and turned it over, wondering whether this whole thing had gone too far.

Not that he didn't want Aubrey. He did. Badly. She embodied everything he craved in a woman, at least when she wasn't playing small-town-country-mouse at that volunteer gig he now regretted suggesting.

Yes, he wanted her sleek elegance on his arm once he moved to New York. Her trim body warming his bed at night. He wanted to cook for her and find out what she tasted like and post so many pictures on social media that everyone in a hundred-mile radius would envy them both.

But he also understood that the letter in his hand had come to him from the far side of a divide. The gulf between the man he knew himself to be and the man who had written these words stretched so wide as to be uncrossable. Not that he wasn't courageous. He was. He would just never be so unrestrained about it. And if Aubrey wanted that, *truly* wanted that, maybe . . . Maybe . . .

He slapped the envelope against the steering wheel, then shut down his half-baked line of thinking and tossed it into a mental trash compactor. Stupid. He'd put in too much effort to turn back now, especially since he'd gotten within spitting distance of closing the deal.

With that sorted, he climbed out and made his way to Aubrey's door. She answered before he even got to the second knock, like she'd been waiting.

"Hi," she said. She'd traced her eyes with some kind of catlike liner. Between that, the purple dress, and the sleek shock of red hair, she looked like a sex goddess. One he wanted to keep up all night.

"Hi." He bit back the instinctive compliment filling his mouth. What would Nick have said? "I . . . missed you. My week was entirely boring without you in it."

Her expression melted into one of delight. "I missed you, too. I'm so glad we're finally getting to do Chicago."

She leaned in for a kiss, surprising him with a bit of tongue. When she pulled back, Gallant smiled. Yes, he could absolutely do this. He could practically taste her eagerness for the next step. With or without the letter.

"Let me just get my coat." She bustled away, her heels clacking on the parquet.

He took the opportunity to step inside and set the envelope on the front hall table. Aubrey returned wearing that elegant, knee-length designer thing he loved so much, then arched an eyebrow at his offering.

"For later." He still had no desire to watch her read Nick's words right in front of him. Especially not *these* words. Let that emotional intensity happen in private.

He offered his arm, then opened the car door for her once outside. The whole time, she watched him with a new focus, one he recognized.

It was the look of a buyer before making an offer.

His blood warmed a degree. He hadn't seen her in over a week, but clearly, something had happened. Some new connection had come together in her mind, and she'd decided—whether consciously or subconsciously—to give him a chance. A real one.

He slid into the driver's seat and gave her his best rakish grin. Already, he couldn't believe he'd ever wavered. Those wide, green cat eyes, that seductive pout, that *dress*—this woman was perfect for him. "Ready? It's a long drive."

She slipped her hand into his and squeezed. "I'm ready."

Aubrey gazed out the window as the Tesla slid between the regal towers of downtown Chicago. Neon reflections streamed across the hood.

The drive had passed pleasantly, and she glanced over to find Gallant smiling, in a way that bore no resemblance to Nick's secret way. It was . . . pleasant. Genial.

She smiled back. He still seemed different in person than in his letters, but she'd decided to simply accept that. What mattered was that those words were in there, simmering. She focused on them now, tying herself to the secrets *behind* the smile. After all, she'd traded away something that had no future for something that did, and she needed to remember the bargain had been worth it.

Gallant raised her hand and kissed it. "What's that look for?"

"Nothing. I'm just glad to be here. With you."

He grinned, administering a dose of sparkling white teeth and vivid eyes. "I'm glad to be here with *you*."

She blushed. Yes, this was good. Normal. Whatever she had with Nick—no, what she'd *had* with Nick—whatever insanity inflamed her whenever he came close, would never leave Henderson. But she would.

At the restaurant, Aubrey gorged on oysters and drank more than she had intended. Probably because Gallant looked more luscious with every additional infusion of chardonnay into her bloodstream—and he'd started off the evening as a solid nine. By the time they canoodled over a shared slice of tiramisu, she could almost believe blue eyes trumped black ones, and that she preferred expensive cologne to the raw burn of a smoking fire.

Gallant leaned in to lick a dollop of custard from her lips. The heat of his mouth zinged into her and pulled her belly tight.

"Don't make me wait so long to see you again," she said. "I was beginning to think you'd forgotten me."

He smiled and played with her fingers over the linen-draped table. "Impossible. I thought of you the whole time. I just barely had a breath away from work."

"Well, I can't blame you for that."

"Which is something I appreciate. All the other women I've dated have hated how much I work. Not you, though."

"No, not me." She gave him a demure smile.

After the meal, they sashayed out of the restaurant with their arms linked. Aubrey leaned into him, though she hadn't drunk so much as to need the support. She just wanted to fill herself with his steady warmth.

They headed for the Magnificent Mile, where they strolled beneath the holiday lights, cocooned in their own laughing, wine-bright bubble. A few sparkling snowflakes drifted from an infinite sky.

"So." Gallant wrapped an arm around her shoulders and anchored her to his side. "Tell me about your week. What did you do, besides miss me?"

She giggled. "Let's see . . . I did a boatload of Pilates. Worked on that project. Oh, and I went and spoke to the high school math club. Nick's daughter invited me. That was nice." No need to mention the weirdness that had followed.

Gallant stiffened. "Nick Thacker's daughter?"

"Yeah. Paige. Have you met her?"

A crinkle formed between his brows. "I've passed her on the street a couple times, I think. How do you even know her?"

The alarm in his tone slowed her steps. "From Hinkley Farm. Megan paired us up. It's been surprisingly nice, getting to know her. She's a sweet kid. Smart, too."

"Huh." He peered down, as if waiting for more.

A frown pulled at her brows, but she had nothing else to tell. Over the weekend, she and Paige had finished up the floats as if the previous day's conversation had never happened. Paige had been cheery, if a few degrees subdued, and had babbled on about math and college admissions and something about newly discovered marshmallow planets.

Which Aubrey had thoroughly enjoyed. Even if Nick's absence had throbbed in her consciousness like a splinter left to fester.

"You haven't talked to *Nick*, though, have you?"

Aubrey disengaged from Gallant's embrace. He'd stopped walking, now. Something in him had gone tense.

"I have," she said slowly. What was he getting at? He certainly wasn't asking whether she'd let Nick push her up against a wall and bite her throat. Which, for some reason, she harbored only mild guilt over. She and Gallant hadn't had the exclusivity conversation yet, and at least she'd tried, with Nick. At least she *knew*. "A few times."

Gallant exhaled through his nose. "And? What'd he say?"

She searched his face. "About?"

"I don't know. How's he doing? What's he, ah, doing for work these days?"

She shook her head. His questions seemed to be driving at something, but she couldn't for the life of her discern what. "He works at the mill. Which you already know."

He gazed at her for a few tense beats. "That's all?"

"Yeah. What're you asking me, exactly?"

He expelled another breath and wrapped his arms around her, tucking her head against his shoulder. "Nothing. Sorry. I just know you two have history. And I don't want this thing between us to end before it's begun."

Ah. That made sense. She steadied herself with the cool musk of his cologne. "You have nothing to worry about."

As Nick had made so abundantly clear the other night.

Nope, not going there. Aubrey shoved the memory into a mental vault and slammed the door. She wanted nothing more than for this pleasant wine-buzz to propel her as far from that evening as she could get.

So she reached up, threaded her arms around Gallant's neck, and kissed him.

He responded with alacrity, his hands finding the small of her back and pulling her in. She sank into the sensation and, even if part of her busied itself keeping that rattling door shut, it was a good kiss. By the time she eased back, her stomach fluttered and Gallant's eyes had darkened to sapphires.

"Let's not talk about Nick anymore," she said.

"Good idea."

They ambled along again, hand in hand. Eventually, they made their way back to the car, and Aubrey's heart lifted when Gallant opened her door. He was, without fail, a gentleman.

As he drove, she memorized the way the dash lights illuminated his features. Outside, pinpricks of white glitter fell, whizzing from the darkness and disappearing again. Inside, the climate control blew hot air, the seat heater glowing against her legs. Aubrey emptied her mind. Nothing existed beyond this sultry bubble but chips of diamond snow and endless black night.

Gallant looked over and met her eyes. Yes, she could get used to looking at that face.

She made a contented sound in her throat.

His lips parted, as if he'd read something in her expression. He reached over to lay a hand on her thigh. Her dress had ridden up over her crossed legs, and his fingers grazed bare skin. The tips edged back and forth, the lightest brush of flesh on flesh, but she recognized the question in it.

Her pulse launched into overdrive. She uncrossed her legs.

Gallant's breathing hitched. He inched his fingers upward, tracing a blazing path along her inner thigh. He slipped beneath her dress, up, up, up, until he brushed against the silk of her panties.

When she held his eyes, his finger ventured beneath the fabric. He quickly found her favorite spot, where he drew slow, exquisite circles.

Her stomach exploded into a flurry of sensation. A broken exhale staggered past her lips. "While you're driving?"

"I can multitask." His tone was low, full of promise. He chased the comment with another swirl of his finger, one that made her clamp down on her bottom lip and lift her gaze toward the sunroof.

He increased his efforts. Aubrey whimpered and squeezed her eyes shut. Which soon proved to be a mistake. His fingers teased a riotous heat to life, but the sensation made its way to her mind in disjointed flashes. There were dark eyes framed by dark lashes. Teeth pressed against her neck. Fire, rushing into her nose, down her throat, incinerating her from the inside out.

Well, fuck.

"Wait," she bit out, and reached down to still Gallant's hand.

He raised an eyebrow and stopped.

The heat he'd kindled floated upward to settle in her cheeks. "That feels amazing, but . . . can we save this for next time, maybe? I'm sorry, I just . . . I don't know. My mind is all over the place tonight."

"Of course. Whatever you want." He cleared his throat, as if trying to strip the coarseness from his voice, and withdrew his hand. He didn't seem angry or disappointed. If anything, he looked heartened, which heartened her, in return.

She smiled. "Thanks."

He chuckled. "Don't thank me. Not until I get the chance to finish."

"I just mean for understanding. And for not being a dick about it."

"I told you I could be patient, and I can."

Something in her chest loosened. Yes, she could definitely get used to this.

They lapsed into soft, casual conversation. When they reached her house, he walked her to the door, where she kissed him with all the unquenched thirst still sloshing around inside her. And if the contact conjured visions of shorn black hair and steel muscle encased in smooth skin, she tried not to dwell on it too much.

Gallant finally broke the kiss. “I’d better go. Before I get carried away.”

She ran a hand down the front of his jacket. “When will I see you again?”

He caught her fingers and kissed the tips. “Thursday evening? We could watch the parade? Drink mulled wine, then go back to my place?”

Her lungs fluttered. His place. For date number five. Which would give her three whole days to exorcise her ghosts and get her head on straight. “I can’t wait.”

He smiled and bade her good-night.

When he’d gone, she went inside and leaned against the door for long minutes, gathering her composure. Gallant’s letter gleamed in the shadows of the hallway, and she plucked it off the table on her way to the living room. It had become tradition to read by firelight, so she kindled a blaze and sat on the chesterfield, the envelope heavy in her hand. This letter weighed more than the others.

She opened it.

As the flames leapt, her blood and breath stilled. She read the pages three times, first in incredulity, then with a relief so profound her lungs ached.

Gallant . . . *loved* her. Not that he’d said so outright, at least not in so many words. No, somehow, he’d found better ones.

Each sentence arrowed into her, a cascade of keys slotting into a series of locks. The last of her hesitation cracked and fell away. She wondered whether people could fall in love in a single moment.

Maybe. Probably. Because if so, she just had.

28.

Nick didn't manage to track down Paige until the day after he returned from New York. When he'd gotten home, she'd been sleeping at Maria's again, so he'd bit back his self-recriminations and spent the night working on his truck, even though he'd remedied the heater problem in twenty minutes with a simple addition of coolant.

Whatever. The truck now ran better than ever, and he'd successfully dodged Tansy's questions.

On Monday evening, Nick dropped into his usual chair at the dinner table, his hair still wet from his post-work, post-gym shower. Tansy nodded a welcome. Paige smiled, though not with her usual enthusiasm.

He studied her covertly. Dark shadows clung beneath her eyes. "Hey, Peanut."

"Hey, Daddy."

"I've barely seen you all week. You okay?"

"Yeah, I'm good." She doodled her fork through her food, then darted a glance at Tansy, who was studiously separating her quinoa from her broccoli—for some reason, she'd never been able to tolerate her food touching.

Not that it mattered right now. Nick got the message. Paige wanted to talk in private.

So he muddled through the meal, trying to keep his mood light. At least . . . as light as it ever got.

Thankfully, Tansy didn't seem to notice the muted atmosphere. When she finished eating, she said, "I'm meeting Betty Klein, over at the salon. She can only do her appointments in the evenings."

"Great." Nick tried to sound casual.

Tansy went to her bedroom to retrieve her work bag. The cords from her many curling irons and straighteners and god-knew-what-else spilled over the sides. She left looking like she was carrying a giant spider under her arm.

The moment the door closed, Nick turned. "Look, if this is about the other day, when your mom and I were talking, I—"

"It's not." Paige's blue eyes flared. "It's really not, Daddy. I mean, that caught me off guard, yeah. But . . . that's not why I've been avoiding you."

He blinked. The sentiment sliced into his gut. "You've been avoiding me?"

"Well . . ." She chewed at her lip.

He sat back. Shit. He'd gotten so knotted up over Aubrey he hadn't even realized. "Aw, hell, kiddo. I'm sorry. I've been a complete asshole."

Paige breathed out something too thin to be called a laugh. "No, you haven't. You really haven't. And you have nothing to apologize for."

"Then why're you avoiding me?"

"I just haven't been ready to talk."

"About?"

Crimson spots appeared on her cheeks. She picked at her food. "A couple things. But, ah . . . if you really wanna know, I found Aubrey's letter. That's one."

Every bone in his body snapped into rigid alignment. "You *what?*"

"The letter Aubrey wrote. In the shoebox under your nightstand. I found it."

He forgot how to breathe. His pulse fired through his veins with the intensity of a machine gun. "Jesus. You should not have looked at that."

"I know." Her expression crumpled. She tossed her silverware down with a clatter and raised empty hands. "And I wasn't trying to snoop, I swear. At least not for *that*. I was looking for something else and found the letter completely by accident. But then I saw who it was from, and . . ."

His throat went dry. "Okay. But she wrote that a long time ago. A *really* long time ago." Shit, why did he sound like he'd crawled across a thousand-mile desert without any water?

"Yeah," Paige said. "But it's obvious that whatever you two had going on back then, it was pretty intense."

Well. He wasn't about to touch that with a fucking hundred-foot pole. He plowed off in the first direction he could think of. "Why were you even in my room? What *were* you looking for?"

Her jaw worked. She held his eyes for an eternity. "My birth certificate."

Static buzzed inside his head. "What? Why?"

"Do you really not know? You have *no* idea why I'd be looking for my birth certificate? None at all?"

The silence turned to stone as he cast about for some sensible meaning in her question. "I don't know? Do you need it for that internship you're doing?"

She stared, then her shoulders lowered and she looked away. "Yeah. For my internship. Except then I found Aubrey's letter. And I know I shouldn't have read it, but it just . . . happened."

He tried to smooth his violent breathing. "It's . . . okay. I mean, it's fine. It's done. And I'm sorry if I raised my voice. I'm not mad. I just wish you hadn't seen that. Like I said, it was a long time ago. Before you were even born."

"Right." She looked up through her lashes. "But you saved it, all this time."

He flinched. "Okay. Yes."

"You were in love with her, weren't you? Like, *really* in love."

Jesus fucking Christ. He wished he hadn't walked into this one so blind. He tried desperately to remember why he made a point of never lying to his daughter. He should just deny it all. Get up, go get the letter, tear it to shreds, tell Paige he didn't care anymore.

Except he didn't move a muscle.

"Not," Paige continued softly, "that it's a problem. I mean, I realize you and Mom aren't together anymore. And that you had girlfriends before her. It would be weird if you hadn't."

A trickle of air made it into his lungs. "It upsets you, though. Knowing."

Paige picked at a fingernail. "That's not the right word. It just . . . It caught me off guard, like I said. There was a lot going on that day."

He stewed over that. "Was that when you mouthed off to Juan?"

She peeked up. "Juan?"

"Mr. Gallegos."

Her eyebrows shot up. "Mr. Gallegos? He talked to you?"

"Yeah. He called to say you hadn't turned in your genetics assignment. And that you were pretty rude to him, even after he gave you an extension."

She buried her face in her hands. "Oh, god. I was hoping you wouldn't find out about that. I don't even know why I said that to him. I was just . . . Like I said, there's been a *lot* going on."

He pushed words out through a rusted throat. "More than just you finding Aubrey's letter?"

"*Yes*," she said, her emphasis so heavy that he wondered if they were talking at cross-purposes. She seemed to expect him to derive some meaning from that answer that he absolutely did not.

"Are you okay, at least? You're not . . ." Fear gripped him, old and pure. ". . . pregnant, are you?"

She stared for an overlong moment, then released a burst of trembling laughter. "Oh, god, what? Pregnant? Really? No, not even close. You have nothing to worry about on that front."

His jaw unlocked. Not that he would've raked her over the coals, considering he'd become a father at eighteen. But he wanted more for her. "Okay. So you talked shit to Juan because . . . ?"

Paige said nothing.

"If you won't tell me what's going on," he said, "how am I supposed to fix it?"

"Oh, Daddy." Her eyes softened. "I'm not asking you to fix it."

"But that's my job. I mean, what do you want me to do, here? Punch someone?"

A flicker of a smile graced her mouth. "I don't think that would help, in this case."

"But I'd do it. You know I would. Or do you want me to swear I'm not going anywhere? That I wouldn't leave you even if the world was ending, even if your mom and I fight sometimes?"

Her eyebrows crooked. "No. Not that. I already know that."

"Well, what, then?"

"Just . . ." She reached over the table for his hands, then squeezed so hard his bones creaked. "Promise you'll always be my dad. And I don't just mean if you find someone new. I mean . . . in general."

He missed a beat, then another. "That's a given. That goes without saying."

His reassurance didn't seem to relax her. Tense lines appeared around the corners of her eyes. "So you promise?"

Jesus, she sounded so vulnerable. Like her whole existence hinged on his answer. "Of course I promise. I'll write it in blood, if you want me to. But I'd sooner jump off a building than stop being your dad. So it's a moot point."

Her grip loosened. Finally, he'd said something right. But goddamn, he had no idea what this conversation was actually about. From what he could tell, Aubrey's letter merely lurked at the fringes of Paige's disquiet. Something else had shaken her to her roots.

"Okay," she said, steadier. "I'm okay."

"Are you?"

She reclaimed her hands and smoothed out her T-shirt. "Yeah. I think so. Or I will be. And I promise I'll tell you everything. Once I sort through some stuff."

He shook his head, which someone had stuffed full of cotton. "You're not in danger, though?"

She smiled faintly. "No."

"Okay, good. And . . . you'll turn in your biology assignment?"

She tucked her lip under her teeth and dropped her eyes. "I'd rather not."

His breath shortened. That damned assignment. Did that lead back to what had freaked her out so badly? "Juan said you'll be lucky to pull a C-minus without it, so I think you kind of have to."

"Right." A cheerless laugh. "Okay, then. If you really, really want me to."

He studied her, hard, as if he might stare his way through the conversational fog. "I do."

"Okay." She heaved a sigh, got up, and kissed his cheek. She carried her plate toward the kitchen, then turned in the doorway. "And Daddy? This thing with you and Aubrey, it doesn't bother me. Not now that I've gotten over the shock. I mean, she's amazing, so I can see why you . . ."

He stiffened, and she trailed off, her cheeks flaring all over again. "Anyway, sorry to be so weird. I'm just gonna go lie down, okay?"

"You're *sure* you're not pregnant? Because you could tell me, if so. You wouldn't be in trouble."

She sighed, but a current of amusement undercut the sound. "That'd be impossible. So yeah, I'm sure."

"Yeah. Okay." His response came out on autopilot.

Paige drifted from the room, but Nick didn't move. He sat at the table, staring past his cold food, unseeing.

The conversation replayed in his mind, over and over. He tugged on a different thread each time, examining where each led, until a picture came together in his head.

That fucking genetics assignment. And a hunt for her birth certificate. Was *that* why Paige had gone quiet after breakfast the other day? Because he hadn't been able to do the tongue-curl thing? At the time, he'd assumed she'd approached him before Tansy, but what if Paige had gotten Tansy's answer, first? And his hadn't been what she was expecting?

Something black and oily coiled his guts. Oh, god. Oh, Jesus fuck.

Was he going to puke? Maybe. His stomach rioted, threatening to turn itself inside out, even as a deep certainty assailed him.

He didn't want to know what had upset Paige so much. Not now, not ever. Because whatever it was, he didn't trust it not to kill him.

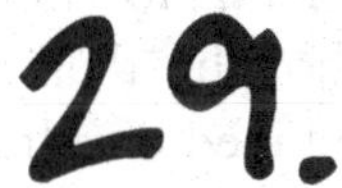

29.

On Thursday, Aubrey dressed with the meticulous intent of a woman who knew she would not be the one undressing herself at the end of the night. On a whim, she'd brought a matching bra-and-panty set from New York, certain she wouldn't actually need it, but now she layered her clothes over the crimson satin, grateful she had something to commemorate the occasion with.

Sleeping with Gallant tonight wouldn't be so much a decision as an inevitability. Over the past three days, she'd read his letter countless times, and with each new pass, a hidden door within her had cracked wider. Now she could peer through, to a future where his words glittered with promise.

She swiped eyeshadow onto her lids and put the finishing touches on her makeup. By the time he pulled into the cul-de-sac, a low hum flowed through every nerve.

Aubrey shrugged on her coat and ventured outside. Gallant's hello kiss added yet another frisson to the anticipation rolling down her spine. She clung to his lapels and breathed an eager sound into his mouth.

He pulled back, heavy-lidded and smiling. "I guess you liked my letter."

"I guess I did."

He gave her a meaningful look and helped her into the car. Downtown, he parallel-parked and came around to open her door. Every brush of his hand carried significance, a secret message for her alone, building toward . . . *later.*

She shivered at the thought, then ambled down the sidewalk with him, their combined breath frosting the air. Most of Henderson had turned out for the parade, and an ocean of light and laughter brightened the chilly dusk. People converged in the square, where an acapella group harmonized in the brightly lit bandstand. Aubrey pulled Gallant toward a row of stalls that offered hot drinks and handmade crafts.

He draped a few silk scarves around her neck, playfully pretending to lasso her, then bought her one in watercolor hues and ordered a round of mulled wine. In between sips, they traded knowing looks that made the crowd fade to white noise.

Aubrey grinned over the rim of her mug. "Promise me something?"

His lips quirked. "Hmm. Depends what it is. Nothing too risqué, I hope."

She laughed. "Risqué? Me? Never. I just don't want you to stop writing letters to me."

His budding smile faltered. "They mean that much to you?"

"They mean everything." She leaned up, planting a kiss on his lips. When she pulled back, he wore an expression she couldn't interpret.

It passed quickly. He took her hand, squeezed it, and tugged her toward the edge of the square. "Come on, let's find a spot for the parade, before all the good ones get taken."

Aubrey followed, forgetting his lack of answer as soon as the procession began. Floats drifted by in a fizzle of color.

"That one!" She pointed at the turkey sailing down the street. "Paige and Nick and I did that! And that one!"

A replica of Indiana glided past, sharing a truck bed with a barbershop quartet. In the gap between floats, Aubrey spotted a familiar pair of blue eyes across the street. She waved. Paige grinned, returning the greeting with a waggle of her fingertips.

Aubrey's attention slid to the hulking shape beyond Paige's shoulder.

Her throat thickened. She hadn't seen Nick in nearly two weeks—not since he'd left her in a tearful puddle on her living room floor—and now her face couldn't decide what to do.

Meanwhile, his betrayed nothing. He held her gaze from across the road, his features carved into grim lines. His eyes were a hard black glint, firmly locked.

Except . . . No, she knew that look. No one else would have recognized it, but she did.

He was miserable. Abjectly, horrifically *desolated.* She didn't delude herself into thinking it had anything to do with her—no, this came from someplace deeper. This was a towering mountain of pain, locked behind an obsidian wall.

Her heart tripped and went splat. In that moment, it didn't matter that he'd refused her, that he'd *left.* A blood-deep desire engulfed every nerve. She needed to go to him, to smooth away the line between his brows with the press of her thumb. To pull him close and lend him a shoulder, like he had for her when she'd first come back.

A float cut off her view. Breathless moments sailed by. When the way cleared again, Nick and Paige had disappeared. Aubrey cast around, but the crowd had absorbed them.

"Damn it," someone said at her side.

She jolted, then turned to find Gallant staring into the blue glow of his phone. For a moment, she'd forgotten him.

"What? What's wrong?"

He gritted out a frustrated sound. "It's one of my tenants.

A pipe burst in the bedroom and flooded the house. Which means I need to go deal with it. Right now."

Her stomach quivered. Briefly, her awareness traveled to the lingerie hugging her body, but she thrust the thought aside. "Then go. We can see each other later, if you want."

He glanced up, his expression anguished. "I'll have to rip up the carpets and get all the water out of there, which'll probably take all night. Even though I really, really don't want it to."

"It's okay." Her lips curled. "You go. I'll catch a ride with someone. It's not a big deal."

He hesitated. "Are you sure? Can I see you tomorrow?"

"Yes. Absolutely. Tomorrow."

"Oh, thank god." He leaned down and kissed her with surprising thirst, considering they stood amid a bustling crowd. He tasted like wine and spice and the promise of more to come. For an all-too-brief moment, he caught her around the waist and buried his nose in her hair. "I can't wait."

"Me, neither."

He gave her one last peck and arrowed away, his leading shoulder cutting through the crowd like a blade.

Aubrey lost him in seconds. She turned back, scanning for Nick, but if he'd had any desire for contact, he wouldn't have disappeared like that. He must need solitude. Not . . . complications.

A small hand clamped around her arm. "Aubrey!"

She pivoted and was immediately pulled into a hug by Megan Shimamoto, whose belly pressed against her, an unexpected combination of firmness and give.

"Wow." Aubrey pulled back. Megan had *definitely* popped in the past few weeks. "Look at your bump!"

"I know." Megan's grin rivaled the sparkling floats. "It's kind of a relief, actually. People have stopped wondering whether I'm overloading on Halloween candy and have started holding the door for me, instead. And someone asked when I was due the other day. Which was surprisingly awesome."

Aubrey chuckled. "You look adorable."

Megan did a little spin. She wore a green maternity sweater and leggings with shearling boots and a knitted pom-pom hat. "Don't I?"

"Yes. And this parade! You should be proud. Look at you, making things happen."

"I couldn't have done it without you." Megan gripped her hand. "But . . . you didn't come alone, did you?"

"No. Gallant was here, but he had to go."

"Oh." Megan's mouth thinned. "Well, come on, you're with me now. Let's go get some cider? I haven't seen you in weeks, and . . ."

Megan chattered on. Aubrey let herself be tugged along, then sipped from the cup she was handed. Megan greeted half the people who passed, thanking them for this, asking about that.

Aubrey hid her smile in her drink.

"Hey, how're you getting home?" Megan piped up, in between chats.

Aubrey glanced around. The crowd had thinned. Empty cider cups rolled across the asphalt while stars twinkled overhead, an icy bluish-white. "I'll probably just walk."

"What? No. It's *miles*."

"It's *a* mile." Aubrey chuckled. She tossed her cider cup into a nearby trash can. "Of which I'm perfectly capable."

"No, no. We can't have that. What if you freeze? What if you get lost?"

"I grew up here. I'm not going to get lost."

"Nuh-uh. I don't care if you built this town, I'm not letting you go off on your own. Here, let's find you a ride. I'd take you myself, but I'm suddenly having a ton of Braxton-Hicks and . . . well, you know how that goes. Time to go home and get in the bath."

Aubrey blinked. She did not, in fact, know how that went. Or what that even meant.

Megan's hand shot out and clamped around a passerby's arm. "Hey, you. Are you leaving?"

The man turned.

Aubrey bit back a sigh. Of course.

"Oh." Megan's tone shot skyward. "Wow, it's you. What're the chances?"

Nick leveled a pointed look at the hand clutching his biceps. Megan's fingers didn't even make it halfway around. "What do you want, Megan?"

"For you to give Aubrey a ride home. You can do that, right? It's only a mile, and—oh, look! There's my husband. I've been looking for him all night. 'Scuse me."

After tossing an apologetic look Aubrey's way, Megan swanned off.

Nick just stood there, his hands jammed in his pockets.

"Wow," Aubrey said. "I'd say that was Oscar-worthy, but . . . Honestly, she didn't even try, did she?"

He shrugged. The iron set of his mouth didn't budge. "You said it, not me."

"Well." She ground a toe into the asphalt, wondering when the temperature had dropped. She hadn't noticed until right now. "I'm fine walking. I know you're with Paige."

"Nah. She went off with one of her friends."

Aubrey tried to smooth over the sudden throb in her throat. "Oh. Okay. Well, I'm sure you've still got better things to do." She started to make her escape.

"Aubs."

The nickname pulled her up short. When she looked back, Nick's shoulders hunched, his muscles piled like boulders. God, he looked miserable. So incredibly, beautifully, gorgeously wrecked.

"Nick?"

"Just get in the truck, will you?"

"Yep. Okay." Because really, what else was there to do? If even a sliver of him desired comfort, she would give it. Whatever had chewed him up and spit him back out looking like *that* transcended any hurt feelings that lay between them.

She followed him to his vehicle and situated herself in the passenger seat. Nick fiddled with the climate control. Within minutes, heated air blasted her face, turning her cheeks hot and prickly.

She raised an eyebrow. "You fixed it."

"Had to, before it snowed."

Silence asserted itself. Nick drove stiffly, every line of his body carved from stone.

Aubrey waited for an in, but he didn't offer one. He didn't say a word. After three minutes of silence, she gathered her breath, but hadn't yet cleared the hurdle of opening her mouth when Nick stopped in front of her house. He shifted into Park, leaving the ignition running.

"Good night," he said, clipped. "Stay warm."

She hesitated, but he couldn't expect her to leave him like this. If she did, sleep would refuse her.

So she reached for his arm and grabbed hold. Her fingers didn't make it all the way around, either. "What's wrong?"

He kept his gaze on the windshield. "Who said anything's wrong?"

"I *know* you," she said quietly. "Something's happened. Something . . . catastrophic."

He scrubbed a hand down his face, then hauled in a few agonized breaths. "Fuck," he said to the night beyond the dash. "Fuck, this is *not* the time for this."

She took it all in—his struggle to control his heaving chest, the posture cast from iron—and unclicked her seat belt. She slid across the seat, gathered him in her arms, and pulled his head to her chest, more than a little shocked at his lack of resistance.

He choked out a ruined sound.

"It's okay," she murmured into the velvet bristle of his hair. What was it he'd said that first night, by the fire? "You can tell me. Whatever it is, I've got you."

"Fucking hell," he gasped, then began to weep. Mostly silently, but with such a glut of feeling that each sob drove a spear of agony into her chest. She blinked back the mist in her eyes and squeezed harder, trying to channel empathy through his skin, to infuse his every straining muscle with comfort.

After long minutes, his breathing stabilized, though the effort clearly cost him, because it took a few tries.

"What happened?" she murmured.

He sniffed wetly against her coat. "It's . . . Paige."

"Paige?" Alarm flared in her gut. "Is she okay?"

"Yeah, she's fine. Or she will be. It's more like *I'm* all fucked-up, and it's about her. Because I'm not sure she's actually . . . That she's . . . I don't think I'm . . ." A dark, broken laugh splintered from his throat. "Jesus Christ, I can't even say it."

Aubrey's stomach swirled. She waited.

He sucked at a racking breath, steeling himself. ". . . I'm not sure she's mine. I'm not sure I'm actually her dad."

She froze, her arms clamped tight. If there was a god, Aubrey was fairly sure she'd just been slapped across the face by him. Or her. Because that . . .

No.

That couldn't be right.

That could *not* be right, not after she'd endured a loss that had hinged around this single, unassailable truth. Paige was *Nick's*.

Her stomach soured and her mind burned, but she forced her reaction to quiet. Whatever this meant to her, he must feel it a thousand times over.

"I don't understand. That . . . can't be true, can it? I mean, you were with Tansy. While I was away. Weren't you?"

Nick unraveled from her embrace but didn't move away. The oceanic tang of his tears joined his singed-metal smell, filling her nose with salt and smoke. Wetness gleamed on his cheeks, and god, no man had any right to look that beautiful when he cried.

Some inner directive demanded that Aubrey lay a hand against his chest. Muscle and bone juddered, his breath coming in tatters. He caught her palm and pressed it flat, sandwiching it between his heart and hand.

"It's not . . . impossible." His voice was as barren as a scorched stretch of earth. "But you won't understand unless I tell you the details. I know you didn't want to hear them, before. But I've always wanted to tell you. All the ugly pieces."

Aubrey groped for her equilibrium and, to her surprise, found it in the thud of his heartbeat against her palm. At eighteen, she'd shut her ears against this, unable to brave the violence of her own shattering. Now, though . . .

"Okay," she whispered. "Tell me."

His eyes flooded with feeling. He tucked her hair back with his free hand, then kept it there to cup her face. "I wouldn't have betrayed you on purpose. Not ever. I'd rather have died. You know that, right?"

"I do," she said. Some part of her always had.

He sighed and closed his eyes. "Good. And please don't hate me for this, but the Tansy thing happened the day you were supposed to get back from your vacation."

Aubrey forced herself not to flinch.

"I went to your house that afternoon, looking for you." Nick gulped. "And your dad answered the door . . ."

30.

Seventeen years ago

Nick wiped a sweaty palm on his button-down shirt and stared at Aubrey's front door. He squeezed the bouquet of flowers so hard the stems oozed.

He should just press the damn doorbell already, instead of standing out here like an idiot. He knew this house better than his own. But he'd only ever climbed through the window when Aubrey's father's silver SUV sat in the driveway, as it did now.

He glanced down at the slacks he'd bought from the Gap. Were they overkill? Probably, but it was too late to change. And this wasn't getting any easier. He squared his shoulders and jabbed the bell. Chimes rang inside the house.

Silence. Then thumping. Nick's heart took up the rhythm of brisk footsteps. Sweat dampened his forehead.

The door swung inward. Green eyes, set beneath bushy red brows, considered him through the screen.

"Mr. MacLean," Nick stammered. "Hi. It's good to see you again. I came to see if Aubrey was—"

"She's gone."

"Oh." He realized he'd offered the flowers and lowered his arm again. Stupid. "Okay. I can come back later."

"No, I mean she's *gone*. To New York."

The wheels inside Nick's mind ground. Afternoon sunlight slanted beneath the portico, searing his cheek. "What? But she said she'd be back today."

"She would've been, but the time away cleared her head. We packed her up last night. She left for NYU this morning."

"She . . . did?" The buzz of Nick's voice reached him like a distant hive of bees.

Mr. MacLean's caterpillar eyebrows crooked. A show of . . . *compassion*, Nick's brain spit out, as if reading the word from a dictionary. A dictionary about ten thousand miles removed from this moment.

"I'm sorry," Mr. MacLean said. "She thought it would be easier this way, without a goodbye. I'm sure you understand."

Nick nodded, then wondered why, because he absolutely did not understand. How could Aubrey just . . . leave, without a word?

Yet as he contemplated, a slumbering dread awakened in his gut. It cracked open a sleepy eye and smiled, its teeth like a row of knives.

Because he'd known, hadn't he? All this time. From the moment he'd first kissed Aubrey, he'd seen this coming. He'd gone hurtling off the cliff without any attempt to check himself, and the fall had gone on for so long he'd almost begun to trust it, yet here it was at last, the ground rushing up to meet him, the crashing end that would splinter his bones to pulp.

He looked up. Shit, was it his turn to say something? And where had his flowers gone? He glanced down. Torn petals dotted his shiny black shoes, like fallen tears.

"Do you want to come in?" Aubrey's father pushed open the screen. "I realize this must be hard."

The offer zapped through Nick like a bullet, lethal. Final. He would never be invited inside if Aubrey hadn't actually left. "She's not waiting for me, in New York?" a small voice said. His. "It's over?"

"I'm afraid so, son."

Son. His own father didn't even call him that. The word seemed significant—one last brushstroke on the heartbreaking tableau of this conversation, the cruelest one of his life. "I . . . I don't want to come in."

"I understand." The screen slapped shut. "And I'm sorry, again. But it's best if you don't contact her. Better for everyone to make a clean break."

Acid scorched the back of Nick's throat. Clean? Right. This was about as clean as having a leg hacked off with a rusty spoon.

"Yes, sir," he said, and walked away.

His shoes thunked hollowly down the steps. When he reached the cul-de-sac, he kept walking, and then he walked some more, each footfall another link in the chain leading him forward, a lifeline dragging him away from the house that would forever contain the bloody wreckage of his ruptured heart.

He walked. And walked. He didn't stop until gravel crunched under his feet. When he looked down, mud caked his brand-new shoes. When had he walked through mud? He didn't remember.

He glanced around. An unpaved lot flanked the highway he now stood beside. The sky had dimmed to a mocking peach while crickets jeered from the shadows. The swaying trees hissed recriminations. In the middle of it all, a neon sign blinked.

Wish You Were Beer.

The bar. The one where all the guys from the mill drank after work. Nick had never been invited, because everyone knew he was underage, but who gave a shit right now?

He crossed the parking lot. Inside, dark paper blacked out the windows. Stale smoke and gloom swallowed him up.

Perfect.

At the counter, he asked for the first thing that came to mind. "An old-fashioned."

He had no idea what the fuck that even was. Just that he needed one. And he needed it now, before his next breath could knife its way free of his chest and splatter blood all over the counter.

The bartender raised a brow. "You got an ID?"

Nick took the guy's measure. He knew him from work. What was his name? Tom? Todd? He was a part-timer, but they'd crossed paths once or twice. "You don't recognize me?"

Tom-Todd cocked his head. "Oh, yeah. You that kid who slings scrap? The new one, from Baltimore?"

"Yeah."

Tom-Todd grunted, friendly. "Well, kid, you look like you got hit by a Mack truck."

"Yeah. Feels that way."

Tom-Todd crossed his arms and pondered. After a long minute, he waved to a stool. Nick tried to sit, but it turned into more of a collapse. His bones caved in, too brittle to prop up his leaden body.

"If anyone asks," Tom-Todd said, "you weren't here, and I didn't serve you, all right?"

Nick bobbed his head.

"I'll hold you to that." Tom-Todd performed some kind of alcoholic alchemy and set a mean-looking drink on the polished wood. Nick downed it in two gulps.

And gagged. Apparently, an old-fashioned consisted of a solid punch to the face, somehow delivered via glass.

Exactly what he needed. "Another."

"Damn, kid. You lose your girl, or something?"

He ignored that. "Please."

Tom-Todd hesitated. "How bad do you need it?"

"Pretend like my life depends on it."

"Okay. Shit. But this is a onetime deal, you got it?"

"Yep."

After that, Tom-Todd left him alone, except for the steady supply of old-fashioneds he kept up.

Nick drank until the floor heaved. He halfway expected his stool to slide down the bar and dump him against the wall. Or was all this movement inside his head? Whatever. Either physics had broken down, or he had. Fifty-fifty chance, either way.

At some point, he paid the tab. Aubrey would be disappointed that he'd dipped into the New York savings for booze, but . . . No. No, she wouldn't. She'd left him. He could drink himself into the ground with that money, if he wanted.

Fuck.

He stumbled out into the balmy night, then picked a direction and started walking. Cars whizzed by, a roaring river of light. Long grass snatched at his ankles. A few times, he fell, but lying on his back was intolerable. The stars wheeled madly overhead, so he got up and walked again, just to hold them still.

His head didn't work right. Thoughts slid over one another, too slippery to catch hold of. Except for one. He should make sure Aubrey was really gone. Check to see if Mr. MacLean had told the truth.

Nick laughed, a violent bark. Pathetic. Of course Mr. MacLean had told the truth. Of course Aubrey had left him.

Still, after a minute or an hour or a century, he found himself in front of her house, more by luck than any real sense of reckoning. The journey around back to her bedroom felt different this time, like mounting the gallows instead of ascending to paradise.

Sure enough, her window offered no light, no movement. He pressed his face to the glass. The bed was neatly made. And empty.

He didn't remember leaving. But somehow, he was on the road again, or maybe in the road, and what time was it, but it didn't matter, nothing mattered, and where was he going, no, who the fuck cared about that, either.

Damn, he needed another drink.

A car pulled up beside him. Nick kept plodding forward, the only direction available to him.

A window whirred. "Hey. New kid."

He glanced down, faintly surprised that someone had acknowledged him. And that the someone looked vaguely familiar. Why had this girl parked here? No, wait, he was moving. Did that mean she was driving?

"You know you're walking on the yellow line, right?"

"Who're you?" he said thickly, then startled. That wasn't his voice.

The girl laughed. "Wow, you are absolutely shitfaced. I'm Tansy. You don't remember?"

He sped up. No, he didn't remember, and he didn't care.

"I saw you kissing Aubrey MacLean outside the basketball game, over the winter."

Aubrey. The name exploded in his gut like dynamite. "She left me," he mumbled.

The girl made a sound he didn't know how to interpret. "Really?"

"Yeah."

She said nothing for a moment. Her car crept along, keeping pace. Lights zoomed out of the darkness, brightening in his face.

A hand closed around his arm and yanked. Nick fell sideways, his body thunking across the sash of Tansy's window. The oncoming car swerved and rushed off into the night, horn blaring.

"You're gonna get yourself killed," she said.

He hissed and pawed his way free of her grip. Then realized she had a point. The double-yellow line glittered beneath his shoes.

"Get in," Tansy said.

He did, even though doing so assaulted him with memories of what had happened the *last* time a girl had convinced him to get in her car. Another dagger joined the array of weaponry already bristling from his guts.

Tansy watched as he puddled bonelessly into the passenger seat. "Put your seat belt on."

"Why? Where're we going?"

"Where do you want to go?"

His head flopped toward her. He left it there. She was . . . pretty, maybe. Sort of. Blond hair, blue eyes, unassuming features that all agreed, like repeated examples of the word *pleasant.*

"You're nice," he said.

She laughed, with an edge. "Not really."

"Oh."

"You want me to take you home?"

"No." He rushed the word out. Was the car moving? Something was. The world, maybe. His soul, sinking to the depths of the ocean.

"Okay. You wanna come home with me, then?"

He did a slow blink. Yes, the car was moving. So was his stomach, burrowing around inside his abdominal cavity like one of those underground animals. Gophers? Moles? What were those things called again?

"I'll take that as a yes," she said. "If not, speak now. Or forever hold your peace."

His forehead got all crumply. *What a weird thing to say*, he decided, then congratulated himself on forming such a coherent thought. "I don't care."

"Okay, then." Tansy laid a hand on his leg. "You can sleep it off at my house. My mom won't be home. She never is."

He glanced down. Her fingers looked wrong. Too short, a shade too pale, with bitten-down nails he didn't recognize.

He wished for a different hand. He wished and wished, but it didn't change, and that was the last thing he remembered, that wrong hand touching him, giving his leg a squeeze.

In the morning, Nick woke with a raging headache and a vicious gurgle in his belly.

He turned his head. Where the hell was he? Someplace with floral wallpaper, dark evergreen carpet, and a fake-wood ceiling fan with gold plastic trim. A pile of blankets straitjacketed him, making him prickle all over.

He pushed at the tangle. An arm flopped to the mattress, not his.

Oh, wait. Shit. Those weren't blankets. That was a woman. A naked one.

He pinwheeled away, and . . . wait, why was he naked, too? Nope, better worry about that in a second. He scooted to the edge of the bed, found a diminutive plastic trash can, and vomited into it.

Not much came up. Just a few mouthfuls of eye-watering yellow bile. He retched again, his stomach roiling.

When he finished, he looked back. The woman was awake now, sitting up. The blanket pooled around her waist. She made no attempt to cover her nudity.

"Hi," he croaked. Hot acid stung his tongue.

"Hey."

"What . . . uh . . . What happened? Last night?"

She shrugged, her bare breasts swaying. They were large, much larger than Aubrey's. "You came home with me. Then we fucked."

He stared for an overlong moment. "We . . . No."

She snorted. "Yeah. You don't remember?"

He didn't. Snippets paraded through his mind, cut-up flashes of last night. The bar. Walking, so much walking. A car rushing out of the darkness.

He shot glances in all directions, searching for evidence to refute her claim. But he was definitely naked. And in bed with this stranger. He grabbed the sheet to cover himself, not liking the way she watched him, like this was all somehow normal.

Oh, Jesus. Aubrey was going to kill him.

He winced. No, Aubrey *wasn't* going to kill him. Which was far, far worse. He twisted around and threw up into the trash can again.

His bed companion didn't move. Didn't rub his back or offer him anything, just waited for him to finish. When he looked back, she regarded him with mild blue eyes.

"You must feel like shit," she said.

He waved away her assessment. "Did we use a condom? Last night?"

"Nope. You didn't want to."

He gritted his teeth. "Did I finish?"

"Oh, yeah. Loudly."

Heat rushed into his face. His mind screamed, trapped inside a body that had frozen solid. *Fuck, fuck, fuuuuuuuck.*

No condom. He hadn't used one with Aubrey, either, but she'd said the risk was nearly nonexistent, given the timing. And really, the idea of impregnating *her* did nothing but set off a bevy of celebratory fireworks inside his head.

But *this* girl . . .

His mind churned, going a hundred miles an hour. His mouth said, stupidly, "What's your name again?"

"Tansy." She scowled. "For the third time."

"Okay, Tansy. Are you on birth control?"

"No."

He dropped his head into his hands. This was a nightmare. This was his honest-to-god, literal worst fucking nightmare, and he couldn't think. Still, Tansy didn't deserve such a callous reaction. But he needed to get the hell out of this strange bed before he started screaming.

He stumbled through an awkward exchange, scribbling his number down, then adding the one for the mill, just in case.

"You'll, uh . . ." He fiddled with the zipper of his slacks, wondering where all the mud permeating the fabric had come from. He'd *just* bought these. ". . . call me, if there's anything to talk about?"

"Yep." Tansy still hadn't gotten dressed. He kept trying to look away, but either she didn't care, or she enjoyed his discomfort.

He escaped as soon as he could, his head a tight ball of agony, the rest of him a hollow shell.

At home, he called into work and went straight to bed. Somehow, he survived the day.

To his dismay, he survived the next one, too. And the next. Three times, he went to Aubrey's window after dark, only to stare through the glass at her empty bed. Three times, his heart tore itself to pieces, a storm inside his ribs he carried all the way home.

Two times, he tried to start a fistfight with his dad, wanting to lose himself in the oblivion of pain and straining muscles, but twice, Noah walked away sneering, not even invested enough to hit him.

Once, Nick reread Aubrey's letter, then decided throwing himself off the top of the quarry would've been less masochistic.

The call came a week later.

A grumbling foreman came and found Nick out in the yard. "Phone call for you. But tell your damned girlfriend to stop calling here."

For the barest edge of a moment, Nick's heart lifted. But when he mashed the receiver to his ear and grated a hello, he knew by the shape of the indrawn breath on the other end that it wasn't Aubrey. That she would never call him again.

He closed his eyes. "Tell me."

"I'm pregnant," Tansy said.

Nick met Tansy downtown.

He bought her ice cream, though afterward, he felt stupid about it. But wasn't that what you did for a pregnant woman? Try to anticipate her cravings before she had them? Pamper her while she was busy growing your child in her belly?

She sat with him on a park bench in the square, haloed by afternoon light. She pushed the plastic spoon around her cup of strawberry ice cream as if she didn't know what to do with it.

"So," she said. "I guess you probably want me to get rid of it."

He curled his hands around the edge of the bench. A glance at her stomach showed nothing much, yet somewhere beneath the torn jeans and laced-up combat boots, tucked into a secret corner of her body, a piece of him grew.

An entire future unfurled in his mind. He imagined sleepy kicks in a darkened womb, a first breath, a smile meant just for him. And later, high-pitched giggles. Shakily written letters. A flashlight shining through the thin walls of a blanket fort.

Despite everything, despite how messed up this had gotten, the daydream planted something breathless in his chest. Something wondrous. Like a far-off star had lanced through the blackened abyss of his life.

"I don't, actually," he said. "Not unless that's what *you* want."

Tansy spooned ice cream into her mouth and watched him closely. "I've thought about it a lot, and no. It isn't."

"A lot?" He frowned. "Didn't you just find out today?"

She expelled a quick breath. "Yeah. You know. The hours have felt like days."

He nodded.

"The thing is," she rushed out, "my mom got pregnant with me young. Like, really young. Fifteen. She tried to abort me. Had the procedure and everything, which obviously didn't take. I don't know why she even told me that, it's kind of a screwed-up thing to say to your own kid. But the point is, she had me against her will, and she's spent my whole life acting like it. Like the fact that I'm even here is basically one giant mistake."

"I know what that's like," he said hoarsely. "I'm pretty sure my dad wishes I didn't exist."

Tansy's forehead pleated. "That sucks. And I never want this kid to feel like that. My mom could've done it so differently, but she just . . . didn't. I would, though. I *will*."

Nick's breathing shortened. Another spark flitted into existence, joining the light of that faraway star. "I respect that. And, yeah. I'm not my dad. I'd do pretty much anything to not be him."

She set the ice cream on the bench. "Most guys would run away from this, you know."

"Most guys are assholes."

"True." She laughed. "God damn, is that true."

"I'm probably an asshole, too," Nick said, "but I'm not going to abandon you. You didn't force me into bed with you. I made a choice. Which means I'll love this kid like that's my only job in life, if you'll let me."

Her eyes sheened over. "Wow. She did say you were different. She wasn't kidding."

His muscles tightened until his bones threatened to pop out of alignment. No part of him wanted to ask who *she* was. "So, now what?"

"I don't know," Tansy said.

He cleared his throat. "Do we get married?"

Her face didn't change. But her voice shook when she said, "I guess so."

"Okay. Should I . . . propose?"

"If you want."

He looked around. He had no ring, nothing to commemorate the decision with. Just a half-eaten, half-melted cup of strawberry ice cream and a few scraggly dandelions that sprouted around the legs of the bench. But he could work with that. He plucked one of the yellow flowers, then split the stem with a fingernail and threaded the bottom back through. He dropped to one knee before Tansy and cinched the makeshift ring around her finger.

"Tansy, will you—"

"Nick?"

His world ground to a halt. That voice. Even shrill and disbelieving, it skimmed across his soul like music. Which didn't make any sense, because Aubrey couldn't possibly be here. He was imagining things.

"Nick," she cried again.

A rush of feeling clogged his throat. He looked up. His angel. She stood ten feet away, paler than winter.

A clenched hand trembled at her side. "What're you doing?"

He stared, wondering why she'd come back from New York.

"I've been calling your house all day." Pained rage leached from her voice. "Trying to find you, only your dad keeps hanging up on me. And why exactly are you down on one knee right now?"

Nick looked to Tansy, then back to Aubrey, his heart doing a slow, confused pirouette straight into the ground. "Um. I'm . . . proposing."

He'd never seen anyone get shot before, except in movies. This was like that, except worse. So much worse. His answer impacted her like a bullet, jerking her back a step. One hand flew to her sternum and pressed so hard it shook. "You're what?"

Tansy cleared her throat. "Yeah. I'm pregnant. It's his."

The following moment proved to be the longest of Nick's life. The concrete sidewalk bit into his knee. A motorcycle roared past, filling the air with static. Aubrey's mouth worked while a glittering tear dove down her cheek. "Tell me that's not true."

He grimaced. And said nothing.

"What the fuck?" she finally managed. "What the fuck, Nick? How *could* you?"

He stumbled to his feet. Her reaction made no sense. She'd *left* him. "You were gone." He reached for her—stupid, stupid, so stupid, but he couldn't control the way his mind screamed at him to ease her pain, even if he didn't understand its source. "You left me."

"For two weeks!" Her shriek drew the eyes of passersby. "And only because I had the flu! Was it seriously too much to ask for you to keep it in your pants for that long? After everything we said to each other? After everything we did? Did that mean *nothing* to you?"

He froze. The flu? The *flu*? No, she'd gone off to New York without him. She'd—

Oh.

Fucking.

God.

Pieces snapped together in his mind, a nauseating whirl of understanding. She'd gotten the flu, which meant that New York . . . She'd never even left.

Oh, fuck. He couldn't breathe. He was going to pass out. He'd been lied to, and, like an idiot, he'd fallen for it. Completely. And now he'd cheated. He'd destroyed the best thing that had ever happened to him in the worst way he could possibly imagine.

And he was his father. Exactly him.

He lurched forward.

"Stay away from me," Aubrey hissed, evading his grasp.

"Aubs, no, you have to listen. I thought—"

"No, you didn't!" she shrieked, pain and anger billowing off her. "You didn't think. If you had, you wouldn't be planning a shotgun wedding with Tansy Burroughs on a fucking park bench without even bothering to break up with me first."

Every word slashed him open. Jesus Christ, he'd hurt the one person he would gladly die for, and now he wanted to take Aubrey's accusations and drive them deeper, stab himself in the fucking throat with the tears knifing down her pale cheeks.

"I'm so sorry," he croaked. "I fucked up. Oh my god, I fucked up so bad. But your dad told me you left. He said you went to New York. That it was over."

"He did *what*?"

"Yeah."

She recoiled, and then she was stumbling back, away from him, opening a distance he couldn't bear.

He scrambled after her, but she didn't have to go far. Her banged-up Subaru hung halfway in the road. She'd clearly jerked it up onto the sidewalk in order to witness his proposal to another woman.

"Aubs, wait!" he shouted.

But she only slammed the door and gunned the engine, squealing away in a whirlwind of tires and acrid exhaust.

He watched her go, his soul peeling from him in long, bloody strips.

He'd cheated on her.

Cheated.

He was everything he despised.

Still, every molecule in his body quivered with the need to chase her. He would go to her window. If she wouldn't talk to him there, he'd walk to New York. He would grovel outside her dorm-room door, write letters in his own blood and push them through the crack underneath until she had no choice but to relent.

Except when he glanced back, Tansy still sat on the park bench, the dandelion limp on her finger, pity in her eyes.

And he knew he couldn't go anywhere, not now that a piece of him had taken root inside her.

No, he'd made his bed. Now he would have to lie in it.

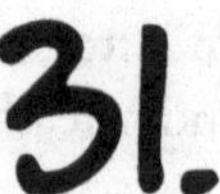

31.

Seventeen years ago

AUBREY WAS FRESH out of firsts. Losing her virginity had been one thing, but everything that had come with it had only piled more bitterness into the empty chasm now gaping inside her. She'd also lied to her dad for the first time. Gotten cheated on. *And* had her heart broken—if that's what this even was, because it felt more like having the thing ripped from her chest, then standing there stunned while it convulsed at her feet.

And now, for the first time, she was screaming in her dad's face.

He faced her from across the living room, legs braced, arms folded over his chest.

"How could you?" she shouted, even though he would only give the same answer he had the last five times. Still, she needed to ask, because if she didn't give voice to the agony stabbing at her ribs, she might crumple to the floor and never get up.

"I did it for you. For your own good." His answer held no compassion. Just solid, bone-deep self-assurance. "Him getting some girl pregnant inside of two weeks was all him. Just be glad you know, now. At least you understand what kind of person he is."

Aubrey bit back a scream. She wanted to throw her keys, except she'd done that already. Her dad hadn't even flinched when they'd hit him in the shoulder and gone clattering to the floor. "I hate you."

"For now, yes. But once you've had time to think, you'll realize this was necessary."

Bile gushed up her throat, burning her sinuses. "No. You ruined my life. I'll never forgive you. Ever."

"You will," he said. "I give it a year. Then you'll see I've done you a favor."

A hiss erupted from her. "A year? Fuck off, try a lifetime."

Pity flashed in his eyes.

Aubrey jerked back as if struck. She could handle misguided resolve. Bullheaded confidence, even. Those, she could rail against, meet force with force. But pity?

"Fuck you," she bit out, then turned on her heel and staggered toward the haven of her room, slamming the door so hard one of her math trophies rattled off its shelf and rolled underneath the dresser.

Her father didn't follow, thankfully, and Aubrey threw herself onto her bed and sobbed. She wanted to be anywhere but inside her own skin. Anyone but this person who'd had their innards crushed by betrayal. Right now, she wanted to be . . . who knew? Tansy Burroughs, probably, which was so pathetic she could barely acknowledge the thought, or maybe she wanted to be someone who'd never met Nick Thacker at all, some naïve person who'd never entrusted her heart to hands that would smash it so unceremoniously to pieces.

She measured the minutes in pain. Agony piled atop misery, followed by woe.

She almost missed the scratch at the window, consumed as she was by the sound of her own breaking. But when she uncurled her aching body and went to the pane, there he stood, the architect of her anguish and yet somehow the only person she wanted to see.

She raised the window. Nick stared up from the yard, his beauty so brutal that she wondered how she'd ever existed without him. Whether she ever could again.

"Fuck you," she said.

He flinched.

"Fuck my dad, yes, but fuck you, too. Two weeks, Nick. I was gone for *two weeks*."

"I know." Where his voice had once been so smoky, now dead ash collected in the spaces between words. "But your dad told me—"

"I know. But how could you not have realized I'd never do that? You didn't trust me that much? You didn't trust *us*?"

He blanched.

"Were you even going to fight for it, Nick? Or were you so ready to let me go that you just hopped into bed with Tansy the moment you thought you were free of me?"

His eyes flashed, a black lightning crack. "Are you kidding? Are you fucking kidding me? I thought I'd lost you. And I was so fucking wrecked about it that when Tansy asked me—"

"Don't." A white-hot arrow raced down her throat. "Don't you dare describe it. I'd rather drown in my own blood than hear the details."

He swallowed hard. "Fine. I get it. And I wish I knew what to say. But I don't, Aubs. I don't know what I *can* say, except that I hate myself and I hate what I've done and I hate the way you're looking at me right now, and I'd do anything to change it."

A corner of her mutilated heart lifted. She tried to command it into quiet, but it strained toward him, ignoring logic. *"Anything?"*

"Anything."

The moment cracked around her. She wanted to throw up. Purge herself of the sharpness slicing at her insides, then army-crawl her way back to yesterday, when the future had lain before them, still. When she'd only had to apply pressure to ensure life followed the course she'd laid out for it. "Does 'anything' mean you'd still go to New York?"

He had never stood so motionless. "What?"

She stared him down. Her eyes ached from crying and someone had clearly pulled her stomach out through her throat, but somewhere amid all that destruction, an eternal candle flickered. Because she loved him. Still. Of course she did. What they had together didn't just vanish with a single snip of the scissors.

No, once her rage cooled, she could find her way to forgiveness. Maybe. Probably. *When life knocks you down, get right back up.*

Because her dad had done this to them. He'd admitted as much without blinking, and she saw no better way to throw his deception in his face than to survive it. The effort would be hard and horrible and leave her with permanent scars, but that was life, wasn't it? And she'd already decided Nick was worth it. Worth anything.

He only had to commit to this, body and soul. Fight for it as hard as she planned to.

"I'm not asking if you'd leave your kid." Her voice warbled, but she ironed out the ripples. "You have a responsibility, I get that. But being a good dad doesn't mean you have to marry Tansy. I mean, what if you did half your time in New York? Half your time here?"

He retreated a step. "What? What're you talking about?"

"After I graduate, we could come back to Henderson, maybe." Her voice stabilized. *If life sticks you between a rock and a hard place, split the difference and aim straight down the middle.* "I could teach, at least until your kid goes off to—"

Horror overtook his expression. "You don't want to teach. You've never wanted to teach."

"No, but—"

"*You don't want to teach,*" he repeated, his tone laced with desperation. "And I can't just . . . bounce back and forth between two places. I have to work. Find some way to pay for this whole new person. I . . . I don't even understand what you're saying."

She clamped her teeth over her lip to keep from screaming. "No? Then what's your solution?"

He looked stricken. "I don't have one. There isn't one, this time."

"Nick. You said you'd do anything. You *just* said that. Four seconds ago."

"Yeah." He gazed up, agonized. "Anything except drag you down with me."

Despite her earlier waterfall of tears, hot prickles stabbed at her eyes all over again. "What?"

He hesitated. The moment lifted and held, a sword primed to fall. His expression collapsed on itself. "I didn't come here to beg, Aubs. I came here to tell you goodbye. And to say I'm sorry. And that I love you. I'll love you for fucking ever, and I'll never forgive myself, but I'm not going to rip away your dream because I turned out to be just like the asshole who raised me."

She'd thought nothing could hurt worse than him proposing to Tansy Burroughs. And she'd been very, very wrong, because Nick might as well have leveled the words against her chest like a gun, then pulled the trigger.

She stared at the boy she loved, the one she would have taken herself apart for if only he'd let her. Anguish swam in his eyes, and hers must have cast back the same, amplifying his pain with her own, some logarithmic function that never ended. An image flashed—of distorted funhouse mirrors, reflecting each other, duplicating heartbreak into eternity.

"There has to be a way," she whispered. "There *has* to."

Nick broke in that moment. She saw it. Felt it in her own bones. "There isn't," he said. "Not this time. I know you didn't believe me before, but life doesn't work that way."

"Only if you don't *make* it work that way."

He shook his head and stepped back. Shadows curtained his face, but the darkness couldn't cloak the glitter of grief coursing down his cheeks. "I can't leave, Aubs. Not now. But I do love you. Forever. And I'm sorry. Sorrier than I have words for."

She stood there and watched him go, too gutted to cry or call out or even move. Long after the yard had settled into stillness, she pulled the curtains shut, then stared at the fabric's weft as if into an infinite distance, where that intolerable candle still glowed, the one she'd thought would light her way until the world went dark.

How long, she wondered—how many *years*—until it would finally burn itself out?

32.

HALFWAY THROUGH HIS STORY, Nick's voice had almost failed him, because Aubrey had started to cry.

He'd faltered when the first tear had rolled down her cheek. But after so many years of regretting and wishing and despising what he'd done, he could no more hold back than he could stop from loving her. He wanted her to know. He needed her to understand.

So he'd gathered a raggedy breath and forced himself to finish. Then he'd listened as she'd told him about her father, how she'd fought with him that night, how the relationship had never recovered.

"I'm sorry," Nick said, once they'd both gone quiet. "I always figured you two patched things up, eventually."

"No." Aubrey sounded so small in the shadows of the truck cab, so broken. "I loved him still, even if I didn't want to. But I never forgave him."

He didn't know how to respond. He didn't relish knowing he'd contributed to the rift between them.

"And whatever I imagined with Tansy," she continued, "it wasn't that. I assumed . . . Well. Something else. I don't even know."

She sniffled. The urge to kiss away her tears swelled, so powerful his back trembled with the effort of restraining himself.

Aubrey scrubbed both palms across her cheeks, then pointed her gaze at the ceiling and breathed deep. She scooted back, opening space between them. It took everything he had not to close it again.

"So it sounds like you don't even know if you two had sex that night." Her voice wobbled in the shadows. "Tansy could've been pregnant already."

He gulped down the sourness creeping up his throat.

She chuckled, thick and humorless. "You know, she asked me about you once, in the pharmacy, the day you fought Brent Reinholdt. She was upset about something, and we got into a conversation about you, somehow. I said you were the kind of guy who does the right thing no matter what. Which interested her. Enough that it freaked me out. And then I just . . . completely forgot about it. Until now."

His pulse surged, charring his veins. He didn't want to examine that revelation too closely. Or at all.

"What will you do?" she finally whispered. "If Paige isn't yours?"

Jesus Christ, he wished she would hold him again. He *needed* her to. He didn't know if he could survive this if she didn't. But he pinned his hands to his sides and gritted his teeth. "I don't know. I honestly don't."

Her fingers crept from the darkness and curled around his. He clung to them, to this lifeline thrown from an impossible height.

"I hope you realize," she said, "that no matter what the truth is, you did right by Paige. She is who she is because you're her father. And she's so, so lucky that you stuck around. What you've done with her is some kind of miracle."

"Thank you," he breathed.

Aubrey exhaled. She unlaced her fingers. "Will you . . . be okay tonight? On your own? Once I get out?"

His throat worked. He felt like he would never be okay again.

For some reason, Jackson's words chose that moment to come rushing in. *Someday, you're going to do something just for you.*

"I don't want you to go," Nick blurted. He didn't stop to consider what he was saying, because if he did, he wouldn't dare continue. "I mean, I know I need to go home. Look Tansy in the eye and ask her this question. But the truth is, I'm scared. I've been scared shitless all week, and right now, I just want to be with you. Because sometimes that's the only way I can actually breathe."

She stilled. "What?"

He fidgeted. Stupid. Too much honesty. Why did he always do that?

"What was that last thing you said?"

He had no idea whether it would be better to repeat himself or pretend he'd said something else. But fuck it. Maybe Jackson had a point. "I said when I'm with you, I can breathe again."

She stared for the longest time. Something deep and infinite moved in her eyes.

He braced. "What?"

"Nothing," she murmured. "Nothing. Just . . . a weird coincidence."

Silence layered between them. He mentally cursed himself for his desperation, for—

"Maybe you should come inside," she said.

He stilled. He waited for the *but*. None came.

"You could . . . stay, if you wanted." Her eyes skewed away. "I promise I wouldn't try anything, like the other day. Which I'm sorry about, by the way. I get why it's a hard line for you.

And I couldn't anymore, anyway, not with the way things've gone with . . ."

She trailed off, chewing her lip.

Gallant, he silently finished. Under different circumstances, the sentiment would have clawed bloody furrows into his ability to function. But his equanimity had gone out the window when Paige had left him at the dinner table Monday night. Now Aubrey's invitation granted him the first ounce of relief he'd experienced since.

"That would mean a lot to me," he rasped. "It would mean everything, actually."

"Then come inside."

She didn't have to say it twice. He silenced the truck engine and followed her out. On her stoop, he inhaled her sunshine scent while she fitted her key into the lock. She looked up from beneath her lashes for a moment before opening the door. Inside, he expected her to go to the living room, but she led him down the opposite hallway.

He hesitated, then followed. At the end of the hall, her bedroom greeted him like an old, familiar friend. The bedspread hadn't changed. Neither had the white dresser along the wall, or the plastic math trophies lining the shelves. Nor had the window, which he'd clambered through countless times. Just looking at it made something tight and painful catch inside him.

Aubrey clicked on her bedside lamp. She sifted through her dresser for pajamas, then disappeared into the adjacent bathroom.

He hovered in the doorway. She couldn't possibly mean for him to sleep in here with her. But when she emerged again, a vision in white cotton, she peeled back the blankets, climbed into bed, and patted the empty half of the mattress.

Heat flooded him, writing words of gratitude in his blood. Aubrey hadn't spoken since coming inside, so he didn't, either.

He just ventured into the room, kicked off his boots, and tossed down his jacket. His fingers hesitated on his belt buckle, but the green of her eyes darkened in invitation, so he thumbed his zipper down and yanked his shirt over his head, then climbed into her bed wearing nothing but boxer-briefs.

She pulled up the blanket to cover them. He lay on his side and, when her hand found his chest, pulled her close. The pressure of her palm burned a brand into his skin, tattooing him with her warmth.

He stared into her eyes as she stared into his. He swore the world grew bigger, all of existence expanding to accommodate the way his heart kept swelling into forever.

It was better than sex, lying with her like that, looking into her. So much flowed between them, the silence more eloquent than any letter he had or ever could write. It was a wordless, naked admission of all that had never been. It was regret and longing and ecstasy all rolled into one, and he would have traded ten years of his life for the undiluted perfection of it.

He didn't remember falling asleep. At some point, she clicked off the bedside lamp, plunging the room into darkness, and then he was somehow studying her again, only now sunlight leaked in through the curtains, painting the lids of her closed eyes silver.

As he watched, her lashes parted, almost like his attention had woken her. He wanted to believe it had, that she could feel the weight of what she meant to him, even in her sleep.

She smoothed the pad of her thumb along his cheekbone. He synchronized his breathing to the rasp of her fingers against his stubble.

She slid a leg over him and tugged. He obeyed the unspoken command by rolling onto her, hardly believing the way her body turned supple and inviting, the way she parted her legs and let him settle within the heated cradle of her thighs.

He stared down and didn't dare try for anything more. She'd made it clear he shouldn't. Even this much counted as a gift beyond measure.

Aubrey breathed deep, as if soaking up his smell. Her fingers painted long strokes against his cheeks. Her attention drifted downward, locking onto his mouth for the longest time, then she looked up again, into his eyes.

Awe coursed through his veins. He almost told her he loved her, but he knew she already knew, and he found the silence so unbearably sweet that he couldn't bear to shatter it. Instead, he reveled in the quiet, gathered it into himself like a held breath he would never exhale.

She eventually pulled him down into a hug, and he curled his body around hers, awed by how perfectly he fit against her, now. He nestled his nose in the crook of her neck and dragged in one drugged breath after another. He clung to her for an eternity before finally pulling away.

He dressed slowly. Aubrey stayed where she'd slept, her eyes traveling across his bare skin like a caress. He smiled before he left, and she smiled back, a sad and somehow perfect thing, and when he closed her front door he stood on the stoop for a long time, gazing at the wide white sky.

He felt changed. Calmer, surer, more awake than he'd ever been.

Just yesterday, he'd considered that evening with her in front of the fireplace the best night of his life. Now he knew this had been.

He just wished he didn't have to follow it up with the worst day he would ever have.

33.

At home, Nick found Tansy bent over the sink in their single cramped bathroom, brushing her teeth. Half an hour remained before his shift, which gave him just enough time to ask. He had to do it now, before this tranquility wore off.

At his approach, Tansy snapped off the water and glanced up, catching his gaze in the mirror. For some reason, that bolstered him, that he could face this reflected facsimile instead of the real live person.

"You didn't come home last night." One corner of her mouth twitched. "I guess you're going to tell me you were with Jackson again?"

"No." To his amazement, he sounded calm. Steady. "I was with Aubrey."

"Mmm. Finally being honest, I see."

"Yeah, well. One of us has to."

The amusement fell right off Tansy's face. She straightened, slotting her toothbrush into the holder without wresting her gaze from the mirror. "What does that mean?"

"I'm sure Paige already asked, but can you roll your tongue into a tube?"

A harsh inhale skated through her teeth. She set both palms against the edge of the counter and squeezed. She didn't answer.

His lungs corralled as much air as they could hold. Point of no return. "I'm not her dad, am I?"

To his shock, she answered without missing a beat, without so much as a flicker of her eyelids. "Not biologically."

Nick swayed on his feet. Hot, white silence blotted out his mind.

He'd already known, on some level. But the confirmation still sent him spiraling into space, unbound by gravity, wheeling into an alien nothingness where he couldn't tell up from down.

Tansy studied him in the glass. "You're her father in every way that counts, though."

When the spinning finally slowed, he forced his spine straight. He had to get through this, all of this, right now, or he'd never marshal the courage to ask the rest. "That night. When you picked me up off the road. What really happened?"

Her lips pressed together. "You mean did we sleep together?"

"Yes."

Her knuckles whitened around the counter. "Which answer would be better for you?"

"The truth."

She chewed on that for a while, maybe shaping the words before setting them loose. Maybe knowing her answer would push them past the breaking point. "You cried. About Aubrey. I tried to fuck you, to make it more believable, but you said you couldn't. I couldn't even get you hard."

His throat closed. He was sucking air through a straw, now. But he hoarded the knowledge, a sliver of gold salvaged from the caustic storm raining from the sky. He wasn't his father, after all. Thank fucking god. "You already knew you were pregnant?"

"Yeah. But . . . Paige's dad didn't want to have anything to do with it. He told me to get rid of her." Her lip curled. "Which I obviously couldn't do. And I needed to give her a better life than the bullshit I got. Which meant she needed a father. A good one."

He had to will his next heartbeat into existence. "Who was he?"

Doubt swarmed Tansy's eyes. "Does it matter?"

"I've spent sixteen years raising his child as mine. So yeah. It matters."

She dipped her chin. "Okay. But you're not going to like it."

He groped for the wall to prop himself up. He had no idea how he was still standing. "Just tell me."

She did.

The name pierced him, a mile-long needle pushed into his chest and pulled out the other side. He fought for a breath. "Are you kidding me? I'll fucking kill him."

"Don't," Tansy said. "Just leave it alone. He doesn't know. He thinks she's yours. I lied to him, told him I'd gone to the clinic. I printed up a fake bill and everything. And I made sure Paige hasn't been anywhere near him, that he's never had a chance to look at her too closely. I couldn't risk anyone destroying this family. You and I are the only people who know."

"We're *not*, though. Paige figured it out."

Tansy let go of the counter and spun to face him, her eyes wide. "How, because of this stupid tongue thing? No, she suspects, but she doesn't know. She *can't*. We'll tell her—"

"No." He brought the word down like an axe, hard and final. Severing. "I won't force this conversation on her, but if she asks me, I'll tell her the truth. It's the least she deserves."

Tansy's lower lip quivered. Her eyes filled and spilled over. She didn't make a sound.

Nick stood motionless, wondering if he'd ever seen her cry before. He couldn't call a single time to mind. And yet her tears summoned absolutely nothing in him, just a blank wall where compassion should have been.

"I know I screwed up your life," she said, "but all I ever did was put Paige first. Before you, yes, but before me, too. And I'm not sorry for that."

"Do you have any idea?" Accusation weighted his words. "What you took from me?"

"Yes." She tipped her chin up. "And the honest truth is I'd do it again. Because if someone held a gun to Paige's head and told me to stab you, the only thing I'd stop to think about is where to aim the knife."

He laughed. Actually laughed, somehow. "And I'd do the same to you. In a heartbeat."

"I know," she said. "That's why I chose you."

It was the most honest conversation they'd ever had. And for a moment, just one, he looked down into her face and found her beautiful.

But that didn't change the fact that she'd taken away his choice. Though maybe that was why she'd pushed him toward Aubrey with such gusto—as some kind of consolation prize, a peace offering for all she'd stolen.

It wasn't nearly enough.

"I want to make one thing clear." His voice dropped. "I'll stay a little longer, for Paige's sake. I'll do whatever I have to in order to help her through this. But I want a divorce, a real one, and I won't live with you anymore. You're the mother of a child I still love like my own, one I'd die for, but I don't owe you a goddamn thing."

Tansy squared her shoulders. "Fine."

He left her there.

In his bedroom, he dressed with record speed, then climbed

into his truck and headed for the mill. He needed heat. Fire. He needed the volcanic roar of the blast furnace to melt him down to numb, dead ash.

And then, when Paige was ready, when she came and asked him, he needed to have a very, very difficult conversation. And somehow, he had to make sure they both survived it.

AUBREY SPENT THE day at the desk in her bedroom, working on her manifesto. Leftover energy from her morning with Nick infused her, and she jabbed at the computer keys, churning out the words that would prove her innocence. She needed to finish this. She needed her job back. She needed to get out of this town. She needed . . .

Oh, god, she just . . . *needed*, so very badly that even her hair throbbed with the intensity of it. But every time she closed her eyes, her mind betrayed her. Flashes swam into focus—upswept black eyes, holding hers. Perfect skin stretched over hardened muscle.

Because holy hell, Nick's body. Running her hands over him two weeks ago had been one thing, but watching him undress, gathering him close, had proved quite another. She recalled every dizzying line—the graceful rise where his shoulder joined his neck, the shadow etched beneath each abdominal muscle, the ridges scored along his side, visible when he raised his arm.

Aubrey slapped the laptop closed and buried her face in her hands. This was pointless. More than pointless, it was destructive. *I love Gallant, not Nick. Gallant, not Nick.*

Yet something had happened to her this morning. When she'd opened her eyes to find Nick's gaze already locked on hers, her entire being had sighed in fulfillment. Waking up to him had plunged her into a sort of nirvana she'd wanted to float in forever.

Which she absolutely couldn't think about, because getting wrapped up in him could only end one way. It only ever ended *one way*.

She wheeled away from the desk and went to the window, but that only reminded her of the countless nights she'd slid up the pane to let in her Romeo, so she abandoned her bedroom for the kitchen, where she filled the electric kettle.

Gallant, she reminded herself. Bubbles rose into existence through the water, whispering his name. *Gallant, Gallant, Gallant.*

She needed to see him. She needed another letter. She needed to slake this horrible need that singed her fingertips and made her hair stand on end.

Aubrey slid her cell from her pocket and punched a few buttons. Are we still on for tonight?

Gallant pinged back in seconds. I was just about to ask you the same. I want to see you so badly I can't concentrate. Everyone at the office keeps asking if I'm okay.

She smiled. Yes. This was what she needed. What time do you get home?

Five, he wrote.

Then I'll see you at 5:01. Be ready.

Bubbles popped up and disappeared. Then, I've been ready since the day you sprained your ankle 😊

She yielded to a shaky laugh and tossed down the phone. A joke, of course. The past couple months had amounted to so much more than just physical attraction. His letters proved that.

After sucking down her tea, she circled back to her manifesto, only to stare at the cursor while her body begged and pleaded for later. Briefly, she considered attending to herself, then decided against it.

She'd probably fly apart the minute she and Gallant came together tonight, but it would be so much better that way.

All she had to do was survive until five o'clock.

Gallant had forgotten to buy more condoms. He realized it the moment Aubrey charged through his door, pushed him against the wall, and kissed him with an aggression that had him hard in seconds.

Shit. The word looped in his mind, even as he fisted his hands in her hair and returned her kiss for all he was worth. *Shit.*

He'd been so eager to leave the office he'd completely spaced on the fact that he'd burned through the last of his condom stash the other night. When Aubrey had shot him down on the way back from Chicago, he'd needed *something*. So he'd texted Jennie Lawson, whose name he'd marked with two stars in his phone.

One for being willing, another for being able to shriek like a banshee.

Now Aubrey broke their kiss, breathing hard. She grabbed the front of his shirt and dragged him toward the bedroom.

Gallant's blood leapt, even as panic swirled into the mix. Where the hell was all this fervor coming from? And what would she think when she realized he didn't have any protection, after telling her just weeks ago that he did?

"Wait," he gasped as she pushed him down on the bed and straddled him.

She froze. "God. Sorry. Is this too much?"

"No. *No*, not even a little. I just . . ." His mind whirled. He had to find a way to spin this, somehow. ". . . I checked the dates on my condoms this morning, and they were all expired. I had to throw them out. It'd been a while."

She blinked, rapid-fire. "And you didn't buy more?"

He forced a smile he hoped looked casual. "You didn't give me time. But I can go now. It'll take ten minutes. Then you can throw me down all over again, and this time we won't have to stop."

Her face fell, as if he'd just delivered the worst news she could imagine. She rolled off, collapsing onto her back on the bed. "Okay, yes. Go. Quickly."

He studied her for a moment, a frown tugging at his mouth. She seemed . . . frazzled, almost frantic. "Are you okay? You seem . . . intense, tonight."

She did a slow blink. She'd done that cat makeup again, and color scorched her cheeks. "I need you."

His pants somehow got even tighter. Damn, he wanted her. Badly. She clearly wanted him just the same.

She would probably shriek like a banshee, too.

"What're you waiting for?" Aubrey said.

Gallant couldn't say what came over him just then. Some new recklessness broke loose inside him, fed by the thirst in her gaze. "Nothing. I'll be right back. You know I can't breathe without you."

Her eyes rounded.

He issued himself a silent congratulations. Maybe there was something to these letters, after all. Maybe he could get used to saying bits out loud, once in a while.

He dropped a kiss on her stunned mouth, then went to the hall, fished his car keys from the bowl, and whipped his jacket on, hoping she'd already be naked when he got back.

Aubrey lay on Gallant's bed and stared at the ceiling, her blood a painful thump in her veins. She hadn't even taken off her coat. God, she'd barged in and jumped on him like an over-eager teenage boy.

But instead of giving her what she'd wanted, he'd thrown her into a tailspin by repeating almost the exact same words Nick had used last night.

Her chest worked, up and down. She tried to placate it with long, deep breaths, but the words circled like vultures.

When I'm with you, I can breathe again.

Nick could've said anything last night. Absolutely anything. But he'd chosen *that.* The very same line from Gallant's third letter, or a version of it. At the time, she'd shrugged it off, but now . . .

Her mind whirred. "Goddamnit," she said to the ceiling, then jumped up and shed her coat.

Where was Gallant? She checked her watch. He'd left . . . wow, four minutes ago. Okay.

She stalked out to the living room, where a half-full glass of liquor sat on the coffee table, the ice barely melted. Flames flickered in the gas fireplace, mocking, and she swigged at the liquor. Hopefully, alcohol would loosen the ever-tighter winding of her nerves.

She replaced the glass and paced Gallant's polished living room. The click of her heels seemed to tap out words.

When I'm with you, I can breathe again.

You know I can't breathe without you.

Different enough, yet so very, very similar, and now, something else rose to niggle at her. Gallant's screens, that night she'd gone into his office. Why would he write a letter on the computer first, and *then* by hand? He hadn't . . . copied those words from somewhere, had he?

Bile rose in her throat. No. Gallant wouldn't do that. And yet the possibility sent out feelers in her mind, which spread like an infection.

Her stomach rocked. She glanced at her watch to find nine minutes had gone by. She cocked an ear, but no key grated in the lock.

She could sneak down to his office and peek. If she was wrong, she'd never doubt Gallant again. If not . . .

She swallowed.

Her heels clacked as she found her way to the hallway with the mirror. God, no wonder he'd asked if she was okay. She looked feral—shiny-eyed and feverish, like predator and prey rolled into one. She couldn't even say which she felt more like.

Aubrey gave her reflection the finger and ducked into Gallant's office. Across the room, the twin monitors glowed.

She held her breath and ventured close. When she jiggled the mouse, both screens blinked to life. The desktop wallpaper showed Gallant posing outside a palatial home. Maybe his first sale, or his most expensive. She didn't particularly care.

She scanned the task bar at the bottom. No word processor, so he hadn't been typing up a document to transcribe afterward. She brought up the browser, which offered her rows of listings on the MLS. Gallant had half a dozen tabs open, and she ran over them from left to right, landing on—

Her blood slowed to an ice-water trickle. Oh, no. No, no, no.

Nick Thacker's Love-Letter-Writing Service.

With a shaking hand, she opened the tab, which brought her to a long message chain. She spun the mouse's wheel, scrolling backward through the exchange.

Her tongue grew heavy enough to choke her, a useless chunk of rubber someone had stuffed into her mouth and left there. Oh god, not again. What the hell was it with this town?

Betrayal after betrayal after betrayal.

Her only consolation, this time, was that Nick hadn't had the faintest clue. Then again, he hadn't the last time, either.

With a cry of revulsion, she tossed the mouse aside. The thing clattered off the desk, dangling by its electronic tail. She stomped out, retrieved her coat from Gallant's bedroom, and burst from the house, leaving the front door wide-open.

Fuck him. She hoped someone came in. She hoped they robbed him blind.

Just as she cleared the driveway, the Tesla jerked to a stop in the road. Gallant jumped out, a plastic shopping bag in hand. "Hey, where're you going?"

She swallowed the fiery brick in her gut long enough to edge out a single word. "Home."

He came around the car, his eyes wide, the bag rustling in his hand.

God, she'd come *so close*. But now the handsome veneer peeled away, and she found herself face-to-face with the boy from high school all over again. The one she'd never even liked.

"Is everything okay?" He sounded bewildered. "What happened?"

"You happened," she snapped. "As in John, from Billings. Or should I say MontanaBirder81?"

Gallant's jaw nearly came unhinged. He tried twice to get out words and failed.

Aubrey whirled and stalked away.

"Wait," he managed, behind her. "Just wait."

She kept going. John from Billings could fuck off into the sun. So could she—she couldn't believe she'd put herself in this position. That she'd handed over her heart in exchange for pretty words. Again. She might as well have given Gallant a knife, then pulled her shirt aside and showed him exactly where to sink the blade.

"Aubrey, wait!"

She didn't.

Cold, black night swirled around her. She wanted to scream. She wanted to sob. Now that she knew, it seemed so obvious that those letters had come from Nick. They'd taken hold of her so easily. She'd fallen in love with him all over again, maybe recognizing on some soul-deep level that all roads led back to him, that no matter what she did or said or pretended, she would never be free of him. He would always be there, blazing inside her like a star, and yet it had only ever brought her pain, pain, pain, because he couldn't leave this town.

And she couldn't give up on Osos. Not without betraying everything she'd ever worked for.

She couldn't torture herself with it anymore. She needed to go—back to New York, to anyplace that wasn't here. She would finish her appeal right now, send it off to Jeff, and if he wouldn't listen, she'd—

Her phone rang. She whisked it from her pocket and lashed out a hello using the sharpest edge of her tongue. She'd only speak to Gallant long enough to tell him to erase her number.

"Hello? Aubrey?"

She faltered, then pulled the phone away from her face. The caller ID showed a New York number. But not just any New York number. An Osos number. *"Jeff?"*

"Yeah, hi. Sorry to call so late on a Friday. Is this a bad time?"

She drifted to a stop on the sidewalk. She hadn't heard Jeff Hutton's voice since he'd fired her two and a half months ago. For a moment, she wondered if she'd accidentally emailed her appeal to him, still unfinished, and he'd called to tell her not to bother. But he sounded . . . warm. Inexplicably so. She reined in her tone. "No, not at all. How are you?"

"I'm good, thanks. Look, I'm calling because I owe you an apology. For that whole debacle in September. I honestly don't even know where to start."

She tried to find her voice, but it had skittered off into the shadows.

He sighed. "The thing is, David Ballard came forward a few days ago, saying you were the true author of the database program. *And* the upgraded daisy chain algorithm. I've been on the phone with HR all week, trying to get this sorted, but the long and short of it is that he's gone, and we're deeply, deeply sorry. Me especially. And we'd like you to come back. I've been cleared to offer you a twenty percent raise, if you'll consider it. *And* you'd receive the Innovation Cup this year."

Aubrey clutched the phone so hard her fingers hurt. "The Cup?"

"Yep. But . . . there's a little more to this, actually."

The sudden tightness in his voice made her stomach flip.

"The thing is," he started, "this new database is supposed to go live in three weeks, along with the algorithm. David assured me it'd all be ready by then, but . . . Aubrey, now that he's gone, I took a look, and it's a mess. It's nowhere even *close* to operational. I could probably untangle what he did to your code, given enough time, but . . . it would take months. And you know how it is. Some of these transplant recipients don't *have* months."

Hot anger blasted through her. He had to be kidding. Not only had David stolen her program, he'd then screwed it up while trying to integrate it with the system? "What are you saying, exactly? That it's broken, and I'm the only one who can fix it?"

Jeff made an uncomfortable sound, halfway between an affirmative and a clearing of his throat. "That's pretty much what I'm saying. Yes."

Her teeth ground. Her life's work. Her single greatest accomplishment, now inoperative because of a scheming man and the fragility of his ego. Not only that, David Ballard had endangered people's *lives*. The same ones she'd spent the last year finding a way to save.

"Aubrey? Are you there?"

"How soon can you get me back there?" she said.

A sigh of relief gusted over the line. "If you can get me all the paperwork tonight, I'll expedite it, get you clearance, and get you back in the system by Monday. I won't lie, you have your work cut out for you. The next three weeks will be rough. But I'll have IT work on getting a keylog, see if maybe we can pinpoint some of the changes David made, so you'll at least know where to start. If anyone can get that database working on time, it's you."

She gulped down the thickness in her throat and tipped her head back. Pinprick snowflakes floated from the abyss overhead. Monday. A mere three days from now.

God, fuck David Ballard. Fuck Gallant Nobel, too. Fuck this whole brightly painted mess. She could just leave it all where it had fallen, put this merciless town behind her, and go salvage the thing she'd always been meant to do.

"Great," she said into the phone. "Monday. I'll see you then."

35.

THE NEXT MORNING, Aubrey packed her bags, then booked a hotel in New York for the following night. She would spend most of Sunday on a Greyhound bus before starting back at Osos on Monday. Over the coming week, she'd have to find a new apartment to lease, but moving wouldn't present much challenge; all her things still sat in storage in Brooklyn.

She'd known, all along, that she would be back.

At noon, Aubrey blocked Gallant's number, then deleted all eight of his voicemails without even listening. Then she did Pilates until her midsection blazed white-hot. Afterward, she drank tea and thought about Nick.

She would have to see him before the day ended. She couldn't just skip town without a word. She'd have to go tell him goodbye, get closure, finally.

Yet her whole body buzzed when she thought about it, all the frazzled energy from yesterday still running rampant. Closure. Ha. Was that what this bone-deep thirst was? This ache that permeated her on a cellular level? She could probably repeat the word until her lips turned blue, yet it didn't soothe the lightning-bolt hum inside her, or quiet her suspicion that coming here had only raveled the knotty equation of her life tighter.

Shit. How was she supposed to look Nick in the eye again, knowing what she knew? That even though his letters had been passed to her through another's hands, he must have, on some level, always intended those words for her?

Except that, for all that everything had changed, *nothing* had changed. She had to go. Nick had to stay. She understood, now, after meeting Paige, why that was true.

At least . . . she understood why it was true for the next two years, until Paige graduated.

Then again, what was two years, in the grand scheme of things? Who the fuck cared about two years, when she'd already endured seventeen without him?

A fragile hope budded inside her.

Outside the window, it began to snow. Aubrey went and looked out. The snow thickened, fat flakes gushing from the sky.

When it began to pile up, she went and took a long, hot shower, which did nothing to soothe the chaos inside her. By the time she finished, evening had fallen, along with a heavy blanket of white. Aubrey reached for her phone, then realized she didn't have Nick's number. She'd have to track him down some other way, so she dug tall snow boots from her closet, paired them with fleece leggings and her overcoat, and ventured outside.

The freshly fallen snow sighed apart before her footsteps. Cold nipped at her cheeks. The sky hung low, the clouds a hazy, reflective orange.

Somehow, she knew exactly where to go, and twenty minutes later, she found herself peering through the lit window of Wilder's MMA Academy.

Nick was inside, alone at the back, pummeling a sandbag to within an inch of its life. The great muscles of his back rippled as his fists blurred. One glance, and she could read the lines of his body like poetry, see anguish written in the hunch of his shoulders.

Her heart squeezed out a thickened beat. Clearly, he'd asked Tansy about Paige. And he hadn't gotten the answer he'd wanted.

His desperate sadness opened up a canyon inside her. Maybe she should leave. Give him some time to process before—

"Are you going in?"

Aubrey startled. A hulking, absurdly tall man stood beside her. She squinted up, recognizing the smiling giant Nick had sparred with the first time she'd stood here.

"I was just trying to decide," she said. Her candor surprised her, but despite this man's size, he exuded an aura of gentleness. Enough that the words had just slipped free.

"You should," he said. "He's waiting for me, but seeing *you* walk through that door would make him a whole lot happier."

Her brows flicked upward. "You know who I am?"

"Oh, yes." He grinned. "Aubrey MacLean. I know all about you."

She groped for a response and came up empty.

"I'm Jackson." He stuck out a mittened hand.

She shook it. "I take it . . . Nick's talked about me, then?"

He laughed, his rich baritone chasing away the cold. "Oh, he never shuts up. It's always Aubrey this, Aubrey that. I've never met anyone who's got it as bad as he does."

She swiveled back to the window, trying to absorb that. Nick landed a punch that sent the bag swinging away.

"Which is why you should go inside," Jackson said. "He's had a rough couple days, and he could really use a friend right now."

"*You're* his friend," she said pointedly.

"Yeah. And I could go in there and beat him up and that'd help him out a little. But you know what'd be even better? A friend who could give him some TLC. If you know what I mean."

She glanced at him wide-eyed. He grinned, his smile bright enough to compete with the snow dusting his woolen cap.

"Do you always talk this way to people you've just met?" she said.

"I just call it like I see it. Anyway. I'll leave you to it. You have yourself a good night."

With a wink, he melted off into the snow. She gaped after him. When she finally turned back, Nick was facing the window. Staring directly at her.

Her heart slammed against her ribs. Well, now she had no choice.

Nick started toward the door, so she did too, slipping into the bright warmth of the gym. He stopped halfway across the mats. The overhead lights gleamed on his sweat-dampened skin. Bruised shadows collected beneath haunted eyes.

A twinge gripped her chest. "Hi."

"Hey. Were you just talking to Jackson, outside?"

"Yeah."

"He's not coming in?"

She fidgeted. "No. He . . . uh, left."

"Huh." Nick's feline eyes slitted. "What'd he say to you?"

"Nothing much." Heat bristled in her cheeks. "Just that you and I should talk. So here I am. Talking. And I wanted to start by saying I'm sorry. About Paige."

He inhaled sharply and closed his eyes. He didn't ask how she knew. She wouldn't have known how to explain, anyway. *I can read your pain in the way you move, and somehow it belongs to me, too.*

He opened his eyes. "Thank you."

"Yeah. Are you all right?"

"I don't know." He shifted. "I mean, no. Not really. I told Tansy I want a divorce. That I'm moving out."

Her blood careened to a stop. It shouldn't have mattered. It didn't. And yet her mouth didn't seem to realize that. "Well . . .

then you should probably know I ended things with Gallant. But I'm leaving Henderson. Tomorrow. I got my job at Osos back."

Nick took a mile-long breath, as if steeling himself. Then his mouth kicked into a brittle smile. "That's great, Aubs."

She hesitated. Hope, wicked and cruel, pricked at her heart. He would ask. Any second, he would ask. *What are you doing in two years?*

"I'll miss you," Nick said quietly. "Forever."

She recoiled, the lights overhead heating to a blistering glare. His words struck her squarely, bringing home a searing realization she couldn't seem to escape—he'd never fought for her. Not the way she'd fought for him. All he'd ever done was let life tear them apart, then shrugged and walked away. And now here he was, doing it again.

Why had she even come? She couldn't remember. "I'll miss you, too," she choked out, then stumbled back through the door.

Outside, the night assaulted her, doubly frigid the second time around. Snow hissed down in sheets. Her boots flung drifts aside as she fled toward home.

Her pulse thrashed. God, when would she learn? When would she stop throwing herself at someone who continually refused to catch her?

She'd made it a quarter of a mile before Nick's truck came roaring out of the darkness. Aubrey backed away, against the nearest building, doing her best to meld with the brick. Anything that might buttress her against the hurt curling around her heart.

The truck jerked to a stop. Nick jumped out, leaving his door wide-open. He arrowed toward her through the snow, his face hard. He looked so unforgivingly beautiful that some inner piece of her crumbled.

"Aubs." He shaped her name into a broken plea. "Come on, don't do that. Don't leave that way."

She pressed herself flush against the wall. "*What* way?"

He came close. "Like you hate me. Like you're mad."

A sob choked her throat, but she pushed it down. "*Like* I'm mad? Of course I'm mad. I'm furious. You're single, and so am I, and even after all that, you *still* don't want me badly enough to try."

"What?" He stared at her. "Jesus Christ, how can you even think that?"

She tried to keep her lip from quivering.

He swallowed a gnarled sound and planted one hand on the brick beside her head, crowding her. "Let me tell you something. If you had any idea of what it's like inside my head, you wouldn't even consider saying that to me. You think I don't want you? That's bullshit. I want you every minute of every day. I want you when I'm dreaming, and when I'm awake, and when I'm so tired I can barely remember my own name. I want you so much that it survives every stupid, desperate thing I hurl at it. Every punch I throw and every letter I write and every shot of tequila I swallow. My whole fucking existence spins on an axis of wanting you."

Her breath thinned and died. Oh yes, he had definitely written those letters. As if she'd had any doubt.

"Wanting you isn't the problem," he growled. "It's that I can't leave. At least not now. Fuck, I wish I could, but I made a promise, Aubs. I told Paige I wasn't going anywhere, and I can't break my word. Not without being the exact kind of person I can't stand to be."

She trembled. Longing clawed its way up her throat. The symmetry of the moment mocked her, like she was staring back across seventeen years to their first kiss, reflected upside down in a water droplet poised to fall. The wall, the winter night, those eyes that threw such impossible heat . . .

The only difference was that he'd already let her go once. And now he was trying to do it again.

"I get that," she spat. "But you could ask. You could fight for it. Just once in your life, you could fight."

"Fight?" He sounded perplexed. "For what?"

"Us," she hissed.

He blinked once, then again. "How the fuck would I do that? You want me to ask you to wait for me?"

She mashed her lips together. She did. Of course she did.

"Because two years is a long time, Aubs. What if you get lonely? What if you meet someone? What if you decide you hate me?"

A pitiless laugh escaped her lips. "I don't hate you. I love you. Still. Always. And if you actually loved *me*, you'd ask."

His eyes flared like she'd harpooned him in the chest. He hovered there, assailing her with the smell of smoke and steel. "Aubs," he begged. His hand came up to cup her cheek, warm and rough and electric.

A dozen different emotions punched her in the solar plexus, reducing her to such a bright, explosive mess that the need to vent the pressure nearly blinded her. "What?"

His gaze dropped to her mouth. "You think I don't love you? Because I do. I've been killing myself for seventeen years with how much I love you. I even have that letter you gave me, the night you left. I've just been reading it over and over and over, like some kind of fucked-up therapy that never actually works. Of *course* I fucking love you. I can't seem to do anything else."

She froze. He'd saved her letter?

Those endless eyes snapped up to hers again. "But I can't ask you to throw away two years for me. You deserve someone who—"

"Shut up," she said.

He blinked. "What?"

"Shut up. Just shut the fuck up. I don't want to hear it."

He made an anguished sound. "Then what do you *want*?"

"Just . . ." She tried to swallow but couldn't, tried to breathe but couldn't, tried to do anything except want and want and *want* and couldn't do that, either. "Kiss me. I don't care about the rest of it right now. Just be mine for one more night. We can figure the rest out later."

A spark of disbelief lit those dark eyes. "What?"

Her control snapped. She anchored her palms to his face and kissed him.

He froze, his mouth unmoving against hers, as if his mind couldn't process what was happening. Or maybe he hadn't done this in a very long time.

Which, she reminded herself, he hadn't. So she'd go gentle. She probed at the seam of his lips with her tongue, coaxing. Hoping.

He made a thick sound deep in his throat, and all at once, whatever force bound him to hesitation shattered apart. He gathered her and pinned her to the wall.

Then he kissed her, hard and ravenous, like he had no other purpose.

Oh, thank god. Heat crashed over her in dizzying waves. She clung to him, so full of his scent and the curl of his tongue that her mind emptied. His mouth drew blossoms of warmth across her lips, then along one side of her face and down the column of her throat. She tipped her head back and offered a drunken moan to the sky. He sucked at her neck, greedily, lavishing it with delirious, toe-curling suction. She ground against him, and he ground back.

Nick found her mouth again, his hunger making her dizzy. Snow was everywhere—pinpricks of cold that scorched her skin—and so were his hands, tangling in her hair, kneading her waist. Every nip of his teeth and slide of his lips asked the same question, over and over again, and her body answered with a low, liquid pulse.

He wrested his mouth away and tilted his forehead against hers. "Where?" No more hesitation. Just desire and need and enough carnal energy to make her combust.

"I don't care." She rocked her hips against his. "Right here, if you want."

"What, up against a wall? In the street?" His breath skimmed across her lips.

"Why not?"

He claimed her mouth in another deep, needful kiss. "Because I don't want to fuck you, I want to savor you. And I still owe you one, from last time. I intend to pay up. With interest."

She tightened her hold around his neck. All the hurt had gone out of her, or maybe it had never existed in the first place, because when he kissed her like that, she understood that she belonged to him in a way she could never revoke. "Are you talking about . . . simple interest? Or compounding?"

He puffed a graveled chuckle against her mouth. "What kind of question is that?"

"Well, don't talk numbers to a mathematician unless you're trying to turn her on."

"I'm definitely trying to turn her on."

"Better go with compounding, then," she breathed. "It's much more complicated and therefore infinitely sexier."

His mouth dropped to her neck, his tongue darting out to lick melted snowflakes from her skin. "Okay, what does compounding bring my debt to, then? Three? Four?"

She whimpered. A dazzle of sparks followed wherever his lips went. "Better call it four."

He made a purely male sound against her throat. "All right. And lucky for you, I took a shower after work. Otherwise, I'd never make it that far."

She meant to ask what a shower had to do with anything, but the words burned to ash in the fire licking through her.

Nick pulled her away from the wall and guided her to the truck, where he slid her in through the driver's side and climbed up beside her. He slammed the door and jammed the gearshift into Drive, then looked down with half-lidded eyes. "Your house?"

"No. In this weather, that'd take longer than I can wait."

He nodded and wheeled the truck around, opening the throttle, roaring through the curtains of snow.

Aubrey held on to the seat, her awareness zeroing in on the place where her thigh pressed against his.

Less than a minute later, he pulled off into an empty, secluded lot, then killed the headlights and wipers. Hot air streamed from the vents, yet the snow came down so densely it blotted out the glass in moments.

He hit the locks. "Here? No one else is out tonight. We might as well be on our own planet."

She nodded, then pulled at him, and his lips crashed into hers again. He guided her down, stretching her out against the long seat, maneuvering both their coats off. He pulled back long enough to whisk his shirt over his head, then dove for her mouth again, stealing her composure with the drug of his kiss.

Her fingers curled against his bare back. She existed in slices of sensation—the tingle of his lips against hers, the glimmer of blue dash light reflected off his sculpted cheek, the ribbed truck seat pressing into her back. The way Nick pinned his hard length against her core when she widened her knees.

He took hold of the hem of her sweater, then got it up and over her head, followed by her shirt. He turned his attention to her boots and leggings, shucking them off and chucking them into the footwell. He straightened and gazed down, his lashes brushing his cheeks.

"Did you know?" he said, husky. He dragged a roughened palm over the flimsy crimson satin of her bra, then the matching thong. "Is that why you're wearing this?"

"Probably," she admitted.

His mouth curled, wry and almost sad. He trailed his fingers across her stomach, making her writhe. When he reached the border of her thong, he slid a finger over the silky fabric, pulling a whimper from her throat.

His thumb grazed the heated spot that cried out for his touch. A gasp raced up her throat. His finger settled there and teased her, back and forth, so slowly that she slammed her fist against the glove box.

"Faster," she commanded.

Nick laughed, dark and sultry. "This is different. Last time, you were shy."

She gritted out a pleading moan. "Please?"

He didn't go faster. "I told you I wanted to savor you. Especially if this is the last—"

She growled, and he wisely dispensed with the rest of that sentence. "Just be with me," she said.

"Okay," he murmured. "Okay."

He redoubled his efforts, and she bucked her hips, forcing more friction from the mind-altering back-and-forth of his thumb. He rewarded her by upping his pace, just enough to heat her muscles and start her body on a slow spiral inward. She anchored both hands to the door handle overhead, needing something to hang on to while her sides trembled.

Without warning, Nick slid down her underwear and replanted his finger against her bare flesh. She swallowed a thick cry, drinking up the heat he poured into her through that one spot. Her eyelids tried to find her cheeks, but she fought to hang on to the sight of him through a slit of fringed lashes. His breath came hard and fast, the muscles of his stomach contracting as his touch sped up.

God, this was torture. The sweetest, most exquisite torture she'd ever endured. Even if he made her come this way, which would happen very soon, she wouldn't stop yearning until she had him inside her.

"Please," she whimpered.

His teeth flashed in the snow-laden darkness—a smile or a threat, who knew. His thumb continued its mission while his other hand roved up and slid her bra aside. He rolled her nipple through his fingers, doubling the electricity coursing into her.

She bit down on a cry and pulled on the door handle so hard her back arched. Black heat piled at the corners of her vision, a gathering wave.

"You're so fucking beautiful," he murmured, throaty.

His hands withdrew. She almost shrieked her frustration, but he whisked her thong off, unhooked her bra and tossed that aside, too, then grabbed the backs of her knees and splayed her wide.

One of her feet ended up draped over the seatback, the other over the dash. The windshield was an icy scorch against her toes, but she forgot it the instant Nick bent and replaced his finger with his tongue.

Her back bowed as her eyes slammed closed. Holy shit. He lapped at her, insistent.

She had no control. She was a pliant, trembling ache. He worked her, relentless, until she coiled so tight that she had nowhere left to go but inward, crashing into a million tormented, glittering pieces that all reflected him.

His tongue slowed as the tremors ran their course. When Aubrey pried her eyes open, Nick had straightened. He gazed down, his black fire half-hidden by heavy lids.

"That's number one." He unbuttoned his pants and slid the zipper down.

She followed the movement with her eyes, her head lolling. She'd never felt so complete and yet so achingly empty. Her palms still stuck to the door handle, glued there by her own sweat.

Nick finagled his pants and boxer-briefs off and flung them atop everything else. He curled over her, propped an elbow beside her head, and reached down to line himself up.

His weight settled against her. Oh, god. She was going to weep. She was going to die.

"Look at me," he said, gruff.

She did, so raw and shaken she had no other choice.

"I love you." His dark gaze lanced into her, as open as she'd ever seen. "I love you so fucking much."

He drove his hips forward. Her eyes rolled back in her head. He sank into her, and then in some more, stretching her, filling her, and just when she thought her hold on herself would shear away, he kept going.

When he was fully seated, he buried his face against her neck and loosed a hot, shuddering gasp in her ear. "Oh, *fuck*. Jesus fucking Christ, I forgot how good you feel."

"I forgot how much of you there is," she gasped. Or maybe she just hadn't appreciated it, before. Whatever the reason, the first time hadn't felt like this. It hadn't even taken place on the same planet.

He slid halfway out and drove back in again, reducing her to a tumult of sensation. There was hot air from the vents, billowing over them both. Nick's scorching scent in her nose. A cave of snow piled around them, lit by the faint blue glow of the dash. And this unstoppable, undeniable, black-haired force, on her, in her, subsuming her with one slide of pleasure after another.

He moved inside her, long and deep, and she came again almost immediately, this time with a quick, ecstatic sigh that washed over her like a wave. Her arms abandoned the door handle and wound around him as she cried her release into his neck.

She fell back against the seat again, her mind a quivering puddle of bliss.

He cocked a brow. "Two?"

"Two," she agreed.

"Halfway there." He upped his pace, his breath quickening to harshness, the most bewitching song in the world.

Of their own accord, her hips rose to meet him. She didn't know where she found the energy. They melted together, a slick of heat and muscle and sweat, his or hers, she didn't know and didn't care, she just wanted to drink him up and glut herself on the way he drove into her with such force she'd probably have to scrape herself off the seat, afterward.

Beautiful curses rolled off his tongue as he lost himself in her. Every touch, every thrust seemed to carry seventeen years of longing behind it, and she swore he was memorizing each moment, as if he expected it to have to last him seventeen more.

But she refused to think about that. Instead, she got lost, too. Pleasure rippled through her, building and building, finally setting off a soundless shock wave that incinerated her, a blinding starburst whiteness.

She heard her own cries, somewhere distant. Nick groaned out her name. Rapture rolled through her, took hold and squeezed for all it was worth, then finally left her spent and exhausted on the warm, sticky seat of the truck. An equally spent, equally exhausted bulwark of muscle lay on top of her, crushing her with his weight.

He groaned in her ear. "Three."

A few last convulsions rippled through her. She stared at the ceiling, wondering if her vision had always been this blurry. If not, she would gladly wear glasses for the rest of her life in payment for what they'd just done. She'd never had sex like that before. Probably nobody'd had sex like that before.

He finally raised his head and looked her in the eye. "Sorry."

She blinked him into focus. Okay, maybe no glasses. His sharp beauty sliced right through the haze. "For?"

His mouth edged downward. "Not making it to four. That felt way, *way* too incredible."

"You're not allowed to apologize. Not for that. That last one . . . Well, I don't even know what the hell that was." God, she sounded drunk. Like she'd had enough whiskey to roughen her vocal cords and turn her mind to smoke. "That was like a hundred all rolled into one."

"Still," he said.

She let her eyes flutter closed. "No 'still.' I think that's all I've got in me, anyway."

He kissed one eyelid, then the other, and slid out of her, drawing a pained squeak from her lips.

"What?" he said. "Did that hurt?"

"No." She opened her eyes to find him sitting in the driver's seat, naked and glistening and carved from granite. "When you come out, it just feels . . . I don't know. Hard to describe. Weird. Kind of like you're robbing me."

His brow creased, as if he didn't quite believe her. "What am I supposed to do, then, just stay there forever?"

"Maybe," she said quietly.

His eyes shied away from hers, and she cursed herself for spoiling the moment. She might as well have opened the door and let snow gush into the cab.

Nick cleared his throat and disentangled their clothes, handing hers over and wiggling into his in a constrained dance.

She lamented the way his jacket stole his sculpted lines from view.

"Should I take you home?" he said, when she'd finished dressing.

She straightened her coat and clicked her seat belt on. "Yeah. Thank you."

"No, thank *you*." He laughed, shaky, then scrubbed a hand over his shorn hair. "That was . . . way better than anything I've ever imagined."

"Likewise. I mean, you promised the second time would be better, but . . . wow."

"Yeah. Wow." He drove with one hand, the other loose in his lap.

"So," Aubrey ventured, after a few blocks.

"So." He flicked a glance at her. "You're leaving tomorrow?"

Her stomach clenched at the reminder. "Yeah." She told him about the database, the damage David had done to her algorithm. "People's actual lives depend on me being at work on Monday."

He nodded along, as if none of this surprised him. Maybe it didn't. "And now what? You're asking me to look you up in two years?"

"Yes. That's what I'm asking."

He drove in silence for a minute. Only after he blinked back whatever emotion that summoned did he answer. "Okay. I can do that. I'll come find you. I don't care if you're in Timbuktu, I'll come. But I want you to know I don't expect anything. In the meantime, you should date. Go meet people, go—"

"Stop," she cut in. "Don't ruin this."

Because she already knew she wouldn't date. She wouldn't even look at another man. She understood now that she never really had, that she only loved *this* one and always would, until the day he came to claim her again.

Still, she could tell by the set of his mouth and the slope of his shoulders that he didn't believe in them the way she did. He didn't trust that she'd be waiting for him.

She'd just have to show him, then.

After another block, she cleared her throat. "How's Paige doing, by the way? Is she okay after . . . everything?"

His mouth bent up at the corner. "Is it weird that I like it when you worry about her?"

"No. You care about her. It makes sense that you would like me caring about her, too."

"I do," he said. "I really, really do."

"So? Is she okay?"

"Sort of." His smile dimmed. "We haven't talked about it, yet. I mean, she knows I'm not her dad. She's figured that out. But I don't know if she wants to know who the real guy is, and I'm not going to dump it on her unless she wants me to. So we've just been kind of . . . dancing around each other, knowing we have to talk and not knowing how to do it. Though I did get an incredibly awkward phone call from her biology teacher after she finally turned in her assignment. He said he'd had no idea that Paige was adopted and he felt like an idiot for not realizing he shouldn't be handing out assignments like that one."

She reached for his hand. "That sounds unpleasant."

He squeezed her fingers. "It wasn't fun. I barely held back from telling him he'd fucked up my entire life. But I'm pretty sure he got the idea, anyway."

The thunk of wipers filled the ensuing silence. "Do you wish you hadn't found out?"

He blew out a long breath. "I don't know. The truth hurts, but maybe pain's better than ignorance. It's not new, anyway. And I like knowing I didn't cheat on you. Thinking I had tortured me. You have no idea."

She gazed at him. He caught her eyes for a brief moment before returning his attention to the road.

"So you weren't with Tansy that night?"

"No. Apparently she tried, and I told her no."

A dark, hollow ache rose inside her. Some part of her almost respected what Tansy had done for her daughter. Almost. But the rest would hate her forever.

"What about you?" he said, after another block of silence. "Are you okay? With the whole Gallant thing?"

She barked an acid laugh. "No, not really. He was writing me love letters. Letters he hired some guy on the internet to write. Which . . . maybe sounds familiar?"

Nick froze, drifting halfway into the other lane before correcting the truck's path. Luckily, there were no other cars on the road.

"Are you kidding me?" The words leached out of him, low and smooth and dangerous, a knife sliding through the dark.

"I wish I was."

"*He's* John? MontanaBirder81?"

"Yep."

"You're Jane?"

"'Fraid so."

He unstitched his hand from hers and clenched it around the wheel. The tendons of his hand stood out like blades. "That motherfucker. That absolute motherfucker. Now I have to kill him twice."

"Twice? Why twice?"

He shook his head, his jaw hardening. "Forget it. I just . . . Did he use those letters to get you to . . . Did you . . . Fuck, I have no right to ask, but—"

"No," she said quickly. "No, thank god. I figured it out before it got that far. You're the only person I've been with in months. *Many* months. Close to a year, actually."

That calmed him some, but he still gripped the wheel like he wanted to rip it into halves. "I never would've written those letters if I'd known. Jesus, I never should have, anyway. I just didn't think it would turn out the way it did. I thought I'd be helping someone. The only reason I even came up with that stupid idea was because Paige had this internship thing—"

"It's okay. You don't have to explain. I read the emails. I know you didn't know."

He ground his teeth so hard they creaked. "That's not an excuse."

The rest of the drive passed in silence. When Nick parked in her cul-de-sac, she hesitated, not wanting to get out. They would have to part before morning, but she couldn't bear it just yet.

"Why don't you come inside?" she said.

He stared at her, an inferno raging behind his eyes.

She chewed her lip. "You *do* still owe me number four."

"What, you want me like this?" His look only burned hotter. "All pissed off?"

A flutter came to life between her thighs. "God, yes."

"Well." He killed the engine and tore the keys from the ignition. "I won't argue with that."

He followed her into the house, a brooding wall of muscle and sinew. She'd barely gotten a fire going in the living room before he stripped them both naked, hoisted her against the wall, and wrapped her legs around his waist. Her vertebrae pushed indents into the plaster.

Heat and anticipation rocketed through her, bringing all her sated nerve endings to life again. She cradled the back of his silky head, studying the way the firelight caressed his angular features. She would miss him, come tomorrow. She would miss him every second for two years.

"I want to have you right here," he said.

"Then take me." She mustered a crooked smile. "Walls *have* kind of always been our thing."

"*You're* kind of my thing." He tilted his head and set his teeth against her throat, the same way he had weeks ago, only this time, the bite turned into a long, bone-melting kiss that made Aubrey splay her hands against the backs of his shoulders. When he looked up again, his gaze had sharpened to laserlike intensity.

"But this time," he said, "I *am* going to fuck you."

She closed her eyes and tipped her head back, pressing the button inside her mind that would allow her to record every detail in the most permanent section of her memory. She would replay this, over and over, until she held him again. Unless, of course, the worst happened and *he* met someone in the next two years. But she couldn't think about that right now, didn't want to.

"For the love of god," she said. "Please do."

As November gave way to December, the skies over Henderson turned as gray as steel.

Six mornings a week, Nick drove to work and prayed for a sliver of sunshine, for some spot of color to open up, but winter had gripped Indiana in earnest. It had gripped him, too. Whenever he turned his attention inward, he confronted a bleak, cold storm even the blast furnaces couldn't thaw.

Because Aubrey was gone. Tansy hardly spoke to him anymore. Even Paige, who'd reclaimed her sunniness inch by inch in the past few weeks, hadn't once brought up the elephantine truth that weighed on him day in and day out. She came and went, kissed his cheek and teased him with bad puns, but a wall had risen between them he couldn't seem to scale. And every time he considered hashing it out with her, his stomach shrank to a queasy pebble.

Today, he donned his protective equipment and nodded at Jackson as he took up his post.

Jackson just shook his head.

Great. Even his best friend had lost all hope.

"Man, you have *got* to talk to somebody," Jackson said. "You look like you haven't slept in weeks."

Nick grunted and wandered off, seeking the violent heat of the furnace. Talking wouldn't do him any good. He'd poured himself out, bled words until he'd run dry, and what did he have to show for it?

Nothing. Except the false, cruel hope that, twenty-three months from now, he might have a shot at happiness. Well, twenty-one, if he worked backward from the time Paige would move out.

Not that he was counting, or anything.

At least, he shouldn't be, because he didn't trust it. He'd once lost Aubrey in the span of two weeks. Two fucking weeks. Compared to that, twenty-one months was a lifetime, and so he knew exactly what awaited at the end of that countdown, what had *always* awaited him when it came to Aubrey MacLean. She'd probably be married by then. It was a miracle she wasn't already.

He would still track her down, of course. Make himself congratulate her. Then he'd proceed to go die a brokenhearted death, somewhere private.

But for now, he read her letter each night until his soul cracked. He took more showers than ever, no longer fueled by memories worn thin by decades, but by the very real agony of knowing exactly what she felt like. She was all cream and silk and sunshine—nothing like the roughened hand he tried to placate himself with.

When the showers failed him, he fought.

He drank too much.

He wondered if his daughter-who-wasn't still loved him.

He filed for divorce. Which felt redundant; his mind had divorced Tansy years ago. But he wanted the law to reflect reality, so he worked out an agreement with her that didn't involve lawyers. She got the house, he kept his retirement accounts. Simple. Now he only had to wait for the decision to grind its way through the wheels of the legal system. Any day now, he would receive an official statement informing him that he was utterly—and now legally—completely fucking alone.

One morning, he sat down to breakfast and realized Paige's winter break had begun. It had crept up on him, somehow. Materialized out of the fog.

"Daddy?" She reached over the table and took his hand. "Are you okay? You don't look so good."

He summoned a bent smile. "I'm fine, Peanut. How're you? How'd exams go?"

She shrugged. "Fine. A's across the board."

A flicker of true warmth heated his smile. "Of course."

"Of course. Hey . . ." Her thumb grazed across the backs of his fingers. "What're you doing today? Do you have any plans?"

He waded through the haze cobwebbing his mind. It was Sunday, which he hated. Sundays were empty and formless, offering nothing in the way of distraction. "I don't know. I'll probably spar with Jackson, later. Why?"

A hopeful spark lit her eyes. "What if we drove up to Chicago, instead? Checked out the holiday lights?"

He almost choked. He couldn't get his agreement out fast enough.

Paige grinned. "Aww. You're excited. That lights me up inside. Get it?"

Everything in him softened, but he still played along. "Wow. Don't quit your day job, kid."

She giggled. "But my day job is being awesome. I couldn't quit that if I tried."

He snorted, then gave in to a full-blown laugh. The sound startled him. He hadn't heard it in so long. "If you say so."

In the car, Paige chirped about one thing after another. Mostly having to do with college admissions. Half an hour in, her phone pinged. She pulled it out and squealed at the name on the screen.

"Maria?" he said, with a lift of his eyebrow.

"No. Aubrey."

The name dumped a shot of ice water into his veins. *"Aubrey?"*

"Yep."

"Why the hell is Aubrey texting you?"

Paige turned. He didn't like the look on her face—much too sly. "Because. I texted her first."

His fingers tightened around the wheel. "About?"

"Here. Read it." She offered him the phone.

He glowered. "I'm driving."

"Fine. I'll read it to you. But at least look at the picture, first." Paige flashed the screen, which showed her at school, flexing beside a line of math trophies longer than his arm. "I sent this to her and wrote, 'Sorry, but the queen has been dethroned. Actually, on second thought, I'm not sorry at all.'"

He snorted. "What'd she say back?"

Paige read off the message. "'Congratulations. I knew you could do it, and I can't think of a more worthy successor.' Then a little heart emoji."

Raw emotion punched him in the chest. "She likes you."

"Yeah. I like her, too."

When he said nothing, Paige sniffed. "Like, a lot. You know that, right?"

He did. He wished he didn't.

He pointed at a sign rising in the distance. "Hey, look. A Waffle House. We haven't been to one of those in ages. What do you say we stop in and have pancakes for lunch?"

"Pancakes?" Paige said flatly. "I want to talk about Aubrey, and you try to distract me with pancakes?"

"Yeah. Is it working?"

"Ugh," she said. "You're impossible."

Yeah. Didn't he know it.

* * *

An hour after lunch, when they finally reached Chicago, they parked downtown, then spent an hour browsing a bookstore that made Nick feel like a kid in a candy factory. Afterward, they bought hot apple ciders from a streetside vendor and wandered down the Magnificent Mile, oohing and aahing at the cascade of lights while the day tilted toward dusk.

The mug warmed his palms through his gloves. He sipped, rolling the sweetness on his tongue and telling himself life wasn't so bad. At least until Paige pulled him onto a bench, set her cider aside, and fixed him with a stare about twenty years too grown-up for his liking.

"So," she said. "We *are* going to talk this out, before the day ends."

He tensed and gulped the cider. It turned rancid on the way down. "Okay. I guess it's been coming for a while."

"Do you have anything you want to say? Up front?"

His throat thickened. "Er, no. Maybe. Just that . . . no matter what, I love you. I love you so much that no one's invented a word for it yet. Whether you're my biological daughter or not, I don't care. It doesn't matter to me. You're still the best and most important thing in my life, and that's never going to change."

Paige's breath whooshed out of her. "Oh. Well, I know *that*. That's not what I meant."

"It's . . . not?"

"Wait." She studied him with no small amount of alarm. "Is *that* what's had you all grouchy and broody for the past month?"

Nick frowned. "I don't brood. Why is everyone always saying that?"

"Come on." Her vivid blue eyes turned thoughtful. "I just . . . I thought you knew I figured out who my dad is weeks ago."

His head rang inside, as if Jackson had just clocked him a good one. "What? How? Did Mom tell you? Because she said—"

Paige flung up a hand. "I don't mean I figured out who the actual guy is. And please don't give me a name. I don't wanna know. I just mean I know who my *dad* is. Because it's you."

Moisture clogged his eyes. He tried to summon words and failed.

"Aw. Daddy." She scooted in and wrapped him in a side-hug. "I'm sorry. I should've realized."

He swiped at his nose. "What, that I've been a wreck over it?"

"Yeah," she said gently. "I mean, I'm not gonna lie, it's been hard for me. Really hard. And at first, I wasn't sure who to question. You or Mom. I thought for a minute Aubrey might be my mom, when I found that letter. The timing lined up, at least. And I always wondered where I got the red in my hair. So I thought maybe you'd gotten Aubrey pregnant and she'd gone off to New York after having me, and . . . thinking about that sucked. Not that I don't love her, I do. But I don't think I could've thought about Mom the same way, if she wasn't really my mom. So I can't tell you how relieved I was when I realized it was you, instead. Because I *do* still think the same way about you. One hundred million percent."

He sniffled. "One hundred million percent isn't actually a thing."

"It is in my world. You've made it that way. I don't care where the sperm came from, or whatever. You're my dad, and anyone who says otherwise can fuck off."

He jolted at her language. He'd never heard her curse before. He decided he loved it, and then he couldn't hold back tears any longer. Warmth welled up and coursed out of him.

Paige hugged him tighter. A woman passed by, pushing a stroller, her gaze widening in alarm.

What, you've never seen a grown man cry? On the shoulder of a sixteen-year-old girl?

He wept himself dry, and when he finished, he felt better than he had in weeks.

Paige didn't let go until he straightened and scrubbed at his cheeks.

"I'll tell you his name, someday," he said. "If you want to know."

She shook her head. "I don't think so. He doesn't even know I exist, does he?"

Nick hesitated, his fist curling of its own accord. "He doesn't know you're his," he said carefully.

"Then no. It doesn't matter to me."

His fingers relaxed. He hoped she never changed her mind. He planned to hoard that secret, strip it from existence by taking it to the grave with him.

She let go and scooted back to her side of the bench. "Well, I'm glad that's out of the way. Because I was *trying* to talk to you about Aubrey."

He braced, or tried to, but his muscles had softened in the wake of his emotional outpouring. "What about her?"

"You love her."

He held her eyes. She'd phrased it as a statement, not a question.

"A lot," Paige said.

His jaw worked. He bought time with a sip of cider. Then dug deep for his courage and said, "Yeah. I do."

Her entire countenance relaxed. "So why'd you let her go?"

He snorted. "Let her go? I didn't. She got her job back. She *chose* to go."

"But you didn't go after her."

"Yeah. Because my life is in Henderson." He didn't say, *Because I have you*. He didn't want Paige to think this was in any way her fault. He'd sooner stab himself in the eye than let the blame so much as touch her.

"But you could move," she said. "Now that you and Mom are finally getting divorced."

Every nerve ending curled tight. "How'd you know about the divorce?"

She rolled her eyes. "Come on. Do you think I'm stupid?"

"I absolutely don't," he ground out. "I just . . . I don't know. Didn't realize you were Sherlock fucking Holmes."

"Enola," she said meaningfully. "Enola Holmes. God, you're so old."

He stared, blank. He had no idea who that was.

"The point is," Paige said blithely, "you could go. I don't need you around every single day anymore. And Maria and I are applying to NYU. That's Aubrey's alma mater, isn't it? If we get in, I could live right down the street from you. You'd never be rid of me. And best of all, you'd be happy. We both would."

He blinked furiously. Oh, fuck. He was going to cry again. He dug his fingernails into his palms, anchoring himself to the pain until the urge passed. He didn't need to go scaring any more passing mothers.

"It's not that easy," he said hoarsely.

"Why not?" Paige's smile reflected the Christmas lights, like she had a mouth full of sunshine. "You know, Aubrey told me this thing, once, when we were out at the farm. 'If life puts something in your way, go around it. If it knocks you down, get right back up. If it sticks you—"

"Oh, Jesus," Nick groaned. "Not you, too."

"What? Don't you think she has a point?"

An ache coalesced in his chest. Yes, she had a point. Maybe. But when he considered going to her, asking to be enough for her *now*, panic spiraled along his nerves. The mere thought made him feel like he'd run into a solid wall, one deep within him. One he tried not to look at, but couldn't help breaking himself against from time to time.

Paige peeked up at him. "Or is it not really me you need permission from? Is it . . . yourself?"

He sucked in a breath.

Surely it couldn't be that easy, could it?

37.

Aubrey was staring out her office window. Again.

She reeled her attention back from the glittering skyline and faced her computer. It was getting late. Probably too late to still be at work, considering her database had debuted two days ago and run smoothly since, and she was still utterly exhausted from the three-week stint of constant coding and lack of sleep.

But she had no desire to go home to that single-bedroom apartment where the radiator knocked and the upstairs neighbors continuously reminded her of how empty her bed was at night.

Maybe she should give herself a reason to go home. Maybe she should get a cat.

She ran her eyes over the code she'd spent the past half hour wrangling with. Or not—a cat would mean one more thing to take care of, and she couldn't even seem to care for herself, these days. She hadn't done Pilates in weeks. Since returning to Osos, she'd poured every ounce of effort into getting the database fixed, and managed to do so just under the deadline. The program had gone live, and the upgraded algorithm had already identified a potential eight-way donor swap—which, if it succeeded, would be the first of its kind. But while Jeff and her colleagues were busy clapping her on the back, Aubrey kept wondering where her heart had gone. Maybe she'd left it in one of those roadstop trash cans on the bus journey back from Indiana. Maybe some hapless cleaner had found it afterward and wondered who on earth had left such a sticky mess.

A knock interrupted her maudlin line of thinking. Jeff stood in her doorway, his dark hair staging its usual mutiny against his efforts at combing. His tie hung askew and a smile lit his face. "Burning the midnight oil? Still?"

She hummed. "Nothing better to do."

"Well, you could always go over your speech for tomorrow. You get that buttoned up yet?"

Tomorrow. What was tomorrow?

Oh, right. The gala. The one at which Osos was awarding her the Innovation Cup. Privately, she figured they were doing it to make a very visible apology for what had happened, but at least Jeff seemed genuinely thrilled that she'd be getting recognition.

She forced a smile. "That's what I'm working on right now, actually."

Not true. She'd put exactly zero thought into what she would say tomorrow.

"Great. Glad to hear it. See you at the party, then?" He rapped a friendly good-night against her doorframe and went whistling down the hallway. Off to his wife and two small children, who would probably piledrive him with hugs the moment he walked into his house. Meanwhile, she was fantasizing about cats.

Aubrey squeezed her eyes shut and jabbed her fingers against her closed lids. God, what was wrong with her?

With a gritty sigh, she wheeled her chair back and gathered her things. She didn't have to go home, but she didn't have to stay here, either. Maybe a walk in the cold would do her good. A movie. Dinner out.

Anything to make the time pass quicker.

Except once outside, she only made it two blocks before veering off into the alcove of an apartment building and pulling out her phone. She scrolled to Paige's text message from last week, hit Reply, then paused with her thumbs over the keys.

She'd done this so many times. Come *this* close to asking for Nick's number, only to lock the phone again and slip it into her pocket, which she did now, too.

Four whole weeks had passed without a word from him. A month.

She'd endured it, because talking would only make things harder. And she would endure another month, then another twenty more. She'd *make* herself.

Even if she had to get a cat.

Christmas Eve Eve.

It was a strange day for a gala, Aubrey thought, but attending a party *did* sound better than sitting at home, doing logic puzzles by candlelight and wondering whether to open a bottle of wine for the express purpose of drinking a single glass.

So she pulled on her black satin evening gown. The dress required several different arm contortions to maneuver the zipper up, but she managed.

She frowned at the full-length mirror. Had she lost weight? The gown sagged where it usually hugged, and the fit across her chest could even be accused of gaping.

Lovely.

She found a safety pin and corrected the deficit, then did her hair and makeup. Those, thankfully, didn't require any thought.

With her overcoat and dangly earrings in place, she took an Uber to the Manhattan Center, not wanting to brave the subway in heels. She tipped the driver and stepped out into a sparkling, frosted holiday tableau.

The Uber drove off, but Aubrey remained on the sidewalk. Across the street, a mother laughed and kissed her rosy-cheeked daughter. A gorgeous young couple strolled by, her dark fingers interlaced with his light ones. The two gave each other the kind of look that could only come from sharing a private joke. All around, lights glistened while the cheerful honks of traffic peppered the air.

Aubrey wondered if it should fill her up. All these people, all this life, and yet she felt hollow in the midst of it, like a hole punched in a piece of sequined paper.

"Aubrey?"

Her shoulders tensed. Oh, god, that voice. She turned.

A man approached, his lapels drawn up in an effort to hide his features.

"David." Her teeth clenched. She'd hoped to never see the man who'd stolen her job again. "What're you doing here?"

He darted glances side to side. "Hi. Sorry to show up like this, it's just the only place I knew you'd be. Other than Osos, of course, but I'm not welcome there anymore, which has been really hard, and—"

"What do you want?" she said coldly.

"Uhm." A nervous flush blazed on his cheeks. "I just came to say sorry. In person."

She waited a beat, then another. A car honked long and loud as it passed. "Really?"

"Yeah. Really. I'm a jerk, and I never should've taken credit for your project. I don't know what I was thinking."

She blinked. And waited for some kind of floodgate to open. Or for the heavens to part and proclaim that everything had righted itself in the world. But nothing happened. "Well . . . thanks?"

"No problem." David bobbed his head. "And I wanted to say I would've told Jeff myself, even if your boyfriend hadn't come and made me. I swear. The only reason I hadn't is because I was still working up my nerve. But I was *going* to tell the truth. You can understand that, right? You know I didn't mean to—"

"Boyfriend?" She waved a hand to stall his soliloquy. "What boyfriend?"

"You know. Big muscly dude? Or maybe he said he was your friend. I can't remember. I just . . ."

David went on. And on. Aubrey heard none of it. All the blood in her body puddled in her feet while static blotted out her mind. *Big muscly dude.*

David's lips stopped moving. Aubrey found her wits somewhere. "You mean a man came *here*? To New York? And made you confess?"

His brows flattened. She could practically see him second-guessing himself. "Well, it was more like he asked. Kind of nicely? Or kind of threateningly? I don't know. Like I said, I would've done it myself, even without him."

The sidewalk tilted beneath her. "This man . . . Did he have dark eyes? Like, really dark?"

"Oh, yeah. Black, basically."

"Oh. Wow. Okay." She turned an aimless circle, wondered why, then floated away on feet that had somehow come unglued from the rest of her. Nick had come here? To the city? While she'd been in Henderson? But *when*?

"Aubrey, wait. You forgive me, right? You—"

She waved a meaningless gesture over her shoulder and aimed for the Manhattan Center's portico. Someone opened the door for her. She glided in. A different someone pointed her down a hallway. She soon found herself in a festive hall filled with violet light and sparkling silver tablecloths, where a third someone took her coat. Music blared. Faces swam by. She recognized most, but struggled to retrieve names for them, even as she shook everyone's hand.

Nick had come to New York. He'd gotten her job back for her.

Just . . . *what*?

Jeff appeared and introduced his wife, who had a German accent and smiling eyes. Aubrey tried to make conversation, but couldn't have said whether her questions made any sense. In the midst of her floundering, someone put a champagne flute in her hand. All the while, the wheels in her mind spun, trying and failing to find purchase.

Why on earth hadn't Nick told her? How could he do a thing like that and not even take credit for it?

She raised her glass to her lips. The warmth of the champagne raced down her throat and blossomed in her belly, then kept going, cannoning outward, suffusing her whole body.

All this time, she'd believed he hadn't fought for her.

Except . . . he *had*. Just not in the way she'd expected. He hadn't fought to keep her, but he'd fought for *her*—her dreams, her wants, her needs. The only person he'd failed to fight for was himself. She'd just been too stupid, too scared and blinded by her own wounded pride, to realize.

"Oh my god." Aubrey put out a satin-gloved hand to steady herself. "Oh my *god*."

Jeff's wife blinked several times. "You are okay, yes? Your color is not looking so good."

"I'm . . ." Aubrey's chest heaved. She guzzled down the rest of the champagne. "Just a little dizzy. I'm sorry, it was so nice to meet you, but I think I need to sit down."

Jeff's wife—Olga? Inga?—looked dubious, but didn't protest as Aubrey teetered away and found a chair to sink into. She thrust the empty glass away and spread her gloved hands against the glittering tablecloth.

God, she'd forgotten herself, hadn't she? All those years ago, Nick had broken her heart, and afterward, she'd lashed the pieces back together with ropes braided from cowardice. And later, she'd expected him to fight for their future, when she herself had quit.

Well. As he would say . . . fuck that.

Aubrey stood. The lights had gone down. Jeff was onstage now, saying her name, delivering a speech about her grit and persistence. She laughed out loud at the absurdity.

Grit and persistence, yes. She remembered now.

Jeff asked her onto the stage. Applause filled the room as Aubrey dutifully threaded her way through the audience. When she reached the podium, Jeff pressed an absurdly heavy slab of etched glass into her hands.

The ballroom quieted. Hundreds of faces turned her way, expectant.

She leaned toward the microphone. *If life puts something in your way, go around it.*

"Good evening," she said. "Thank you all for being here. I'm honored to accept this award, tonight. But I'm going to break form a bit here and ask you all to excuse me, because I have to leave for Indiana. Right now."

The audience members exchanged uneasy glances.

Jeff's eyes popped. "Aubrey?" he whisper-hissed. "What're you doing?"

"Thanks again," she said into the microphone, "for the recognition."

She descended from the stage, arrowing through the crowd toward the coat check. Once there, she handed over her ticket, took her jacket, and fished in the pocket for her cell phone. *If life knocks you down, get right back up.* She'd take an Uber to the nearest car rental place. Then drive all night. If the car broke down, she'd walk. If her legs broke down, she'd crawl.

Jeff caught her arm on her way out of the ballroom.

"Aubrey." He looked worried. Not angry, but genuinely concerned. "What're you doing? Are you okay? Do you have some kind of emergency?"

"Yes," she said. "And I'm sorry I have to go. But since I have you here, consider this my notice that I'll be working remotely, going forward."

He stared. "Remotely? What? No. You know it's against company policy to—"

"I know," she cut in. "But it's the twenty-first century. That policy doesn't make sense anymore. And that algorithm I built, Osos doesn't own it. I made it on my own time. At home. And I never signed over the rights for you to use it. You fired me before I could. At which point I spent two months writing a document that proves all that, actually."

He gaped. She hoped he wouldn't make her spell out the rest. She *really* didn't feel like dampening the mood by threatening him with a lawsuit.

"Okay," he finally said. "But . . . where's this coming from?"

"It doesn't matter. I should've told you I'd be working remotely when I agreed to come back. But since I didn't, I'm doing it now."

He surveyed her as if looking at a stranger. "Remotely. As in, full-time?"

"Yes," she said, calm as a summer's breeze. "Full-time."

He pulled at his bow tie, then ran a hand through hair he still hadn't managed to tame, even for this. His frown gave her the impression she'd strained his goodwill to breaking. "I . . . okay. If you're not giving me any other option, then I'll make it happen."

"Thank you." She kissed his cheek, which only deepened the groove between his brows. "I'll be available by Zoom, if you want."

"Uh. Sure. We'll work out the details. But . . . you're really leaving? Right now? It's that important?"

She checked her phone. The Uber driver was seven minutes away. "Yes, it's that important." She handed him the Innovation Cup.

"You don't want this?"

"Put it in my office. You can have it shipped to me, okay?"

"O . . . kay."

She flashed a smile and left him standing there.

In the bright, airy lobby, she scrolled to Paige's name in her phone, then hit the call button. She needed more than just Nick's number. She needed to know where he was so she could do this face-to-face. But she had no idea where he lived these days, whether he was still sharing a roof with Tansy, or—

"Eeeeeee!" Paige shrieked in her ear. "What'd you say? Tellmetellmetellme!"

Aubrey blinked and held the phone out, giving her ringing ear a reprieve. "Uh, Paige? Hi, it's Aubrey MacLean."

"Oh my god, I know who it is, you weirdo. Just tell me the news!"

"News? What do you mean, news?"

Paige rushed in a breath. "Wait. Is there not news? Oh my god, you didn't say no, did you? Because if you're worried it's going to upset me or something, it totally won't, and—"

"I have absolutely no idea what you're talking about," Aubrey said. "I just called to see if you could tell me where your dad is. If he has a new address. There's . . . something I want to ask him."

The line went silent.

"Paige? Hello?"

"You haven't seen him?" Paige sounded subdued now.

Aubrey rocked back on her heels. "Um, no? Should I have?"

"Uh . . . Where are you right now? The Manhattan Center? For the Osos gala?"

Aubrey swallowed her bewilderment and glanced around, halfway expecting to find Paige hiding behind a potted plant, her hand cupped around a cell phone. "How'd you know that?"

"Oh my god," Paige rushed out, smearing the words together. "Wait, so you just randomly called, wanting to find him? Okay, this is seriously too perfect. Hold on, lemme check my app and see where he is."

Aubrey's head swam.

Paige squealed again, some distance from the phone. Then the line crackled and her voice erupted in Aubrey's ear again. "Okay, just walk outside. Right now, okay? Go quick."

"What? Why?"

"Just do it! And please . . . don't say no, okay? It'll make him so happy. And call me back! OhmygodI'msoexcited! Bye!"

The line went dead. The moment collapsed on itself, then spun into the next, bringing with it a tremulous hope that started in Aubrey's marrow and seeped into her limbs. Go outside. Well, she could do that.

She took a step, then another. By the time she reached the revolving doors, she'd gathered enough inertia to burst through, then had to stumble to a stop on the sidewalk.

Because there was the most beautiful man in the world, wearing a tuxedo, staring up at the portico and steeling himself with an indrawn breath.

38.

NICK WONDERED IF he was going to throw up. Or chicken out and drive all the way back to Henderson without even going inside. The brightly lit sign over the door of the Manhattan Center dared him to do it.

Sweat slicked his palms, everything in him screaming to run away, that this would only amount to another fall with a painful end. That painful endings were all he could ever hope for.

But he steeled his jaw, because fuck that. He'd doubted himself all his life, and where had that gotten him, except lost and heartbroken and alone? For once, he would go to war. For himself, just like Jackson had said.

If that meant going out in a blaze of glory, so be it.

Nick lowered his eyes. And immediately encountered a pair of jade ones that nearly knocked him off his feet.

Aubrey. Fuck, she looked stunning. Stunned, too, but still every bit as beautiful as the day he'd first sat down beside her in English class and tried to ignore her siren call.

Holy shit, how he'd failed in that endeavor.

"Hi." His voice came out rough, but the sight of her smoothed the emotional riot inside him. Yes, he would do this. His whole life had only ever been leading him here, to this moment. He suddenly had no idea why he'd ever fought it.

"Hi." She took a step. "I was just, uh, coming to see you. In Indiana."

He blinked. "You what?"

"Yeah." She pointed behind him. He turned as a silver sedan with a lit Uber icon pulled up to the curb. The driver rolled the window down.

"Sorry," Aubrey called to him. "It looks like I don't need you after all."

The driver made a rude gesture and zoomed off. When Nick turned back, her face had melted in a smile.

"You were going to take an Uber to Indiana?" he said, disbelieving.

"More or less."

"And . . . then what?"

Another step. Her eyes shimmered a shade of green he swore he hadn't glimpsed in seventeen years. "I was going to grovel. Tell you I love you. That I always have, and I'll do whatever I have to if you'll just be with me. I'll work remotely from Henderson, if that's what it takes, or . . . whatever. We can figure it out. But I want you now, not in two years. And I'm so sorry I didn't say so sooner. You deserved so much more than what I've given you, but I'm going to do better. And I hope it's not too late."

Every word crackled lightning down his spine, then sank into him, a molten glow. This had to be what heaven felt like.

"I . . . had a whole speech," he said, and didn't recognize his own voice. The distance between them became unbearable, so he closed it. Aubrey tipped her face up, allowing him to count each beloved freckle.

"And?" A smile infused her voice. "What was it?"

"I forgot." His fingers found her cheeks. Pure wonder flowed through him. Amazement that he could ever even hope to call a woman like this his.

"You?" she said. "At a loss for words? Of all people?"

His mouth curled. "It was something about deserving you, I think. How I've always told myself I don't, but I'm calling bullshit on that."

"You finally figured that out?"

"Well. Paige may've had to beat it into my head a little. Jackson, too."

She gazed up. "Good. I'm glad. Because you deserve the world. Everything you want. You're the noblest, most incredible, stubbornest, most gorgeous, foulest-mouthed, most ridiculously intelligent human I've ever met. Not to mention phenomenal in bed. And . . . there's just no end to it. You're like a number that equals the sum of its divisors. Perfect."

He searched her eyes. Light crested inside him, a sunrise burning away shadows. He cupped her face and kissed her, soft and sweet and endless, and it occurred to him that he'd never done that before, crossed the distance first while trusting he had every right to.

When he pulled away, with her sweetness clinging to his lips and her sunshine filling his nose, she looked up from beneath her lashes, almost shy.

"Paige made it sound like you had a question for me."

His heartbeat hitched. "Paige? You talked to her?"

"I did."

"When?"

"Just now. When I was going to drive to Henderson and find you."

He tried to process that. "Did she tell you what my question was?"

"No." A knowing smile curved her mouth. "But god, do I have a strong opinion on what I want it to be."

"All your opinions are strong," he said.

She laughed. "True."

He swallowed. His nerves wakened. This was so different. No park bench or sad dandelions. Just the only woman he would ever love, plus a proper box this time, filling his pocket like a grenade.

"Just one thing," Aubrey said.

He raised an eyebrow.

"Ask me standing up."

"You don't want me down on one knee?"

Her breath caught. "No," she warbled, then swallowed. "If anything, I should be the one getting down on the sidewalk. I would, if this damned dress wasn't so restricting. I have so much to make up to you."

The ridiculousness of that notion made him chuckle. "You don't."

"I do."

"Fine. You can spend all night making it up to me. Just let me do this, first."

She laughed wetly. He pulled the box from his pocket. Her gloved hands cradled his as he flipped the lid to reveal a rose-gold confection with a polished black gemstone at the center.

His pulse sped. This part made him nervous, no matter how many times he'd practiced beforehand. "I'm sorry it's not a diamond. It can be, in a couple years. Once I get back on my feet from the divorce."

A thick, happy sound fell from her lips as her eyes locked on the ring. "Oh, wow. I don't want a diamond. This is so much better. It's the same color as your eyes."

"So . . . is that a yes?"

She looked up. "You haven't asked me anything yet. But you know what? I don't want you to do that part, either. I'll just say yes. A million yeses. If you'll say yes to me, too."

Relief choked him, and his heart sang as he plucked the ring from its velvet, peeled away Aubrey's left glove, then slipped it on her finger.

"I fucking love you," he said.

"I fucking love *you*. So much."

He kissed her again, long and deep, until a flame kindled in his belly, the kind that would burn him up unless he got her somewhere private. He kissed her until her she clung to him, and when he finally pulled away her eyes had gone glassy, her pupils shot wide.

"Do you want to go back to your party?" he said.

"No," she breathed. "Take me home."

"To your place?"

"Yeah. Where I can spend all night making things up to you. And one-upping the upstairs neighbors. And then, in the morning, I want to go to Henderson. To my house. Or . . . *our* house, now, I guess."

He blinked. "Is that how this is going to work? Because I was going to move here."

A drunken smile spread across her lips. "What about Paige?"

"We talked and . . . it's okay. We're okay."

The grin that lit her face was so sweet he felt an answering happiness rise in his chest. "Why don't we stay in Henderson 'til she's done with school? Then we can move back here or . . . whatever you want. Okay?"

Pure joy shot along every nerve. "Okay," he said, gathering her in his arms. "Absolutely okay."

She laughed. He buried his face in her hair and breathed her in like sustenance, until he could think of nothing but finding the nearest wall as soon as possible.

* * *

The night passed in a delirious, blurry haze. There was a phone call to an overjoyed Paige. An Uber he kissed Aubrey all the way home in. A heap of formalwear shed on the floor of her bedroom. There was the sheer ecstasy of burying himself in her softness and heat, the way her lashes fluttered against her cheeks as she tipped her head back and let her tongue trip over his name.

And there was definitely a wall, somewhere in the mix.

Many hours later, as the sun came up, Aubrey lay naked and wild-haired in the crook of his arm, smiling her way into sleep.

She whispered one last thing, just before her eyes closed.

"I'm so glad I don't have to get a cat."

AUBREY SAT ON the closed toilet lid and stared at the plastic stick in her hand, her blood a chaotic tumble.

Two blue lines.

Two.

Moisture flooded her throat. She'd suspected already, back in New York. Well, sort of. But she was glad she'd waited until now, four whole days after she and Nick had returned to Henderson. It felt right, somehow, to have sorted things out *before* she sprung the news on him that he'd be having yet another shotgun wedding.

Dazed, she flushed the toilet and lurched from the bathroom, one hand pressed to her belly. She felt nothing out of the ordinary, could only be six or seven weeks along, because it must have happened that night in his truck. Or maybe up against the wall, beside the fire.

Either way, she should call the OB and make an appointment.

She found the chesterfield and sank onto it, the rest of the living room a blur. She saw nothing except a future full of Nick—his long fingers playing with pudgy hands, his laugh echoing a high-pitched giggle, his dark eyes peering out from a rounded face. Or maybe their child would inherit her green gaze.

It didn't matter. Either way, their child would be perfect. Just like her husband-to-be.

Aubrey sat there for the remainder of Nick's shift at the mill, which amounted to two and a half hours. She cradled her belly and cried the most joyful tears she'd ever shed.

When a knock interrupted her reverie, she didn't stop to wonder why Nick would ask to be let in to what was now his house. She just drifted to the door in a trance, wondering if he'd know simply by looking at her.

But Nick wasn't there. Instead, electric blue eyes regarded her from the stoop, chasing away her effervescent joy.

"Gallant?" Her voice turned to stone.

"Hey." He shifted from one foot to the other. "I was hoping we could talk."

She ran her eyes over him, but her body offered no reaction. No shift in her heart rate, not so much as a stitch in her breathing. Like she'd never cared about him at all. Which, she supposed, she hadn't. No, she'd spent all that time falling in love with Nick.

She had to be the only woman in the world who'd fallen for the same man twice, without unfalling in between. "About what?"

"What happened. The letters. Which I shouldn't have given you, I realize that now. But it was only because I liked you so much. That part was real. It really, really was, and I was hoping you might give me another chance. Get to know the real me. Because I never faked the way I felt about you."

She anchored her grip to the doorframe. Cold air leached in, pebbling her skin. "You don't even know me, Gallant."

"Yeah, I do. Of course I do."

"No. You have an idea of me. But it's made-up. The letters fooled me, but you don't actually know what I dream about at night, or what my deepest secret is, or what scares me most in the world. We never talked about any of that."

"Okay." Bronze brows crooked as his eyes pleaded with her. "I can find out."

"I'm sorry," she said, "but no."

He slid his hands into his pockets. The naked regret on his face surprised her. "But what—"

The roar of an engine cut him off. Gallant turned as Nick's truck screeched to a stop in the driveway.

The rest happened so quickly Aubrey didn't have the chance to protest. Not that she would have, anyway. Nick came streaking up the walk, his boots punching through the crusted snow. He didn't slow when he came up the steps, just wound up a fist and smashed it straight into Gallant's face.

Gallant reeled, stumbling off the stoop and into the yard, but he managed to keep his feet, somehow. Nick hit him again, this time with the other fist, then spat at Gallant's feet and stood there, his back heaving, his breath puffing silver streams into the air.

Gallant swayed. Blood leaked from his nose and a corner of his mouth. "What the hell? What'd I do to you?"

Nick hissed air through his teeth. "A lot of things, you absolute bag of dicks. But that wasn't for me. That was for them."

Aubrey's breath thinned.

Nick glanced back and met her eyes, a spark of pure love flaring before he faced Gallant again. "One for each."

"One for each of *what*?" Gallant touched his face, wincing when his fingers came away red and glistening.

Aubrey kept silent. She had an idea of what Nick meant, one she would never ask about, because some things truly weren't her business.

But she figured she understood.

"Get the fuck out of my yard," Nick growled. "And leave my fiancée alone. If I so much as see your face again, I'll beat the shit out of you. Are we clear?"

Gallant's eyes bugged, whether over the threat or the word *fiancée*, Aubrey didn't know and didn't care.

When he'd gone, Nick stomped up the steps and into the

entryway. She closed the front door behind him, shutting out the rest of the world.

He stood staring down at her, breathing hard, clearly trying to leash his rage. His fingers balled into fists at his sides.

She pressed a hand to his chest. "Wow. You hit him first. I've never seen you do that before."

"Yeah, well. He deserved it. Are you okay? He didn't touch you, did he?"

"No." She couldn't help it. She chuckled. "No way in hell was he getting close enough to try."

Her laughter relaxed him; the corner of his mouth curled, just slightly. He held her eyes until the air thickened and heated. His fingers straightened at his sides.

God, this man. Just looking at him set her nerves aflame. "How was your day?" she said, breathy.

"Better, now. About to be fucking spectacular, in a minute."

"Oh? Why's that?"

He grinned, then lunged for her, hoisting her up and wrapping her legs around his waist. He held her there, suspended, like it cost him nothing. "Because. I'm about to make good use of a wall. Which one do you want today?"

She planted her palms on his shoulders and lost herself in the infinity of his eyes. Her skin prickled with the knowledge that she was about to change his whole life. Again.

"How about the one we used when we made Paige's sister or brother?"

He blinked. Blinked again. His fingers dug into her thighs. "What?"

"Yeah." She risked a smile. "Because it was either there, or in your truck."

An eternity passed while he stared up at her with parted lips. Then a broken, joy-soaked sob burst from his mouth. He hugged her so tight the air gusted out of her.

"You're suffocating me," she wheezed.

"Oh, shit." He set her down like she was made of glass and stepped back, hands spread. His cheeks were wet. "Oh fuck, I'm sorry. What do you need? Space? A fire? Ice cream?"

She laughed. "I think I was promised a wall."

His nostrils flared. "But . . . with a baby in there?"

She pressed her lips together to rein in her amusement. "It's perfectly safe. I mean, I've never done this before, but I know that much, at least."

"Oh. Okay. But . . . are you sure? When Tansy was pregnant, we never . . ." His words died away while red splashed across his cheeks. "I mean . . . Sorry. You didn't need to hear that. I just . . . Fuck. Sorry."

"It's okay. You were married before me. I get it. We don't have to pretend you weren't."

He swallowed. "Okay. Just tell me what you need."

"You," she said simply.

In the end, he took her into the living room, drew the curtains, and built a fire, insisting that walls would have to wait another seven months or so. She didn't argue, just captured his tear-damp cheeks with her hands and laid soft kisses along the side of his neck when he stretched her out on the fur throw he'd spread before the hearth. Seventeen years had passed since she'd last lain with him here, yet none of them had dulled the way her nerves flowered beneath his touch or the way she gazed into his eyes and saw forever written there.

"What do *you* need?" she murmured when he paused.

"Three things," he said, staring down. "You. Paige. And this." He laid a warm palm against her bare belly.

"Well." Her heart filled, growing at least two sizes, threatening to overflow. "We're your family. Which means you have us, all of us. And you always will."

★★★★★

Author Note

THANKS FOR READING! For a bonus excerpt from Nick and Aubrey's wedding night, please visit: www.shaylingandhi.com/bonus.

Acknowledgments

THANKS FOR READING *Love Letters for Other People*! I hope you enjoyed Nick and Aubrey's story. I'd be remiss if I didn't first express my gratitude to you, the reader, for being here, because let's be honest: you're the reason I write. Every message and comment I've received is enshrined in a permanent corner of my heart, and WOW, you guys have really made this otherwise solitary pursuit worthwhile. Thank you, truly. (And, for anyone who's ever wondered whether it's worth contacting an author whose book you've enjoyed: yes. Unequivocally yes. It fuels us. Sometimes we ride that high for days.)

Of course, no book is created in a vacuum, and I'm endlessly grateful to those who've had a hand in bringing *Love Letters for Other People* to shelves. Thank you, always, to my incredible agent Beth Miller for your support, thoughtfulness, and sheer badassery. I'm continually awed by your organizational skills and count myself lucky to have you in my corner.

My deepest thanks, also, to my wonderful editor, Cat Clyne. You have the most valuable insight. Every. Single. Time. My books always shine brighter after they've passed through your hands, and I'm beyond grateful that you're so adept at teasing out what I'm *trying* to do, even when I haven't quite done it. I wouldn't be able to dig to the heart of these books without you; your guidance is so very appreciated.

To my audiobook narrator, Carly Robins—thank you for bringing my books to life so vividly and with such skill. Your performances wow me, your voice is beautiful, and our meet-cute remains one of my favorites of all time.

Of course, every author also needs other authors to thrive. I'm no different, and I'm fortunate enough to be surrounded by the best community out there—not because I'm particularly deserving, but because book people are some of the most generous and supportive souls in existence. Nisha Tuli, my writing wife, I count myself lucky beyond measure that we happened to swap beta reads all those years ago. What would I do without you? (Don't actually answer that, it doesn't bear thinking about . . .) To the other equally incredible women of the Mouse Jiggler society, I LOVE YOU GUYS. Neely Tubati Alexander, Melissa O'Connor, Emily Matheis, Tina Mars, Keshe Chow, Kate Robb, and Alex Kiley . . . our unhinged conversations nourish me and keep me going, and I love that I get to swoon over your beautiful books long before anyone else does.

To Windy Prasert, the very first person who read this book, thank you for your insight and undying support. I was so nervous to share this one, but your reaction both bolstered me and convinced me that maybe I actually had a decent story here. As a result, I hope you enjoy being immortalized in print as the proprietor of a fictional café in an equally fictional town in Indiana.

To my friends, readers, and neighbors, and all the booksellers, librarians, and other incredible people who've supported me on this journey: I'm genuinely flabbergasted by the kindness you've shown me. I hope you all know how appreciated you are. I wish I had space to name each and every one of you, but since I don't, special thanks go to Chelsea and the entire crew of House of J's in Arvada: you're amazing. Everyone in the Denver area should make your place their home coffee shop. Lyndsey Gantert, you're still my favorite broken pencil ever. Ruthie Wilson, your generosity of spirit is incredible, and I'm so glad we connected. You can pitch my books to strangers in front of me anytime, lol. Stephanie Pao, I'm still giddy every time I see my book on your truck (readers, if you're in LA, check out the Fleuria Romance Book Truck!). Jess (@jessabibliophile), I will never forget the post where you said you felt like *When We Had Forever* was staring into your soul (I'm not crying, you're crying!). To Hannah and the entire Colorado-based crew of CO Book Besties, I'm honored to be part of one of the best chat groups on Instagram. Not only are you guys hilarious, but your enthusiasm for books is unparalleled and very much appreciated.

To my wonderful family, both by blood and by marriage—how'd I get so lucky? I couldn't do any of this without you, and I'm so glad my children have such a loving village to grow up amongst. That said, I hope you skipped over the sexy bits, like I asked you to last time. But since I'm pretty sure you didn't, PLEASE DO NOT SPEAK OF THEM TO ME. We'll just pretend this didn't happen, okay?

Finally, my ultimate thanks go to my husband, Krishna. I still don't know what I did to deserve you, but I think about how lucky I am literally every single day. You make it so easy to write an epic love story, because even though I'm making it up . . . I'm not really making it up, you know? I love and appreciate you so very, very much, and am eternally grateful you bit my neck during Twister at that random house party all those years ago.

bar. I'm [illegible] one of my favorite author friends. [illegible] your generosity of spirit is incredible, and I'm so glad we connected. [illegible] [illegible] [illegible] [illegible] every time I see my books on your stack, readers, at [illegible] [illegible] [illegible] [illegible] the possibilities [illegible] [illegible] [illegible] [illegible] and the [illegible] Book [illegible] I'm honored to be part of one of the best [illegible] group on Instagram. Not only are you [illegible] but your enthusiasm for books is unparalleled and very much appreciated.

To my wonderful family both by blood and by marriage—how'd I get so lucky? [illegible] any of this without you, and I'm so glad my children have such a loving village to grow up amongst. [illegible] I hope you skipped over the sexy bits, like I asked you to last time. But since I'm aware you didn't [illegible] Well, we'll pretend that didn't happen. Oops.

[illegible] my husband. [illegible] [illegible] didn't deserve you, but I think [illegible] every single day. You make it so easy to write [illegible] love story, because [illegible] [illegible] [illegible] I love and appreciate [illegible] so very, very [illegible] grateful [illegible]